UNDER AN AMBER SKY

UNDER AN AMBER SKY

Pamela Evans

headline

First published in 2008
by HEADLINE PUBLISHING GROUP

2

Cataloguing in Publication Data is
available from the British Library

ISBN 978 0 7553 3058 4

Typeset in Bembo by Palimpsest Book Production Limited,
Grangemouth, Stirlingshire
Printed and bound in Great Britain by
Clays Ltd, St Ives plc

Headline's policy is to use papers that are natural, renewable and
recyclable products and made from wood grown in sustainable
forests. The logging and manufacturing processes are expected
to conform to the environmental regulations of the country of origin.

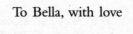
To Bella, with love

Chapter One

'Flamin' blackout; it's more trouble than it's worth if you ask me,' grumbled Alice Porter to her friend Peg Mills as they walked through the back streets of Chiswick one morning in early September 1940. They were heading for the shops in the High Road to get the day's provisions, the youngest of their children – in the dying days of the school summer holidays – going on ahead.

'Why? What's happened? Did you bump into a lamppost in the dark or something?' responded Peg.

'No, not me. It's my Ernie. He tripped over a pushbike when he was out on patrol last night and took a nasty tumble. He's got a whopping great bump on his forehead where he hit the ground.'

Peg tried unsuccessfully to stifle a giggle at the thought of Alice's po-faced husband coming a cropper in the dark. It wasn't very dignified for a man whose serious nature verged on the supercilious at times. Air-raid wardens in general were the butt of many jokes, being unpopular with the public for their zealous enforcement of blackout regulations and constant cries of 'Put that light out!' 'That's irony for you,' she said. 'A lord and master of the blackout having an accident in the dark.'

'It isn't funny, Peg,' said Alice in a tone of mild admonition. 'He really hurt himself, and he *had* been out doing his bit for the war effort after being at work all day. I don't take the mickey out of your Tom when he does his ARP duty.'

'I know you don't, love, and I shouldn't laugh. But you know what a clown I am; always seeing a joke when there isn't one. Peeling an onion can have me in fits,' said Peg, a woman of generous proportions, hearty and gregarious, with greying dark hair tucked into the black straw hat she

1

was wearing. She was dressed in a faded floral frock that had been dragged out of the wardrobe every summer for more years than she cared to count. 'But seriously, people really should be more careful. Whoever left the bike there ought to know better. Poor old Ernie. Is he all right?'

'He'll live, but he's none too happy,' Alice replied. 'He grazed both his knees and was left with a rotten headache so he had a face like a fiddle when he went off to work this morning.'

Nothing new there then, thought Peg, since Ernie Porter wasn't best known for his sunny smile. But she said, 'The blackout is causing more problems than the war at the moment for us here at home. The bombs we've all been living in fear of still haven't come.'

'It makes you wonder if quite so many precautions are necessary, doesn't it?' suggested Alice as they passed a disused pub that was now a first-aid centre heavily protected by banks of sandbags. 'What with our gardens being dug up for underground shelters and not being able to see a thing when you go out at night.'

'We have to be prepared, Alice,' Peg pointed out in a more serious mood. 'Especially now that all these dogfights in the skies between our planes and the Germans are happening so regular. It pains me to say it, but I reckon it's only a matter of time before we get bombed. That little rat Hitler means business.'

'We've been saying that ever since war broke out a year ago, and nothing's happened,' Alice reminded her. 'The blackout is so damned dangerous.'

Alice was a mousy-haired, brown-eyed woman of rather a sober person-ality; the result, in Peg's opinion, of being married to such a taciturn man for so many years. Constant gloom was bound to erode even the most buoyant sense of humour. By some miracle it didn't seem to have rubbed off on the couple's daughters, probably because Alice was such a devoted mother.

'Not half as dangerous as bombs raining down on us with no protection, though,' Peg responded now. 'Mind you, I always find those beauties up there a comfort.' She paused, looking up at the glorious blue sky where the silver barrage balloons were tinged with gold from the morning sun. Londoners had become accustomed to seeing the balloons since the Battle of Britain had begun in July. Watching the vapour trails left by the fighting planes had become something of a pastime for many people too.

'I think most people do.' Alice looked around her at the sunlit street, the privets dusty and dry, and a few tired geraniums here and there in front gardens. 'It's another beautiful day.'

'The weather is one thing we can't complain about. It's been a glorious summer,' agreed Peg

'Yeah. I'm glad we didn't send the kids away on the evacuation scheme, aren't you?'

'Not half,' replied Peg without hesitation. 'Things would have to be really dire here before I'd send young Lenny away.'

'I feel the same way about Pansy,' said Alice. 'Whatever comes, we'll face it together, as a family.'

'At least you don't have sons who will be sent away to fight,' Peg mentioned.

'Neither do you at the moment, as Ed's only seventeen,' Alice pointed out.

'If the war goes on for any length of time . . .'

'It won't,' her friend was quick to assure her. 'Everyone says it won't last much longer. It'll be over long before Ed is of an age to be called up. And we can both be truly thankful that our husbands are too old to go to war.'

'That's a fact,' agreed Peg.

'Nell was saying that she wouldn't mind joining one of the services, though,' Alice remarked, referring to her eldest daughter.

'Ooh, I don't suppose you'd like that very much, with the women's forces having such a bad name.'

'You're right, I wouldn't,' Alice confirmed. 'You hear such stories of what those ATS girls get up to in their spare time. Still, I don't think she'd pass the medical if she were to apply. Even though she's grown out of her asthma, I think it would probably still go against her.'

The two women were both in their mid-forties and had been close friends since primary school. They lived in adjoining streets and saw each other most days if they could possibly manage it. Through joy and tribulation, marriage and motherhood, their friendship had endured and was of great value to them both, even though they had very different personalities.

Peg had two sons: Ed, who was seventeen, and Lenny aged ten. Alice had two daughters: seventeen-year-old Nell and her little sister Pansy, who was nine. Having been raised under the aegis of their mothers' stable friendship, there was a natural sense of kinship among the children which pleased both women. The bond between the two families was a warm and enriching element in all of their lives; there was a sense that no matter what problems arose, they were never entirely alone.

Alice had a sudden thought. 'Your Ed is in a reserved occupation anyway, isn't he?' she reminded Peg. 'Engineering workers are needed here at home. So he won't have to go in the services even when he does come of age.'

Peg gave a dry laugh. 'That won't stop him joining up if he thinks he should. King and Country and all that,' she said. 'No matter what they do at Barker's Engineering to stop him from signing on, he'll do what he thinks is right. You know what some young fellas are like for a spot of adventure.'

'As you say, I'm lucky having daughters; at least I don't have to worry about them getting sent away to fight,' said Alice. 'Even if Nell were to join up she wouldn't go into action. They'd draw the line at putting women into combat, surely.'

'Talking of Nell, is she still doing well in her job?' enquired Peg chattily.

'Yeah, she's doing fine, thanks,' Alice nodded. 'She's very conscientious in her work; puts a lot into it because she's hoping to get promoted to personal secretary eventually. Even though she's a qualified shorthand typist she's still a bit young for a position as a secretary. She's gaining valuable experience in the stenographers' pool, taking dictation from different people on the management.'

'That's good.'

'She was saying that her shorthand has to be book-perfect so that if she's away for any reason and there's work outstanding, it's readable for someone else to type up.'

'I suppose it would have to be, when you think about it,' opined Peg. 'I've always had a soft spot for Nell. She enjoys a bit of a lark with her friends like all young girls, but she's got her head screwed on.'

'I'm glad she persevered with her evening classes. Her training will stand her in good stead.'

'I was pleased that Ed decided to get a trade behind him too,' said Peg.

'It's more important for him, of course,' remarked Alice, 'since a man has to work all his life.'

'Whereas Nell will give up when she marries.'

'Exactly! But don't mention wedding bells just yet,' said Alice laughingly. 'That's one expense Ernie and I can do without at the moment.'

'One of the drawbacks of having daughters is that you get lumbered with the wedding expenses,' said Peg. 'Tom and I are lucky as far as that's concerned.'

'Listen to the two of us, talking so far into the future,' remarked Alice lightly. 'Goodness knows what's brought that on.'

But they both knew perfectly well that it was just a diversion from the present time and the ghastly war that instilled fear into the hearts of everyone, even if they were at pains not to show it. So far it had been quiet in London, but the threat of annihilation was always there and had grown stronger recently, with the air attacks and news of bombing on the outskirts of the capital.

Pansy and Lenny approached them at full pelt. 'Can I have some sweets, Mum?' asked Pansy, a thin, rather nondescript child with the look of her mother about her. She had large round eyes and brown hair tied with ribbon into bunches.

'If we can get any,' Alice replied.

'Can I have some too?' asked Lenny, fair-haired and freckle-faced with the wickedest grin.

'If there are any about,' nodded his mother.

'We'll go on ahead and look in the sweet shop,' said Lenny, and they both hurried away.

'I reckon sweets will be the next thing to go on ration,' opined Alice as the children ran off. 'A good thing too. At least the distribution would be fairer.'

'Don't talk about sweet rationing, for Gawd's sake, Alice,' joshed Peg. 'I haven't got used to tea being on ration yet. You know how I love my cuppa. Talking of sweets,' she went on, 'I wouldn't mind a few suckers for the show tonight.'

'Me neither.'

'You're still coming then?'

'Not half. It isn't often I get a night out. You know what a home body Ernie is.'

To say the least, thought Peg. She couldn't remember the last time Ernie

Porter had taken his wife out, but she just said, 'Tom and I will be round to call for you about seven o'clock to drop Lenny off at your place, then the four of us can walk to the theatre together. All right?'

'Smashing. I'm looking forward to it.'

'Meanwhile, let's do the sweetshop first to keep the kids quiet, the butcher's next, then the greengrocer's, same as usual,' suggested Peg as they arrived at the shopping parade.

'Suits me,' agreed Alice.

They made their way along the crowded street under the coloured awnings, stopping every so often to exchange a few words with acquaintances. They had both lived in Chiswick all their lives and knew a lot of people.

The noise in the stenographers' pool at Barker's Engineering factory was loud and relentless, the continuous clatter of typewriters creating a harsh metallic din.

'Fancy the pictures tonight?' came the voice of Nell Porter's friend Polly Brown, who sat at the next desk and never allowed such things as noise or the strict 'no talking' office rule to interfere with the organisation of her social life.

Nell, a bright-eyed brunette with loose shoulder-length hair, paused momentarily and turned towards her, shaking her head. 'I can't tonight, I'm sorry. I've got to look after my sister and my mum's friend's little boy. Mum and Dad and their friends are all going to see a show at the Chiswick Empire.'

'Can't you get out of it?' asked the hedonistic Polly.

'No. Not without ruining my mum's night out,' replied Nell. 'I wouldn't want to do that because she hardly ever goes out anywhere nice.'

'She shouldn't expect you to baby-sit,' opined Polly with an air of outrage. 'They're not your kids.'

'She doesn't expect me to,' Nell came back at her, fiercely defensive of her mother. 'I'm doing it because I want her to have a break from the house. Anyway, I don't mind.'

'You must be mad if you don't mind staying in to look after a couple of nippers,' expressed Polly in disgust. 'You wouldn't catch me doing anything as boring as that.'

'It isn't as if they're babies that will need attention,' Nell pointed out. 'Once they've gone to bed I'll read and listen to the wireless. My hair needs washing so I'll do that as well.'

'Blimey, Nell. I thought you were seventeen, not seventy. You'll be old before your time at this rate.'

'That's just too bad.'

'Whoops, look out!' Polly cut in swiftly. 'The Crow is heading this way.'

As both girls became glued to their work as though their attention hadn't strayed for a second all day, the aptly named supervisor Miss Crow swept on to the scene.

'Miss Porter and Miss Brown.' She was almost shouting to make herself heard, and her mouth was tight with irritation. 'How many more times must I remind you that you are paid by the company to work, not to gossip?'

Polly shook with an attack of nervous giggles, which did nothing for the older woman's temper. 'Sorry, Miss Crow,' she managed to splutter eventually.

'I'm glad you find it amusing, young lady,' responded the supervisor with withering sarcasm. 'I hope you'll find it as funny when you're at the labour exchange looking for another job as good as this one.' She paused before adding triumphantly, 'Without a decent reference from Barker's.'

Nell was having a struggle not to laugh, the fact that it would be entirely inappropriate heightening the compulsion to an almost unbearable level. 'We weren't talking for long, Miss Crow,' she was able to utter in a voice distorted from containing herself. 'And we didn't actually stop work for more than a minute.'

'I have a very good view of all the staff in my section of this office, thank you very much,' announced the supervisor, who was a spinster in her late thirties and very diligent in her work. 'I can see exactly what is going on at all times, so I know exactly how long you stopped work for, and it was a lot more than a minute. It's my job to notice these things. We don't tolerate time-wasters here at Barker's Engineering. There's a war on and our contribution in the office is just as important as what they do out on the factory floor. Without administration the whole place would fall apart. So you two need to get on with your work, instead of chattering.'

'Sorry, Miss Crow,' said Nell, and meant it.

'Me too,' added Polly, who didn't.

'I'll let it go this time. Back to work now, and don't let me catch you talking again or I shall have to report you to the overall head of department, who may see fit to mention it to Mr Barker himself. He likes to be kept up to date with what's happening in every aspect of his business. So for your own sakes, don't make me have to come over to reprimand you again.'

'Old cow,' said Polly later, when the two girls were walking home along the riverside from the factory at Hammersmith to the leafier banks of Chiswick.

'It's over and done with now, so I should forget all about it if I were you,' advised Nell, enjoying the scent of incipient autumn mingled with the familiar mixture of oil and tar. A gentle river breeze shivered across the undulating surface of the water and made itself felt through the navy-blue cardigan she was wearing over a white blouse and grey skirt, which was suitable attire for her job. Swans and ducks enjoyed themselves in the outer reaches of the sunlit waters, not bothered by the busy flow of commercial craft carrying such essentials as coal and coke, wood and food.

'She needs a man to give her something to think about other than what's going on in her rotten old office,' Polly went on, as though Nell hadn't spoken.

'Maybe she has a man,' her friend suggested. 'She isn't married but she could have a boyfriend.'

'If she has, he doesn't put much of a smile on her face, does he?' said Polly. 'Still, anyone willing to go out with her would have to be desperate. She looks like the back of a bus. Anyway, she's too old.'

'Don't be so horrible,' chided Nell, who didn't have a malicious bone in her body. 'She's only doing her job, and we don't know what her life is like outside of the office. We know nothing about the woman. She might have all sorts of terrible problems and be very lonely.'

'Can you wonder that she's lonely, the way she carries on? Anyway, I don't know why you are sticking up for her.'

'She isn't the sweetest-natured of people, I admit, but she has a job to do,' Nell pointed out. 'Anyway, all offices have strict rules. It's a well-known fact.'

'Factory girls have a laugh and a joke. They even sing while they're working,' said Polly enviously.

'So I've heard.' Nell chuckled. 'Can you imagine what Miss Crow would do if we burst into song at our desks?'

'It would probably give the old bag a heart attack, and good riddance too.'

'Polly, that's wicked . . . you shouldn't say things like that.'

'Honestly, Nell, I wonder about you sometimes, the way you take her side,' admonished Polly. 'Anyone would think you were on the management too. It's almost as if you want a job like hers where you can boss everyone around.'

'I certainly do *not*. I want to be a personal secretary, you know that very well.'

'I can't imagine anything on earth more boring.'

'At least it's higher up in the office pecking order, and the money's better.'

'You sound just like my mum,' Polly sighed, her voice heavy with discontent. 'I only went to work in an office because she practically forced me into it. She thinks it's a cut above working in a shop or a factory. I think it must be the dullest job there is.'

'Why don't you do something else then?' suggested Nell patiently. 'There are a lot more opportunities for women in wartime, with the men away.'

'I don't want to do men's work,' Polly said definitely.

'Go into something really worthwhile like nursing then.'

'Ugh, no thanks. I can't stand illness; it makes me feel sick,' she said. 'I want to do something glamorous and exciting.'

'What is there that's glamorous and exiting for girls like us unless you have some special talent?'

'I might have special talent by the bucketful. Who knows? There could be a great actress inside of me waiting to get out. I'm not likely to get the chance to find out, am I? I mean, you have your fourteenth birthday and you have to pay your way at home. So it's out to work you go; unless you're a rich kid.'

'I think acting must be very hard work,' Nell remarked thoughtfully. 'All those lines to learn . . .'

'Not acting especially,' her friend cut in impatiently. 'Just something that's more fun than working in an office. Ordinary girls can go on the stage, can't they? You hear of them going on the halls.'

'If they can sing or tap-dance,' Nell pointed out. 'Perhaps you could take some dancing lessons, then do some sort of voluntary entertaining in your spare time.'

'I'd still have to work here during the day, though, wouldn't I,' Polly said. 'So there would be no point.'

'It would bring some glamour into your life and it might lead to something else,' Nell told her. 'You'll have to make some sort of an effort if you want to change your situation, Polly. It isn't likely to happen unless you do.'

'Taking a few dance lessons won't help,' Polly responded in her usual negative manner.

'Oh well, you'll just have to make the best of what you've got and count yourself lucky that we haven't had to go into domestic service, like women of our mothers' generation.'

'I'd sell my body sooner than wait hand and foot on some posh family.'

'You wouldn't . . .'

'I bloomin' well would,' she affirmed hotly. 'I wouldn't, *I couldn't* bow and scrape to a crowd of snobs.'

'I really don't know what you can do that's glamorous then, if you're not prepared to do anything but moan,' Nell told her. 'I mean, work is work. It isn't meant to be a picnic, especially now that there's a war on. We have to make a contribution to the war effort.'

'I'm talking about after the war.' Polly was thoughtful. 'What about a mannequin? I'd love to be one of those.'

Wouldn't we all? thought Nell, but she said, 'Why don't you make some enquiries about it then? Find out how you get into it so that you'll know what to do after the war.'

'Nah. No point. You probably need to have contacts in the right places and a rich daddy who'll support you and pay the training fees.' She sighed wistfully. 'Oh, why can't some wealthy film producer discover me and make me into a film star? That's more the sort of thing I'd be suited to.'

'I don't think there are any film producers around here.' Actually, Nell thought Polly was better-looking than a lot of the film stars they saw on the screen. She had a cloud of golden hair, peachy skin and a gorgeous figure that she wasn't afraid to show off. 'But I think you'd do well in films if you could learn to act.'

'Ooh, fat chance of that while I'm tied to this place.' Polly emitted an eloquent sigh. 'I know I was meant for more than being stuck in a typing pool all day under the beady eye of the Crow.'

'Why not join the Land Army?' proposed Nell, clinging tenaciously to her sorely tried patience. 'That would be an adventure, and it looks like good fun in the recruitment posters.'

'No thanks. That's far too much like hard work for me. Long hours; out in all weathers. Messing about with smelly animals.' She made a face. 'Ugh, not likely!'

'In that case, why not knuckle down to this job and get to be a secretary?'

'Ooh, how can I resist?' Polly said with irony.

'You never know, it could turn out to be the way to this better life you want so badly. Your boss might fall for you,' said Nell. 'You do hear of bosses marrying their secretaries.'

'Men in that position are always married,' declared Polly, sounding about thirty-five. 'A bit on the side is what the secretary would be. Not that I would mind that if he gave me lots of presents and somewhere nice to live.'

'You're terrible,' rebuked Nell, but she was smiling.

'So my mother is always telling me,' Polly said. 'But no, I don't think the secretary route is a plausible way out, so I'll just have to hope that some rich single bloke will come along and rescue me from my boring life. Meanwhile I have to find someone to go to the flicks with tonight, since you can't come.'

Nell and Polly weren't lifelong friends and had only palled up when they'd started work at Barker's together as school-leavers. Nell liked Polly and thought she was good fun, but was sometimes irritated by her constant craving for a different sort of life. Being non grammer school, and working class, a job as a secretary was probably about as good as it got for girls like them, especially as Polly wasn't prepared to make any sort of effort to change things.

Now Nell said, 'Sorry, kid, but I can't let my mum down; another time perhaps.'

'That's all right. But honestly, Nell, you are getting to be so boring lately.' Polly sighed. 'I mean . . . baby-sitting and wanting to be a secretary. Really!'

'At least I'm living in the real world.'

'With people like Miss Crow on your back all day. I want more from life than that.'

'I hope you get it, Polly, I really do.'

They turned off the towpath and crossed the road towards Chiswick High Road, where they parted company. Nell was still thinking about Polly as she made her way home through streets of suburban houses. It must be awful to be that dissatisfied with your life, especially as Polly stood little chance of achieving her fanciful notions, mainly because she expected something wonderful to drop into her lap without her lifting a finger.

'Hello, my little chickadees,' boomed Tom Mills that evening when Nell and Pansy answered the door to him and his wife. 'How are my two favourite girls?'

'Fine thanks, Uncle Tom,' replied Nell.

'How about you, Titch?' enquired Tom, smiling warmly at Pansy. 'Have you been good?' He always gave Pansy plenty of attention; she was a particular favourite of his.

She nodded, giving him a bashful smile, her cheeks suffused with pink, because she was sometimes rather a shy child.

Nell turned her attention to his wife, who appeared behind him wearing a navy-blue hat with a matching feather and a long blue crêpe de Chine dress. 'My, my, you're looking very smart tonight, Auntie Peg,' she complimented.

'I've had this frock a million years, but thank you, ducks.' Peg swept past her husband as he took off his trilby hat and put it on the hall stand. A thickset man, the handsome looks of his youth still vaguely detectable, Tom had kind blue eyes and greying fair hair. This evening he was spruced up in a navy-blue striped suit with a waistcoat, a white starched collar and a dark red tie. 'I hope your mum and dad are all ready to go,' Peg said. 'We want a bit of time to have a swift one before the show.'

'I'm sure they won't be long,' said Nell hopefully.

As Peg headed for the living room, Tom looked towards the front door.

12

'Where's that lad of ours got to, I wonder.' He shouted through the doorway: 'Lenny . . . come on in now, boy. I want a few serious words with you before we go. I want to make sure you behave yourself.'

No response.

'Get in here when I tell you,' Tom persisted, increasing the volume substantially. 'What are you doing out there?'

'I'll find him while you go and hurry Mum and Dad up, or else you'll all be late,' offered Nell, and Pansy trotted along after her.

Like the rest of the terraced houses in the street, of which the Porters' was the end one, the front garden was just a narrow strip the width of the house. It had a tiny lawn, an untidy privet hedge and a tall cherry tree that never bore fruit. The girls found Lenny up the tree, which wasn't surprising since he tended to be anywhere that was forbidden.

'Your dad wants you indoors, so you'd better get down here sharpish,' advised Nell.

'I can't come down yet,' he called.

'You won't half cop it if you don't get down and come indoors quick,' warned Pansy with concern. 'You know you're not supposed to climb trees.'

'I had to climb this one because Tiddles is up here and he's stuck,' he explained, referring to the Porters' long-haired and much-loved tabby cat.

'Oh dear, the poor little thing.' This was Pansy, who was devoted to the animal.

'Come on, puss,' cajoled Lenny. The tabby promptly shot down the tree and into the house, passing Tom, who was on his way out to find his son.

Lenny slid down the tree trunk, catching his trousers on a small twig, which produced a loud ripping sound. 'Crikey, that's done it,' he said, looking down to see the pocket hanging off his short grey trousers, as well as a large tear in the leg material. 'I'll be for it now.'

'It's your own fault. How many more times do you have to be told not to climb trees?' his father admonished.

'I had to; the cat was stuck up there,' he explained.

'Now you're telling porkies,' stated his father. 'That moggy has just run past me at high speed. Stuck, my eye!'

'I thought he couldn't get down,' Lenny explained. 'He was acting like he couldn't. He was meowing like mad.'

'I believe you, thousands wouldn't.' Tom looked at the large rip in the leg of his son's trousers. 'Oh my Gawd. Your mother will do her nut.'

At that moment Peg emerged from the house.

'Oh no,' she exclaimed, taking in the scene in a second. 'You've been up that tree, Lenny. Just look at the state of those trousers. You've torn them nearly in two.' She cuffed him round the ear. 'You're a little heathen, Lenny Mills, and I'm very cross with you.'

'It wasn't Lenny's fault. He went up the tree to get Tiddles.' True to form, Pansy leapt to the defence of her friend and hero. 'The poor thing couldn't get down.'

'I admire your loyalty, love, but it's wasted on this one,' snorted Peg. 'That child just can't resist getting into mischief.' She inspected the damage to the trousers more closely. 'Lord only knows how I'm going to mend these. Honestly, Lenny, you are the limit.'

'Sorry, Mum,' he said.

'Sorry is all very well, but when are you going to learn to do as you're told?'

He shrugged.

She looked about to explode. 'You're asking for another clip round the ear with that attitude, my lad,' she warned.

Alice appeared at the front door in her best black dress worn to the lower calf and a hat with a long curling feather. 'What's going on out here?'

'It's this little monkey again,' explained Peg. 'He's only been up your cherry tree. I don't know what we're gonna do with the little perisher, I really don't.'

'Oh dear.' Alice was diplomatically noncommittal. It wasn't wise to criticise someone else's child, even if his mother was your best friend. Peg would blow her top if anyone else suggested that Lenny was anything less than perfect, no matter what she said to the contrary herself. Anyway, he was a good-hearted child for all his devilment and would go to the ends of the earth for Pansy. For that reason alone Alice could forgive him anything.

'We'd better be on our way,' suggested Tom, slipping his arm around his wife in a natural gesture of affection. 'Is Ernie nearly ready, Alice?'

'I think so but I'll go and give him a shout,' she said.

'I've put Lenny's pyjamas and toothbrush on the bottom stair, Nell,' said Peg. She turned to her son. 'Be a good boy or Nell won't look after you again.'

'Yeah, you behave yourself tonight, my lad,' added Tom supportively. 'Don't give Nell any trouble.' He turned to her. 'You have my permission to use whatever form of discipline you feel necessary if he gives you a hard time.'

'He won't do that, will you, Lenny?' Nell said, ruffling the boy's hair. Like her mother, she was very fond of him for all his mischievousness. 'You lot just go off and enjoy yourselves and forget all about what might be going on here.'

'Enjoying ourselves is something Peg and I never have any trouble doing,' Tom grinned. 'Isn't that right, love?'

'Too true,' agreed Peg, beaming at him. 'Life's too short to miss out on the fun.'

Nell found herself smiling too, because Peg and Tom Mills were the sort of people who could turn a fish queue in the rain into a party. She sometimes wished her own parents were a bit more like them, but they never seemed to let their hair down.

They emerged from the house now. Her father – who worked in the stores at a war factory – was a tall, pale man with pointed features and worried eyes peering through horn-rimmed spectacles. He was soberly dressed in a dark suit and stiff collar, his greying brown hair slicked back close to his head. As usual his features were arranged in a serious expression.

'Have a good time, you two,' enthused Nell. 'Just sit back and enjoy yourselves.'

'We will.' Alice looked concerned. 'Make sure the children go to bed on time.'

'I will, don't worry. I'm not having them running about all night, getting on my nerves,' Nell assured her. 'Once they've settled down I'm going to wash my hair and listen to the wireless, so I'll want some peace.'

Alice kissed both her daughters good night in her normal affectionate manner. Ernie, who never indulged in such intimacies, stood aside.

'Have a good time, Dad,' said Nell.

'That's the general idea,' he responded with only the glimmer of a smile.

Watching the four of them walk down the street, Nell felt a pang. There was something piercingly poignant about her parents somehow. It was almost as though there was a vital ingredient missing between them, which always seemed especially noticeable when they were with Peg and Tom Mills. Nell's father had never been a sociable or cheerful man, and it occurred to her in that moment that she had always regarded him as a stranger; a familiar but shadowy figure who was always there in the background but never actively involved in family life.

Maybe he was warm and loving towards her mother in private. He certainly never had been in Nell's presence as far as she could remember, and for some reason at this particular moment she felt a painful empathy with her mother. She comforted herself with the thought that they both seemed content with the way things were. They occasionally had words, but Nell had never heard any serious arguments, unlike other children in the street when she was growing up. Some of those poor kids used to be sent out to play while their dad was giving Mum 'a pasting'.

So she and Pansy were lucky in that respect. But she couldn't help wishing that their father was a bit more like Uncle Tom, who was so jolly and warm-hearted. There was always plenty of fun and laughter in the Mills house.

'All right, you two,' she said now to the younger ones. 'Let's go inside so that you can get ready for bed.'

'Already?' objected Pansy. 'It's much too early. We're not little kids, you know.'

'You're not adults either, and while Mum isn't here, I'm the boss,' asserted Nell. 'But how would it be if you were to get ready for bed, then we'll all have a game of Ludo for a little while until you get sleepy?'

'Ooh yeah, that's better.' Pansy brightened considerably, slipping her hand into her adored elder sister's as they went inside. 'Isn't it, Lenny?'

'Smashing,' he agreed.

Nell had just finished washing her hair at the kitchen sink when there was a knock at the front door. Wrapping the towel turban-like around her head, she went to answer it.

'Wotcha, Nell,' said a tall, blond-haired young man with the bluest of blue eyes.

16

'Hello, Ed,' she responded, ushering Ed Mills inside without any preamble because he was almost like one of the family. She stood at the door of the long, narrow kitchen. 'Cuppa tea?'

'That would be nice, but are you sure your mum won't mind us dipping into the precious family ration?'

'Of course she won't. It balances out between the two families, since we are always in and out of each other's houses.'

'I don't mind if I do then.'

He followed her into the kitchen and stood by the wooden draining board at the side of the deep square sink while she filled the kettle and put it to boil on the gas cooker.

'It's all quiet upstairs, so I presume you didn't have any trouble getting the kids to bed.'

'They've only just stopped giggling and larking about up there but I left them to it and got on with washing my hair. I knew they'd go off to sleep eventually.'

'You're bound to get high jinks if my little brother's around,' Ed remarked. 'He's a right horror.'

'You were no angel when you were his age, if I remember rightly,' Nell reminded him.

'I'm sure I wasn't as bad as he is.'

'You gave your mum a few headaches, I reckon.'

'It doesn't seem to have done her any harm.'

'No, it doesn't; she's always full of beans.' Nell got the tea things out of the kitchen cabinet and put them on the table while she waited for the kettle to boil. Turning to the kitchen mirror by the back door, she removed the towel and rubbed her hair vigorously, then ran a comb through it. Its near black shade emphasised the green in her eyes. 'It'll take ages to dry and I hate going to bed while it's still damp. That's the trouble in the summer; you can't dry it by the fire.'

'You'll have to put your head in the oven,' Ed chuckled. 'But don't forget to light the gas or they'll be laying you out.'

'Very funny,' she smiled, completely unabashed to be seen by him in such a natural state. 'It's all right for you boys with your little bit of hair.'

She poured the tea and they took it into the living room, a homely part of the house that was at the centre of family life. It had a bulky beige

17

three-piece suite standing on polished brown lino patterned with squares, and a large rug in the centre. There was a sideboard with a wireless set sitting on top, a table and chairs, occasional furnishings and a multitude of ornaments dotted about.

'Did you call in just to see me or do you have an ulterior motive?' Nell enquired as they sat down in the armchairs near the fireplace, unlit at this time of year.

'Ulterior motive,' he admitted without shame.

'Why doesn't that surprise me?'

'Because we're friends, and friends ask each other favours,' he replied.

'I hope you don't want to borrow any money, because I'm skint until pay day.'

'As if I would come to you on the cadge,' he said, offended. 'Honestly, Nell, surely you know me better than that.'

'Keep your wig on, I was only joking.'

'That's all right then.' He sipped his tea, looking at her over the rim of the cup. 'The reason I'm here is, a mate of mine down Hammersmith way is having a party on Saturday night and we're a bit short of females. His parents are going to the country for the weekend to see his little brother, who's been evacuated down there, so we'll have the house to ourselves.'

'Oh,' Nell said knowingly. 'I see.'

'Anyway, I wondered, if you're not doing anything special that is, if you might fancy rounding up a few of your girlfriends and coming along to join us.'

'Will we be safe on our own with you lot?' She wasn't being serious. She knew Ed could be trusted.

'Leave off. A few bottles of beer and some records on the gramophone. You'll come to no harm.'

'That's a shame,' she joked. 'Seriously, though, it sounds like a good laugh and I fancy a party. I'll see what I can do about getting some others to come along with me. I know Polly from the office will jump at the chance. She'll never say no to a knees-up, or anything of a social nature.'

'Is that the blonde I've seen you with at work?'

She nodded.

'That'll please the lads. She's a real cracker.'

18

'I'll tell her you said that.' She gave a wry grin. 'No . . . on second thoughts, maybe I won't. She's big-headed enough already, and I'm not saying anything that I wouldn't say to her face.'

'There'll be a few there who will fancy you, as well,' he told her. 'So I shall be keeping a brotherly eye on you.'

'And spoil my fun? You'd better not.'

'I'll just make sure no one takes liberties.'

'Don't you dare embarrass me,' she warned. 'I mean it, Ed.'

'That's what brothers are for, isn't it?'

'You're not my brother.'

'As good as.'

She couldn't argue with that.

'So, what are you up to tonight when you leave here?' she enquired chattily.

'Nothing much. I'm going home.'

'Ooh, no hot date lined up?'

'No.'

'You must be losing your touch,' she joshed. Having fared so well as far as looks and personality were concerned, Ed never lacked for female admirers.

'Cheeky madam. There's nothing wrong with my technique, I can assure you, but I can't afford to take a girl out during the week on my wages. It's an expensive hobby, this courting lark.'

'I suppose it would be.'

'Anyway, it was my night for duty but I've been down the depot and there's nothing doing, so they said there was no need for me to stay.' He was a volunteer for the Auxiliary Fire Service a few nights a week, running messages on his bike. 'None of my mates are around tonight either. They're all out doing their bit for the war somewhere, I suppose.'

'Still no bombs, though the siren has been a good few times, hasn't it?'

'Mm. There was an air raid out Croydon way the other night, so I heard,' he mentioned, his expression becoming grave. 'Some people got killed apparently.'

'Someone told me about that too,' she said, looking serious. 'Do you reckon Jerry is working his way towards London?'

'I think we've all got that feeling, even if we don't like to admit it. But who knows? We all thought our end had come a year ago and we're still alive and kicking.'

'Let's hope it stays that way.'

He stayed chatting for a while longer. They knew each other so well, they were never lost for words.

'I'll do my best to get some of the girls lined up for the party,' Nell assured him as she saw him off at the gate.

'Thanks, kid.'

The night was clear and warm, the air infused with the ambrosia of autumn. 'It's so quiet out here at the moment, you'd never know there was a war on, would you?' he said. 'Apart from the stirrup pump and bucket,' he added, glancing towards the two items at the side of the front door.

'Never once used.'

'Let's hope they never are.'

'I'll second that.'

'Anyway, about Saturday,' he began. 'The lads are meeting up at my place, so if you come round about half past seven, we'll all go off together. Will that suit you?'

'Fine.'

'G'night, Nell.'

'Night, Ed.'

Standing at the gate watching him in the moonlight as he strode off down the street, she was imbued with a warm feeling towards him. He was a smashing bloke and a dear friend. Fortunately there was nothing of a romantic nature between them to complicate matters. As he turned the corner, she went back inside, pleasantly anticipating the party on Saturday.

Chapter Two

Polly welcomed the invitation to the party with such eagerness, an eaves-dropping stranger might have assumed that she was socially deprived.

'Thank God for a chance to go out and have some fun at last,' she enthused. It was Saturday and she and Nell were walking home from work in the late afternoon sun. 'I can't wait to get there.'

'It should be a bit of a giggle anyway,' responded Nell with less dramatic fervour. It was just a party, she thought, not a life-changing event.

'I reckon we deserve a good night out after having to work all day on a Saturday,' declared Polly with her habitual air of complaint. 'What a bloomin' pain that is.'

'It's the same for everybody during wartime,' Nell reminded her. 'They need the extra productivity so it can't be helped. At least we get away a bit earlier on a Saturday.'

'The difference is so small it's hardly worth bothering about,' Polly said.

'We don't have to go in tomorrow, though, and that will be nice.' Nell was determined to stay positive. 'It'll be the first Sunday we've had off for ages.'

'Mm, there is that, I suppose,' Polly conceded with reluctance. 'It's just as well we don't have to go in to work, since we're gonna be up all night enjoying ourselves.'

'I don't know if it's going to be an all-night party,' Nell mentioned. 'Ed didn't say anything about that.'

'It's bound to go on until the small hours anyway, as the old folks are away,' Polly informed her knowingly. 'These things always do. And I plan to be the last one to leave. I shall probably get home with the milk.'

'You must have a very understanding mother,' remarked Nell. 'My mum would have forty fits if I stayed out all night.'

'So will mine, but that won't stop me doing it if I'm having a good time,' expressed Polly jauntily. 'I just shut my ears to their nagging and let them get on with it. You're only young once, so you might as well make the most of it while you can. In fact, I see it as my duty to do so. Which brings me to the subject of boys at this party. Will there be any worth getting dressed up for?'

'I don't know exactly who's going,' replied Nell. 'But I should think so, because Ed has some nice mates.'

'Would you have any objection if I went after Ed himself?' Polly enquired. 'I wouldn't be treading on your toes or anything, would I?'

'Of course not. Ed's just a friend.'

'You must be mad. He wouldn't be just a friend if *I* was on pally terms with him, I can tell you,' Polly said, giggling. 'I only know him by sight through seeing him around at the factory, but he's gorgeous, and I've been dying for the chance to get to know him properly. Oh yeah, not half! A party is the perfect opportunity to make him notice me. What's the competition going to be like?'

'I've no idea,' Nell told her. 'I invited a few girls I've kept in touch with from school.'

'I hope none of them are lookers.'

'They are all absolutely beautiful.'

Polly halted in her step and looked at her worriedly. 'Are they . . . honestly?' she asked.

Nell burst out laughing. 'You are so vain, it would serve you right if I meant it, but I'm only joking.'

'I'm not vain. I want to get my man, that's all,' Polly retaliated. 'A bloke like Ed Mills can take his pick.'

'Don't worry. All the girls I know who are going to the party are quite ordinary to look at.' Nell chuckled and added jokingly, 'Except for me, of course, and I'll steal the show.'

'You're not interested in Ed Mills, so I'm not counting you.'

'And there was me thinking you didn't rate me as any sort of competition.'

'I didn't think you were bothered about those things.'

'I'm not, you dope. I'm just teasing you. It isn't difficult to pull your leg, because if you're not hankering after a different sort of life, you're worrying about the way you look. Why not take things as they come a bit more?'

'It isn't in my nature.'

'No. I don't believe it is.'

The weather was still lovely; just a few wispy clouds smudged here and there on the clear blue sky, the sun feeling warm on Nell's face. The river looked sage green in places and various shades of brown in others, and the trees were still luxuriant, their colours as yet unchanged by the coming season. The two girls turned off the riverside towards the town.

'I shall wear the lowest-necked blouse I can find,' announced Polly brightly. 'I don't want the delectable Ed Mills to be left in any doubt as to the extent of my charms.'

'Might that not give the wrong impression?' queried Nell.

'It wouldn't be the wrong one as far as I'm concerned,' she said. 'I intend to have a good time.'

'You don't mean . . . ?'

'Yes, I do,' she cut in. 'It won't be the first time either.'

'Ooh, Polly.' Nell was deliciously intrigued. Polly was the most daring friend she'd ever had. Girls did sometimes make claims of a similar nature, which were received with a mixture of awe and disbelief. But Polly's had the ring of truth about it. Nell wouldn't put anything past her.

'Don't sound so shocked,' admonished Polly. 'We're grown women and it's the most natural thing in the world.'

That didn't make it any the less a taboo subject within earshot of the older generation, though, thought Nell, and definitely forbidden in prac-tice until after they were married.

'What's it like . . . ?'

'Find out for yourself,' Polly advised in a worldly-wise manner. 'Don't take any notice of all this rubbish they ram down our throats because they're scared stiff we'll get pregnant. Supposing Hitler was to bomb us to the ground tonight? You'd die never knowing, wouldn't you?' They reached their parting point. 'Anyway, what time shall I call for you?'

'Just before half past seven will be fine,' said Nell. 'It only takes a few minutes to walk round to Ed's.'

'I'll see you later then.'

As she walked home, Nell was wondering what she had to wear that was suitable for a party. She didn't possess anything very glamorous because her lifestyle didn't demand it. She certainly didn't own anything of the sort Polly was planning on wearing, with a neckline that dug deep into her cleavage.

Tom Mills was a highly skilled metal-worker who was employed in an engineering factory in Acton. Before the war they had manufactured engines and parts for a variety of items including buses, trams and factory machines. Now they made such front-line essentials as tank engines and guns. Because the products were so urgently needed by the military, the hours were punishing and the work physically exhausting when carried out over such long periods of time.

But on Saturdays they finished earlier, and Tom had just left the factory and was on his way to the pub nearby with his pal Bert; they planned to have a quick pint before Tom caught the bus home. His normal means of transport – his bicycle – was out of action because of a puncture.

'I reckon we need something to take away the taste of the factory filth,' remarked Bert as they walked along the street together. 'I feel as though my mouth is full of metal dust.'

'Mine is the same,' agreed Tom, relishing the lovely autumn weather after being inside the factory all day. Even now, in the incipient evening, with a sweet coolness spicing the air, it was still mild, though the sun was low in the sky. 'I'm feeling parched.'

'It'll be a treat not to have to go into work tomorrow,' mentioned his friend as they stood at the bar, each making short work of a pint of bitter.

'I'll say,' nodded Tom. 'It'll be the first Sunday we've had off for weeks, with them being so short-staffed. I reckon I'll sleep till dinnertime, won't you?'

'Fat chance of that for me,' said Bert. '"Get up, you lazy sod!" the wife will shout up the stairs. Lying about in bed is strictly forbidden in our house without a doctor's certificate.'

'I'm sure you're exaggerating,' grinned Tom.

'You wouldn't say that if you knew my missus, mate,' said the other man with an air of feigned gloom. 'I gave up trying to fathom the workings of her mind years ago. Funny things, women, and my wife's the strangest of the lot, as I've told you before, especially when it comes to my having any pleasure. That really gets up her nose.'

Tom smiled. Bert fancied himself as a bit of a comedian and was well known for his tales of woe about his wife, all of which were taken with a pinch of salt by his workmates. Everyone knew he was devoted to her, and the anecdotes were all a part of his comic routine.

'I don't believe a word of it,' Tom told him. 'I bet she runs around after you like a housemaid.'

Bert puffed out his lips. 'Don't make me laugh,' he snorted. 'We don't all have wives like your Peg, who brings you tea in bed of a morning. A wet flannel in my face to wake me up is more the sort of thing I can expect.'

'Now you really are having me on,' said Tom.

'Well, maybe I am a bit,' conceded Bert with a wry grin. 'But she's an awesome woman just the same. You cross her at your peril. You don't know how lucky you are, mate.'

'I do, you know.' Tom's wife and family were everything to him. He knew he had a real diamond in Peg and there was nothing he wouldn't do for her.

The conversation moved on to the state of the war, the watered-down wartime beer and the new football season. They were in the middle of a discussion about the technicalities of their work when the fearful wail of the siren cut them short.

'It's probably just a false alarm,' suggested Bert.

'I'm off mate, just the same,' said Tom, emptying his glass. 'You never know when it might be the real thing. I don't want Peg worrying about me. I need to be home.'

'Yeah, me and all,' said his pal.

The two men left the pub and hurried towards the bus stop. Overhead there was a roar of aircraft, which wasn't unusual since the skies were often busy lately.

'Gawd Almighty, Tom, look up there,' said Bert, pointing towards the east, where the sky was flame-coloured.

'Bloody 'ell,' gasped Tom. 'It's started. Someone's getting it good and proper. Some part of our town is on fire.'

'That'll be the docks, I reckon,' speculated Bert. 'They say that's one of the Germans' prime targets.'

'I think you're right.'

Wherever it was it was of huge significance, as it meant that the waiting was over. Tom's blood turned to ice. After a whole year of being tensed up and ready, with precautions in place to confront the worst, only to find that there were no bombs to face, they had come at last. Imbued with fear for Peg and the boys, he broke into a run towards the bus stop.

Nell was in her underwear, still trying to decide what to wear to the party, when the siren went.

'Come down here quick, Nell,' her mother shrieked up the stairs. 'We've got to go in the shelter right away.'

She went to the bedroom door and called down, 'I don't think I'll bother, Mum; it'll only be another false alarm. I'm in the middle of getting ready to go to the party, and I don't want to be late in case the boys go without us. I don't know where the place is, you see.'

'Never mind all that; just come outside and have a look at the sky,' urged her mother in a tone of barely stifled panic. 'You'll soon change your mind about wanting to go out to the party when you see it. I want you down here, and make it snappy.'

Recognising the urgency in her mother's voice, Nell pulled on the first clothes to hand – a blouse and skirt – and sped down the stairs and out of the back door, where her parents were making their way across the garden to the Anderson shelter. Dad was laden down with blankets, and Mum was carrying a shopping bag in which Nell guessed there would be food of some sort. Alice turned to her daughter and pointed towards the rooftops of the houses backing on to theirs.

'I think that's reason enough to go down the shelter, don't you?' she said shakily.

'Blimey, I'll say it is.' Nell was breathless with fear.

Pansy had discovered that the cat was missing and was worried about him. 'Where is he?' she asked, peering around anxiously. 'Tiddles, come on, puss, puss.'

'He's here,' said Nell as the cat brushed passed her legs. He was quickly scooped up by Pansy.

Staring up to see the dusk sky suffused with amber above the chimney-tops, Nell was in no doubt about the gravity of the situation. Even though the fires must be a good distance away, London was now under attack. The moment everyone had been dreading was here. Forcing herself to stay calm, she mentally ran through the advice given in a government leaflet about what to do in the event of an air raid. 'Have you turned off the gas and electric, Mum?' she asked.

'I've taken care of it,' said her father. 'You'd better pop indoors and get your handbag, gas mask and identity card. Your mother's got the ration books.'

'Hurry up, Nell,' urged Pansy, happy now that she had the family pet safely in her arms. She was excited too, her mother having made the whole thing seem like an adventure in an effort to protect her from the terrible reality. 'We're all going down the shelter. Isn't it a lark? Mum's got some candles and food. She says we might sleep down there.'

'You'd better bring your winter coat, Nell,' shouted her mother as an afterthought. 'It'll be cold down there.'

'I'll be as quick as I can,' said Nell, running back inside to get her belongings, her insides quivering, the party forgotten.

'I'm sure Dad will be home in a minute,' Ed tried to reassure his worried mother as they sat in the chilly, damp Anderson shelter, a candle in a jam jar flickering over the dismal corrugated-iron walls. 'He's probably just missed the bus and had to wait a long time for another.'

'The raid is for real this time,' she said gravely. 'The colour of the sky is evidence of that.'

'That glow is coming from miles away; the other side of London probably,' Ed pointed out, hoping to comfort her. 'But don't worry. I'll stay here with you until Dad gets back.'

'What about the party?'

'Forget that.'

'You can go if you want to, son,' she said. 'I don't want you missing out on fun because of me.'

'Don't be daft. I'm not going anywhere until Dad gets back, and then, if I go anywhere at all, I shall go down to the AFS depot in case I'm needed there.'

'We'll be all right here on our own if you want to go now, won't we,

Lenny?' Peg said, putting on a brave face to hide her terror. 'But be careful out there.'

'We'll be fine,' said Lenny cheerfully; he was sitting on the wooden plank next to his mother, while Ed was seated opposite. 'Got anything to eat, Mum? I'm starving.'

'I've got some cheese sandwiches here, love,' she said, unwrapping a tea towel and handing him a doorstep, which was munched with enthusiasm.

Ed was dressed in his best suit, as he'd been ready for the party when the siren had sounded and they'd spotted the ominously coloured sky. That had been a moment of huge significance, he reflected, even though there had been no nearby explosions yet. The much-feared German bombs had arrived somewhere in London a year later than expected. It was only a matter of time before they came to their locality. The war on the home front had begun, and alongside the fear in his heart, there was also relief. At least now they could get on with whatever horror lay in store for them, instead of just worrying about it.

'Wotcha, you lot,' said Tom, climbing down into the shelter, squeezing in next to his wife and giving her a peck on the cheek. 'Sorry I'm late, love. I had to walk home. Don't ask me what happened to the buses. There just weren't any around.'

'The drivers are all in the shelter, I expect, and I don't blame them.' She handed him a sandwich. 'This might help to keep your strength up. I didn't get round to making any tea. I got a bit flustered when I saw the colour of the sky.'

'It shook me too,' he said.

'You must be worn out, you poor dear, having to walk all the way home,' she said warmly. 'I hope we don't have to stay down here all bloomin' night. You need your proper rest.'

'No more than you or anyone else. Ed's been at work all day too,' he pointed out.

'He's young.'

'Oh yeah, so I'm an old codger, am I? Is that what you're saying?' was his jovial response.

'You are getting on a bit now, Dad,' joshed Ed, entering into the bantering spirit. It was curious how they were all acting as though nothing out of the ordinary was happening.

'Maybe he is, but he's my old codger and it's my job to look after him,' said Peg.

'I've got the day off tomorrow, which will give me a break,' Tom mentioned. 'The all-clear will probably go in a minute anyway and we can all get back to normal.'

'Anyone fancy a game of cards?' asked Lenny.

'Not me, mate,' replied his brother. 'Now that Dad is back I'm going down the depot to see if they need a hand.'

'Be careful, son,' warned his mother, her stomach lurching with worry for him. 'Take shelter somewhere if the bombers get close.'

'I won't take any chances, don't worry, Mum. Shan't be long,' he said breezily, moving towards the shelter opening. 'See you all later.'

Peg almost added 'God willing' out loud, but managed to restrain herself because there was a child present and it was her duty to hide her feelings from Lenny even though she was terrified. No intelligent adult could be otherwise now that the Germans had finally arrived with their deadly weapons. For all the government's advice, no one could be truly prepared for the reality of being bombed.

'Finish your sandwich, Lenny, and I'll have a game with you,' she said. 'We might even get your dad to join in.'

'It'll help to pass the time,' agreed Tom in his usual easy-going manner.

Pansy thought the air-raid shelter was terrific fun, especially as it meant she had her elder sister's wholehearted attention.

'Snap!' she squealed as she spotted two Mr Buns in the candlelight.

'You're beating me hollow,' said Nell, pretending to care. 'I shall have to put a stop to that.'

'I always win when I play this with Lenny,' Pansy announced proudly. 'He gets ever so narked.'

'I reckon you must be having a crafty peek before you put the cards down,' Nell teased her.

This light-hearted accusation produced exactly the reaction Nell had hoped for: giggling outrage. Anything as long as it kept her sister happy and unafraid. Every child was entitled to that, in her opinion. This was the first proper air raid they'd had and it felt surreal; all of them sitting on wooden planks they had rigged up as benches in the sour-smelling candlelit bolthole, all trying to behave as though it was perfectly normal.

'Can Lenny come in our shelter next time?' Pansy enquired.

'No,' said her monosyllabic father.

'Why not?'

'Because I said so,' he replied irritably.

'He needs to be with his own family, love,' explained Alice in a softer tone.

'Why?'

Alice thought for a few moments before replying. 'Because it will probably be bedtime for the two of you,' she said. She could hardly frighten the child by pointing out that families needed to be together if they were going to get blown to bits. 'Anyway, we don't know that there'll be any more air raids after this.'

From outside came the sharp click of high heels on concrete; someone was walking up the garden path.

'Who on earth is that?' wondered Alice.

Nell went to the opening at the end of the shelter and poked her head out.

'Who is it?' she shouted loudly; it was almost completely dark now, and she couldn't see anything.

'It's me, Polly,' was the reply.

'We're out the back in the Anderson. Come round. The side gate isn't locked.'

There were more footsteps, and as Nell's eyes got accustomed to the dark, she could make out the figure of her friend picking her way across the garden.

'What are you doing down there?' asked Polly.

'There's an air raid in progress, in case you haven't noticed,' said Nell. 'What are you doing here anyway?'

'I've come to call for you for the party.'

'Oh Polly, don't be so daft.'

'What do you mean?'

'Isn't it obvious?'

'No . . .'

'Then it ought to be. I'm not going to the party while bombs are dropping, and I doubt if anyone else will either.'

30

'Oh for goodness' sake,' was Polly's irritable response. 'So what if there is an air raid? We can't stay at home just because of that.'

'It's dangerous out there,' said Alice from below. 'Tell her to come down here, Nell, or go home to her own shelter. She shouldn't be out on the streets at a time like this.'

Nell passed the message on.

'No thanks. I'm not hiding away in some smelly shelter,' Polly declared. 'The bombs are miles away.'

'They can't be that far off or they wouldn't have sounded the siren,' Nell pointed out.

'Even so, we've got to get on with our lives or that snake Hitler will have won,' Polly stated categorically. 'We'll be expected to go to work, air raids or not, so I don't see why we shouldn't go out and have some fun as well.'

Nell couldn't help agreeing with her up to a point and admiring her spirit, but there was no point in deliberately putting yourself at risk. 'It's up to you what you do about the party,' she told her, 'but I'm not going and I don't think you'll find many people out tonight.'

'Miserable lot,' complained Polly. 'What about the bulldog spirit we're all supposed to be showing? There won't be much evidence of that if everyone disappears into their shelters at the first sign of trouble. I thought the idea was to carry on regardless; showing Jerry what we're made of.'

'I think that means with regard to things of national importance,' suggested Nell.

'A party is important to me.'

'It isn't going to save anyone's life or keep the country going, though, is it?' Nell pointed out.

'It could do; a party is good for people's morale,' Polly retorted. 'I thought that was what we were all supposed to be doing; keeping our spirits up.'

'You pick out the bits of government advice that suit you,' chided Nell, 'and ignore the rest.'

Just then there was an explosion that shook the ground and shattered everyone's nerves.

'Blimey!' cried Polly into the ensuing silence. 'That sounded a bit dodgy.'

'Tell her to come down here, for heaven's sake,' urged Alice again. 'It isn't safe out there.'

31

'I suppose I'd better,' Polly agreed reluctantly, climbing down and complaining bitterly as she nudged in next to Nell. 'Honestly, what a comedown for a Saturday night. I was all dressed up and ready to get off with Ed Mills at the party, and I end up in a hole in the ground.'

'Stop being such a misery,' admonished Nell lightly. 'None of us want to be here any more than you do, but there's no point in moaning about it.'

'Won't your parents be worried about you, Polly?' enquired Alice with concern.

'Dunno. They'll be mad with me for going out, though, so I can be sure of a right earful when I get back,' she replied, without so much as a smidgen of empathy for her parents. 'But as I'm always telling them, I'm a grown woman. If I'm old enough to earn my own living and pay my way, I'm old enough do just as I please.'

'It's a question of consideration, dear, whatever your age,' Alice pointed out in a tone of mild admonition. 'It isn't fair to have people who care about you worrying, if it can be avoided.'

'I suppose you're right, Mrs Porter, and I'll be more thoughtful in future,' said Polly, deeming it wise to seem to agree with the older woman since she was sharing her shelter. 'What a flippin' to-do, isn't it, eh? This stupid war, ruining innocent people's lives. The government should get it sorted out sharpish. They're supposed to be running things, and they're not making a very good job of it, if you ask me.'

'We're not asking you, so give over grumbling and pick up your cards,' requested Nell, changing the subject swiftly before the outrageous Polly said something to really offend Nell's gentle-natured mother. 'We're playing snap to amuse Pansy.'

Polly heaved a sigh of irritation. 'It isn't my sort of thing, but all right, if you say so,' she said, picking up her share of cards from the upturned wooden box they were using as a table.

'I know it's a bit babyish,' said Pansy, taking Polly's comments personally. 'But we don't have any other games down here. We were in such a rush we didn't stop to find any.'

'Take no notice of me, kid. I probably couldn't manage anything more difficult anyway,' said Polly.

'She's just miffed because her social life has been upset,' Nell told her sister.

'I flippin' well am,' admitted Polly. 'I hope we're not going to have this performance on a regular basis.'

'I think we are all hoping that,' said Nell, tensing as another explosion could be heard in the distance.

Not only were the raids regular after that; they were long and lethal. The blazing sky that had marked the beginning of what was now known as the Blitz had been the London docks on fire, they had discovered the next day. Miles of dockside warehouses had been burned to the ground by an incendiary attack, whole streets of houses in the surrounding areas flattened and people killed, injured and made homeless. The East End of London was only the beginning; the bombs soon spread to west London and beyond.

But somehow life went on and people still went to work even after nights spent in the shelters with little or no sleep. One morning, a couple of months after what was now known as Black Saturday, Nell and Polly got to work to find broken glass everywhere and the office bitterly cold and draughty because the windows had been blown out.

'If we all pull together we can clear the mess and get back to work without too much delay,' said Miss Crow, showing amazing sangfroid and with hardly a hair out of place as she worked with a broom to clear the glass from the floor. 'The factory is still operating, so we need to do the same. If you can each get the broken glass off your own desk, then help me with the floor, we'll soon have a workable office. You'd better keep your gloves on to protect your hands, and you can use cardboard folders to sweep the glass off the desks as there aren't enough brushes for us all. You'll need to keep your outdoor clothes on until the men come to put something in the windows to keep out the draught.'

Everybody got on with it without argument. They were becoming accustomed to being cold, frightened and uncomfortable, and there was an excellent sense of team spirit among the typists. Even Polly did her bit with good grace, admitting to Nell that Miss Crow wasn't quite such an evil old bag after all, since she was willing to muck in and help with all the rest.

When they were sent home early so that they would have time to get settled into the shelters before the siren wailed its nightly warning, a cheer went up.

'Another night underground; what a thrilling prospect that is,' grumbled Polly as she and Nell walked home in the dusk. 'It's the sheer boredom of it that gets on my nerves. Just Mum and Dad and me, sitting there hoping our end doesn't come. It's dead weird and enough to give you the flippin' creeps.'

'I spend my time amusing Pansy,' Nell told her. 'It keeps my mind occupied.'

'At least you've got a sister, which is more than I have,' said Polly. 'I know she's just a kid, but at least it's someone young to give things a lift.'

'Can't you invite the neighbours into the shelter for a chat?' suggested Nell. 'Some people make a social occasion of it, even though it's a bit of a squeeze to get anyone else in. They have singsongs and games.'

'Mum and Dad wouldn't have that. They aren't the type to socialise,' Polly explained.

'You obviously don't take after them.'

'No, thank goodness,' she said with emphasis.

'I've noticed one thing about myself,' began Nell as something occurred to her. 'I don't think I'm quite as terrified when the siren goes as I used to be when the raids first started. I must be getting used to them, I suppose.'

'I still nearly wet myself with fright every night when the bombers start coming over, but when you're still alive after the all-clear has gone time and time again it does give you a bit of confidence.'

'Once the raids ease off a bit, perhaps we'll have a night out somewhere,' suggested Nell. 'I've heard that some of the cinemas have reopened and are staying open for longer, though the punters are told that they're there at their own risk.'

'I can't wait to go out at night again,' confessed Polly predictably. 'It might make us feel normal again.'

'Let's wait and see if things quieten down a bit first, though,' suggested Nell. 'I wouldn't want to desert the family the way things are at the moment, with the bombing being so bad. It would be asking for trouble anyway.'

'Okey-dokey.' They reached their parting point. 'Meanwhile it's another night of listening to my dad snoring and belching. Ta-ta, Nell; see you tomorrow.'

'Ta-ta, Polly.'

*　　*　　*

'Try not to be too long, love,' Nell said to Pansy that same night, coming up to the house out of the shelter during a lull in the bombing with her sister, who needed the lavatory. 'We need to get back underground before any more planes come over.'

'I'll be as quick as I can, Nell,' said Pansy, and hurried upstairs.

All seemed quiet outside, so Nell thought she might as well make some tea to take down to the shelter. Having turned the electricity back on at the mains so that they could see, she also turned on the gas, filled the kettle and put it on the stove. There were already cups and milk in the shelter, so she would just take a fresh pot of tea down with her. That would please Mum and Dad.

'You can go on back down if you like while I make the tea. Take the torch. I'll find my way in the moonlight,' she said when her sister appeared at her side. 'Tell Mum and Dad I'll be there in a minute with a pot of tea for them.'

'I'd rather wait for you.'

'All right then. I'll only be a few minutes.' Even as she said it, she could hear the drone of enemy aircraft. She made the tea, turned the gas and electricity off at the mains and gave the torch to Pansy to guide them back across the garden while she carried the tray. 'Here they come again.'

She was only thinking aloud, but her sister picked up on it. 'They won't bomb us, will they, Nell? Mum says we'll be safe, and we always are.'

'That's right, love. Mum hasn't let you down so far, has she? So don't you worry.' They were at the back door now, ready to go. 'Don't forget to keep the torch beam facing downwards because of the blackout regulations.'

'I won't.'

'Let's go, then.'

But before they had a chance to go anywhere, Nell heard the sound of a bomb descending close by. It was horribly different to the whistle of one at a distance; like the massively magnified sound of material being ripped.

'Get down, Pansy love. Get down on your tummy on the floor,' she yelled.

The tray slipped from her grasp and the last thing she felt before she blacked out was the scalding-hot tea stinging her leg.

★　★　★

When Nell came to, it was dark and her mind was a blank. Where was she? What had happened? Then she remembered the sound of the bomb in descent and the rest came crashing back to her. She and Pansy had been in the kitchen, so this must be the ruins of it. But where was her sister?

'Pansy,' she called, but her mouth was so full of dust no sound came out. There was a sharp pain in her leg and she couldn't move because something was packed against her. She realised with horror that she must be buried by debris. She couldn't see anything, but she could hear voices; men were shouting to each other and there was a strong smell of fire. 'Pansy!' she called again. 'Help, somebody please help me. I have to find my sister and my mum and dad.'

Her cries were so weak they went unanswered, and the pain in her leg was almost too much to bear. She felt nauseous and faint. Vaguely she was aware that she was screaming in agony, and she was shivering though her skin was burning and suffused with sweat. She drifted in and out of consciousness until she was finally granted the mercy of oblivion.

'Oh my God,' gasped Peg, clinging to her son's arm, when she and Ed arrived in Parkin Street and saw the piles of rubble that had once been a row of houses; one of which had been the home of their closest friends, the Porters. The postman had been the bearer of the news that this street had caught it last night, and the whole Mills family had been thrown into a state of despair. Peg had managed to persuade Lenny to stay at home with his father for fear the worst had happened. And it had. There was nothing left of the Porters' home. That and the rest of the houses in the terrace were now just broken bricks and concrete littered with bits of broken furniture.

'Shocking, innit?' said one of the residents, coming out of her house on the opposite side of the street, crying openly. 'I haven't been able to stop shaking since it happened.'

Peg couldn't speak. She was too distressed.

'It's one thing hearing about someone copping it, and quite another actually being there when it happens.' The neighbour wiped her tears with a rag handkerchief. 'By God, it was close. I feel guilty for being glad it wasn't us that got it, but you can't help it, can you? It's only human nature.'

Still Peg wept.

'But even so, those people were neighbours and we're all shattered by their loss,' the woman went on.

'Surely they must have got some of them out alive,' Peg managed to utter, thickly.

The woman shook her head. 'They reckon there were no survivors,' she said. 'It was terrible; really awful. We were all in our shelters, too scared to come out after the crash. When we did eventually venture outside, the rescue people wouldn't let us anywhere near. You couldn't see what was happening anyway in the dark, and there was so much smoke and dust we were all choking with it. The emergency services were doing what they could, but there wasn't much hope of survivors. The poor souls were in bits all over the place, so I've heard.'

Ed tightened his hold on his mother supportively as she swayed and seemed about to pass out.

'Most of us went back down the shelters until the all-clear sounded,' the woman continued. 'I felt as sick as a pig. I still do.'

'The Porters might have got out alive because they would have been in the shelter,' said Peg through her tears. 'They always went underground when the siren started. Alice told me they were scrupulous about that. They never took a chance on it.'

'Their shelter took a direct hit, apparently,' the woman informed her, shattering Peg's last hope. She put her hand on Peg's arm, tears running down her own cheeks. 'I'm so sorry, dear. I know they were friends of yours. I've seen you around here a lot. I hate to upset you, but no one in that shelter could have lived.'

'Come on, Mum,' said Ed kindly, putting his arm around her as Peg emitted a strangled cry. 'Let's go home.'

As they turned to leave, there was a pitiful meowing and Tiddles ran up and rubbed himself in circles around Peg's legs. Unexpectedly and profoundly moved by this evidence of life among the death and destruction, Peg choked out, 'If only people had nine lives.'

'That's a fact,' Ed agreed.

'Oh, Ed, all of them gone, I can't bear it.'

'I know, Mum. Neither can I.' He was at pains to hide the fact that he himself wanted to weep. 'We'll just have to help each other through it as best as we can.'

The cat's cries became guttural; the poor thing was obviously bewildered by the change in the landscape and the absence of his family.

'Come on, Tiddles,' said Ed, picking up the distressed animal and stroking it gently. 'You're coming home with us, old fella. We'll look after you.'

'It's what Alice and the others would want,' said Peg thickly, 'and the very least we can do.'

Chapter Three

Nell was in a hospital ward crowded with extra beds to accommodate the bomb victims. She was still feeling nauseous and woozy from the effects of the anaesthetic, and the pills they were giving her to dull the pain in her leg had a sedative effect. A piece of an iron girder had become embedded in her shin in the explosion and she'd had surgery to remove it. The skin in that area had also been scalded by the hot tea she'd spilled on it, and this had exacerbated the problem. Apparently, she had lost a lot of blood while she was buried in the rubble and she was still feeling very weak.

But the news she had been given by the rescue team was far more agonising than any physical pain. They had told her there was definitely no hope that her parents could have lived through the direct hit to the shelter. But no one seemed to know what had happened to Pansy.

Nell had repeatedly begged the nurses to help her find out, but they were extremely overworked and had more than enough to do caring for the patients. Although Nell knew there was very little chance of her sister having survived, she couldn't bring herself to give up hope altogether.

'Nurse, I hate to bother you,' she said now to the nurse who had brought her medication. 'But is there some way I can get news of my sister? She wasn't in the shelter with our parents. She was up at the house with me, so she could be alive.'

'It's nothing short of a miracle that you came through it, dear, so don't get your hopes up too high,' the nurse advised kindly. 'Anyway, you must concentrate on your own recovery and stop worrying about anyone else. You're in no condition to do anything but rest at the moment.'

'You don't understand,' Nell persisted with as much strength as she could muster. 'If she is alive she'll be lost without me. She needs to know that I'm all right and will bring her home as soon as I'm better.'

'But your home has gone, dear,' the nurse reminded her gently.

'I'll find us a home somewhere else.' Getting through to these people was like wading backwards through a sea of porridge. It was so upsetting! 'If she is alive she'll be missing me like mad. We need to be together.'

'And you need to rest; all this fretting isn't doing you any good at all,' advised the middle-aged woman. 'You are our patient; our responsibility is to you. It's our job to make you well again, and you are not making it easy for us by upsetting yourself about something you can do nothing about at the moment.'

'But . . .'

'Look, my dear, when you're feeling stronger, that's the time to be worrying about your sister,' the nurse pointed out, impatience creeping into her tone because she had so many patients to look after and only one pair of hands. 'You'll be no good to anyone if you hinder your progress, will you? Once you're back on your feet again you can find out about your sister.' She handed Nell two tablets in a small container and picked up a glass of water from the top of the locker. 'Take these. They'll ease the pain in your leg and calm you down.'

Tears of frustration and grief meandered down Nell's cheeks as she did as the nurse asked. She felt utterly helpless to do anything but sleep.

On the outskirts of a small town in Hertfordshire stood an old grey building with narrow windows and tall locked gates. A black-painted board situated at the front of the building was inscribed with the faded words *St Catherine's Home for Destitute Girls*. It was an uninviting stone structure containing dismal dormitories, draughty classrooms, a refectory, a recreation hall and various other cheerless areas. Staff quarters and the more salubrious visitors' rooms were out of bounds to the children.

At the front of the orphanage was an imposing entrance hall, immaculately tidy and furnished with religious ornaments, the wooden floors kept highly polished by the young girls of unfortunate circumstances who resided here. Across a concrete yard was a chapel near to the convent where the nuns lived.

The children received their education here until they reached secondary school age, when they went to school in the town, escorted under strict supervision by staff, rigid discipline being of the essence in this institution.

This particular morning, a few days after the bombing of Parkin Street, inside one of the overcrowded classrooms the little girls were sitting at well-worn wooden desks having an arithmetic lesson conducted by a nun called Sister Margaret. She was the strictest nun in the orphanage and feared by one and all. Currently she was in the process of testing her pupils on their times tables. Her small, grey eyes darted around the room as she chose her next victim.

'Pansy Porter,' she decided in an awesome tone, fixing a small, pale faced girl with a frightening stare and causing every other head in the class to swivel as the children focused their attention on the newcomer. 'Tell me what seven eights are, please.'

Traumatised and bewildered by the orphanage and its austere regime, Pansy's mind was blank.

'Come on, child. Don't keep the class waiting. You should know this, a girl of your age.'

Somewhere in the mists of Pansy's troubled mind was the answer, but she was in such a state of trepidation it refused to reveal itself. 'I don't know, miss,' she admitted meekly.

'*Miss*,' the nun bellowed. 'You do not call me *miss*. You call me Sister – Sister Margaret – and don't you forget it.'

Petrified, Pansy stared at the nun, knowing that she should apologise but unable to utter a word. Her lips were glued together and simply would not work. The other girls started to laugh behind their hands, but Pansy was far too frightened and miserable to be mortified. The barely hidden amusement in the room caused the nun to become even angrier, and she thumped her hand down on her desk, making the entire class jump and bringing the laughter to a halt.

'Come out here, girl,' she ordered harshly.

Somehow Pansy managed to do as she asked, but her legs were like jelly and her stomach was griping to the point where she needed the lavatory but was too afraid to ask. The nun took her by the arm and led her to the corner of the room.

'You will stay here with your back to the class until I say otherwise,' she declared, her voice ringing out as a warning to the others. 'You've been here for long enough to know how we do things at St Catherine's. You're a disruptive influence in my class, and I won't have it.'

Although Pansy felt quite ill with terror, her agonising longing for her family forced her to speak out.

'I want my mum and dad,' she gulped, as a hush fell on the other girls at her temerity. 'I want my sister. Please . . . I want them so badly.'

Sister Margaret didn't know the history of this particular child personally, though there would probably be some sort of record in the Mother Superior's office. Because of the chaos caused by the heavy bombing in London, it wasn't always possible for the details to be recorded, and it certainly wasn't feasible for Sister Margaret to be familiar with every new child's background, given the huge numbers that had been sent to them since the Blitz had begun. It had reached the point where they were unhealthily overcrowded here. They were admitting children from outside the faith because all the other orphanages were full up. Someone had to look after the poor wretches, and everyone had to do what they could in these terrible times.

When children came to St Catherine's, the nuns' aim was to look after them and give them the best possible start in life, which required – in the opinion of the order – strict discipline, total obedience, a rigid moral code, cleanliness, holiness and respect for their elders and betters. This was the character-building regime that would make decent human beings of them. With so many children to care for, pandemonium would break out if authority wasn't maintained. On the other hand, this little girl had been recently bereaved and the nun wasn't entirely without a heart. She daren't let the others know that, though, or they'd run rings around her.

With this in mind, she grabbed Pansy by the arm and pulled her towards the door. 'I will be back in approximately one minute,' she announced, turning to the rest of the class. 'Use the time I'm away wisely; make sure you know your tables, as I will be testing you all on my return. If I hear so much as a whisper from this classroom, there will be trouble.'

Outside in the corridor, the nun spoke to Pansy in a softer tone.

'Look . . . it will be easier for you to settle in here if you stop thinking about your family so much,' she advised. 'I know that you are hurting, but you must try to fit in here. Many children have been killed by these awful bombs, so you are lucky to be alive, as indeed we all are. Be grateful to God for that, and accept the fact that we are your family now.' She stared hard at Pansy, her hard eyes glinting in her scrubbed face, her skin suffused with pink patches and shining against the starched white of her wimple. Discipline was so deeply ingrained in her, she couldn't let her personal feelings interfere with it for long. 'One thing that is very import- ant here is respect for your elders.' She gave Pansy another meaningful look. 'So what do you have to say?'

'Yes, Sister Margaret,' Pansy managed to croak.

'That's better. Now you will stay out here until I say otherwise. You will say a prayer for your family and thank our Lord for sparing you and sending you to us. You are not to move from this spot until I say so. Is that clear?'

'Yes, Sister Margaret,' Pansy said again.

As the nun went back into the classroom and closed the door behind her, Pansy could feel the tears burning at the back of her eyes. As they escaped, she wiped them with the back of her hand and tried to stop a fresh flow from forming, because she'd be in big trouble if the nun saw her crying. But there was a terrible dragging sensation in the pit of her stomach that tightened her throat and forced the tears out.

What had happened to her life? Why was she here? She tried to reflect on the events of the past few days. It was all a bit vague, but she could remember the air raid and being at the kitchen door with Nell and the torch in her hand ready to go back to the shelter. There had been a terrible crash and somehow she had been outside in the dark with the rough edges of wreckage all around her. There were flames, too, and smoke in her eyes. A man with a kind voice had lifted her up and carried her to an ambulance. Then she was in a place called a rest centre, where women in green uniforms were giving out food and drink. A lot of the people had been crying.

As soon as she arrived here, she'd been scrubbed with carbolic soap by one of the nuns to make sure she was properly clean before she started life at St Catherine's. She'd been too miserable to be indignant about the fact that she was more than old enough to bath herself and was used to doing so. All she wanted was to go home to her family. But every time she asked, she was told she must forget all about them.

No one had actually said so, but she feared they might all be dead. This made her ache so hard she wanted to be sick. She even missed her father, and she'd never had much to do with him. But he'd always been there, a part of the fabric of her life that had somehow disappeared, and she wanted it back so much. How could it all have gone so wrong when her mother had promised they would be safe?

The classroom door opened and Sister Margaret emerged, the black folds of her habit sweeping the floor.

'You can come in again now,' she told Pansy. 'But behave yourself or you'll be back out here.'

'Yes, Sister Margaret.' Pansy spoke in a compliant manner, but she was hurting desperately and in deep despair.

In the dormitory that night, Pansy was curled up in a foetal position with the bedcovers over her head, shivering from the cold and trying to stifle her sobs. If the matron heard her she'd be in terrible trouble for disturbing the other girls. Crying wasn't allowed here. It was called self-indulgence, whatever that was supposed to mean. But she couldn't help it. She felt so wretched she couldn't stop the tears from coming.

Feeling a tap on her shoulder, she jumped, a bolt of fear shooting through her body.

'It's all right,' someone whispered. 'It's only me; Jane from the next bed.'

Slowly Pansy turned over and poked her head out from under the blanket. The dormitory was in darkness because of the blackout, but there was a light in the matron's office at the end and she could just make out the dark outline of the girl sitting on her bed; a girl she had judged earlier to be a bit older than she was herself.

'I heard you crying,' Jane went on in a whisper. 'Just wanted to tell you that it's nothing to be ashamed of, whatever the nuns say. I cried in bed every night at first.'

'Really?'

'Yeah.'

'How did you stop doing it?'

'Dunno. I just did,' the girl replied. 'You probably can't imagine it now, but you do get used to it here after a while and it isn't so bad. I know the nuns seem like witches at first, and they are very strict with us, but they're not all as nasty as Sister Margaret. She's the worst of the lot. We all hate the sight of her. Some of the other nuns are quite nice.'

'She's got it in for me.'

'No she hasn't. She just happens to be picking on you at the moment. It'll probably be my turn tomorrow or the next day. She does it to us all at times.'

This unexpected hand of friendship warmed Pansy's heart. 'Have you been here long?' she hissed.

'Yeah, ages,' the girl replied. 'I came when I was four.'

'Your mum and dad didn't get killed in the bombing then?' Pansy assumed.

'They're not dead,' Jane told her. 'Dad left and Mum didn't want me, so she abandoned me and I ended up here.'

Such a thing was so alien to a girl from Pansy's background, she didn't know what to say. As it happened, she wasn't required to say anything.

'Look out, the matron's coming,' warned Jane. 'Night, Pansy. See yer tomorrow.'

'Night, Jane.'

Pansy curled back into a ball and pretended to be asleep as the matron did her rounds. At least she'd managed to stop crying; that was something. It was nice to know she had a friend.

She didn't feel better for long. The next day things went from bad to worse because of a remaining spark of spirit that refused to be crushed by Sister Margaret.

'Your hair is in a mess, Pansy Porter,' admonished the nun when Pansy went into the classroom. 'It's all over the place and an utter disgrace. Go to the dormitory at once and tie it back, and you will stay behind in the classroom after school to make up for the time you have missed.'

Pansy turned scarlet. She didn't move. She couldn't; she was too mortified and frightened. But there was something else too suddenly; a flash of anger.

45

'You're not my mum, you know, so you can't tell me what to do,' she heard someone say, and had a terrible suspicion that it might have been her.

The classroom was electrified; every child waiting for the explosion they knew would come.

'No, I am not your mother, but while you are in my care you will do as I say.' Visibly seething, Sister Margaret swept up to Pansy's desk. 'You will go to the dormitory and get your coat and hat, then you will stand on the drain in the yard until I tell you to come in.'

There was a communal intake of breath; the drain was almost as serious a disgrace as a hiding.

'Go *now!*'

Pansy left the classroom with her cheeks flaming. In the dormitory she put on the awful brown coat that was too big for her, and the navy-blue pixie hood she had been issued with at the rest centre. Then she went out into the cold and foggy yard and stood on the grille of the drain, feeling utterly desolate. Would she really never see her family again?

Even as she slept, Nell was in a state of turmoil about Pansy. She feared her sister was dead, but was unable to dismiss the notion that she might be alive but lost and alone out there somewhere. All appeals on the subject to the medical team here continued to fall on deaf ears. She was just told to rest and they would help her when she was stronger. In one of her less drowsy moments she thought of Peg and wondered why she hadn't come to see her. Perhaps she'd been killed too. She felt cut off from everything; she was in mental chaos and had no idea what was going on in the outside world. All she knew was that the bombs were still coming; she heard the explosions every night.

Everyone working on the wards was exhausted, so it wasn't fair to pester them for news of Pansy when they had no way of knowing anyway. They had far more serious cases than hers to deal with: patients who'd lost limbs and had terrible head injuries. It tore at Nell's heart to see them.

All of this didn't make her own loss any easier to bear or stop her from fretting about her sister. It was hard to believe that she would never see her parents again. Life without Mum seemed unbearable. The terrible thing about losing her father was that she felt as though she had never really known him that well. She'd never get to know him now; would never feel her mother's comforting presence again. Maybe she had seen the last of her sister too. That would be too much to bear.

It was Ed Mills' dinner break and he was sitting at a table with his workmates in the factory canteen; they were all tucking into sausage and mash with gravy and boiled cabbage.

'You've been a bit quiet this last couple o' days, Ed. Not your usual chipper self at all,' remarked one of the older men. 'Woman trouble, I suppose.'

'No, nothing like that,' responded Ed, looking bleak. 'Some close family friends of ours got killed in a raid the other night. The whole lot of them wiped out. It really shakes you up when it's people you know. It was a hell of a blow.'

'Sorry to hear that.'

'Thanks, mate.'

Ed had been utterly devastated by the bombing. The Porters had been a part of his life for as long as he could remember, especially Nell. Although he would never ever admit it to anyone, he'd actually shed copious tears of grief for her in private. She'd been the nearest thing he'd had to a sister and he couldn't bear the thought of life without her.

He'd found Lenny sobbing in his bedroom too. Pansy had been his friend and soulmate. As for his mother, he didn't think she'd ever be the same again. She tried not to upset the rest of them by showing it, but it was obvious that she was suffering; understandably so, since she and Alice had been friends for most of their lives. Because they had always had each other, they hadn't made much of an effort to nurture other female friendships, so Mum was going to be lost without her. His father seemed cut up about it too. Although he'd never been close friends with Ernie, he had always seemed very fond of the family as a whole.

'It's shocking what's happening to people these days,' said Cyril, one of the other men at the table.

'You never know who's gonna still be about from one day to the next,' said someone else.

'My brother-in-law works for the rescue service, and some of the stories he's told me are enough to make your hair curl,' put in Cyril with a morbid shake of his head. 'Human remains strewn far and wide in the wreckage; they can't tell who's who so they count so many portions as one body.'

'Ooh, leave off,' complained another of the men. 'You're putting me off my dinner.'

'How do you think the poor rescue workers feel, being in the thick of it?' Cyril asked him. 'One bloke was dismissed from the service because he lost his nerve and couldn't go down into an Anderson shelter that had taken a direct hit. He knew it would be too gruesome and he just couldn't do it. A big strong chap by all accounts too.'

The men all listened intently. People talked about the air raids a lot of the time. They all had their own particular story that outshone the others as far as drama and bravery were concerned. Trading anecdotes had become a bit of a national hobby.

'Strange how things work out sometimes, though,' Cyril went on to say. 'You'd think you would stand the best chance of survival by going in the shelter as soon as the siren starts, wouldn't you?'

'Of course, it's bound to be safer,' said one of the men. 'It stands to reason.'

'Not always,' Cyril told him. 'My brother-in-law was saying that he went out to an incident the other night and the daughters of the family were saved because they *weren't* in the shelter. It took a direct hit and the parents were wiped out. But the two girls had gone into the house for something and they came out of it alive, even though the house was in ruins.'

'Well stone me,' said one of his mates.

'In fact the little girl had barely a scratch on her.'

'What's her life gonna be like without her mum and dad, though?' queried one of the men.

'Exactly,' agreed Cyril. 'The poor little mite. Her older sister was pretty badly hurt. She was buried for quite a while, apparently, with a serious injury to her leg. She was absolutely soaked in blood when they got her out. They nearly missed her too. The rescue boys were just packing up to leave when they finally heard her calling for help. A few minutes later and they'd have gone. She wouldn't have survived if that had happened.'

'God Almighty,' said the other man.

Cyril shook his head sadly as he continued. 'A terraced row of houses was completely flattened,' he said gravely. 'No survivors from any of them except the two young girls. There was nothing left of the shelter either, apparently.'

Things were happening in Ed's mind. It was a mere morsel of hope but he couldn't let it go unquestioned. 'Where was this?' he wanted to know.

'Ooh, now you're asking, mate,' replied Cyril, frowning as he tried to remember. 'There's been such a lot of bombings lately, I can't recall where they all were. I think he said it was in one of the side streets that lead off the High Road.'

Ed leapt up. 'Tell the foreman I've had to go out, will you, lads? I'll be back as soon as I can,' he told the astonished group, taking off his boiler suit.

'What about your dinner?'

'You can have the rest of it.'

'You can't just leave in the middle of the shift,' one of the men pointed out.

'I've got to, mate. It's *that* important. Anyway, it's my dinner hour,' he reminded them. 'I'll be late back but I'll make the time up tonight. Can you tell the guv'nor?'

'Will do,' said Cyril, and they all watched, puzzled, as the tall young man marched purposefully from the canteen.

That evening Peg Mills sat at Nell's bedside sobbing her heart out.

'You poor love,' she wept, holding Nell's hand. 'I should have been here before. You must have thought we'd all deserted you.'

'Of course I didn't think that,' Nell assured her. 'I knew there must be a reason.'

'I could kick myself for believing that woman in Parkin Street who said there had been no survivors.'

'She wasn't to know what had happened,' Nell pointed out. 'She obviously thought everyone had been killed.'

'It didn't look as though anyone could have lived, I must admit, but I should have checked with the authorities,' Peg said through her tears. 'I think I must have been in such a state of shock, my mind wasn't working properly.'

'Don't cry, Mum,' said Ed, who had come to the hospital with Peg after he'd finally finished work. 'Nell knows we would never let her down. We were both too grief-stricken to question it, especially given the state of the bomb site. There's a lot of chaos after the raids so it's no wonder the neighbour got the facts wrong.'

Peg looked at Nell and then at Ed. 'Thank God my son had more sense than me.'

'I only went to the police station to check because of what Cyril at work was saying,' he explained. 'It wasn't because of any special savvy on my part.'

'You're here now, that's what matters,' Nell told them, her eyes brimming with tears. 'And you've given me the best possible news.'

Peg put a comforting arm around Nell. 'Your little sister, safe and well. The poor mite has been put into care, they told Ed at the police station,' she said. 'But they didn't know exactly where she is.'

'With my being laid up in here, I suppose they didn't know what else to do with her.'

'I would have taken her home with us if I'd known she was alive,' declared Peg. 'I can hardly bear to think what she must be going through.'

'Could you please find out where they've sent her so that I can write and tell her I'll come and get her as soon as I can,' Nell pleaded. 'I'll have to find us somewhere to live, but I must have her with me. She needs to be with me.' She was still close to tears.

'I'll go to the Children's Department, find out where she is, and tell them that the two of you will be moving in with us. Then I shall go and fetch Pansy. There's no need to wait until you come out of hospital,' Peg stated.

'But we can't impose on you in that way,' said Nell.

'You wouldn't be imposing,' Peg was quick to assure her. 'We'd love to have you, wouldn't we, Ed? The boys won't mind sharing a room to make space for you and your sister.'

'But . . .' Nell couldn't believe what she was hearing.

'Where else will you go, love?' asked Peg sadly. 'Your home isn't there any more.'

'Oh Peg, it's all so awful. Poor Mum and Dad. We didn't even have a chance to say goodbye. Our home gone, all our things, all our memories.'

'You haven't lost your memories, love, you'll always have them with you.'

The two of them were weeping now. Ed stood back quietly.

'Poor Pansy. She'll be feeling so miserable wherever she is, in a strange place without anyone of her own.'

'I'll see to Pansy; you can stop worrying about her,' assured Peg, blowing her nose and composing herself. 'I'll get on to it first thing in the morning. But I might need a note of authority from you before they'll let me take her.'

'You're so kind.'

'I can't bring your mum and dad back but I'll do what I can to help you and Pansy,' Peg told her kindly. 'There will be a home for you and your sister with us for as long as you need it. Having you there will be good for me; it will help to fill the void left by the loss of my dearest friend.'

'Thanks, Auntie Peg.'

'Er . . . I'll wait for you outside, Mum,' muttered Ed, deciding to make a diplomatic exit because he felt so choked up. He put his hand on Nell's arm. 'See you, kid. Get better soon.'

'See you, Ed,' Nell said thickly.

The news that the Porter sisters were alive soon spread among the neighbourhood and reached the factory. Even Polly was misty-eyed when she went to the hospital to visit Nell a few days later.

'I could have jumped for joy when I heard that my best friend was still alive after all,' she told her. 'Well, I did actually do quite a bit of squealing, and I didn't get told off by the Crow either. Even she was smiling; something never before seen in Barker's typing pool. You produced a miracle, kid.'

Nell was feeling a little better, and less drowsy. Now that she wasn't so groggy her grief was more violent, but at least she knew that Peg had traced Pansy's whereabouts through the Children's Department and was doing everything she could to get her home. There was red tape to be dealt with, which was causing a delay, especially as all Nell's papers – her birth certificate and identity card – had been lost in the bombing, so she had no proof of who she was until her replacement documents came through. At this rate she would be able to collect Pansy herself. Still, at least her sister would know that rescue was on the way, because Nell had written to her.

'I'm glad to hear that something good has come from it,' Nell said now.

'Poor you, though,' said Polly, becoming serious. She pointed to the hillock in the bed covers covering the protective cage in which Nell's wounded leg was encased. 'Does it hurt?'

Nell nodded. 'I'll say it does,' she replied. 'But not as much as it did at first, thank goodness. They were giving me stuff for the pain and it was sending me to sleep.'

'Lucky you,' teased Polly. 'I feel as if I could sleep for a year, given half the chance.'

'No let-up in the raids, then?'

Polly shook her head. 'I'm sick of spending every night in the shelter. It didn't do your mum and dad any good either, did it?' she said tactlessly.

'No, but they were an exception. Generally speaking the shelter is the safest place.'

'I suppose so, though I've heard that people are risking it and going to the pictures instead of the shelter to take their minds off the raids,' Polly went on. 'I think I'll have to start doing that. I can't stick many more nights in the Anderson. What with Mum clicking her knitting needles and her teeth and Dad snoring like a ruddy pig. Honestly, it's worse than being at the flamin' zoo.' She bit her lip, looking sheepish, and put her hand on Nell's. Polly hadn't been blessed with a great deal of sensitivity but she wasn't quite devoid of it altogether. 'Sorry, Nell. I know you'd give anything to have your mum and dad back and here I am complaining about mine. Take no notice of me. It's just my way. I don't mean half of what I say.'

'I know, and don't worry about upsetting me.' Nothing anyone said or didn't say made any difference to the level of Nell's grief. It was there inside her every waking moment; a dull, gnawing pain. She didn't want to talk about it or share it with anyone, even though it hurt so much. It was as though she needed the agony to make it seem real; to grieve was all she could do for them now.

'Anyway, have you any idea what's going to happen to you and Pansy when you leave here?' Polly enquired on a more practical note. 'I mean, as regards accommodation.'

'We're moving in with the Millses,' Nell informed her. 'They've told me that we are welcome to stay there more or less indefinitely.'

'Oh good. I'm glad you've got somewhere nice to go,' Polly said. 'I've heard some bomb victims have to stay at the rest centres for ages because they don't have anyone to take them in and the council can't find anywhere to rehouse them.'

'We're very lucky,' said Nell.

So am I, thought Polly, because Nell had just provided her with the perfect opportunity to get to know the wonderful Ed Mills. When she went to call for Nell, he'd be there. Oh joy! Once she got to work on him with her sex appeal, he'd be hers. To be seen on the arm of the best-looking bloke around would really be something to boast about in the office. It would certainly put a bit of oomph into her life.

She was very sorry for Nell, of course, losing her parents like that. But life went on and a girl had to make the most of any break that came her way. Polly had, after all, missed the chance of getting to know him at the party that had never happened.

'So, when do you think you'll be coming out of here?' she asked, all concern.

'I don't know. They want to make sure that the infection in my leg has cleared up before they discharge me,' Nell explained. 'But they won't keep me a moment longer than they have to because they need the beds.'

'The sooner the better, eh?'

'I'll say.'

For me too, thought Polly, selfishly excited. The funny thing about luck was that it could change for the better when you were least expecting it.

It had been deemed unwise by the powers-that-be at St Catherine's for Pansy to be shown the letter that had arrived from her sister. After inspecting the contents, they had thought it would be in the child's best interests to keep it from her until she was actually collected, in case something went wrong and she was disappointed, which would be a very unsettling experience for her indeed. After all, nobody knew what was going to happen from one minute to the next these days.

So Pansy had no idea that help was at hand and was now in trouble with Sister Margaret yet again. The girl had got too much ink from the inkwell on her pen and spilled it all over her exercise book and the desktop. Furtively trying to clear it up with her handkerchief before the nun spotted it, she had managed to stain that, as well as her blouse and grey tunic.

The girl at the next desk tried to help by passing her a piece of rag she was using as a hanky. One of the other girls was unable to suppress a nervous giggle and all of this was noticed by Sister Margaret, who wouldn't miss so much as a change of heartbeat in her classroom.

'Oh no, not Pansy Porter causing disruption again,' the nun bellowed, marching across to Pansy's desk and surveying the dark blue mess with disdain.

Dry-mouthed, Pansy stared at the floor.

'I do believe you must have been sent here to try my patience to the limit.'

'Sorry, Sister Margaret,' Pansy muttered nervously. 'The ink just went all over the place.'

'It did it by itself, did it?' said the nun, causing a ripple of laughter in the classroom which stopped immediately she turned her head towards the class.

'Well, no . . .' began Pansy.

'It happened because you weren't paying proper attention to what you were doing,' Sister Margaret cut in. 'You were day-dreaming.'

'No, I . . .'

'Yes you were, and don't answer me back.'

'Sorry . . .'

'Come out here while I decide what punishment to give you,' she ordered.

The little girl followed the nun nervously to the front of the class, whereupon the classroom door opened and the Mother Superior glided in. She spoke to Sister Margaret in low tones, then they both looked at Pansy and the Mother Superior left the room.

'You are to go and wash your hands and tidy yourself up straight away,' commanded Sister Margaret. 'Then you are to go to the front hall.'

Pansy didn't dare to ask why, but guessed there would be some sort of punishment in store for her.

Nell knew that she would never be able to smell floor polish again without wanting to cry as she studied the gleaming wooden floor in the entrance hall of St Catherine's. Her emotions were heightened to such an extent she was physically trembling. The nun who had greeted her had made a diplomatic exit, telling her to go to the Mother Superior's office down the corridor when she was ready, to deal with the paperwork related to Pansy's release.

It was only a matter of weeks since Nell had last seen her sister, but it felt like for ever. The world they had shared had gone and they had both been plunged cruelly into a new one. They had never needed each other more than they did now.

It had taken Nell a long time to get here because of the delays on public transport. She'd caught the train from King's Cross to Potters Bar, then she'd had two bus rides and a long walk, which had been hard going because her leg wound was still painful.

But when a small figure appeared at the end of the corridor, she knew she would have walked from London to Land's End to see the smile of pure happiness on her sister's face when she spotted her.

'Nell, oh Nell!' Pansy cried, running up to her and throwing her arms round her. 'I've missed you so much.'

Nell burst into tears with the joy of seeing her beloved sister again. 'Oh love,' she gulped, holding Pansy close, her body racked with sobs. 'You'll never know how good it feels to see you. I've been so worried about you.'

'Are you going to take me home to Mum and Dad?' Pansy asked, holding Nell as though she would never let her go. 'Oh please say you are, please, please, please.'

'I'm going to take you with me,' Nell replied, knowing that she was going to have some painful explaining to do to her sister before they got back to Peg's. 'But first let's go to Mother Superior's office. I have to sign some papers.'

It was a strange feeling for Nell, walking down Parkin Street and seeing the house she had lived in since birth now just a cavity; even the rubble had been cleared away, so there was nothing left at all. She was glad she'd come on her own. Pansy would come eventually; it was, after all, only a few minutes' walk. But not now, when the child's grief for her parents was still so raw.

It was a bright sunny morning in early December and Nell was still on sick leave because of her leg wound, which was better but not completely healed. She had felt compelled to come here while Pansy was at school; had felt she must face up to it by way of saying a final farewell to her parents. Because of the grim circumstances of their death – their bodies hadn't been recovered as such – there hadn't been a funeral. So this was her way of saying goodbye to her parents and to her life with them.

Staring at the bomb site in the heatless winter sunshine, the air smoky from last night's raid in the area, every part of her ached with sadness. Everything had gone. The essence of the house that a family gave to bricks and mortar: the smells, the sounds, and most of all the feelings that washed over you when you came in the door; all taken for granted at the time but so very precious now. There had always been a sense of cosiness and safety that could never be recaptured anywhere else, because this had been Nell's roots; hers and Pansy's.

Maybe it hadn't been the cheeriest of homes because of her father's gloomy nature. Perhaps as she had got older she'd sometimes experienced a sense of wanting to escape and taste freedom, which she presumed was the natural thing when you grew up.

The Mills' house had always been far more fun than the Porters', and she could remember envying the Mills boys for the laughter they had in their home. Now she would give anything to have that sober household back again.

It wasn't that she didn't like living with the Millses. Peg and Tom were kindness itself and the boys were welcoming, and she loved them all to bits. But they weren't her flesh and blood. The rock on which her early life had been built had gone; blown to pieces.

The memories were strong, though. That was one thing that Hitler's bombers couldn't take from the bereaved. How easy it was to be careless about things that were always there. She and Pansy had been the most precious things in their mother's life and Alice would have done anything for them. That was the greatest gift a growing child could have. Nell realised that now.

Because they'd never known anything else, she and Pansy had accepted it as normal, expecting it go on for ever because parents were indestructible. But it hadn't, and they weren't, and it was too late to thank their mother; to thank either of them. Their father hadn't been warm towards them but he had probably loved them in his way. He'd never been unkind; just remote. And he had, of course, provided for them. As a clerk in a factory stores, his earnings would have been modest, but there had always been food on the table and enough money for the clothes they needed. Maybe there hadn't been many treats, but the essentials had always been there.

She stood in silence, deep in thought, painfully aware of how fragile life was. But although she was still racked with grief and would always keep her memories alive, she knew she had to get on with her own life as best as she could and live every moment as though it might be her last. That was what her mother and father would want.

They would also want her to look out for Pansy and try to put some stability back into her shattered life, as difficult as that was in these dangerous times. That was uppermost in Nell's mind. It had broken her heart to tell Pansy that their parents were dead. Even though the child had suspected it, actually knowing for sure had hit her little sister hard. She was at first inconsolable, then bewildered and sad, and looked to Nell for comfort, even though the Mills family were the salvation of them both. There were times when Pansy had quiet moods; she seemed to withdraw into herself, and that worried Nell.

Would her sister ever trust anyone ever again after having complete faith in her mother, who – with the very best of intentions – had promised her something that was beyond her control: immunity from the bombing?

Sadly Nell had no option but to inflict another cruel blow on the poor girl. She took one last look at the empty space where her home had once been, then – realising that she was shivering from the cold – pulled her coat collar up around her ears and turned away. Walking back down the street, she wiped the tears from her eyes and braced herself for what she was going to be forced to tell Pansy when she got home from school.

Chapter Four

'But Mum said I wouldn't have to be evacuated, Nell.' Pansy's brown eyes were hot with tears and accusation.

'I know, love, and I'm ever so sorry to do this to you, but I have to think about what's best for you,' Nell explained.

'It isn't best for me and Mum wouldn't like it. She said that we'd all stay together and face the bombs no matter what happened,' Pansy went on, desperate to stay in London with her sister. 'If you send me away you're going against her wishes. You just want to get rid of me.'

'That isn't fair and you know it isn't true.' They were in the bedroom the sisters shared in the Millses' house. Pansy was sitting on her bed nursing Tiddles. Nell was perched on the edge of her own bed consumed with guilt about having to inflict evacuation on Pansy. 'It's the very last thing I want and I shall miss you like mad, but I'm responsible for you now that Mum isn't here, and it's too dangerous for you to stay in London now. What happened to Mum and Dad is proof of that. Surely you must see that.'

'Why don't you come with me then, if it's so dangerous here?' Pansy asked sulkily.

'Because I have to work and my job is here,' Nell told her.

'Supposing you get killed by a bomb too?'

This wasn't an easy question to answer. On the one hand Nell didn't want to give assurances about something she had no power over; equally, she didn't want Pansy to live in fear for her sister. 'We'll both just have to hope that that doesn't happen and try not to think about it.'

'I don't want to be away from you.'

'Nor me from you, but none of us can do what we want because of

59

the war,' Nell explained. 'Even aside from the war I have to work to support us both. We can't expect Auntie Peg to keep us for nothing.'

Knowing she was beaten but still not quite willing to accept it, Pansy fondled the cat's head, putting her face against his fur. He was always a comfort to her when she was troubled.

'Look, love, you might not be away for long.' Nell knew she must stand her ground for the sake of Pansy's safety. 'Anyway, it isn't as if you're going to be staying with strangers, and you won't be going on your own. Lenny will be with you. You've been to his Granny Maud's cottage in the country lots of times before. And you always enjoyed yourself.'

Saying nothing, Pansy fixed her eyes on the cat.

Peg and Tom had decided to evacuate Lenny to Tom's mother in the Essex countryside, and Nell had known she must accept their invitation for Pansy to go with him. The death of her parents had really brought home to her the danger of keeping a child here in London. 'Please don't make it harder for me than it already is,' she urged her sister. 'Help me out here, sis. Having to send you away is breaking my heart.'

There was a long pause, then, 'Oh, all right, I suppose I'll have to go,' Pansy agreed, a tear running down her cheek and dropping on to Tiddles' soft fur.

'Good girl,' said Nell with a sigh of relief.

'We'll have a great time at my gran's,' Lenny said to Pansy that evening as they sat around the table having just finished their meal of corned beef and mashed potato. 'We always have fun there. You've been with us before in the summer holidays so you know all about it.'

'It's lovely there,' Nell cut in to encourage her sister. 'I wish it was me who was going.'

As a child Nell used to go with the Millses to stay at Tom's mother's cottage for a week during the summer holidays. More recently – until the outbreak of war – Pansy had sometimes gone with Peg and Lenny on her own. It had always been thought of as a treat. Not this time, though. Now it was a painful wrench for her.

'Remember the river, Pans,' Lenny went on, thrilled at the prospect of a prolonged stay with his grandmother, who was much less heavy on the discipline than they were at home. 'We'll have good fun messing about there.'

'You certainly will not, Lenny,' declared his mother sternly. 'You know you are not to go near that river without an adult.'

'The kids who live there play by the water all the time,' he told her. 'They paddle and everything.'

'They're used to it and they know about the tides and currents. You don't, so stay away.'

'Yes, Mum,' he said with the air of one who wasn't intending to take the slightest notice.

'I mean it, Lenny. I don't want you giving your grandmother any worry or trouble,' Peg emphasised, picking up on his attitude. 'She isn't of an age to have a drama inflicted upon her if you get into bother. There are plenty of other places to play on dry land.'

'Yeah, all right.' He paused thoughtfully. 'Do you remember the well in Gran's garden?' he asked Pansy.

'Yeah, I thought that was smashing and I can't wait to see it again.' Lenny's enthusiasm was so infectious, Pansy was gradually beginning to warm to the idea.

'We won't have to go to school or anything like that,' Lenny effused, fervour growing with every syllable.

'You have to go to school wherever you're living, son,' put in his father, frowning. 'What on earth gave you the idea that you wouldn't?'

Lenny gave him a pitying look. 'No one goes to school there, Dad. It's the country. The kids play out all day.'

'You'll be lucky,' chortled his father.

'Oh, I know what this is all about,' deduced his mother, looking sad because she didn't want to send her boy away. 'You've only been there in the school summer holidays; that must be what's put such daft ideas into your head. They certainly do go to school, and you and Pansy will be going with them.'

'Oh well,' shrugged Lenny, not seeming particularly bothered.

Tom turned his attention to Pansy, feeling a strong empathy with her as she faced yet another disruption after all she had already endured. 'I'm sure you'll like it at the school, love. It'll be smaller than the one you go to here; the teachers will have more time for you, and you'll have Lenny to look out for you.'

Pansy smiled her shy smile and melted his heart.

'Granny Maud will look after you as well,' he went on, hoping to take the frightened look out of the little girl's eyes. 'There's not a kinder woman in the whole of Essex.'

'That's very true, luv,' added Peg. 'You'll soon feel at home with Maud.'

The Porter girls were the nearest thing Peg had to daughters and she loved the bones of them both. Although desperately sad at the awful circumstances that had brought them into her home, she was glad of the opportunity to try to make life at least bearable for them in their grief.

'We're relying on you to make sure that Lenny behaves himself, Pansy,' Tom went on to say. 'If he gets up to any mischief, you must tell his gran.'

'Fat chance of her splitting on him,' said Ed.

'You've taken the words right out of my mouth,' added Nell, because they all knew how much Pansy adored Lenny. 'You don't tell on a best mate, do you, Pansy?'

She shook her head.

'Anyway, don't be fooled by that sweet little face; she's no angel herself,' Nell continued in a light-hearted manner. 'She doesn't need much persuading when it comes to a spot of mischief.'

'I don't believe a word of it,' said Tom.

'You wouldn't,' responded Peg, because Pansy could do no wrong in his eyes.

The air of false levity was painfully tangible, observed Nell. Everyone was putting on a brave face to hide their real feelings about the parting tomorrow.

Just then the siren went, as though to endorse Nell's decision to send Pansy away.

'Here we go again,' said Tom, rising. 'You lot get your coats and go down the shelter. I'll fetch the blankets and turn everything off before I come down.'

'Tiddles,' said Pansy. 'We mustn't forget Tiddles.'

'Don't you worry about him, love,' Peg soothed. 'We'll find that moggy and take him with us. We don't want him using up any more of his nine lives, do we?'

The cat obligingly appeared and was scooped up by Pansy. Thank God this is the last air raid the kids will have to endure, thought Nell, knowing that she'd made the right decision.

★   ★   ★

'That Polly seems a bit of a flighty piece to me,' Peg remarked to Nell one evening a few weeks later. The two women were ensconced in the living room knitting for the troops with the wireless turned low. Unusually the siren was quiet, so Tom had gone to the local for a pint and Ed was on duty at the AFS depot. 'She's certainly no shrinking violet.'

'You can say that again,' Nell agreed.

'She wears her jumpers so tight it's a wonder her chest doesn't burst through. Man-mad, she seems to me,' expressed Peg. 'A bit too forward in my opinion.'

'I don't think she's man-mad exactly,' said Nell, not wishing to be disloyal to her friend. 'It's more that she wants to have fun and isn't afraid to admit it. She talks quite openly about the sort of feelings the rest of us are embarrassed to mention.'

'Well she'd better not mess my Ed about,' declared Peg. 'I can see she's got her eye on him. I don't think any of us could miss that.'

There was no room in Polly's life for subtlety, and since Nell had been home from hospital she'd come calling at the house at the slightest excuse in the hope of gaining Ed's interest. She flirted with him so outrageously, nobody could be in any doubt as to what she was after. It was rather embarrassing really, especially as Ed seemed to let it all go over his head.

'It's just her way,' Nell defended. 'Her heart's in the right place.'

'It may very well be,' chortled Peg. 'It's the other parts of her that worry me.'

'A lot of it is just talk with her, I think,' said Nell.

Peg gave a wry grin. 'Take no notice of me. Mothers and sons, eh?' she said lightly. 'It's true what they say. We're hard to please when it comes to the women in their life. It's the same with fathers and daughters. No one is good enough.'

Nell's father had never shown the slightest interest in any of Nell's friends of either sex. But it seemed disloyal to say so she just said, 'That's true.' She paused. 'Polly really is all right, you know, Auntie Peg. She likes to enjoy herself and doesn't care who knows it, that's all. Anyway, he hasn't even asked her out yet.'

'Not for want of trying on her part,' said Peg. 'Talk about determined. She simply won't give up even though he doesn't give her any encouragement.'

Nell deemed it wise to change the subject. Polly was her friend, after all.

'The kids seem to be settling in all right with Granny Maud.' Both Nell and Peg had received short letters in the post this morning, having previously provided the children with several stamped addressed envelopes to make sure they kept in touch. 'Pansy sounds all right anyway.'

'Lenny does too, though the little perisher only wrote a line or two. That's him all over, bless him. He'd sooner be out looking for mischief than writing a letter.'

'Pansy didn't write more than a couple of lines either, but that's kids for you.'

'As long as they're safe and not homesick, that's all that matters.' Peg looked at the clock on the mantelpiece. 'It's nearly time for the news.'

'I'll turn up the wireless,' said Nell, getting up and going over to the bulky brown wireless set on the sideboard and turning one of the knobs. The nine o'clock news had become compulsory listening since the outbreak of war.

'Thanks, love,' said Peg.

Suddenly Nell experienced a moment of sheer gratitude for the endless kindness and hospitality of Peg and her family. The feeling was so fierce it brought tears to her eyes. Nell's grief was still raw, of course, but no one could wish for more, under the circumstances, than she had, living with this lovely family.

It couldn't be easy for Peg, having to get along without the company of her best friend. The length of their friendship outmatched Nell's entire lifetime. But the older woman kept going, staying cheerful so as not to upset anyone else.

Now, instead of going straight back to her chair, Nell went and sat next to Peg on the sofa. Peg put down her knitting and rested her hand on Nell's arm for a moment. Neither of them spoke; there was no need because each knew how the other was feeling.

'How have you been feeling today, love?' enquired Tom that night when he got into bed beside his wife, grateful to be sleeping in the bed instead of the shelter.

'I miss Alice something awful, Tom,' she confessed, appreciative of his thoughtfulness in asking. 'There's an emptiness inside me all the time. When I go to the shops I keep going to talk to her because I'm so used to her being with me. But she's on my mind whatever I'm doing, whether I'm cleaning the grate or pegging out the washing, I can feel this awful tight feeling that makes me want to weep . . .'

'Aah,' he said gently, putting his arm around her. 'I miss them too but it isn't quite the same for me. Ernie and I were never close like you were with Alice. It's you and the girls I feel for.'

'Nell is a great comfort to me,' she confided. 'Having her here keeps me going, and I don't mean any disrespect to you when I say that. You know how much you mean to me and how you're helping me through this.' She paused, mulling it over. 'It's just that she's a woman. I know she's only young, but she's mature in her outlook and she's like a pal to me.'

'I'm glad.'

'It's with us having no daughters of our own that I value female company, I suppose,' she continued thoughtfully. 'I think the world of our boys and would walk through fire for them if I needed to, but I would have loved to have had a daughter as well, wouldn't you?'

He didn't answer; just stared into the darkness, glad that she couldn't see his face.

'Tom . . .'

'Yeah, it would have been nice,' he said at last. 'But it just wasn't to be, and we have many other blessings.'

'I'll say we do,' she agreed wholeheartedly.

'Anyway, we'd better settle down and go to sleep, though we'll probably just drop off and the damned siren will go,' he said, moving his arm and shifting about to get comfortable.

'Let's hope we get a night off,' she said, kissing him lightly. 'Night, Tom.'

'Night, love.'

As the raids continued, the number of people defying them and going out of an evening for entertainment was increasing. Pubs, cinemas and dance halls were crowded at the weekends. The management at Barker's Engineering showed true patriotic spirit and decided to go ahead with their annual staff dance, bombs or no bombs.

'Hurray,' cheered Polly in the canteen at dinnertime. 'A bit of normality at last. It'll do us all the world of good. We'll have a great laugh.'

'I won't be going,' Nell told her.

'Not going! Why not?'

'I should have thought that was obvious,' said Nell. 'I'm still in mourning.'

'Oh yeah, I forgot about that for a moment.' Polly gave the matter some thought. 'But no one bothers so much about that sort of thing since the war, with so many people losing relatives and no one knowing if they will be the next to go. I think you should come. It'll take your mind off things and cheer you up.'

'I don't want to go,' Nell made clear. 'It's too soon, Polly.'

'But it'll be a bit of a giggle,' she persisted. 'People won't think badly of you. Anyway, so what if they do?'

'What other people think isn't the issue,' Nell informed her. 'It's me; how I feel inside. I'm not ready.'

'You can't stay at home moping for the rest of your life,' stated Polly categorically.

'I have no intention of doing that.'

'The sooner you start to go out the better.' Polly held forth in an authoritative manner. 'You're young. We've spent enough time in the shelters. Now that we've the chance of some light relief, don't let it pass you by.'

'Leave it, Polly,' Nell said sharply. 'I don't want to go and I'm not going to change my mind. So show a bit of respect for my feelings, for good-ness' sake.'

'All right, don't get narked.' Polly was indignant. 'I was only thinking of you.'

'No you weren't. You were thinking of yourself,' Nell corrected. 'You want me to go because you don't want to go on your own. I don't blame you for that, but don't try and bully me over such a personal matter. There'll be lots of the other girls from the office going, so you'll have plenty of company.' She gave her a knowing look. 'Ed will be there.'

Polly's eyes glinted. 'Oh will he now?' she said. 'I did wonder if he might be.'

'I thought that would please you.'

'It'll be easier for me if you're there, though,' decided the self-seeking

Polly. 'He's bound to come over to talk to you even if he is with his mates. If I'm with you . . .'

'Don't be so soft,' cut in Nell in a tone of friendly admonishment. 'You're more than capable of getting off with a bloke on your own. Since when did you need me?'

'This isn't just any old bloke. It's Ed Mills; there'll be a lot of competition,' Polly reminded her. 'Anyway, he hasn't shown much interest in me so far and I've given him enough opportunity. I've flirted my socks off and he hasn't responded.'

'There are always too many people around when you come to the house. He might be put off by that, especially as his mum and dad are there,' Nell suggested. 'The mood at the dance should make it easier for you, seeing that flirting is what people do at dances.'

'Mm. Maybe you're right.' Suddenly Polly saw the whole thing in a new light. If Nell wasn't there, she could be as brazen as she liked in her quest for Ed Mills without fear of criticism or embarrassment. 'I can see that you wouldn't want to go so soon after your loss. Don't worry about me.'

She was so transparent Nell couldn't help but laugh. 'He's a friend of mine, remember.'

'Meaning what?'

'Meaning treat him right or you'll have me to answer to,' Nell explained.

'What world are you living in, Nell? It's the men who call the tune. They're the ones who play around and let us women down, not the other way around. Everybody knows that. Honestly, Nell, you can be so naïve at times.'

'And you can be so cynical.'

Just then a couple of their colleagues from the stenographers' pool walked by and stopped at their table.

'Are you two going to the dance on Saturday?' asked one of them, an attractive brunette called Maggie.

Nell explained the situation.

'You can come with us if you like, Polly,' invited Maggie in a friendly manner.

'Thanks, Maggie. I'll see you there.' The girls would be useful to stand with until she got into her stride, but she didn't want to be tied to them all evening, because she had other plans.

'We'll look out for you then.'

'Likewise.'

'There you are,' said Nell when the others had gone. 'You're all fixed up. You won't even notice that I'm not there.'

I'll be too busy beating off the competition, Polly thought, especially as the women would outnumber the men, who would either be under the age for conscription or wrinkled old blokes who were past it, with the exception of those in reserved occupations. But she said, 'Course I will. We're pals, aren't we? I'd much rather you were there.'

It was Saturday night and Ed was at the dance, standing with a group of mates. The subject under discussion was the talent here tonight, and there was a great deal of boasting and bravado about their chances with the opposite sex, all of whom were sitting or standing on the other side of the dance floor. Some older couples were twirling to a slow waltz, but it was still early in the evening and the dance hadn't really got going yet.

The canteen had been transformed into a dance hall with a stage on which a group of musicians of the older generation – smartly dressed in dinner jackets and bow ties – were playing 'A Nightingale Sang in Berkeley Square'.

'That little blonde from the typing pool is a bit of all right, isn't she?' said one of the boys. 'Cor, yeah, I wouldn't mind some o' that. She doesn't look the sort to say no.'

'I wouldn't mind burying my head in her assets, would you?' laughed someone.

'No I would not,' said another. 'She doesn't look as though she'd mind either. The way she's flashing them about. She's asking for it by the look of her.'

For some reason their bawdy talk about Polly annoyed Ed.

'Her name is Polly and she's a friend of a good friend of mine, so watch what you're saying about her,' he admonished.

'Ooh, hark at him,' said the first boy in a joshing tone. 'I didn't realise you knew her. No offence meant, mate.'

'None taken,' said Ed, not sure why he had over-reacted, since Polly was nothing to him. He assumed it must be because of her connection with Nell.

'That's why she keeps looking over here, because she knows you,' said one of the others. 'And there was I thinking it was me she was after.'

Ed was fully aware of the fact that Polly had spent most of the evening so far giving him the come-on, in the same way that he was conscious of it when she called to see Nell at home. He fancied Polly; what man wouldn't? She was a beautiful girl. But he found her relentless obviousness a little intimidating, which was why he hadn't responded to her. Where was the challenge in going after a girl who was dead set on you? On the other hand, she was definitely the best-looking girl here tonight.

His mates were egging him on.

'Go and ask her to dance,' one of them encouraged. 'She obviously fancies you. You're well in there.'

'Nah.'

'Not scared of a busty little blonde, are you?' teased another.

'Leave off.'

'Two bob says you are scared,' said a third lad. 'I bet you two bob you won't go over and ask her.'

'Right. You're on. Have your money ready, mate,' pronounced Ed. 'Some extra dosh will come in handy.'

'I thought you'd never ask,' said Polly as she and Ed glided round the floor in a quickstep. 'It's taken you long enough.'

He knew she was referring to the signals she'd been sending out for weeks and that he had been studiously ignoring. 'What's worth having is worth waiting for. Isn't that what they say?' he said saucily, looking down into her face and approving of what he saw. She was even better-looking close up.

'Yeah, they do say that,' she replied, leaning back slightly and looking into his eyes, blatantly inviting. 'So I hope I'm not going to be disappointed.'

Blimey, she was a fast one, he thought, his heart beating wildly, partly with fear but also with excitement; she certainly didn't mince her words, and he had the distinct impression that she was far more experienced than he was. It was enough to scare a bloke half to death and a novel experience for him. All the girls he'd been out with had been chaste and determined to stay that way.

'You don't hold back, do you?' he remarked.

'No. What's the point of that?' she said breezily. 'We could all be dead tomorrow.' Just then the siren wailed, as though to prove her point. 'See what I mean. It's our youth this war is messing with. Seize the moment; that's my motto.'

'There's something to be said for that attitude.' He looked at her. 'Do you want to go to the shelter?'

'No. Not unless you do,' she answered. 'I'd rather take my chances here.'

'Me too.'

'Let's carry on dancing then,' she said, smiling and moving closer to him.

Some of the older members of staff left the dance after the siren; most of the young ones, stayed. Ed's mates were keen for details when the music ended and he returned to join their ranks.

'What's she like?' asked one of them.

'She's a nice girl,' he replied.

'Is that all you're gonna tell us?' said another in disgust.

'There's nothing else to tell.'

'What about her chest? What did it feel like up close?'

'Don't be so disgusting,' Ed heard himself say, 'talking about the girl like that. She's a human being, not a piece of meat.'

'Keep your hair on, mate,' said his pal. 'I dunno what you're getting so ratty about. It's only a bit of fun.'

'Go and find a girl of your own,' Ed told him. 'This is a dance, a social occasion. You're not meant to stand in a huddle all night, eyeing the girls up and taking the mick. The idea is to ask one of them to dance.'

The music struck up again and Ed made a beeline for Polly. He danced every dance with her after that. The sound of the music and the buzz of conversation took the edge off the noise from outside: the roar of aircraft, the anti-aircraft guns and the explosions. By the time they played the last waltz, the all-clear had gone and he and Polly were smooching.

'Can I see you home?' he whispered in her ear.

'Yes please,' she said, resting her head on his shoulder. 'You certainly can.'

★　★　★

Maud Mills put on her best hat in front of the mirror that hung over the fireplace in the parlour of her cottage. A short, dumpy woman with white hair, plump cheeks and the same laughing blue eyes she had passed on to her son Tom, she was dressed all in black in keeping with her age, though she did have a red feather in her hat. Having satisfied herself that her hat pins were secure, she turned to her two young charges, who were sitting on the sofa. Lenny was reading a comic, Pansy was looking at a book.

'Now, you two little 'uns, I'm going down to the pub for my Sunday dinnertime glass of beer. I won't be more than half an hour and you know where I am if you need me. Just open the pub door and shout my name. The dinner is cooking and I shall serve it out when I get back. Be good kids while I'm gone.'

'Yes, Gran,' said Lenny.

'We will,' added Pansy.

As soon as the door closed behind her, Lenny said, 'Shall we go down to the river?'

'We're not allowed.'

'Gran won't mind. It's only my mum and dad who say we mustn't do it. Gran's different to them. She doesn't fuss because she knows we'll be all right. Anyway, she won't know.'

'She won't be gone long and the pub is only a few doors down on the corner, so she might see us.'

'We'll sneak out the back way and down the alley,' he suggested. 'We'll be back before she is and still have time to have a bit of fun. It's boring indoors.'

'All right then,' agreed Pansy.

They got their coats and scarves off the hall stand and went out of the back kitchen door into the cold December weather. Hurrying through the narrow garden past the well, the chicken run and the vegetable patch, they opened the gate, sped furtively along the alley and down the hill to the river.

'Morning, Maud,' said the landlord of the Waterlow Arms. 'The usual, is it?'

'Yes please, duck,' Maud said, putting some money on the counter.

He handed her her change and said, 'You go and sit down and I'll bring it over to you.'

'Ta, dear, that's very kind.'

She sat down at a table by the fire, exchanging greetings with other locals; all men, mostly elderly because the others were away at the war. Being such a small community, everyone knew everyone else and there was a friendly atmosphere. Because she was such a well-known local character and something of a free spirit, no one thought it odd or inappropriate that Maud came into the pub on her own, as they most certainly would of other women.

Maud had come back to live in the village after her dear husband had passed on. They had both been born and raised here but had gone away to London for him to find work and had brought their family up there. With her husband gone and Tom settled with his wife and family, she'd felt drawn back to her roots. Being a countrywoman at heart, the ethos suited her.

'How are the nippers you've got staying with you, Maud?' asked a man who was sitting nearby with another man playing dominoes. 'Keeping you busy, are they?'

'Phew, I should say so. They're a couple of right little livewires and that's a fact, especially my grandson Lenny,' she told him. 'He takes after his dad at that age. He's up to all sorts. Still, I like a boy with plenty of go in him. The little girl's a sweetheart. She lost her mum and dad in the bombing, the poor love.'

'Shame about that,' said the man,

'Mm, it is. I'm doing what I can to make the poor mite feel welcome. Truth is, I enjoy having them to stay. I don't bother so much with rules as they do in London. It's more free and easy here in the country, and they love that.' The landlord brought her glass of stout and she took a sip. 'They have to do as they're told, mind. I don't take any nonsense from them but I do give them a bit of leeway. I know I can leave them for half an hour of a Sunday morning without them coming to any harm, especially as my place is only a few doors away so they can come and get me if they need to.'

'It's company for you,' said the man.

'It is, duck, it is.' Although she was the only woman in the pub, Maud felt completely at ease. A Sunday lunchtime glass of stout in her local was her weekly treat and all the locals knew that. She never had more than one drink and never stayed long. It was just her way of feeling a part of things.

Digging into her pocket, she took out a tobacco tin and some papers and began to roll a cigarette. No one paid any attention. Maud was a one-off and was very well liked in the village.

Situated on the banks of a river flowing into the sea, Waterlow was a maritime village with a busy boatyard, a school, a pub, a church and a village shop. The butcher operated his business in the front room of his house, as did the baker, the shoemaker and the lady who ran the post office. There was a ferryman who took people across the river to the larger village on the other side, where there was a train station with a direct link to London.

Today the wind was sharp and the sky a grey dome of shifting white and black clouds. There was no one about in this cold weather except fishermen working on their boats. Nearly all the men earned their living fishing, though the younger ones were currently away at war.

'Come on, Pans,' said Lenny, climbing down the river bank by a wooded area out of sight of the village.

'There's quicksand down there, Lenny,' she told him. 'It'll suck us under and we'll suffocate.'

'It isn't quicksand, it's just ordinary mud,' he assured her. 'But we'll stay on the stony part if you'd rather. Come on.' He held out his hand. 'Here, hang on to me.'

Warily Pansy climbed down the bank on to the wet foreshore. Holding her hand, Lenny led the way along the pebbly ground away from the village and any prying eyes that might be looking in this direction. Pansy loved the taste of the open air and the feel of the wind; even the strange, slightly sour smell of the river pleased her. It didn't smell of smoke like it did at home. The smell of smoke made her stomach churn because it reminded her of the terrible night the house had been bombed.

Lenny stopped to pick up some stones and aimed them towards the river so that they skimmed the surface.

'Here, you have a go,' he said, handing her one.

'I'm not as good as you,' she said as her aim fell short of the water's edge.

73

'You're doing all right.'

After a while they became bored with this, so explored further along the river's edge until they came across a tree that might have been made especially for Lenny in that it had long branches reaching right out over the tideway, leafless at this time of the year and perfect for climbing.

'Cor,' he exclaimed with awe at this perfect opportunity for adventure.

'No, Lenny,' warned Pansy, fearful for her friend, especially as there was no one around. 'If you climb out on to one of those branches you might fall off.'

'No I won't,' he assured her with confidence. 'Anyway, the tide's out so I won't drown. Are you coming?'

She shook her head. It was a bit too adventurous for her. 'And I don't think you should either,' she told him. 'You'll really cop it if your gran finds out.'

'She won't, will she?' he pointed out. 'How can she? There's no one around.'

'I'm ever so cold, Lenny,' Pansy said, hugging herself as the wind stung her cheeks and seemed to cut right through her coat.

'Are you? All right. I won't be long,' he said, scrambling up the bank towards the tree. 'I'll just have a quick go at this, then we'll go home.'

He had started to climb the tree when there was a shriek from Pansy, who had stepped beyond the pebbled area and had her foot stuck deep in the mud.

'I'm in the quicksand, Lenny!' There were all sorts of stories about quicksand in the area, which was why she was so terrified. 'It'll suck me under.'

Lenny was down the bank in a trice. 'Here, hold on to me and I'll pull you out.'

'It'll take me down.'

'It isn't quicksand, I told you. Stop panicking.'

'How do you know?'

'I just know; that stuff you hear about quicksand around here is just stories people make up. Here, take my hand.'

She did as he said, whereupon Lenny slipped and fell on his bottom, the soft mud splashing on to Pansy.

'That's done it,' he said, looking at the dark river mud all over their clothes. 'Gran'll go mad.'

Pansy wasn't made of such strong stuff as Lenny and burst into tears.

'Don't cry,' he said kindly, clambering to his feet. 'At least we know it isn't quicksand. We'd have sunk by now if it was.'

'There is that, I suppose,' she said, brightening slightly.

As soon as he was steady on his feet, he took hold of Pansy's hand so that she was able to draw her foot out of the mud without losing her balance.

'You all right now?' he asked, digging into his pocket and producing a rather grubby rag handkerchief.

'Yeah.' She was fine now the fear of quicksand had receded.

'Here, you can use this to wipe your eyes.'

'Thanks.'

'We'd better try and get some of this mud off before Gran sees it,' he suggested. 'It's a pity the tide's out or we could wash ourselves in the water. Still, let's have a go with the hanky.'

He might as well have rolled them both in a mud bath for all the good the handkerchief did. It simply spread the dark sludge to a wider area.

But, ever the optimist, he said, 'That's better. Perhaps Gran won't be back and we can change our clothes and rinse these before she comes home.'

'You think of everything, Lenny,' Pansy said admiringly, and they climbed up the bank and hurried towards the cottage.

'Oh good Lord above, just look at the state of you both,' exploded Maud when they appeared in the kitchen, where she was straining the cabbage at the sink. 'What in God's name have you been doing? As if I can't guess.'

'Sorry, Gran,' said Lenny sheepishly. 'We fell in the mud. It wasn't Pansy's fault.'

'How can I trust you when as soon as I turn my back you get up to mischief?' ranted Maud. 'You've been down to the river, and don't bother to deny it.'

Lenny bit his lip. Pansy said, 'Sorry.' They were both shivering.

'You know your mother doesn't like you going down there, Lenny. She told you you weren't to go near the water unless you were with an adult. And what do you do? You're down there the minute you get the chance.' Maud wasn't fool enough to destroy her authority by admitting it to them, but she had done the same thing herself as a child. The times she'd come home in the same state they were in now couldn't be counted on four pairs of hands.

'We won't do it again, I promise,' said Lenny.

'You promised your mother and it counted for nothing,' she reminded him. 'You're one of those children who just can't help himself from poking around until you find some sort of adventure that leads to trouble. The only way I can stop you is by keeping you indoors, and then you'll probably set fire to the place or something. But you will stay in except for school until further notice. And I shall think of other ways of punishing you as well.'

'It wasn't Pansy's fault,' Lenny said again. 'So it isn't fair for her to get punished.'

'She was with you, so you'll be treated equally,' his grandmother informed him. 'Sorry, Pansy dear, but I want to be fair.'

''S all right,' she said solemnly.

'Now get those wet clothes off and clean yourselves up before dinner,' Maud instructed. 'I'll have to heat some water up so that you can have a bath later on. Lord knows how I'm going to get that mud off your clothes.'

'Are you going to write and tell Mum about it?' asked Lenny. A wigging from his grandmother was a glass of Tizer compared with one from his mother.

Maud looked at him thoughtfully and answered him with a question of her own. 'Are you going to tell her that I was in the pub when you went to the river?' she said.

'I dunno.' He found himself fixed with her questioning stare and caught on. 'Well no, I don't suppose I have to.'

'It can be our little secret then,' she said, her blue eyes resting on him shrewdly. 'You keep shtoom and so will I.'

'Thanks, Gran.'

'Just stay out of trouble in future or you really will find out that I'm not such a soft touch.'

'Thank you,' said Pansy, smiling her shy smile.

'Go on with you,' said Maud. 'Just get yourselves into some clean clothes so that we can have our dinner.'

* * *

76

'So, how did the dance go last night?' Nell asked Ed that same day over Sunday dinner, a meal made up to a large extent of swede mixed with potato, and Yorkshire pudding; the meat ration was such that they each had just a mouthful of roast beef.

'It was good,' he said, looking extremely pleased with himself. 'I had a smashing time.'

'Judging by the soppy grin on your face, there was a young lady involved,' said his mother.

'Lady' wasn't the word best suited to describe Polly, but he said, 'There were lots of girls there.'

'Don't be cagey, son. You know very well what I mean,' grinned his mother.

'Yeah, all right, there was someone I was with for most of the time.' He looked at Peg with a hint of defiance, knowing instinctively that she wouldn't approve of Polly. His mother saw even the most casual female acquaintance as a future wife for him, even though he wasn't yet eighteen and had no plans to marry for years to come. 'I was with Polly, as it happens. Nell's friend.'

Peg's brows shot up, despite her attempts not to show her reaction. 'Oh, really? At least it's someone we know.'

'She seems a nice enough girl,' remarked Tom, a little too casually. 'Always cheerful and full of fun.'

'Yeah, she is a lively spark,' added Nell, exchanging a glance with Ed to let him know that he had her support.

Nice didn't go anywhere near to describing Polly in Ed's opinion. Having spent an evening with her, he thought she was the most exciting girl he had ever met and he couldn't wait to see her again. She was fast, daring and passionate; she knew what she wanted and wasn't in the least bit embarrassed about getting it. He was an innocent compared to her but he'd been a very willing learner. Oh yes! His heart beat faster at the mere thought of her.

'I'm taking her to the pictures tonight, as it happens,' he announced.

'What if the siren goes?' asked his mother.

'We'll go anyway and take our chances,' he told her. 'Might as well make the most of a Sunday off. I'll be working all day next Sunday. In fact, I might as well make the most of my freedom. I'll be eighteen soon so I'll be getting my call-up papers.'

'You're in a reserved occupation,' Peg reminded him.

'Yeah, yeah, I know.'

'There's no question about it. You'll have to stay put if your firm won't release you.' There was a note of desperation in her voice. 'So don't go getting any ideas about volunteering.'

'All right, don't go on about it, Mum,' he urged her. 'As you say, there's a few months to go. Anything could have happened by then.'

'Thanks for cheering us all up,' said Nell with irony, and, deciding on a swift change of subject to defuse the rising tension, added, 'Now you've done that, you can give us all the gossip about the dance. Who got off with who and so on.'

Ed had been far too engrossed in Polly to have noticed much about anyone else.

'It went off very well and everyone enjoyed themselves, I think,' he said thoughtfully. 'Most people carried on dancing when the bombing started. A few of the older ones left, though.'

'No scandal to report, then?' probed Nell.

'Sorry to disappoint you, but no,' he said. 'There was nothing out of the ordinary at all.'

'You men never notice anything,' said Nell lightly. 'I'll hear more about it from Polly at work tomorrow.'

Polly wouldn't have noticed what was going on around her any more than Ed had; she'd have been far too busy lavishing all her attention on him. There would certainly be a scandal if anyone had spotted what the two of them had got up to after the dance under cover of darkness. Oh boy! He'd never be the same again.

Chapter Five

Although Nell didn't yet feel ready to go out enjoying herself, she did find, unexpectedly, that she was prepared for a new challenge. It happened a week or so later, when she just happened to be idly glancing through the situations vacant column in the local paper and spotted a job advertisement that interested her. On impulse, she applied for it and was invited to go for an interview.

'Shorthand speed?' asked Ted Bigley, the editor of the *Chiswick and Hammersmith Herald*.

'A hundred and twenty words a minute,' she replied.

'Typing?'

'Seventy-five.'

His brows rose approvingly; this exceeded the minimum requirement.

'Can you make tea?'

She nodded.

'Answer the phone?'

'Yes.'

'Do filing if necessary?'

'Of course.' She looked at him, puzzled. 'But I thought the vacancy was for a shorthand typist.'

A large, florid man of about fifty in a crumpled pinstriped suit and bright red waistcoat, Bigley had scarlet cheeks and wild grey hair that resembled a well-worn floor mop. He peered at her over his spectacles from the other side of his chaotically overloaded desk.

'There's a war on,' he pointed out unnecessarily and in a tone that was almost aggressive, 'and we are a weekly newspaper struggling to keep going

79

despite a crippling paper shortage and very little of all the other materials we need.'

Beginning to get the gist of what he was getting at, Nell nodded politely.

Looking down at her letter of application, he studied it for a few moments. 'Our office routine is entirely different to that of a big company like the one you are with at present, where everyone keeps well within the confines of their own duties,' he said, looking up. 'We are a small company made up of a flexible team and I am looking for someone to work primarily as a secretary to me but also willing to turn their hand to anything else if the need arises. We have a common aim here, and that is to produce a good local newspaper which myself and my staff care passionately about.'

Consider yourself told, Nell thought, but said, 'I see.'

'No doubt you use a reliable typewriter in your current position,' he went on.

'Of course,' was her natural reaction.

'There's no "of course" about it here,' he informed her somewhat sharply.

'Oh, and why is that?'

'We don't have enough typewriters because we can't get them replaced or repaired when they go wrong. Priority goes to government offices and typists in the war factories such as the one you currently work in.' He stubbed his cigarette out in an ashtray already overflowing with the detritus of his nicotine habit. His untidy office was small and looked out over the general office, which wasn't very big either; the newspaper was based in an old house converted for commercial use and situated at the far end of Chiswick High Road. His desk was piled high with bits of paper and newspapers. 'We've reached the stage where my reporters have to write their copy by hand if there isn't a typewriter available.'

She nodded again.

'So it isn't the sort of job you are used to at all,' he continued, in a manner she found slightly threatening. 'The hours aren't consistent. We have a newspaper to get out once a week and it's all hands on deck to make sure that happens on time. If it means working late then that's what we do.'

'I understand.'

This was the oddest job interview she'd ever had and seemed to be a complete disaster as far as she was concerned. Bigley obviously deemed her to be unsuitable and seemed the sort to come right out and say so, which she guessed he was about to do at any moment.

But instead he became reflective. 'Like a lot of other areas of business, the newspaper industry is having a hard time because of the war,' he told her, lighting another cigarette.

'I've noticed that all the papers are a lot thinner these days,' she remarked.

'Some are folding altogether,' he informed her gravely, inhaling on his cigarette as though his next breath depended on it, then practically disappearing behind a pall of smoke. 'They just can't keep going under the circumstances.'

'That's a pity.'

'It is indeed, and I am determined that this one will survive,' he declared gruffly. 'The residents need to know what's going on in their local area more than ever in a time of war. It's an essential social service we provide here. Our reporters search for the stories behind the news; the human element. We may just be a local rag, but we do a hell of a lot more than just reporting on the latest weddings and funerals and who's up in court for being drunk and disorderly.'

'I'm sure you do,' she responded courteously.

'Apart from anything else, the paper is my livelihood,' he seemed to find it necessary to inform her. 'I'm the proprietor as well as the editor. I started it from scratch.'

'Really?' She wondered when he was going to get to the point.

He looked at her shrewdly. 'Are you likely to join the services?' he enquired bluntly.

'No. I would be turned down on medical grounds,' she told him. 'I had asthma as a child.'

'That's good.'

'Oh?' She threw him a look.

'I mean it's good as far as the job is concerned, in that I wouldn't want to take someone on who's likely to join up before they've had a chance to settle in,' he explained. 'The person you'd be replacing is leaving because she's managed to get herself in the family way and is having to get married at the end of the month.'

'I see.'

He rested his steely gaze on her, raising one eyebrow questioningly. His attitude was so outrageous, she was almost beyond anger; more in a state of disbelief. She looked him directly in the eyes.

'I don't even have a boyfriend at the moment, so the same thing isn't likely to happen to me.'

'I'm glad to hear it.'

Why was she here? She was well suited at Barker's and had had no intention of changing her job until this advertisement had caught her eye. The premises here were shabby, this man was arrogant, patronising and downright rude, and they apparently didn't even have any decent office equipment.

But for some reason the job excited her. She felt drawn to the idea of a more personal working environment, and flexibility would add interest to the office day. Being a part of a small team must surely be more rewarding than the faceless environment she worked in now, typing correspondence that held no personal interest for her for hours on end. But what attracted her most about the opportunity was the idea of being at the hub of what was going on in the local area.

'Well that seems to be about all,' Bigley was saying now.

'Thank you.' Nell rose, expecting him to tell her he'd give her a decision when he'd seen the rest of the applicants.

Much to her surprise he said, 'Can you start the first Monday of the new year? The other girl will have left by then. I can't afford to have her stay on to show you the job, I'm afraid, so the others will have to show you the ropes.'

Although she was pleased by this unexpected turn of events, she was niggled by his manner, which seemed to challenge her intellect somehow. 'I am a fully trained shorthand typist and used to office routine,' she reminded him. 'I don't think I'll have any trouble getting the hang of things.'

He raised his eyes, his steady gaze resting on her. 'Every office has its own way of doing things and you have to get to know it no matter how many certificates you have,' he came back at her in a scathing tone. 'As I've already said, you'll need to be versatile to work here. So . . . do you want the job or don't you?'

He was nothing if not direct. 'Yes, Mr Bigley, I do,' she heard herself say.

'The name is Ted,' he informed her. 'We don't go in for all that office formality here.'

This interview was getting more peculiar by the second. She'd never heard of such a thing as staff calling the boss by their Christian name. Heaven only knew what she was getting herself into. 'I'll bear that in mind in future,' she said, not quite brave enough yet to address him as Ted.

'We'll confirm your appointment in writing in the next few days,' he told her.

'Thank you.'

As she left his room and walked through the general office, she noticed the informal atmosphere. The place was a hive of activity, though. There seemed to be several conversations in progress at once, all concerning the paper. There was a discussion going on by a desk, another on the telephone; a phone was ringing somewhere and a young man – she thought he might be a reporter – came in, took off his coat and hat and sat down at a typewriter with a notebook, obviously working on his own initiative. She couldn't help comparing this with Miss Crow's department, where conversation was strictly prohibited and you even had to ask permission to leave your desk to answer a call of nature.

Maybe a new job was just what she needed to take her mind off her grief. Meanwhile Christmas had to be endured. For the first time in her life, Nell was dreading it.

It was Christmas afternoon in the Millses front room, which was only used on special occasions. The fire was glowing in the hearth, home-made paper chains hung from the ceiling in loops and a gold cardboard bell they had had for years was shining from the sideboard among an array of Christmas cards.

Tom was dozing in the armchair with Tiddles snoozing at his feet, Polly and Ed were sitting close together on the sofa holding hands, and Nell and Peg were knitting and listening to the wireless. Not exactly a party atmosphere, but no one had the heart for the usual fun and games without the children, though they had all struggled to create a festive mood.

Nell and Peg had toyed with the idea of having the children home for the holiday as there was currently a lull in the air raids, but had finally decided not to risk it. After what had happened to Alice and Ernie, they were bound to be overly cautious, and no one doubted that the raids were far from over.

Being essentially a family time, Christmas had magnified Nell's emotions to an almost unbearable level. Ostensibly cheerful, she was actually weeping inside at the crippling absence of her parents, the feeling of sadness exacerbated by the fact that her sister wasn't here either.

She and Peg had travelled to Essex to see the children last weekend, setting off when Nell finished work on Saturday and returning Sunday night in time for work on Monday. They had taken presents that had been queued for, bargained for and bought second hand, as toys were in short supply. But for all the kindness Maud would undoubtedly bestow on Pansy, it would be Nell her sister would want to be with today. However, it just wasn't possible for Nell to get up there, because of the lack of public transport over the holiday, and work commitments immediately after.

'Cor blimey, it's like a flamin' morgue in here,' piped up Polly, who was now a regular visitor at the Mills house and had been accepted as Ed's steady girlfriend. 'Surely we can do something to cheer the place up? It's supposed to be the festive season. It's more like Doomsday than Christmas Day. I want to enjoy myself this holiday, as work will be worse than ever with Nell deserting me.'

'You'll be all right,' said Nell.

'It won't be the same without you and I'm dreading it.'

'I'll put the kettle on when I've finished this row,' said Peg. 'And we'll start on the Christmas cake.'

'Tea and Christmas cake won't do the trick. A nice drop of booze would be more like it,' said the intrepid Polly. 'That would soon liven things up.'

'We don't want to liven things up at the moment,' said Peg in a tone of admonition. 'It's Christmas afternoon, for heaven's sake. We'll have a few drinks tonight.'

'I reckon we should bring the drinks forward,' Polly carried on regardless. 'You lot look as though you need something to cheer you up. What a bunch of miseries!'

'Polly,' rebuked Ed, looking embarrassed and glancing towards Nell. 'Have a bit of respect, will you?'

'Yes, we'd all appreciate that,' sniffed Peg. 'You'll wait till tonight for the booze, my girl. It's tea and cake for now.'

'I was only trying to inject some Christmas spirit into the proceedings,' Polly explained, apparently immune to the discomfort she was causing. 'It only comes once a year so we might as well make the most of it. We need to loosen up a bit and have some fun. It's supposed to be a time for celebration. There's enough misery about during the year without having to suffer it at Christmas as well.'

'I'll go and put the kettle on,' said Nell, and left the room hurriedly in a desperate bid to escape. The last thing she wanted was to spoil Christmas for anyone else. She had tried so hard to seem cheerful, but obviously she hadn't convinced anyone.

'Honestly, Polly, you don't half know how to put your foot in it,' reproved Ed when Nell was out of earshot. 'It must be hard for Nell this Christmas, having lost her parents so recently and not being able to be with her sister.'

'Which is why I'm trying to jolly things up,' Polly told him. 'She needs taking out of herself; to help her forget.'

'That isn't what she wants at all,' he said, and got up and left the room.

Polly looked from Peg to Tom, spreading her arms in a baffled gesture. 'Honestly, some people aren't half quick to take offence. I was only trying to help.' She looked extremely miffed. 'I didn't mean any harm. There's no need for everyone to take umbrage. Anyone would think I'd committed a murder or something.'

Polly's lack of depth probably had something to do with the fact that she was young, Peg told herself. Perhaps she'd improve with the years. She certainly hoped so, because as she was at the moment, she wasn't the sort of person you could take to your heart. Ed was very keen on her so Peg had respected his feelings and welcomed her into their home, trying to make her feel like one of the family whilst hoping it would just be a temporary thing between the two of them. Ed was far too young to settle down anyway.

'We're all very fond of Nell, and are feeling especially sensitive to her feelings today of all days,' explained Peg. 'That's why we're upset on her behalf.'

'She can't expect everyone to go into mourning just because she is,' remarked Polly, huffy and on the defensive.

'Now that isn't a nice thing to say at all,' Peg rebuked. 'That's the last thing Nell would ever expect or want. You're her friend. You must know that.'

'Well, yeah, I do, I s'pose . . .'

'Why can't you show it a little more, then?' asked Peg.

'I dunno. It isn't in my nature. I can't help the way I am. I just can't stand all this gloom and doom.'

'It isn't gloomy; it's just a bit quieter than usual, that's all,' said Peg. 'And we are not going to have a party in the middle of the afternoon just to cheer you up.'

'All right. I'm sorry.' Polly looked sheepish. 'Should I go and apologise to Nell, do you think?' she asked.

'I think you'd better leave Ed to sort things out with Nell for the moment,' intervened Tom from his armchair.

'Good idea,' agreed Peg. They were both aware of the close friendship that existed between Nell and Ed. 'If anyone can make Nell feel better, it's him.'

'I'll stay here then,' said Polly dismally. A fine Christmas this was turning out to be! She'd had such high hopes of it too, being her first with Ed.

'Christmas is a bit much for you to take this year, isn't it?' Ed said to Nell, who was getting the cups and saucers out of the cupboard and setting them out on a tray.

She shrugged. 'Just a bit,' she said.

'It's understandable,' he said. 'Polly doesn't mean any harm. She isn't very tactful, that's all.'

'You don't need to defend Polly to me, Ed. I know she doesn't mean it; it's just the way she is. She likes to enjoy herself, especially at Christmas, and I don't blame her.' Her voice was ragged with emotion. 'Anyway, I don't want people treading on eggshells around me. The last thing I want to do is spoil Christmas for other people.'

'You're not spoiling anything,' he assured her. 'You've been amazing. It's any excuse for a party with Polly.'

'And why shouldn't she have fun?' said Nell. 'She's young. It's only natural. I'd want the same thing myself normally.'

'Anyway, I haven't come out here to talk about Polly,' he told her. 'I'm here to make sure you're all right.'

She and Ed had always been honest with each other, and she couldn't lie to him.

'I don't feel as though I'll ever be all right again, to tell you the truth,' she admitted. 'On top of everything else, I feel as though I've let Pansy down. I wish I'd brought her back here for the holiday. She'll need me so much today, the poor little thing. I'm an adult and I feel bad enough about Mum and Dad. She's just a kid. She should be here with me.'

'You have not let Pansy down,' he stated categorically. 'You did the right thing. There could be a raid at any time. She could get hurt or worse here in London. It broke Mum's heart to leave Lenny where he is, but she knew she had to. It's no more than our duty to protect the little 'uns.'

'I miss her, Ed,' Nell said, finally breaking down in tears. 'I miss Pansy, and I miss my mum something awful.'

'Come here, you,' he said, wrapping his arms around her while she sobbed, releasing some of the pain and tension. 'You have a good cry. You've been holding it inside for too long.'

'How do you know?' she asked when she was able to speak.

'I've known you for ever, remember.'

'I'd have thought you were too busy with Polly lately to notice anyone else.'

'I hope I never reach the stage where I stop caring about my friends because I'm seeing a girl,' he told her.

'Even one you're besotted with?'

He didn't deny it. 'Even then,' he said gently.

He held her until there wasn't a tear left in her, then dabbed her eyes with his handkerchief.

'I'd better get on and make the tea,' she said thickly. 'They'll be wondering what we're doing out here.'

'They'll know exactly what we're doing,' he told her, 'but a cup of tea and a slice of cake would be nice.'

'Coming up,' she said, forcing a smile and turning the gas up under the kettle.

'Just one thing about Pansy,' Ed began. 'The thing to bear in mind is that although she will feel upset today, she will get over it. She might not live to do that if you'd brought her back to London. We all know we haven't seen the last of the raids.'

'I know, Ed,' Nell sighed. 'I know.'

The light had already faded when Maud went into the kitchen to cut the cake late on Christmas afternoon. It was the saddest Christmas she'd ever had; even worse than the first one after her dear husband had passed on. She'd been with Tom and his family then in London. She had always spent Christmas and New Year with them until this year, when the situation had made it necessary for her to stay here with the children.

It was for them she was sad, especially young Pansy. Maud had done her best to keep them entertained; she'd put up paper chains and holly and had got what she could in the way of festive treats. In the run-up to the big day the children had taken an active part in local events: the carol-singing, the party in the village hall, and special festive activities at the school. They'd spent hours making Christmas cards with old bits of cardboard and a painting set she'd managed to get hold of when they'd first arrived here.

They'd made friends of their own age in the village, but on Christmas Day everyone was at home with their families, and Lenny and Pansy were missing theirs. Even the indomitable Lenny had been somewhat subdued this afternoon, though both children had an assortment of gifts to keep them occupied.

It was Pansy who was breaking Maud's heart. It was the expression in her eyes; the haunted look of longing for something she could never have again. Today of all days she needed her big sister, and because of the ruddy war she was denied even that. Oh, it made Maud so mad.

As she drew the curtains across the kitchen window, she noticed how clear the sky was, with stars beginning to sparkle as darkness fell. It was a lovely sight and gave her an idea.

'Fancy coming out for a walk, kids?' she asked, going into the parlour where Pansy was looking at a sewing set she'd been given and Lenny was playing with some toy soldiers. They each had their presents in a neat pile, keeping them special because it would be a long time before they got any more. 'It'll do us good and give us an appetite for tea.'

'No thanks. I'm playing with this,' said Lenny.

'I'll come,' said Pansy dutifully. It would be good to go out because she'd been feeling peculiar today; kind of sick in her stomach and close to tears, which was wrong of her because it was Christmas and you had to be happy, especially as she had nice presents she was grateful for. She couldn't stop thinking of home in Parkin Street and remembering that it wasn't there any more. She had flashes in her mind of Auntie Peg's house and Uncle Tom making jokes and the warm softness of Tiddles purring on her lap.

The slightest thing reminded her of them today: the familiar sound of the wireless, which had always been on, the bath salts Nell had given her that smelt like her sister, the taste of Granny Maud's gravy, which was the same as Auntie Peg's. But she couldn't tell Maud because it was rude to tell someone whose house you were in that you wanted to go home. Anyway, she didn't want to upset her, because she was such a nice person.

'I think you might as well come too, Lenny. It will do you good to get some fresh air,' his grandmother informed him firmly. 'Get your coats and scarves and wrap up well, because it'll be cold out.'

Outside the air was pure and sharp, the village dark and silent beneath the brilliant stars. Maud shone the torch downwards as they walked down the hill to the riverside, where the reflection of the moon shone on the water. There was a magical quality about it somehow, Maud thought, drenched as it was in the special silence of a Christmas Day.

'It isn't half cold,' said Lenny, who couldn't run about to get warm as he usually would because it was too dark.

'Yeah, it is a bit nippy, love, so we won't stay out long,' Maud told him. 'Just long enough to give us a bit of exercise, then we'll go back and have tea by the fire. It's time to feed the chickens anyway. I should have done it earlier, before it got dark. The poor things don't know it's Christmas. They want their grub the same as we do.'

'It's nice out here,' said Pansy, feeling a little better. 'The stars are lovely and bright. Why are they there sometimes and not others?'

'They're always there,' replied Maud. 'But sometimes they're hidden behind the clouds.'

'Do they have different stars in London?' wondered Pansy.

'Course not, dimwit,' chipped in Lenny; then, because he wasn't actually sure, 'They don't, do they, Gran?'

'I'm not a dimwit,' Pansy protested. 'You don't even know yourself, birdbrain.'

89

'Now, now, you two,' rebuked Maud. 'And the answer is no, they are not different in London; they see the same stars as us. If Nell is looking out of the window, she'll see what we are seeing unless it's cloudy there. That very bright one is called the North Star.'

They had halted in their step and were all looking up at the sky. 'Can Mum and Dad see them?' asked Pansy.

Maud didn't answer right away. 'I don't know for sure, love,' she said eventually. 'But I am sure they are looking out for you.'

'Can I make a wish?'

'Course you can,' said Maud. 'How about you, Lenny? Are you going to wish on a star?'

'Nah, that's soppy girls' stuff. Boys don't do that sort of thing,' he said scornfully. He thought for a moment. 'I suppose I could do one for Pansy, though.'

'That's a nice thought.' Maud knew the two children were devoted. Falling out from time to time was just part and parcel of childhood. Lenny was a right little scallywag at times, but it was touching to see how gentle and protective he was towards Pansy. Whether his wish really was for Pansy or for the shiny new bike he wanted after the war was debatable. He was just a kid after all. But she decided to give him the benefit of the doubt.

As they walked back to the cottage, Pansy took Maud's hand. The gesture warmed the old woman's heart. Maybe the short outing had lessened the homesickness she knew had besieged the child all day.

'Can I help you to feed the chickens?' Pansy asked.

'Yeah, course you can, love.'

'I will too,' said Lenny.

'That will be a great help,' Maud said, though of course it would be much quicker for her to do it alone. But if they were willing to give her a hand, she wasn't going to stop them. Let this be the last Christmas they had to be away from home.

As everyone had known they would, the raids returned soon after Christmas. On 29 December the City of London was devastated by incendiary bombs on a night that was dubbed the Second Fire of London. Flames leapt through buildings in a conflagration that left offices, business premises and historical churches in ruins, though miraculously St Paul's Cathedral remained standing, due in part to the courageous band of volunteers who made up St Paul's Watch.

Although the damage was less spectacular in the suburbs, the return of the raids finally convinced Nell that she had made the right decision in leaving Pansy where she was.

Indeed, she herself had to pick her way through rubble to get to work on her first morning in the new job, after a night in the shelter with very little sleep. But she still managed to look smart in her office clothes, her hair combed neatly into place.

There was no time to be nervous; she'd hardly had time to get her coat off when Ted Bigley asked her to go into his office for dictation.

'Your predecessor left before Christmas and we couldn't get a temp, so there's a lot of catching up to do,' he explained.

She'd filled the whole of her shorthand book by the time she went to her desk to start typing, and before she'd even had a chance to get the carbon paper into place, Ted Bigley asked her to make tea for everybody, explaining that the production staff were all too busy. She herself had enough work to last her for several days, but she didn't argue or query the fact. She knew the rules; being young and female, tea-making was expected of her, especially as there didn't seem to be an office junior.

There was only one other female on the staff besides Nell: a middle-aged spinster called Elsie who was an accounts clerk. She looked after the books and the wages and so on. She had her own office, whereas Nell worked in a cubbyhole outside Ted's office, separated from the others only by some filing cabinets.

The rest were men past the age for military service, except for the junior reporter, who was too young. There was a clerk in charge of the classified advertising and a couple of subeditors. The latter checked the copy, corrected it, wrote headlines and marked it all up for the typesetters, from whom it would be passed to the compositors prior to being printed on huge metal printing presses in a room downstairs.

'Welcome on board,' said Elsie when Nell took her a cup of tea. 'How are you getting on?'

'It seems a bit hectic.'

'Yes, it is mad here at times, but they're a nice bunch of people when you get to know them. Ted keeps losing his staff to the war, which leaves the rest of us with more to do. It isn't so easy to get replacements as it used to be.'

'Have you been here long?'

'Oh yes. I'm a part of the furniture. I've been with the paper since the beginning.' Elsie had iron-grey hair set in neat waves and clipped back with kirby grips, and the sort of bone structure to suggest that she had once been beautiful. 'Ted can be a hard taskmaster, but that's because he's such a hard worker himself.'

'He does seem devoted to his work.'

'Yes, he is. He's determined to keep the paper going against all the odds,' Elsie said. 'He's a bit blunt, but his bark is worse than his bite. I must say he has treated me well over the years; I've no complaints. I've never married, so I have to work. Not that I mind. I enjoy my job.'

'It's very different to what I'm used to.'

'You'll either love it or hate it here. It's that sort of an office. It isn't predictable like most jobs, and not everybody's cup of tea.' She gave Nell an appraising look, taking in her lively smile and intelligent eyes. 'I think you'll fit in very well.' She gave a wry grin. 'It isn't always mad and you won't always have to make the tea, I promise. I'll take my turn every now and again. Obviously the men never do it.'

'Thank you,' said Nell.

When she finally left the office around eighty thirty that night, after a day when she hadn't had time to eat her sandwiches until three o'clock in the afternoon, she wondered what she had got herself into. She had done hours of dictation and typing, interrupted continually by other demands, including making tea, going to the post office for stamps and the baker's for buns for everyone to have with their tea, and answering the telephone umpteen times. This was why she'd had to stay until she'd finished all the letters, which she'd then posted on the way home because Ted had wanted them to go out today. She'd been too busy to wonder whether she liked the job or not.

Walking home carefully in the blackout, she felt something she had never experienced at Barker's: a feeling of exhilaration and fulfilment. The day had flown by because she had been interested in what she was doing. She was still thinking about it now. Even the fact that there was an air raid currently in progress didn't take her mind off the job completely, though she would be glad to get home. The explosions, although not sounding too near, were frightening nonetheless. For all that it was frantic at the paper she realised that she was looking forward to going to work tomorrow.

Over the next few weeks Nell became increasingly engrossed in the job and began to enjoy office life. Although everyone was busy, the informal atmosphere suited her. The staff collectively knew that their responsibility was to produce the newspaper, and they didn't need someone of the Miss Crow variety inflicting discipline. If someone spent a little time on office chatter that put them behind, they worked later to get the job done.

'I hope they are paying you overtime for all these long hours you are working,' said Peg one night when Nell got home from work very late. 'By the time you get in it's nearly time to go to bed. You don't have a chance to relax.'

'It's an office job, Auntie Peg,' she explained. 'It isn't paid by the hour so your salary is the same however long you work.'

'That isn't right,' put in Tom. 'If you work extra hours you should be paid for it. The women in our factory get paid overtime. We're not living in the Dark Ages now.'

'It's just the way it is for office workers,' Nell explained. 'It's always been like that for clerical staff.'

'That doesn't make it right,' said Peg, protective of her young friend. 'There's all this talk about the long hours the factory workers are putting in because of the war. No mention of office staff doing all this unpaid overtime.'

'Just one of those things,' Nell told her. 'I like the job and I want to stay on top of it, so I have to work late to give me a clean start the next day. I enjoy being part of a team working together to create something, rather than just typing endless letters. It's given me a new challenge and I thrive on it, so I don't mind the long hours.'

'Oh well, as long as you're happy,' Peg accepted. 'Come and have something to eat. I've kept your meal warm for you.'

'Thanks, Auntie.' Nell sat down to a plate of bubble and squeak. 'Where's Ed?' she asked casually, adding, 'Though I don't really need to ask, do I? He'll be with Polly.'

'Where else would he be of an evening these days if he's not on duty at the AFS?' answered Peg.

'He might as well make the most of it while he can,' Tom cut in. 'He'll be eighteen soon, and he's still set on joining up.' He looked at his wife. 'Sorry, Peg love, but we have to get used to it.'

'He doesn't have to go.'

'He doesn't seem to see it that way,' said Tom. 'And we mustn't stand in his way whatever he decides. He has to do what he thinks is right.'

'I know,' said Peg with a wistful sigh. 'Oh, what it is to be a mother. It's like being put through the mangle on a regular basis. First Lenny has to go, then Ed.'

'You'll still have me,' said Tom.

'And me,' added Nell. 'You won't get rid of us so easy, will she, Uncle Tom?'

'Depends how much she nags me,' said Tom, teasing her. 'If she gives me a hard time, I might go and join up myself.'

'You're miles too old,' joshed Peg, 'so there's no point in threatening me with that one.'

The atmosphere was jolly and Nell enjoyed it. She was so lucky that they had taken her in.

In the event Ed didn't sign up for the army. He joined the navy in his dinner hour the day after his eighteenth birthday in March.

'Because I volunteered they gave me a choice of which one of the services I could join,' he told his parents that evening over their meal. 'Sorry, Mum, I know you don't want me to go away, but it's something I feel I have to do. I'm young and strong, I want to see some action and I've often fancied going away to sea.'

'I understand, son,' said Peg, accepting the situation. 'There's a war on and we all have to do our bit. A mother has to play her part and let her sons go with good grace. It doesn't stop it hurting, though.'

'At least you'll get to see something of the world, son,' mentioned his father.

'That's the intention,' said Ed. 'I certainly won't get the chance otherwise.'

The sound of the key being pulled through the letter box heralded the arrival of Nell home from work.

'We've got a sailor in the family,' announced Tom when she came into the room. 'Or at least we will have very soon.'

'You've joined the navy, have you, Ed?' guessed Nell.

He nodded.

'Uh-oh, Polly had better watch out now,' she said, taking off her coat. 'You know what they say. All the nice girls love a sailor; a girl in every port and all that. I might even fancy you myself when I see you in uniform.'

'Why else do you think I joined?' he grinned, adding quickly, 'Only joking.'

'We'll miss you around here,' said Nell.

Ed looked at his mother, who was putting on a brave face. 'I'll be back before you know it,' he said.

'I'll look after them, Ed, don't worry,' Nell assured him lightly.

There was a knock at the front door.

'That'll probably be Polly,' said Ed, making as though to get up and go to the door.

'You stay where you are,' said Nell. 'I'm already on my feet so I'll go. I've got to hang my coat up anyway.'

Much to Nell's astonishment, Polly practically fell inside when Nell opened the door and greeted her as though she hadn't seen her for years.

'At last you're here,' she burst out, sounding relieved. 'I never get to see you since you started this new job. You're always out when I come to call for Ed.'

'I work late most nights,' Nell explained. 'Anyway, it doesn't matter, does it? You come to see Ed, not me.'

'It does matter, because I need to talk to you urgently, as it happens.'

'Go ahead then,' urged Nell. 'I'm listening.'

'Not here,' Polly said, speaking in a whisper. 'I need to talk to you in private.'

'They can't hear us,' said Nell in a low voice, looking towards the closed door of the parlour.

'I'd rather not take the chance,' hissed Polly mysteriously. 'Can you meet me somewhere tomorrow night?'

'I'm not sure what time I'll finish work. Shall I come round to your place on my way home?'

'God, no. Mum and Dad will be there,' she said. 'I'll meet you in the

High Road. Outside Goodbans. Do you reckon you could make it for eight o'clock?'

Something about Polly's tone of voice made Nell say, 'I'll be there come hell or high water.'

'Thanks, kid.' Polly put her finger to her lips. 'Not a word about it to the others.'

'All right,' said Nell, wondering what was so secret it couldn't be discussed here. 'Now get your coat off and come in. Ed's got some important news for you.'

Chapter Six

Polly was waiting for Nell in the doorway of the closed department store the following evening.

'We have to stop meeting like this,' said Nell jokingly, stepping into the doorway out of the wind. 'It makes me feel shady; like a spy or something.'

'Sorry about that, but it isn't something I can discuss with ears wagging, and there's nowhere open where we can go inside and get a cup of tea,' Polly said. She obviously wasn't in the mood for levity.

Nell shivered as the blustery March wind whistled around the buildings and gusted against her legs. 'Come on then; now that I'm here, tell me what's so urgent so that we can go home,' she urged reasonably. 'It's chilly and I need something to eat.'

'I'm in big trouble,' Polly confided.

'Oh . . . really?' Now Nell's mood was grave. 'Er . . . what sort of trouble?'

'The worst sort for a girl,' she replied, her voice trembling.

Nell looked at her. 'Oh no. You're not . . .'

'I flamin' well am.'

'Blimey,' gasped Nell. 'No wonder you're worried.'

'Worried is an understatement. I'm at my wits' end,' Polly told her. 'Mum and Dad will throw me out into the street if they get wind of it, and I'm terrified they'll hear me throwing up in the mornings. Oh Nell, it's so awful. Why did it have to happen to me?'

'You know the answer to that.'

'Other people get away with it.'

Nell saw no point in continuing along these lines, as Polly obviously saw herself as a victim and in no way responsible for her own plight. 'Have you told Ed?'

'Of course I haven't,' she replied sharply. 'I'm not daft enough to tell him a thing like that. I wouldn't see him for dust if I did, like all blokes in that position.'

'You don't know that.'

'I can have a bloomin' good guess, though,' she proclaimed. 'Anyway, what's the point of his knowing when he isn't going to be around for much longer?'

'I think you might be misjudging him, you know,' opined Nell. 'He's a decent chap, and the fact that he's going away is all the more reason to tell him as soon as possible. You can at least give him the chance to do the right thing before he leaves. Apart from anything else, he has the right to know that he's about to become a father.'

'Oh God, don't say that.' Polly clutched her throat, sounding frightened. 'It makes it seem too real and serious. I don't want to be pregnant, and I can't bear to think about things further down the line when there will be an actual baby. The pregnancy is just a flamin' nuisance; something that's making me feel ill, and the last thing on earth I want. Oh Nell, what am I going to do?'

'I think your best bet is to confide in Ed.'

'I've just told you, I'm not doing that. He doesn't need to know anything about it.' Polly was irritable now. 'There are women you can go to who see to this sort of problem. It's a bit pricey, though, and I don't have anything put by.'

'Polly, you'd never forgive yourself if you were to do something like that.' Nell was horrified. 'Personally I don't think you can even consider that option until you've spoken to Ed about it. It just wouldn't be fair to him.'

'All right, you've made your point. But there's no need to be so high and mighty,' objected Polly, on the defensive. 'Abortions happen all the time. It's a fact of life and there's no point in your pretending otherwise just because you don't approve.'

Nell gritted her teeth and held her tongue because she knew Polly was genuinely in despair.

'Oh Nell, I just don't know which way to turn,' cried Polly, her voice breaking. 'I'm feeling so sick and ghastly all the time. I've been rubbing lipstick into my cheeks because I'm so pale and terrified my mum will notice and put two and two together. All hell will break loose if she does.

You know what parents are like; they pretend they never did it until after they were married.'

'It isn't my business and it must be your decision, but I think you'd be very wise to tell Ed.' Nell was adamant about it. 'After all, it's his responsibility every bit as much as yours.'

'He's only just had his eighteenth birthday; he won't want a kid,' Polly said.

'He should have thought of that before, shouldn't she?' Nell pointed out. She was angry with Ed for getting her friend into this predicament. 'There's a baby on the way and he needs to know about it.'

'Do you have to be so self-righteous?' Polly snapped. 'You don't think about the consequences when you're enjoying yourself with someone you really like. Still, you wouldn't know anything about that, would you, little Miss Iron Knickers? You're far too sensible for that.'

'If that's your attitude, I'll go,' threatened Nell, her patience tried to the limit. 'I don't have to stay here in the cold while you give me a tongue-lashing, and I really do need some food. It's way past my suppertime and I'm starving.'

Polly's attitude changed in an instant. 'Please don't go, Nell,' she entreated.

'Why should I stay here to be insulted? You ask me what you should do, and when I offer my opinion you turn on me.'

Polly took hold of Nell's arm in a persuasive gesture. 'I'm sorry; I shouldn't have said those things. I didn't mean them, honest. I'm in such a state, I hardly know what I'm saying. I'm really sorry, Nell. Please don't desert me.'

'Oh come here, you daft thing,' Nell said, hugging her. 'I won't desert you so long as you don't get nasty.'

'Sorry,' Polly said again.

'It's all right. You're forgiven. But we can't stay here all night. It's too cold,' Nell pointed out. 'Honestly, Pol, I think you'll have to tell Ed. I can't see any other way around it. I think you know that in your heart. The sooner you do it, the better.'

Polly didn't say anything at first, then, 'Yeah, I suppose you're right. I will have to pluck up the courage to tell him,' she said with a sigh of resignation.

★　★　★

99

She broke the news to him at her front gate when he took her home that same night.

'Pregnant!' He stepped back from her as though he'd been pushed. 'Oh bloody hell!'

'I thought you'd be pleased,' she said with withering sarcasm.

'It's just such a shock.'

'Well, I was none too pleased either,' she told him. 'It's your fault. You said it would be all right.'

'I thought it would be.' He clamped his hand to his head. 'Oh God! What a nightmare.'

'Don't panic,' she said quickly. 'I can get it seen to, but it's expensive and I don't have any dosh.'

Ed was in mental chaos. How could he have been so careless? Passion was the answer to that. It had ruled his life ever since he'd danced with Polly that night at the firm's dance. He'd been so besotted with her he'd thrown caution to the wind. His inexperience hadn't helped either. But marriage and children? Not with her; not with anyone yet! He was far too young and had seen nothing of life. He wasn't ready to be a married man.

'I want nothing from you except the money to get it fixed,' she was saying haughtily. 'So there's no need to make such a big drama out of it.'

'Money? What are you talking about?' He was still preoccupied; trying to come to terms with it and work out what to do.

'Do I have to spell it out for you?' she snapped miserably. 'We're in a situation that needs sorting sharpish and I don't have the dough to get it fixed.'

What she was suggesting suddenly registered fully. 'Oh no. You're not doing that,' he stated categorically.

'What else do you suggest then?' she asked.

'You have the baby, of course. There isn't an alternative as far as I'm concerned.'

'It's all too easy for you, isn't it?' She was vehement in her accusation. 'You can just walk away from the situation. Or sail away in your case. I'm the one who will be branded as an outcast; me and your child. My life will be over, and I don't think much of the nipper's chances either.'

'I'm not walking away from anything,' he made clear. 'What do you take me for?'

She narrowed her eyes on him. 'I'm not sure what you mean,' she said.

'I mean that I'll do right by you and the baby,' he told her impulsively. 'We'll get married.'

'Married! Flippin 'eck!' Polly exclaimed. 'You don't want to get married. Be honest. You just feel trapped.'

She was right; he felt completely cornered. But he didn't see he had any choice under the circumstances. As the physical side was so good between them, perhaps marriage wouldn't prove to be too difficult; not so long as they both made an effort. Anyway, the deed was done and the decision made, and Ed vowed there and then that he would do his level best to make the marriage work and be a good father to their child.

'I hadn't planned to get married at this stage in my life and would rather we hadn't been forced into it,' he admitted. 'I won't insult your intelligence by lying to you about that. But this has happened and we have to make the best of the way things are; not how we'd like them to be. We get on well enough together, so I'm sure we can make a go of it. I'll do everything I can to make you happy, Pol. It won't be the wedding of the year and it'll have to be done quickly before I go abroad, but your good name will remain intact.'

'How can we get married?' responded Polly gloomily. She wasn't at all sure if it was what she wanted. Domesticity wasn't something she was eager to explore. She'd rather resolve the problem by making it disappear. 'We've got no money; nowhere to live. My mum and dad won't help. I can tell you that right away. Getting married won't alter the fact that I've put the cart before the horse, so to speak. They'll be disgusted.'

'Leave everything to me and stop worrying,' he said kindly, the life-changing development beginning to grow on him

Ed's chivalrous attitude was heartening, Polly had to admit. She didn't want the baby, but as he obviously wasn't going to come up with the cash she needed to get rid of it, maybe marriage wouldn't be such a bad idea. At least as a married woman she'd be protected from disgrace. She'd be supported too, so would be able to give up that awful job in the stenographers' pool, she thought, the idea of marriage and motherhood becoming more appealing by the moment.

'You really are the most gorgeous man,' she said to him now. 'Is it any wonder that I got myself in the club?'

'It it any wonder that I put you there?' he responded, taking her into his arms and holding her gently. 'Everything is going to be fine; just fine. I'll take care of you. I'll find out what we have to do to get a special licence.'

Peg rose to the occasion magnificently. A rushed wedding with a kiddie on the way wasn't what she would have wished for her eldest son, but as things had worked out that way and the situation was irreversible, she did everything she could to help, organising a small wedding party at the house and telling the couple they could have Ed's room as their own until Lenny came home, when she would adapt the front room to accommodate them and the new arrival.

Whatever the circumstances, they were going to provide her and Tom with their first grandchild, and that was a cause for celebration as far as she was concerned. Polly's parents – a miserable couple of prudes in Peg's opinion – had been tight-lipped and uncooperative, so Peg and Tom managed without them, though they did make an appearance at the wedding, which Peg was pleased about for Polly's sake.

Because of rationing there wasn't a banquet for the guests when they came back from the register office. But there were sandwiches and Peg had made a cake, albeit that she couldn't ice it because it had been made illegal to use sugar for that purpose while everything was so short. Tom managed to get some beer and a couple of bottles of sherry so they were able to toast the happy couple.

Nell was happy for them, and glad that Ed had done the decent thing as she had guessed he would. But she had to admit to feeling sentimental as she raised her glass to the bride and groom; kind of sad and nostalgic. It was the end of an era. Ed was a married man now. Would the special friendship she had with him continue under the new circumstances? She couldn't imagine that it wouldn't, but she was aware that things were different now.

They were certainly a good-looking couple; Ed in his best suit, Polly in a blue dress she'd found on a second-hand stall and a feathery hat she'd borrowed from a girl at work.

'You look lovely,' complimented Nell when they managed a few words together. 'I'm sure you'll be very happy.'

'I hope so, kid,' Polly said. 'We won't have a chance to quarrel, that's for sure, as he's going away to Portsmouth to start his navy service on Monday.'

Another change, thought Nell. She would probably feel Ed's loss as much or even more than Polly, because he'd always been there; all her life. She was going to miss him, that was for sure.

Ed wasn't the only one going away to the war. So was Micky, the junior reporter at the *Chiswick and Hammersmith Herald*.

'He was coming on very well in the job too; he had a nose for a story and the stamina to pursue it,' Ted said to Nell one day when she went into his office for dictation. 'It's a damned shame these young fellas are having their careers interrupted; a nuisance for me as well. I knew it was only a matter of time before he got his call-up papers, of course, but you can't get a replacement until you know when they are actually going, can you? God knows how long it will take to find someone suitable. All the young men are away.'

'Why not have a woman then?' Nell suggested impulsively.

He looked at her as though she'd just suggested he take on a team of tabby cats to collect and report the news. 'A woman?' he said incredulously.

'Yes. Why not?'

'There are very few women reporters,' he informed her knowledgeably. 'Generally speaking, and certainly in my opinion, it's a man's job.'

'So are plumbing and chimney-sweeping, but women are doing those jobs while the men are away.'

'That's a different thing altogether,' Ted said. 'Journalism is highly specialised work.'

'So are those other things, but they have learned how to do them and are doing a good job by all accounts.'

'That is highly skilled work, I agree,' he conceded. 'But to be a reporter you require talent too, and initiative.'

'Someone with a good education?'

'Not necessarily. They'd need to be bright, of course, and to have a way with words. But a woman wouldn't be tough enough to get out there and find the stories.'

'Women can be intrepid when they need to be,' Nell told him. 'They have been proving that ever since war broke out.'

'I know there are a few women journalists working in Fleet Street, but they are very much in a minority. I don't want female reporters working on this paper,' he made clear. 'No offence meant against you and the rest of your gender. It just isn't the way of things in this profession.'

'It seems a bit short-sighted to me,' Nell blurted out. 'You need someone and men are in short supply, so the obvious answer is a woman.' Without any prior intention she added, 'In fact, why not give me a try?'

She received another pitying look. 'I've just told you I don't have women reporters on my team. Anyway, you have no training,' he pointed out.

'I can learn on the job and I have very good shorthand,' she replied, enthusiasm rising with every syllable. She'd been interested in the journalism side of things ever since she'd joined the paper. Now, because of the war, here was an opportunity that might never come her way again; if only she could manage to persuade him. 'I'm sure I could make a success of it. I've fancied working on that side of things ever since I joined the paper and learned something about how journalists operate. Surely being keen counts for something.'

'You probably have the idea that the job would be some sort of an adventure; something different and glamorous,' he suggested. 'But I can assure you it is very hard work, extremely demanding and often very boring.'

'I'd still like to have a crack at it.'

'You're too valuable to me on the secretarial side of things,' was his latest excuse.

'It'll be easier to get a replacement for a shorthand typist than for a reporter, since almost all the young men are away,' she pointed out, realising as she spoke what a valid point this was. 'And at least I've been here long enough to know how a newspaper office works.'

'Mm.' He was obviously beginning to think it over, but still needed a little more coaxing.

'Anyway, it wouldn't be as if you'd be breaking with tradition, since it would only be temporary – a means to an end for you – until the boys come home. I'll make a success of it if you give me a chance.'

'How do you know?'

'Gut instinct,' she replied. 'I've got a feel for it.'

He heaved a sigh of resignation. 'You'd better get an ad in this week's edition for a shorthand typist then, hadn't you?' He gave her a grim look. 'You've talked me into giving you a chance. Don't let me down.'

'I won't. I promise.'

Nell was to remember that promise many times during the first few days on the new job; a married woman who had returned to the workplace because of the war having replaced her on the secretarial side. The first lesson she learned as a reporter was that news didn't come from sitting at a desk waiting for the phone to ring. You had to get out there in the community looking for it. Among other things, you never missed the magistrate's or coroner's court or a council meeting. You visited the fire station and the police station at least once a day.

The senior reporter – a middle-aged man called Frank – went with her the first time to show her the ropes.

'Morning, Frank,' said the desk sergeant at the police station, passing him the incident book and looking at Nell. 'Well, well, who do we have here?'

Frank introduced her and explained that in future she would be calling at the police station to look at the incident book and find out what had been going on in the area.

The policeman raised his brows. 'You've got girls out on the job now then?'

'We get in everywhere these days,' joked Nell, to pre-empt a similar remark from him.

'Nice to see a different face,' said the sergeant and grinning at Frank added jokingly, 'We get tired of seeing his ugly mug. A bit of glamour is just what we need to cheer our day up.'

'You'll have to watch him, Nell,' joked Frank.

'Don't worry, love,' the sergeant assured her. 'I'm a happily married man with a wife who keeps me well in order, so you'll be quite safe with me.'

'I can take care of myself,' Nell said, aware that she had entered a different world to that she was used to; she was now in a male-dominated working environment. Their patronising attitude niggled her slightly but there was no point in letting it rankle, because it was synonymous with the way society was run and she was sure to come across plenty more of it before she'd finished her stint as a reporter.

'Been busy?' Frank enquired of the policeman.

'When are we not in this job, mate?' he replied. 'There are always plenty of villains about to keep us on our toes. They're having a field day in the blackout.'

'Anything major?' asked Frank.

'I wasn't on duty last night but I've had a look at the book,' he replied. 'I think there were a couple of domestics, a few burglaries, and they managed to nab one of the black-market boys. You'd better have a look for yourself.'

Possessing an enquiring mind, and having been instructed by the editor to ask questions, Nell said, 'Is there much racketeering going on around here then?'

'Phew, I should say so,' said the sergeant. 'The black market is thriving everywhere at the moment. The war is paradise for spivs, especially in London, which has always been a magnet for rogues. All over the capital, not just around here, and some of them are big operators, dealing in everything from false identity papers to goods stolen direct from the factories; tinned food and so on.'

'It's just as well you caught one of them then, isn't it?' she remarked naïvely.

'Small fry, love; just the tip of the iceberg,' he told her. 'It's the big boys behind it we're after, but they're too artful to get caught, and the small dealers who work for them won't grass; they're too scared of what'll happen to them if they do. The criminals behind it are hard men of the worst kind. They're not just blokes peddling a few knocked-off tins of salmon for pocket money. They're running well-organised operations and making a fortune. They'll go to any lengths to protect their lucrative businesses which is why they're so dangerous.'

'If they are so tough, why haven't they been called up for the services?' Nell wondered.

'Bogus medicals,' he replied.

Nell looked puzzled. 'How do they manage that?' she asked.

'A crafty villain will always find a way,' he told her. 'What they do is

106

pay someone with a health problem to go in front of the medical board for them; someone who has already been exempted on medical grounds so that they can be sure they'll get away with it. They take the criminal's birth certificate and National Registration Card in with them and come out with an exemption certificate made out to the criminal. The racket caught on fast in the underworld as soon as conscription was introduced. A young man with a dodgy ticker or some other serious complaint can make a good bit of money from it. They charge a hefty sum for every phoney medical they do.'

'Well I'll be blowed,' said Nell. 'If they're as clever as that, it must make it hard to catch up with them.'

'It is, but we'll get 'em in the end.'

'Well you know where we are when you do,' said Frank

They finished going through the book, Nell taking notes in shorthand. When they left the police station, they went straight to the fire station to find out if anything newsworthy had been happening there.

Later that day they paid what Nell found to be a distressing visit to the hospital to see a woman who had been beaten up in the street by her husband. He had been taken to the police station but released later because the woman didn't press charges. Frank and Nell had followed it up after seeing the event recorded in the police incident book.

'Don't come poking your nose into my business,' said the woman, whose face was a mass of cuts and bruises; her arm in a sling.

'We just came to see how you are,' explained Frank.

'No you didn't; you came looking for a story. Well there isn't one because I ain't bringing any charges so they can't do anything to my ole man,' she said, her speech indistinct because her lips were so swollen. 'I tripped up the kerb and went flying. That's how I hurt myself. Never mind what they've told you at the police station. If you print one word different I'll have you done for libel. Now go away before I call a nurse and have you thrown out.'

Outside Nell said to Frank, 'Her husband could kill her next time if she lets him get away with it.'

'She's scared stiff of what he'll do to her if she does take him to court; that's why she's lying about what happened,' explained Frank. 'Not only that, who's going to keep her and the six kids if her husband is in prison?'

'Mm. I see what you mean.'

'It happens all too often,' he went on. 'If her husband hadn't lost his temper while they were out in the street, no one would have known anything about it and she would have struggled on with broken bones and black eyes, like so many other battered wives.'

'The poor thing; that's terrible.'

'It is indeed. You'll really see the other side of life in this job. You'll have to toughen up.'

'I'm beginning to realise that.'

Because they were such a small team, Nell was out working on her own within a very short time; too soon it felt like at first. But determined to make a success of it, she soldiered on, learning fast; exhilarated at times, disillusioned at others.

One day the editor sent her on an assignment to interview a woman who had been buried alive under the rubble of a shop for days in the early part of the Blitz. Against all the odds she'd survived and gone on to run a hostel for the homeless. This was Nell's first serious creative challenge and she enjoyed it, working hard on the article to make it a compelling piece of writing.

As it happened, it didn't even make the paper because more important news came in and her piece was deemed to be disposable. Although it was disappointing, it proved to be a defining experience in that it introduced her to the joy of words, which she knew somehow she would never lose. Those meaningless black things she had typed for years had become tools that she could use to bring events to life; she could make them leap off the page.

She had barely scratched the surface of the job but knew she had made the right decision in persuading Ted, against his better judgement, to let her have a go at it. There was so much more she had to give, and the best was yet to come.

'Shall we go out tonight, Nell?' suggested Polly one Sunday afternoon when they were all sitting around in the living room. 'I'm bored stiff with staying in night after night.'

'You might as well get used to it,' advised Peg. 'You won't be able to go out enjoying yourself when the baby arrives.'

'People have baby-sitters for that, don't they?' returned Polly breezily. 'I'm sure you'll want to oblige every so often.'

'Of course I will,' said Peg, smiling because Polly was so damned cheeky. 'But what I mean is, you won't be able to just go when you feel like it as you've always done before. You'll have to make provision for the little one before you do anything. Things change when you become a mother; including your priorities and your perspective on life.'

'I'd better go out and enjoy myself while I can then, hadn't I?' Polly laughed. 'Anyone know what's on at the pictures?'

'There's an Arthur Askey film on locally. *The Ghost Train*, it's called,' Peg informed her.

'That should be a laugh,' Polly approved.

'There's bound to be a long queue, though, with him being so popular,' Peg pointed out with genuine concern. 'It isn't good for a woman in your condition to be on her feet for too long.'

'I'm not in the final stages of consumption, you know,' Polly retorted sharply. 'I'm only having a baby.'

'You need to look after yourself just the same.' Peg really did care about her daughter-in-law's wellbeing. 'Do it for the baby's sake as much as for your own.'

'You make me feel as if I'm serving a flamin' prison sentence,' complained the ungrateful and outspoken Polly. 'It's bad enough having to put up with morning sickness and heartburn and backache and all the rest of the miserable symptoms. Now I can't even go out for a break to try to feel half normal.'

'Of course you can go out,' said Tom from his armchair. 'Peg's just concerned about you, that's all. That's why she's being overly protective.'

'It's our duty to look out for her since Ed isn't here to do it, and I'm not being overly protective,' objected Peg, throwing her husband a furious look.

He met her eyes and made a face. 'I was only defending you,' he said.

'I don't need it, thanks very much.' Cheeks flaming, Peg turned to Polly. 'I haven't said you can't go out. It isn't my place to tell you what to do and I wouldn't dream of trying. Surely you must know that. All right, perhaps I am a bit of a mother hen now and again, but I really do have your interests at heart. Anyway, you don't need me to tell you how things change when you become a mother because you'll find out for yourself soon enough.'

'Meanwhile we'll go to the flicks tonight and forget all our troubles,' said Nell to defuse the rising tension; turning to Peg she added, 'You can come with us if you fancy it, Auntie Peg. You'd be more than welcome.'

'No, you two young things go on your own,' replied Peg, who was no fool and knew that the last thing Polly would want was her mother-in-law tagging along. 'I'm quite happy to stay here. I might even go for a drink with Tom if there isn't a raid.'

'As long as you're sure,' said Nell.

'I am, love, but thanks for asking.'

'Why on earth did you ask Peg to come with us?' demanded Polly as she and Nell walked to the cinema. 'For one awful moment I thought she was going to say yes.'

'So what if she had done?' asked Nell. 'That was why I asked her. She's very partial to a night out at the flicks.'

'She's my mother-in-law . . .'

'What does that matter? Auntie Peg is a lovely woman and smashing company. She's been very good to both of us, taking us in and looking after us.'

'I'm not denying that, but I don't want to go out with old people,' declared Polly. 'Being married and pregnant hasn't taken away my youth, you know.'

'Honestly, you don't half get some daft ideas,' stated Nell. 'I invited Peg to go to the pictures with us. I didn't enrol you for the Darby and Joan club.'

'No need to be sarky,' Polly rebuked. 'I'm young. I want to have fun, and I can't do that with my husband's mother breathing down my neck, can I?'

'I don't see why not,' said Nell. 'It isn't as though she's some awful old dragon.'

'Having her around is restricting for me, can't you see that?' Polly tried to explain. 'By the very fact that she's Ed's mum.'

'If we were going out looking for blokes, yeah, I could see that might be a stumbling block,' conceded Nell. 'But not just for a night out at the pictures.'

'I can't be myself and let go with her around, can I? And I don't see how you can either,' Polly pointed out. 'She's a different generation. We're young. We talk about different things to what she does; have different opinions.'

'Mm, there is that, I suppose,' Nell agreed reluctantly. 'I've never thought of Peg as old, though. I think she's only in her forties.'

'That's ancient compared to us,' declared Polly.

'She's young at heart, and I enjoy her company.'

'Honestly, Nell, I really am beginning to worry about you,' exploded Polly. 'You're getting far too serious for your years. What with all the extra hours you're working and the interest you're taking in the job. You're not much fun any more.'

'I'm sorry if my taking an interest in my job offends you,' said Nell in a barbed tone. 'I can't help it if I enjoy my work, can I? It really gives me a buzz.'

'How can work give anyone a buzz?' Polly said mockingly. 'It's just something people do to get money.'

'It used to be like that for me until I started at the paper,' Nell told her. 'Now it's more than that.'

'Seems a bit queer to me.'

'Well it doesn't to me. I'm glad to have been given the opportunity to do something interesting,' she explained. 'It wouldn't have happened if it hadn't been for the war.'

'That's one good thing to have come out of it then.'

Nell nodded. 'I'll have to hand the job back when it's all over, but I'll have learnt a lot,' she said.

'For all the good it will do you.'

'Experience is what it will have given me,' said Nell. 'It's opened my eyes to my own potential, which is a damned sight more than I got under Miss Crow's regime.'

'Don't remind me about her and ruin my night out,' reproached Polly.

'You won't be there for much longer, will you?' Nell reminded her.

'I certainly won't. Another couple of months and I'll be out of there for good, thank goodness,' she said. 'That's one of the few perks of pregnancy. At least you get to leave work.'

'Are you looking forward to the baby?'

'Course I am,' she said casually. 'I'll be glad to be shot of all this extra weight and feeling off colour.'

'Exciting, having a baby, though,' enthused Nell. 'Are you looking forward to the time when it's actually here? Wheeling it out in the pram and all of that?'

'Can't say I've thought much about that part of it,' Polly admitted airily. 'I'm more interested in getting my figure back and feeling normal again.'

'I'm really looking forward to having a baby around,' Nell told her. 'I'll be an unofficial aunt like Auntie Peg has always been to me. I'll do everything I can to help you with the baby when I'm at home.'

'Until then will you please forget all about the flippin' baby and help me by having a laugh like we used to?' Polly said.

'I'll do my best,' agreed Nell.

But somehow the mood wasn't right despite the fact that the film was a comedy. Polly's desperation to have fun put a damper on things somehow. Her frivolous attitude to life was entertaining at times, but her lack of interest in anything outside of herself could be hard to take. Still, Nell reminded herself, she was a friend, and you accepted your friends for all their faults.

They were in the middle of the main feature when a message was flashed on to the screen advising them that an air-raid warning had just been sounded outside. The notice requested those who wished to leave the cinema to do so as quietly as possible, and reminded those who wished to remain that they did so at their own risk. It ended by saying that the film would now continue.

There were a few sharp bangs as people left their seats, but along with the majority Nell and Polly stayed where they were, deeming it equally dangerous to head off into the streets.

'Auntie Peg will know we've stayed on, won't she?' said Nell anxiously. 'I don't want them worrying about us.'

'They'll guess,' responded Polly, who hadn't actually given a thought to Peg and Tom and the fact that they might be concerned. She had no intention of cutting the evening short by rushing home just because of an air raid.

'I hope they'll be all right,' fretted Nell.

'Course they'll be all right. Our going home won't change anything anyway,' Polly pointed out. 'If their number's up, they'll have had it whatever we do.'

'That's a bit callous.'

'I'm just saying it like it is.'

'Well I wish you wouldn't,' reproached Nell. 'I don't need to be reminded.'

'All right. Keep your hair on.'

When the big picture ended, the raid was still in progress so the cinema organist rose up majestically on his Wurlitzer to give them a second recital of popular tunes, having already done his normal session before the picture started. After that the manager came on stage and said that the raid was still on and either he could show the film again to entertain them or – if the audience preferred – the usherettes would lead them in a singsong.

The latter suggestion was greeted by loud cheers, so the usherettes came on to the stage and started things off with 'I've got Sixpence', followed by a string of other favourites. Nell and Polly sang their heads off. The singing was loud, mostly out of tune and wonderfully uplifting. It soothed the nerves and drowned out the noise from outside.

They were in the middle of 'We'll Meet Again' when the manager came on, held his hands up for quiet, then announced that the all-clear had sounded. There was hearty applause and a loud chorus of whistles. People were still singing as they left their seats, and talking to anyone who happened to be near them.

'Wasn't it wonderful, the way everybody stayed?' said Nell as they went out into the street, pausing while their eyes grew accustomed to the dark. 'Such community spirit.'

'Yeah, it was good.'

'You got the laugh you wanted so badly then,' said Nell.

'Mm, I did. In fact I felt almost normal for a while. Quite like old times.'

'You are normal,' Nell pointed out.

'How can I be when I'm pregnant?'

'There's nothing more normal than that.'

'This isn't normal,' Polly disagreed. 'This is purgatory.'

★　★　★

Nell was in the office early the next morning, typing up the shorthand notes she'd made last night when she got home from the cinema and it was all still fresh in her mind.

'This is pretty good,' said Frank when she showed him the article. 'We can't mention the actual name or location of the cinema because of security, but it'll be good for morale. It's the human interest stories behind the news that are the lifeblood of papers like ours. Well done, Nell.'

The editor also liked it. The subeditor came up with the headline WE SHALL NOT BE MOVED, and Nell's description of her visit to the cinema appeared in that week's edition of the paper. She had managed to capture the cheerfulness and indomitable spirit of the cinema-goers, the warmth and friendliness that filled the auditorium that night. Her colleagues said that the piece leapt off of the page, and she was enormously thrilled.

She wondered what her mother would have made of it and was pierced with sadness that she wasn't here to share it with her. But Peg and Tom were full of praise and enthusiasm, to the point where Nell thought there could be few people left in west London who hadn't had the piece waved under their nose.

Polly couldn't get the point of it at all.

'Why would you want to turn a night out for pleasure into work?' she wanted to know.

'I don't know the answer to that, Polly,' Nell replied. 'It's just something in me. I don't know where it comes from, but I feel blessed that I have it.'

Chapter Seven

Nell's eighteenth birthday in May happened to fall on a Saturday, which she thought was rather nice because she was home from work earlier than on a weekday, and there was always a sense of holiday at a weekend.

'Well, you might not officially come of age until you're twenty-one, but I reckon we can give you the key of the door on this birthday,' proclaimed Tom that evening after gifts had been bestowed. They'd enjoyed a birthday cake that Peg had managed to produce despite no eggs or icing, and upon which sat one pre-war candle she'd come across at the back of the sideboard drawer.

'Hear! Hear!' added Peg.

'You're old enough to have a legal drink in a pub now, too,' Tom reminded Nell.

'I suppose I am.' Not being much of a drinker, this aspect of her birthday hadn't occurred to her.

'Bags I buy her the first one,' put in Ed, who was home on leave, fit and fine-looking in his naval uniform. 'Why don't we all go down to the pub for a bit of a party, the whole lot of us?' He paused, looking at Nell. 'If you've nothing else planned, that is.'

'No, I've nothing planned.' She gave his wife a wary glance. 'But wouldn't you and Polly rather spend the evening on your own, seeing as you're going back off leave tomorrow?'

Realising that he might have been too hasty, Ed gave Polly a sheepish look. 'Sorry, Pol, I should have asked you first,' he apologised. 'I just assumed you'd want a get-together as it's Nell's birthday, but if you'd rather we were by ourselves, you only have to say.'

Polly would much rather go out to a dance hall full of vibrant young people with thriving hormones than a pub full of middle-aged husbands and their boring wives whose only topic of conversation would be what to do with corned beef to make it go further. But as she had a stomach like an ever-growing hillock and ankles to match, the pub was about the best option she had. At least she had Ed to cheer her up. He looked gorgeous in uniform and she could hardly keep her hands off him. It was a pity he was so nervous about harming the baby during their intimate moments, though, because it reduced the passion. God, what a life! But she said, 'No, it's all right. The pub will be fine for me.'

'Good, we'll have a bit of a knees-up, bombs or no bombs,' Ed said. 'Look out, Chiswick, here we come.'

'We'd better get going if we want to get a table,' suggested Peg sensibly. 'It gets very crowded down there on a Saturday evening and we don't want Polly to have to stand up all night.'

'I'll make sure that doesn't happen, don't worry,' assured Ed, slipping his arm around Polly and brushing the top of her head with his lips in a casually tender gesture. 'I'll get her a seat somehow. She and the nipper are precious and it's my job to look after them.'

Polly seethed at what seemed like constant reference to her condition, but she didn't get a chance to make an issue of it because there was a general rush to get ready. Then they all piled out of the house and headed down the street towards the pub on the corner.

'This is gonna be a whole lot of fun, I don't think,' Polly grumbled to Nell as the others walked on ahead.

'What's the matter with an outing to the pub?' Nell wondered.

'It'll be you me and Peg sitting at a table talking about the fish shortage and the men up at the bar chatting among themselves,' she explained.

'How do you know?' asked Nell.

'I have been to pubs, you know,' she declared. 'I do know what the procedure is.'

'You might enjoy it. You never know.'

'I'll have to sit down all night because of my flamin' *condition*,' Polly ranted on as though Nell hadn't spoken. 'Honestly, what have I come to?'

'It won't be for too much longer,' said Nell patiently.

'I've still got months to go and I'm fed up with it.'

'I think we're all fully aware of that,' said Nell meaningfully.

'Are you suggesting that I keep on about it?'

'I'm not suggesting; I'm stating a fact.'

'So would you keep on if you were in my position,' Polly pointed out. 'You don't know what it's like.'

Nell heaved an eloquent sigh. 'A lot of women would give an arm and a leg to have what you have,' she felt compelled to say. 'You're married to a smashing bloke who really looks after you and you have a baby on the way. I wouldn't call that punishment. Quite the opposite. So stop moaning and cheer up. It is my birthday, remember.'

'Not much of a birthday treat for you, is it?' Polly said mournfully. 'A night down at the pub? We should be out dancing.'

'Who said so?' Nell wanted to know. 'What law is there to say that if you're young and single you have to be out dancing at every opportunity?'

'Now you're just being awkward,' objected Polly. 'You know very well what I mean.'

'Yeah, course I do,' Nell admitted. 'It's just that there seems to be no pleasing you, Polly. You were determined to get your claws into Ed, and now you've got him good and proper so I can't understand why you keep complaining. Anyway, there'll be plenty of other times to go out dancing. This is just one night out with the family; a family that I think the world of and you are officially a part of. So let's do our best to enjoy ourselves for their sake, shall we?'

'As I've told you before, you're too old for your years.'

'Yes, you have told me before on several occasions, so I don't need telling again, thanks very much,' reproved Nell. 'I probably have grown up a bit since I lost Mum and Dad; it's natural that I would, and it wouldn't do you any harm to do the same.'

'All right, keep your wig on,' Polly retorted, as they went into the saloon bar of the pub.

It was still quite early, so Peg had managed to get a table and was waving at them.

'The men are standing at the bar,' disapproved Polly to Nell as they made their way over. 'I told you, didn't I?'

'They're getting the drinks,' Nell pointed out. 'This isn't the Ritz; they don't have waiter service.'

'They'll find an excuse to go back there when they've brought the drinks over to the table,' whined Polly. 'Why do men always want to stand at the bar talking?'

'I've no idea,' replied Nell. 'Perhaps it's to get away from women like you going on at them.'

'You're a traitor to your sex,' admonished Polly, giving her a friendly slap on the arm.

Things got very lively in the pub as the evening wore on. The place was packed to the doors, a jolly, enveloping roar of conversation and laughter filling the bar, the air smoggy with cigarette smoke. There was a piano going and a few aspiring performers got up in turn and provided some entertainment. One man played the spoons, another told some risqué jokes and a woman with white hair stood up and sang 'The White Cliffs of Dover' to riotous applause.

When the pianist went for his break, Ed proposed a toast to Nell and they all chinked glasses and wished her a happy birthday. Although she tried not to show it, she felt dangerously close to tears as she became acutely aware that this was the first birthday she had spent without her parents or sister.

Sensitive as ever to her feelings, Ed said, 'To absent friends and loved ones.'

They all raised their glasses again and Nell tried to dispel the sudden gloom by saying, 'I was pleased to get a birthday card and a present from Pansy, bless her.' She looked at Peg. 'Reminded, I suspect, by some thoughtful person.'

'I'm saying nothing,' grinned Peg.

Nell's thoughts were diverted from her sadness when a stranger appeared at their table, a tall, attractive man with slicked-back dark hair, and wearing a sober grey suit with a white shirt and dark blue tie. Nell judged him to be quite a bit older than she was but not enough to put him in the same generation as Peg and Tom. Despite his immaculate appearance, there was a toughness about his face somehow, Nell observed, possibly caused by the square set of his jaw or his craggy complexion. It was as almost as though the man didn't quite match his conventional apparel.

'Wotcha, Tom,' he said, tapping Tom on the shoulder.

Turning, Tom smiled and stood up, shaking the man's hand heartily. 'Hello, Gus,' he greeted warmly. 'What are you doing round here? This isn't your usual local.'

'I came over this way to see someone,' the man explained. 'We've just popped in for a quick one.' He looked towards the company. 'Are you having a celebration?'

'This is Gus Granger, everyone, a pal of mine from the ARP.' Tom went on to make the rest of the introductions. 'It's young Nell's birthday,' he explained. 'She's a very close family friend; lives with us as a matter of fact. She's eighteen today and having a drink out legally for the first time.'

'Happy birthday, Nell,' Gus said, giving her the most melting smile. His compelling eyes rested on her in such a way as to turn her cheeks crimson.

'Thank you,' she responded graciously.

'Eighteen, eh,' he said wistfully. 'Oh happy days. My eighteenth is further back than I care to remember.'

'It can't be all that long ago,' probed Peg, giving him the once-over.

'Twelve years.'

'That's nothing compared to me. I'm not going to tell you how many years have passed since mine,' she said, flushed from a few glasses of port and lemon.

'And I'm far too much of a gentleman to ask,' he laughed. 'So you're quite safe.'

'Would you like to join us, mate?' invited Tom. 'You'll be very welcome.'

'Thanks, but I'm with someone over there.' He pointed behind him, but the pub was far too crowded to see who his companion was.

'Oh, I see; a lady friend, eh?'

Gus nodded. 'I'd better be getting back or I'll be in trouble.' He turned his gaze directly on to Nell and she felt a strong connection. 'Enjoy the rest of your birthday.'

'I'll do my best.'

As soon as he was out of earshot, Polly made an observation. 'He liked the look of you, Nell. I thought his eyes were going to pop out of his head.'

'Don't be daft,' protested Nell, even though she had sensed the same thing herself. 'He's too old for me; anyway he's with someone, he said so. He's probably married.'

'He isn't,' Tom informed her. 'Not as far as I know anyway.'

'Even if he is, when did that ever stop a bloke from going after someone else?' This was Polly.

'Honestly, you're such a cynic,' said Nell in a tone of light-hearted admonition.

'She is, and so young too,' Peg put in.

'Take no notice of them, love,' said Ed, who was sitting next to Polly. 'I think you're lovely, cynic or not.'

'Aah,' approved Nell. 'Isn't that sweet?'

'Yeah, they're a proper couple of lovebirds.' Peg paused as though remembering something. 'Why isn't your pal Gus in uniform, Tom?' she enquired. 'Does he have something wrong with him?'

'No. He's in a reserved occupation. A civil servant of some sort, I think. He works in central London somewhere; something to do with the war,' explained Tom. 'He doesn't talk about it much. I get the impression that it's all a bit hush-hush.'

'Ooh, a white-collar worker, eh?' remarked Peg. 'Very nice too.'

'He's a really good bloke actually; very down to earth,' Tom told them. 'He gets on well with everyone down at the depot, and always does more than his fair share.'

'He's a real dish, whatever he does for a living,' remarked Polly, whose mood had been improved by the lively atmosphere.

'Trust you to lower the tone,' teased Nell. 'And you a married woman too.'

'I'm not the one lowering the tone,' retorted Polly in the same style of friendly banter. 'I saw the way you were looking at him. You fancied the flamin' pants off him.'

All eyes turned to Nell and she flushed a beetroot colour.

'Shut up, Pol,' she said, objecting good-humouredly. 'You're embarrassing me.'

'We just want to see you fixed up with a fella,' Polly told her.

'It would be nice to see you with a suitable young man,' added Peg, 'but not someone twelve years older.'

'Honestly,' said Nell in exasperation. 'I can find a man for myself when I'm ready, thanks very much, so will you all stop going on about Gus Granger, for goodness' sake.'

The conversation was brought to a sudden conclusion by the wail of the air-raid siren.

'Are we going home or staying?' asked Peg.

'Normally I'd suggest we stay here and let Hitler do his worst,' said Tom. 'But because of Polly's condition I think we should head home to the Anderson.'

'And a bit sharpish too, before the bombs start raining down,' agreed Ed.

They hurriedly finished their drinks and left along with a few others. Most people stayed. On their way out they saw the pianist take up his position back at the piano, and they could hear the singing down the street as they made their way home.

Ever since the terrible raid that had robbed Nell of her parents, she turned to jelly at the sound of the siren, and was terrified underground in the Anderson. She was sometimes tempted to stay up at the house, but her common sense told her it was safer in the shelter, so she went along with the others, mostly because they would be worried if she stayed in the house on her own.

'That cat is completely oblivious to what's going on around him now that he's used to the raids,' mentioned Peg. Nell had Tiddles on her lap, stroking him, to comfort herself as much as the cat. 'He gets spoilt rotten when we are down here with all the extra attention we give him.'

Nell's mouth was so parched with fear she could hardly speak, but she managed to say in a relatively normal tone, 'I've got to look after him. I dread to think what Pansy will do to me if her beloved Tiddles isn't fit and thriving when she comes home.'

The drone of aircraft and the whistle of a descending bomb caused a hush. It all came rushing back to Nell. The tearing sound of the bomb falling had been the last thing she remembered before she'd blacked out. Her skin dampened as she relieved the terror of being buried, calling for help to no avail, the grinding fear for Pansy and their parents. Now it felt as though there was an iron clamp in her stomach pulling so tight she couldn't breathe.

'I hope we're not gonna be stuck down here all night long,' said Polly in such a matter-of-fact tone that not only did it break the silence, it reduced the tension.

'Don't we all,' said Peg.

'I realise that, but it's especially annoying for Ed and me because we have some serious catching-up to do in the bedroom,' Polly announced crudely. 'He's going back tomorrow and away to sea, so who knows when I'll see him again.'

Tom and Ed laughed, but Peg wasn't amused.

'Really, Polly,' she said, embarrassed rather than disapproving. 'Is nothing sacred with you at all?'

'I only said . . .'

'I know what you only said, and some things are best left private,' she interrupted. 'I've never known anyone talk about such personal subjects. You're one on your own, you really are.'

'It's just her way, Mum,' defended Ed. 'No offence meant.'

'Even so . . .'

Because Nell's nerves were in such a state of heightened awareness, Polly's outrageous lack of decorum seemed very comical at that moment, and she collapsed into a fit of nervous giggling.

Gradually the others became infected, until they were all helpless with laughter.

'It isn't funny,' began Peg, only to have her voice shake as she started to chuckle.

The situation was about as serious as it could get. They were in a hole in the ground while the earth around them shook from the force of explosions which sounded unnervingly close, their lives hanging in the balance. But they cackled and giggled until they were crying with laughter. Nerves worked that way sometimes, Nell thought. This wasn't laughter; it was hysteria.

Pansy could hear the explosions and feel the brick dust in her mouth choking her as the house fell down around her. It was black everywhere and she didn't know where her sister was. She tried to run to the shelter, to her mum and dad, but there were broken bricks everywhere and her legs wouldn't move. She opened her mouth to scream and nothing came out. Then a nun with an angry face came at her and she couldn't get away. There was no way out. She was terrified, and it was dark, dark, dark . . .

'Pans, what's the matter with you? Shush, shush. You're all right. I'm here with you.'

She was sitting bolt upright in bed. Lenny was perched next to her on the edge of her bed with his arm around her. The light was on. She was deathly white and trembling.

'Did you have a bad dream?' he asked. 'You weren't half screaming.'

'Sorry. Did I wake you?'

'That don't matter,' he assured her. 'You can't help dreams. No one can.'

'What's going on here?' This was Maud, appearing in the doorway in a billowing winceyette nightdress. 'Gawd Almighty, what a racket! I thought someone was being murdered in here.'

'Pansy had a bad dream,' Lenny explained.

'Aah, did you, love?' she said, instantly concerned and sitting on the bed beside Pansy, holding her hand.

'There were bombs. I couldn't move,' Pansy told them. 'A nun was after me.'

'There, there, you're all right now. It was only a dream and it'll fade soon enough,' said Maud kindly. 'I'll go and make you some cocoa. That'll calm you down.'

'I'll have a cup too, please, Gran, if there's one going, and a biscuit would be nice,' said Lenny, pushing his luck as usual.

'You cheeky article,' she rebuked. 'But yes, all right, I'll see what I can do. I'll bring it up here. As we're awake we might as well all have a drink. You look after Pansy while I'm gone, Lenny.'

Maud realised afterwards that her request was unnecessary, because Lenny looked out for Pansy as a matter of course, which was unusual for a boy of that age, especially one like Lenny who was such a tearaway in other ways. In fact she'd rarely seen two children so close; even more so than siblings.

As she made her way down the creaky old wooden stairs, she thought what a toll this war was taking on this generation of children. For how long would the poor mites be haunted by bad dreams? she wondered.

After the worst night of bombing that Nell could remember, the pale light of dawn was visible before she and the others finally crawled out of the shelter. They found the air clouded with smoke and the remains of some houses at the end of the street still smouldering.

'We've been lucky, by the look of it,' observed Tom.

'I'll say we have,' agreed Ed, looking down the road at the damaged buildings.

The others murmured in agreement, but they were all too tired and dispirited to say much, so went indoors quietly to bed.

After a few hours thrashing about in the sheets but only sleeping fitfully, Nell got up and went to the office to see if it was still standing. Some of the windows had been blown out and there was a thick layer of sooty dust covering everything, but the building was structurally unharmed.

Although it was Sunday, both Ted and Frank were there.

'What a night, eh?' said Ted. 'Glad to see that you're safe, Nell.'

'I thought I'd better come and see if the office was still here,' she explained.

'You don't know what to expect after bombing like that, do you?' said Ted. 'I reckon that must be the worst night we've had since the Blitz started. I thought the German bombers would never stop coming.'

'There's quite a lot of damage over our way,' mentioned Nell, who had been shocked by the carnage she'd seen on her way to the office. There had been people standing by their ruined homes weeping; others in groups with their few remaining belongings talking in sad, desperate tones.

'It's been bad all over London,' Ted informed her. 'I've been on the blower to colleagues in other parts. East, west, south and north have all had the worst night anyone can remember.'

Nell felt tearful with the reaction, but she got a dustpan and brush from the cleaner's cupboard and helped the men to clear up the glass, then got busy cleaning off the filthy black soot that was clinging to everything.

When she left the office, she didn't go straight home; instead some impulse sent her on a detour to a school that was being used as a rest centre for those made homeless by the bombing. It was being run by volunteers who worked tirelessly for the bomb victims, most of whom had lost everything except the clothes they were wearing. The unfortunates were gathered in the school hall. Some of the children were crying; others looking bewildered.

'We've only the clothes we've got on,' Nell was told by a woman who was sitting on a mattress with a baby in her arms and two little girls beside her, both looking very tired but surprisingly tidy; their mother had obviously made sure they'd used the facilities here to clean themselves up. Nell found that hugely admirable under the circumstances. 'I don't know what we'll do, I really don't. I'd just bought the kids new stuff an' all. What a waste o' money that was.'

'I'm sure you'll receive compensation to get yourself and your family re-clothed,' suggested Nell, hoping she was right. 'I was bombed out early on in the Blitz so I know how awful it feels.'

'I hope to God we do get some help or we'll all be arrested for going about naked,' the woman announced. 'I'm not having my kids wearing dirty clothes. Never have done and don't intend to let Hitler make me start now.'

'Do you have any relatives or close friends you can stay with temporarily?' Nell enquired.

'No. Not now.' She started to cry softly, and Nell realised that all the talk about clothes for the children was just a diversion from what was really on her mind. 'We were living with my mum and dad and they didn't make it. My sister lived next door and she was killed too. Everyone gone, just like that.'

'I'm so sorry,' Nell tried to comfort, swallowing hard on her own tears.

'Don't mind me, dear,' said the woman, dabbing at her eyes with a grubby handkerchief. 'I'll be all right. I'm a survivor. They'll find us a billet somewhere, eventually.' She drew her children close to her. 'I've got my kids and they've got me. We'll keep each other going until, God willing, their dad comes home.'

Nell was humbled by the woman's courage and wished she could do something to help. But she had nothing to offer except kind words, since she had no home of her own and only enough money to support herself and Pansy week by week. Thinking about it, though, maybe there was something she could do . . .

Instead of going home, she hurried back to the office. Ted was still there at his desk.

'Can we do a campaign through the paper to help the people who have been bombed out?' she said breathlessly. 'Appealing for clothes and money and so on?'

Ted leaned back in his chair, stroking his chin. 'It's a nice thought, Nell, but we have to be realistic. Something like that would mean a lot of extra work and we just don't have the staff. We're rushed off our feet as it is.'

'But it's so awful for them,' she pleaded, distraught at their plight. 'They've lost everything. No one can make them feel better about losing their loved ones, of course, but we can give them a bit of material support.'

'I know this might sound very hard-hearted, but we're not a charity,' he pointed out. 'There are plenty of organisations already involved in that sort of thing.'

'I know we're not a charity, but as a local paper surely we have a social conscience. We care about the people in our neighbourhood.' She looked at him with awesome directness. 'If we don't, we jolly well ought to.'

'All right; point taken. But look at it from my point of view. We have to make the paper pay or we'll go out of business, and that would be a loss to a lot of people,' he reminded her. 'We have little enough space as it is because of the paper shortage.'

'I know, but . . .'

'Good causes are all very well, but they take up column inches that we don't have,' he went on. 'Then there's the time it will take organising it.'

'I'll do all that.'

'You have more than enough to do as it is.'

'I'll come in earlier and work later to get it all done. Anyway, we could lessen our workload if we were to team up with a charity on this,' she suggested on the spur of the moment. 'If we get all the donations directed straight to them, it will make it a lot easier. Our job will mainly be to raise public awareness.'

His brows rose and he moved so that he was sitting forward in his chair meditatively.

'I can find out which charity to approach and go and talk to their local organisers; find out if they are prepared to cope with the response and distribute the stuff accordingly. I'm sure they will be, as they are experts at it,' Nell went on with ardour. 'I'll go out collecting as well after I've finished work here, to help out. Please, Ted. We have to do this. We can't just sit back and do nothing when people are in such dire straits.'

He rested his chin on his steepled fingers, mulling it over.

'Please, Ted. You know it would be the right thing.' She wouldn't give up.

He sighed. 'You'd better start getting it organised then, hadn't you?' he said at last. 'I'm obviously not going to get any peace until you do.' Ted was not an uncaring man, but he had a responsibility to keep the paper going which called for a commercial mind as well as an altruistic one. 'But make sure that your everyday work doesn't suffer.'

'I promise.'

'I shall be keeping my beady eye on you.'

'I'm sure you will.' Nell paused thoughtfully. 'I think I'll make a start on the project right away by doing a piece about the rest centre that I've just been to visit,' she said, going over to her desk. 'That should get people thinking and – hopefully – dipping into their wardrobes and pockets.'

'Tomorrow will do,' he pointed out. 'There's plenty of time for it to get in this week's edition.'

'I'll do a draft now while it's still fresh in my mind,' she told him. 'It won't take long. I'll polish it up tomorrow.'

'As you wish.'

What his junior reporter lacked in experience she certainly made up for in initiative and enthusiasm, he thought. She was a very talented girl and seemed to improve with every passing day. What a blessing he had taken her on.

By the time Nell got home, lunch was finished, the dishes washed, and Ed was almost ready to leave.

'We wondered where you'd got to,' he said.

'I've kept your dinner warm for you in the oven,' Peg told her. 'I hope it isn't too dried up.'

Nell apologised for being late and told them what she had been doing.

'You must be off your head, going to work on a Sunday when you don't have to,' said Polly. 'Especially after getting hardly any sleep last night.'

'I didn't go to work as such. I went to see if the office was still there, and this campaign I've got involved in is something I'm doing off my own bat,' she explained. 'I've been bombed out and left with nothing so I know how terrible that feels. I was lucky because Peg and Tom took Pansy and me in. A lot of people aren't so fortunate.'

'Very commendable of you, dear,' Peg praised. 'But you must be feeling tired now.'

'Not half as tired as those poor people at the rest centre,' said Nell worriedly.

'You can't change the world,' Tom told her.

'She'll have a bloomin' good try, though, won't you, Nell?' said Ed. 'And good luck to you.'

She gave him an affectionate smile. He would support her to the ends of the earth; he always had. That was what true friends did for each other.

'Thanks, Ed,' she smiled. 'I'll touch your sailor's collar before you go. That's supposed to bring good luck.'

'So they say.'

'So when are you off?'

'In a minute,' he replied.

'Oh dear, that soon. I almost missed you and I'm very glad I didn't,' she said ruefully. 'I hadn't realised you were going this early.'

'I'm glad you got back in time too,' he told her. 'Because I don't know when I'll be home again. It's the navy proper for me now. Out there on the high seas and all that.'

Ed had been at Portsmouth up until now. Because of his engineering experience and specialised knowledge he had been trained for a job in the engine room of a ship which he was due to join shortly after he got back.

'Let's hope it won't be for too long,' said Tom, forcing himself to stay positive to cheer his wife up. This parting was difficult for Peg, as for any mother.

'I'll turn up like any bad penny, don't you worry,' replied Ed making a joke of it. He patted Polly's bump. 'If his nibs arrives before I do, tell him I won't be long.'

'It might be a girl,' Polly pointed out.

'Tell her nibs then.'

An effort at laughter was made but there was no real substance to it. They all trooped to the front door, where Ed hugged and kissed his mother, and shook hands with his father, who slapped his back. He gave Nell a friendly peck on the cheek.

'I'm expecting you to be the chief reporter on the *Daily Mirror* when I come back,' he laughed.

'Fat chance,' she came back at him.

'I wouldn't put anything past you,' he said. 'Good luck with the campaign.'

'Thanks. Good luck to you too. Look after yourself, and none of this heroic stuff.'

'We'll see.'

He put his cap on, and Nell, Peg and Tom stood at the front gate and watched him and Polly – who was seeing him off at the station – make their way down the street, Ed very upright and with a slight swagger, his bell bottoms flapping, his kit bag slung over his shoulder. Polly was holding his arm and moving in an awkward way because of her extra weight.

At the corner they turned and Ed gave a final wave.

Peg sniffed into her handkerchief and Tom put his arm around her. 'He'll be all right, love,' he said in a comforting tone. 'He'll be back before we know it.'

The unity between the two of them was so tangible it brought tears to Nell's eyes. She was feeling anxious for Ed herself. Despite the prevailing optimism that most people clung to as a way of staying sane, the loss of life at sea was horrific, and none of them knew if he would make it back.

When she went inside and removed her dinner from the oven, she found herself without any appetite. What with the terrible events of last night and Ed going away to sea, she was feeling a bit quivery inside. But she cleared her plate because she needed to keep her strength up. Anyway, it was a sin to waste food when there was so little of it about.

That evening a visitor called at the house.

'Just popped round to see if you're all right after last night,' explained Gus Granger when Tom let him in and led him into the living room, where Nell and Peg were listening to the wireless and knitting for the baby. Polly was reading a woman's magazine; she was a hopeless knitter with no plans to improve, because knitting and sewing were both anathema to her.

'That's kind of you,' said Peg.

'Phew, what a bugger of a night it was, eh? It's a wonder any of us are still here.'

'They must have used every bomber and bomb they've got, I should think,' remarked Nell. 'Perhaps that's why there's no sign of them tonight.'

'It would be nice to think they'd run out of ammunition, but we all know there's plenty more where that came from, don't we?' said Gus.

'You're a real Cheerful Charlie, you are,' responded Nell, grinning at him. Once again she felt a strong sense of chemistry between them as their eyes met.

'Sorry. I didn't mean to be a doom and gloom merchant. I was just being realistic.'

'I think we all had enough realism last night to keep our feet planted firmly on the ground.'

'That's very true.'

'I'll put the kettle on,' suggested Peg in a friendly manner. 'Have a seat, Gus, and make yourself at home.'

'Thanks for offering, Peg, but I can't stop,' he told her. 'I'm on duty down the ARP depot.'

'Not even time for a quick one?'

'Another time perhaps,' he replied. 'I'd better shoot off. They'll be expecting me.'

'Thanks for calling in,' said Peg warmly. 'It's nice of you to worry about us.'

'No trouble,' he said, his eyes lingering on Nell again. 'See you again sometime. G'night, all. Let's hope it stays as quiet as this to give us all a break.'

There was a general response.

When Tom came back from seeing Gus out, Peg said, 'Wasn't it good of him to come round to check on us?'

'It wasn't us he came to check on,' said Polly knowingly. 'It was Nell.'

'Don't start that again,' objected Nell.

'He practically had his tongue hanging out.'

'Polly,' rebuked Peg sharply. 'I wish you wouldn't be so crude. You know I don't like that sort of talk.'

'What was crude about that?'

'Everything,' Peg replied. 'There are ways of putting things without being vulgar.'

'Don't take on, love; she doesn't mean any harm,' said Tom, hoping to smooth things over between them. 'She's right about Gus too. He's really taken a shine to Nell. He can't keep his eyes off her. Even I noticed that.'

'Honestly, you lot really are the limit,' tutted Nell. 'Anyway, if what you say is true, why hasn't he asked me out?'

'Because we're all here, of course,' opined Polly, looking towards Tom for support. 'He's just waiting for the right opportunity, don't you think?'

'I do,' agreed Tom wholeheartedly. 'The poor bloke can't ask you with us lot gawping at him.'

'As I said before, I think he's too old for her,' said Peg. 'He's thirty, for goodness' sake.'

'Mm, there is a bit of a gap there, I suppose,' agreed Tom.

'What does it matter?' demanded Polly. 'Someone a bit older might be the best thing for her. He might have a few quid put by. He doesn't look short of a bob or two.'

'Oi,' interrupted Nell lightly. 'I am here in the room, you know, so I wish you'd all stop behaving as if I'm not. You'll be taking bets on whether he asks me out next.'

'What a good idea,' laughed Tom, teasing her. 'I'll say he'll have asked you within a week.'

'I'll say within two days,' Polly chipped in. 'How about you, Peg? What's your bet?'

'I'm not betting, and you can stop, the pair of you,' admonished Peg. 'Can't you see that you're embarrassing the girl?'

'Let them get on with it, Auntie,' said Nell, who hadn't taken umbrage in the least, since there were far worse things in life than a spot of teasing. 'I'm not taking any notice of them; they're both as daft as brushes.'

She was however, wondering if she might hear from Gus Granger, because there was no denying the fact that he fancied her. Oh well, only time will tell, she thought. She wasn't going to dwell on it; she had far too many other things on her mind.

As Gus Granger made his way to the ARP depot his thoughts were all of Nell. She was absolutely gorgeous: young and fresh and beautiful; intelligent too. That was obvious the minute she opened her mouth. She was quite different from the women he generally went out with, who were older than Nell and had usually been around the block a few times. That was the way he liked it.

His circumstances were such that he had to be careful not to get too involved, so he went for the brassy types who weren't looking for a happy-ever-after ending. Often they were married and just wanting a fling, which suited him perfectly. It was too risky for a man in his position to lose control of his feelings. Serious relationships were not on his agenda.

Nell was in a different league altogether. He'd been smitten the minute he'd first clapped eyes on her. He knew nothing about her apart from her name and age and that she was closely involved with the Mills family, but he wanted to know more; he wanted to know everything about her and longed to be with her. He hadn't felt this way about a girl since he'd been in his teens; thrilled with the joy of looking at her, the excitement of getting to know her.

But he'd be taking a risk in more ways than one if he did get involved. She was young and vulnerable and he'd have Tom and his family and the chaps down the depot after him if he didn't do right by her. Anyway, she probably wouldn't be interested in someone who was twelve years her senior. A girl like her could have anyone. But that argument didn't hold water, because he'd seen the look in her eyes; felt the connection.

No, it just wasn't on. He would have to steel himself against tempta-tion. If he went down that road he would lose his head and get careless. That mustn't be allowed to happen, because the price was too high. He must put her out of his mind. No more acting on impulse and chasing round to her house as he had tonight just to catch a glimpse of her. That sort of lack of control could only end in disaster.

Sadly, he had to accept the fact that romance with Nell Porter was absolutely out of the question.

Chapter Eight

Since the horrific night of intensive bombing in May, Londoners were treated to a series of blissful Blitz-free ones, leading some to dread that something big was about to befall them; everyone knew that Hitler hadn't finished by a long chalk. But as the respite continued, confidence grew. People began to relax and enjoy sleeping in their own beds, and waking in the morning feeling refreshed after a proper night's sleep.

Peg and Nell were beginning to think in terms of having the children home if things stayed quiet in the long term, but they were still only cautiously optimistic, aware that this might be the calm before the storm. Finally they decided that if the air raids continued to stay away they would bring them home in time for Christmas.

Nell's campaign for bomb victims took a lot of organising but received a satisfying response, which delighted her. With that behind her, she was kept busy chasing the stories behind the news as well as doing the daily rounds of the courts, police station and so on; her enthusiasm for the job never waned. The more she learned, the more enthralling she found it.

Contrary to expectations, she didn't hear from Gus Granger. He disappeared from her life as suddenly as he'd appeared, though Tom said he still did his voluntary work for the ARP. It was disappointing for Nell because she had been excited about his possible interest in her; probably because he was so different from boys of her own age and simply oozed a charisma they didn't have. But she had plenty of other things to occupy her mind. In her limited off-duty time, she sometimes went dancing with girls she used to work with at Barker's; occasionally she accepted an invitation out on a date, but none ever developed into anything because there was no one for whom she felt so much as an inkling of that special spark.

As the warm and sultry days of summer sharpened into autumn, Polly's time drew near. She went into labour one night in October. Characteristically, she didn't embrace childbirth but fought it every step of the way. The swearing was shocking; so bad that the midwife threatened to walk out, whereupon Polly tried to physically attack her and Nell had to calm her and make her promise to tone her language down, while Peg placated the midwife, who only agreed to stay for the sake of the poor unborn child.

'Men ought to be castrated, every flamin' one of them. It's nothing short of cruelty to subject a woman to such terrible pain and should be against the law,' Polly ranted in between the screams she was letting rip during the contractions. 'I'm never letting a single one of them near me again and that's definite. And as for Ed, I'll kill him for putting me through this purgatory. Separate beds in future. Oh yes!'

Finally, just as dawn was breaking, she gave birth to a beautiful baby boy.

'There now, hasn't it all been worth it?' said the long-suffering midwife, handing her the little boy. 'Isn't he just the loveliest thing you've ever seen?'

'Yeah,' she muttered, visibly uncomfortable as she stared down at the bloodstained bundle in her arms. 'Lovely.'

'Here, let me have him,' said the nurse in an efficient manner. 'I'll get him cleaned up and looking presentable.'

She looked at Polly, who had started to cry.

'It's a very emotional thing, giving birth,' the nurse said kindly. 'It's the joy of it that makes us weep. It's only natural.'

Joy was the last thing Polly was feeling. She was weeping with sheer terror at the situation she was in. The pregnancy and the labour pains were as nothing compared to how she felt now. She had created this human being and in doing so had been plunged into a world of darkness and fear. For the first time in her life she was entirely responsible for another human being, a tiny fragile one at that, and she didn't know how she was going to cope.

'He's beautiful,' said Nell, leaning over the crib beside Polly's bed later on that day. 'Can I pick him up?'

'Course you can.'

'He's got a look of Ed about him, don't you think?' suggested Peg predictably as Nell cradled him and Peg peered at the pink mottled face wrapped in a shawl.

'Mm, I think you're right,' agreed Nell. 'But he'll probably change as he gets bigger.'

'What do you think, Polly?'

'About what?' She seemed distant and preoccupied.

'About the baby looking like his dad.'

'Isn't it too early to tell?' she said flatly. 'Babies all look the same to me.'

'I can definitely see his father in him,' opined Peg.

'That's only because you're Ed's mother,' responded Polly without much interest. 'I expect all grannies think like that.'

'I can see it too,' remarked Nell. She had rushed home in her lunch hour to see how things were going. The whole house was buzzing with the new arrival. Peg was in her element with her first grandchild.

'If you say so.' Polly sounded bored.

'Have you got any ideas about what you're going to call him yet?' enquired Nell excitedly.

Oh for heaven's sake, why didn't they all go away and take the baby with them so that she could be left in peace? thought Polly. She felt so exhausted and miserable, she just wanted to be left alone to sleep. Her breasts hurt, her stomach ached, she was sore from the delivery, and when the baby cried it tore her nerves to shreds. She didn't want to talk to anyone. All she wanted was to bury her head under the bedclothes and shut out the world.

'Polly, what name do you fancy for him?' Peg asked.

Would they never stop pestering her? She hadn't the faintest idea what to call him and didn't even want to think about it. But she had to shut them up so she said the first name that came into her head, which was her father's. 'Joe,' she said.

'Oh, that's nice,' responded Peg, unable to hide her disappointment. 'You're not calling him after his dad then.'

'Joe Edward,' she added on the spur of the moment, to keep the peace.

'Oh, Ed will be so thrilled.'

'He will,' added Nell.

Good, now perhaps you'll all go away and leave me alone, Polly thought, but no such luck; a knock at the door heralded the midwife on a routine visit.

'And how are mother and baby now?' she asked, bounding into the room. Nell handed the baby to Polly, and she and Peg made a diplomatic exit, at which point the baby launched into a screaming fit. 'Oh dear. It sounds as though someone needs some attention. When your milk comes in and you're feeding him he'll soon be content.'

'About the breastfeeding,' began Polly.

'Yes . . . ?'

'I don't want to do it.'

'Nonsense, of course you must do it,' the midwife stated in a domineering manner.

'You can't make me.'

The nurse flushed angrily. This patient must be one of the most difficult she'd ever had to deal with. 'I don't need to. Your conscience will do that.' She paused, looking at Polly in a fiercely direct manner. 'Some women do find it a little difficult to begin with, but you must persevere. The baby comes first, remember, and breast milk is the best thing.'

'But I . . .'

'No argument,' she said dismissively. 'It's nature's way. You'll soon get used to it.' She took the baby from Polly. 'Now, let's get this little fellow checked over.'

Old cow, cursed Polly furiously. How dare she come in here bossing her around, behaving as though she had no rights? The sooner her visits stopped, the better. Usually Polly had no trouble in standing up for herself, but she felt completely incapable of asserting herself to this ghastly harridan. In fact she didn't feel able to do battle with anyone. Childbirth seemed to have sucked the confidence out of her. She was determined to get her own way about the feeding, though, once she was up and about again and that awful midwife was out of her life. Ooh, her nerves were so much on edge, they were tingling. If only that child would stop screaming. It was driving her mad.

Since Nell had been working on the paper, she had really had her eyes opened to the sleazier side of life, especially with relation to the war.

In the world that she inhabited people were patriotic and selfless in the face of the adversity they were living under. But there was a darker minority of criminals who were cheating the system and making money from the shortages.

Her naïvety was brought home to her one day a week or so after the birth of Polly's baby, when she was in the court reporting on the locals who had been misbehaving. There was the usual mix of miscreants, including several men charged with being drunk and disorderly, one who had exposed himself in the foyer of a cinema, and a small-time burglar.

But her heartstrings had been tugged by a young man with ill health who had been caught in possession of stolen goods. He'd obviously been driven to crime by desperation. The poor chap wasn't well enough to work and would have been unable to join the services for the same reason. He was a pallid, skinny, blond-haired man who looked to be in his early twenties. His speech was interrupted by fits of coughing and sneezing.

Nell was surprised and somewhat outraged when he was sentenced to three months in prison.

'You'd think the judge would have shown some compassion under the circumstances,' she said to Frank back at the office. 'The man has no money and is in poor health; it's no wonder he's been driven to break the law. He's been in court before, apparently, and I'm not surprised, given his circumstances.'

'He wasn't a fair-haired fella by the name of Percy Wood, by any chance, was he?' asked Frank.

Nell gave him a puzzled look. 'He was as it happens. How did you know?'

'I've worked on the paper for a long time and done plenty of court reporting,' he explained. 'Percy is a regular. He'll be back to the same old tricks as soon as he's done his porridge. He'll probably have a nice little stash put by for after the war. A few spells in prison are worth it to him.'

'I'm sure you must be wrong about him,' she insisted. 'The man is ill. You can tell that just by looking at him, not to mention his shocking cough. I felt very sorry for him.'

'A bit of flour rubbed into his face, and pepper on his hanky to induce coughing can make anyone seem ill.'

'No. I can't believe that, Frank.' Nell was adamant. 'Anyway, he must have a medical certificate or he would be conscripted for the services or war work.'

'He probably paid someone else to go for his medical; someone with a genuine complaint. You remember what the policeman told us about the scam that's going on in the underworld,' Frank reminded her.

'Mm.' She did remember but still didn't want to believe it of the man in court because he'd been so convincing. 'It doesn't mean that he did that.'

'Either that or he's got forged papers,' stated Frank. 'You can get almost anything if you're prepared to pay for it and have the right contacts. False identity cards, stolen goods, even clothing coupons; it's all run by the same bunch of crooks.'

'If you're so sure of all this, why don't you report it to the police?' she asked.

'They know. Everybody knows it goes on. It's finding out who's behind it that's the problem, as the police sergeant told us when we were down the nick that time.'

'I knew about the black market, of course, but I didn't realise it was on such a large scale until I started this job.'

'Everybody who's in the law enforcement or news business knows the full extent of it,' he said. 'Anyway, you know now, and that's the important thing.'

'I almost wish I didn't.'

'You need to be aware of that sort of thing in our line of business,' he told her. 'There's no point in having a blinkered attitude when you're working in journalism. You're dealing with human nature in all its forms; the best and the worst of it.'

'All right, I admit it, I was completely taken in by Percy,' she confessed. 'It seems I wasted my pity.'

'You did indeed.' Frank nodded. 'But on the other hand, he is being used by people who are making far more out of it than he is. The men he works for – whoever they are – will dispense with him if he stops being useful to them. He takes the stuff off their hands and sells it, so they need him and plenty of others like him. Selling it on themselves would be too risky, so they prefer to stay in the background.'

'Where do they get it?'

138

'It's stolen from factories; from the docks, warehouses; places where there are goods in bulk.'

'Where do people like Percy sell it?'

'Any and everywhere. Pubs, clubs, on the street, to shopkeepers who fancy bigger profits,' he informed her. 'There are plenty of customers, with everything being in such short supply.'

'I suppose so.'

'If Percy were to grass up the men he works for or start getting difficult, they'd have him removed, just like that,' he went on. 'They are hardened criminals; men who would have someone killed without turning a hair, especially loners like Percy who don't have anyone to miss them. They wouldn't dirty their hands by doing it themselves, of course. They are far too cowardly for that.'

'How terrible!' Nell was outraged. 'It makes you feel like going out there and nailing them yourself, doesn't it?'

'Don't you dare,' he warned. 'There's nothing we can do. We're journalists, not coppers.'

'Journalists do sometimes expose scandals.'

'On the big national newspapers maybe,' he said. 'But they always make sure they have proof.'

'It's enough to make you lose faith in human nature, all these criminals cashing in on the war when our boys are losing their lives at the front,' she said.

'It is only a very small minority who are lining their pockets,' he reminded her. 'The war has brought the best out in the majority of people.'

She knew that he was right, and couldn't count the number of kindnesses and acts of courage she had witnessed since war was declared.

'Yeah, that's very true,' she agreed.

HMS *Benwall* was in a mid-Atlantic storm, and Ed was up on deck during a break from his duties in the engine room. Some sailors might be glad to stay below deck in such dramatic weather, but Ed preferred to experience the storm full on. Now that he had got over the awful initial seasickness and had his sea legs, he enjoyed the sway of the ship and being so close to the elements.

The ship rolled and heaved, thundering through the mountainous waves and soaring to the top to provide a magnificent glimpse of the sea beyond. Doors swung almost off their hinges and the boat creaked and rattled so hard it seemed to Ed as though it might split into pieces, while white foamy water – ice cold and salty – burst into his face and ran down his oilskins.

Since he'd been at sea he'd had experiences unlike anything he'd had before. Living in London he'd been rather sheltered from the wilder elements. On the ocean, he'd seen and felt Nature in the raw and had found it to be an almost spiritual experience. It frightened and thrilled him simultaneously.

He'd also been involved in enemy action, which had turned his insides to water, but somehow he'd found the strength to carry on down in the engine room, despite leaks which flooded the room and threatened to drown the men. Another time there was a fire down there that nearly roasted him alive.

Still, he'd lived through it, and today he felt as though he had the strength of ten men, because in his pocket was a letter from Polly to say that she had given birth to a son. His son! He was a father and his pride knew no bounds.

Aye aye, now there's trouble, he thought as there was an explosion nearby which shook the ship even more. He assumed it had been fired from a long-distance bomber, though he couldn't see anything yet. More often their ship was attacked by submarines. I'd better get back down the hatch to duty, he thought. Every man to his post when the enemy was about, and there were plenty of gunners up here.

Him a dad; it felt really awesome. He hoped there would be some leave coming up before too long. He couldn't wait to get home to his wife and son.

Peg's grandson had given her a new lease of life. Tom adored him too, but he was out at work most of the time, so it was Peg who took a large part in looking after him. She welcomed any opportunity to give him his bottle or bath or dress him, talking to him and singing all the while. The love just poured out of her. When he smiled for the first time, a passing stranger could have been forgiven for thinking that peace had been declared.

It was a treat for Nell to see. Peg had taken it hard when Ed had gone away to sea, even though she tried not to show it, and little Joe created a much-needed diversion. It was good to see her enjoying life.

Less buoyant was Polly, who had become subdued and serious since Joe's birth. She didn't complain noisily about every single thing as she had before; nor did she utter embarrassingly vulgar remarks. But neither did she giggle or chatter as she used to. In fact she didn't say much at all, which wasn't a bit like her. It wasn't that she was miserable exactly; more detached and vague. That wicked gleam had gone out of her eyes.

Although excessively dutiful towards the baby, she didn't cuddle or fuss him as his grandmother did. Her movements were fast now and efficient, as though she wanted to get on to the next job, unlike the old days when she didn't lift a finger around the house unless she was nagged into it. Now she cleaned up and did the dishes without even being asked.

'Are you all right, Pol?' Nell asked one evening when they happened to be alone together in the living room. Nell was listening to the wireless with half an ear. Polly was perched on the edge of the armchair, not looking at all relaxed.

'Course I am. Why wouldn't I be?'

'You seem so quiet these days.'

'Do I?'

'Yes. You do. You seem to have changed altogether,' she told her. 'You're a lot more serious than you used to be. You don't lark about any more.'

How could she be light-hearted with such a crippling responsibility weighing her down twenty-four hours a day? thought Polly. You couldn't laugh and lark about when you had a baby to look after because the whole thing was such a serious obligation. It squeezed all the fun out of life.

She shrugged. 'I'm not purposely being a misery-guts. But motherhood is a serious business,' she explained. 'I suppose I'm bound to have been affected by it.'

'You're feeling all right, though, are you?' Nell persisted, concerned. 'Not worried about anything in particular?'

'No.'

'If there's anything I can help with, you only have to say.'

'I'm fine.'

Nell didn't believe her but she said, 'As long as you are, that's all right. But I'm always here if you need a listening ear.'

'I'll bear that in mind, but there's nothing I want to talk about at the moment.'

'That's all right then.'

They sat in comfortable silence. Nell opened her knitting bag and drew out the blue sweater she was making for the navy. She had her needles poised ready to start when Polly made an unexpected announcement.

'I'd like to get Joe christened as soon as possible,' she said, out of the blue.

'Oh really; how lovely!'

'Actually, I was wondering if you might consider being his godmother.'

'Polly, I'd love to,' smiled Nell, putting her knitting on her lap. 'Oh, thank you for asking me. I'd be very honoured.'

'That's settled then,' said Polly in a hurried manner. 'I think people usually have a godfather too, and sometimes more than one of each, but I don't have anyone to ask to be godfather, so one godmother will have to do.'

'I'm sure that will be fine.'

'I'll go down the church tomorrow to see the vicar and get it organised,' said Polly.

'There's no great hurry, is there?'

'As I've decided to get it done, the sooner the better.'

'I didn't realise you were that religious,' mentioned Nell.

'I'm not particularly, but you have to get your baby christened, don't you?' she stated. 'It's what people do, so I might as well get on and do it or it might look bad.'

'I know it's the usual thing, but it really is a matter of choice,' Nell pointed out. 'You certainly don't have to treat it as urgent.'

'Once it's done, it's off my mind and I can relax,' Polly explained. 'I'd rather get it organised straight away.'

'I see,' said Nell. She was worried by Polly's attitude. There didn't seem to be any joy in her son's christening. It was as though it was just another obligation that had to be dealt with, like changing the baby's nappy or feeding him. 'It's a good excuse for us to get something new to wear anyway. If you've got any clothing coupons we could go to Oxford Street, if you like.'

'I won't bother to get anything new,' Polly said, sounding uninterested. 'As long as I'm clean and tidy, and the baby looks nice, that'll do.'

Nell could hardly believe she was hearing this. The Polly she'd known wouldn't have been able to wait to hit the dress shops in the West End. It had always been any excuse with her for something new to wear, and throughout her pregnancy she'd talked of her longing to wear smart clothes again.

'I shall splash out as I'm going to be his godmother,' Nell mentioned. 'But I'll have to see how many coupons I've got.'

'Yeah, that will be nice for you,' said Polly absently, as though she had other, more important things on her mind.

'Would you like to come with me?' invited Nell. 'To help me choose something. It'll be fun. We haven't been clothes shopping together for ages.'

'I can't drag the baby round the shops.' Polly sounded horrified at the suggestion. 'It would be far too much of a performance. He'd probably scream the place down.'

'I don't see why he should.'

'It's what babies do,' she said sharply. 'Don't tell me you haven't noticed.'

Nell held on to her patience. 'Peg will be happy to look after him for a couple of hours while we're out, I'm sure,' she suggested.

'No. I'd rather not if you don't mind.' Polly yawned. 'It'll be far too much of a fuss and will upset his routine. Anyway, I think I'll go off to bed now.'

'Bed!' Nell glanced at the clock on the mantelpiece. 'It's only eight o'clock,' she said.

'I don't care what the time is,' she responded, getting up. 'I'm tired and the baby will have me awake in the night, so I might as well get some sleep while I can.'

'Just one thing before you go,' began Nell. 'Don't you think you ought to have a chat with Peg and Tom about the christening? To sort out a suitable date with them, as the christening party will be here.'

'I'll do it in the morning before I go to the church,' Polly told her. 'I'm too tired now.'

'G'night then,' said Nell. 'Sleep well.'

'Night.'

143

There was something disturbing about this sudden eagerness to get little Joe christened, thought Nell. What it was she couldn't imagine, but all was not well, she was sure of it.

Nell didn't have enough clothing coupons to buy a new coat but she did manage to scrape together sufficient for a hat — a red one with an artificial flower on it which gave her grey coat a new and dressy look — so she was feeling pleased with herself when she finished shopping and made her way to the station to get the train home.

She'd managed to get the afternoon off in lieu of all the extra hours she'd put in at the office, and a wander round the shops had been enjoyable. Unfortunately she hadn't taken enough notice of the time so found herself caught up in the rush hour when she got to the station. What with homeward-bound office workers and early Christmas shoppers, there was a suffocating crush inside Oxford Circus station as she made her way down on the escalator to the platform.

'Hello there,' said someone, tapping her on the shoulder from behind as she headed for the westbound trains. 'Fancy seeing you here of all places.'

Turning, she saw that it was Gus Granger, smiling and looking very pleased to see her.

'Hello there,' she responded cheerfully.

'Do you work in the West End then?' he enquired by way of conversation as they left the escalator.

'No. I work local to home. I had the afternoon off to do some shopping,' she explained.

'Been buying anything nice?' he asked chattily, glancing towards the shopping bag she was carrying.

'Yes, I have, as it happens,' she told him as they struggled through the crowds surging towards the platform. 'I've blown most of my coupons on a hat for my friend's baby's christening on Sunday. I'm going to be his godmother.'

'Being a godmother sounds like a very good reason for a new hat to me; not that I know much about christenings.'

'There will be a church service, then a small get-together at home afterwards; nothing extravagant,' she explained. 'But I'm absolutely thrilled to be asked to be his godmother. I'm nuts about him. We all are in our house.'

'I'm sure you'll do a really good job.'

'I certainly intend to take the commitment seriously, now and into the future.'

People were pushing and jostling around them as they finally made it on to the platform.

'Are you changing at Notting Hill Gate and taking the District Line to Chiswick Park?' she enquired in a conversational manner.

'No, I'll go on to Shepherd's Bush and walk from there,' he replied. 'I live somewhere between the two.'

'You work in the West End then?' she surmised.

He nodded.

'So you have to put up with this crush every day,' she said. 'Poor you.'

'You get used to it.' He paused, looking at her. 'What do you do for a living?' he enquired with interest.

'I work for the *Chiswick and Hammersmith Herald*.'

'Typing, that sort of thing?'

'That does come into it, yes,' she told him. 'But I'm a reporter actually.'

'Well, well, I am impressed.'

'There's no need to be,' she said. 'I'm very junior and I only got the job because all the men are away. Sadly, it's only temporary until the end of the war. But I enjoy it enormously so I'm making the most of it and learning as much as I can.'

'Even though you'll have to leave after the war?'

'You bet,' was her buoyant reply. 'It's all good experience. It might come in handy at some time in the future, you never know. A career in journalism wasn't available to me when I left school, so the war has done me a favour.' She paused, looking sad. 'In one way anyway.'

'Tom mentioned that you lost your parents in the bombing,' he said. 'I was sorry to hear that.'

'Thank you.'

'So . . . do you report on weddings, funerals and school sports days; that sort of thing?' he said moving on swiftly because she was looking upset.

She nodded. 'But not only those sort of events,' she told him. 'We report what's going on in the neighbourhood in general. What's on. Who's done something good; those who have been misbehaving. You know what local

145

papers are like. People usually buy them to find out what's on at the pictures and for the situations vacant column, but I hope they enjoy the human interest stories we run as well. Most readers like that sort of thing.'

'I'm sure they do.'

The train came and they managed to get on, but it was packed to the doors and they both had to strap-hang.

'So what do you do in your spare time?' he asked.

'The same as most girls of my age,' she replied. 'Dancing sometimes, the pictures; the usual sort of things.'

'A special boyfriend?' he enquired.

'Not at the moment.'

'It can't be from any lack of offers,' he said, looking at her with unveiled approval. 'A lovely young woman like yourself must have legions of admirers.'

'That's very kind of you.' He was about a head taller than her so she had to look up at him when she spoke. 'Are you flirting with me by any chance?' she asked jokingly.

'I think perhaps I am.' Their eyes met, the chemistry sparking. 'But it's a bit cheeky of me, since you wouldn't be interested in an old geezer like me.'

'You don't know that, do you?' She was excited by him and enjoying the repartee. The tough look she had noticed when she'd seen him before was even more noticeable close up. It wasn't anything she could pin down. His features were firm and well carved and his mouth nicely shaped, but there was a harshness about it somehow. It must be his solid jaw and his large hands, which she could see because he wasn't wearing gloves. At close proximity he wasn't good-looking in the traditional way – his face was too chunky for that – but he was very attractive and had a powerful presence. 'Anyway, you've got a girlfriend, haven't you? You were with someone when we saw you in the pub on my birthday.'

'That was over ages ago. It wasn't serious anyway.'

She was holding her breath, absolutely certain that he was going to ask her out. But he said, 'Well, this is my stop. Nice to see you, Nell. Enjoy yourself at the christening.'

'Thanks. I will.'

She spent the rest of the journey wondering what was wrong with her that he hadn't asked to see her again. It was obvious that he was interested in her and she'd made it plain that she felt the same. So why hadn't he taken the initiative?

Gus was admonishing himself severely as he left the station and started to walk down the street. What on earth had he been thinking of; going up to her and making himself known as soon as he set eyes on her? She hadn't seen him so he could easily have avoided her. But oh no, he had to follow his instincts and push through the crowds to get to her, where-upon he'd embarked upon a blatant flirtation, only managing not to ask to see her again because the train had made a timely arrival at his station.

Although he had wanted to know more about her ever since that first meeting back in the summer, he'd resisted the temptation to ask Tom Mills too much because he'd been trying to put her out of his mind. Now he'd blown all that by rushing up to her like some lovesick schoolboy. It was ridiculous!

She was a young and lovely straightforward girl. Her life was a world away from his and to pursue her would be madness, especially as she was a journalist, which meant she would have an enquiring mind. It was far too risky for him.

Forget about her, he warned himself. There were plenty more fish in the sea, especially now that so many men were away at the war. There were lots of lonely married women looking for a good time with someone like him. They were much less complicated than squeaky-clean young girls like Nell Porter.

The christening was a small affair; just Polly's parents and a few friends and neighbours of Peg and Tom. Nell swelled with pride when they stood at the font, even though Joe bawled the place down when the vicar splashed the water on him.

'He isn't the first baby to do that and he certainly won't be the last,' said Peg that evening after all the guests had gone. Nell, Peg and Polly were sitting by the fire in the living room enjoying a companionable glass of sherry that had been left over from the party. Now Tom had gone for a pint with the man next door and Joe was asleep in his cot.

'He hasn't half got some lungs on him, hasn't he?' said Polly. 'I thought he was going to blow the roof off the church with his yelling.'

'His father did the same thing at his christening, if my memory serves me correctly,' recalled Peg. 'I suppose you can't blame them; suddenly having water thrown all over you must be frightening for a little one.'

'It was only a drop, Peg,' Polly pointed out. 'Anyone would think the vicar had thrown a full bucketful over him, the racket he was making.'

'Didn't he look sweet in the christening gown?' mentioned Nell. 'I was so proud to be holding him.'

'Yeah, it washed up very well,' agreed Peg. 'You'd never guess it has been around so long, would you? I got it for Ed's christening and we used it for Lenny's as well. Just as well I hung on to it, as you can't even get a bit of material to make one without coupons.'

'Thanks for putting on a spread and making a little do of it,' said Polly unexpectedly. Acknowledging someone else's generosity wasn't something she normally did.

'No need to thank me, love,' Peg assured her warmly. 'He's my grandson and I consider it a privilege to do what I can for him, especially as you don't have a place of your own.'

'It was good of you anyway when you already have such a lot to do,' insisted Polly.

Nell could hardly believe she was hearing this. Polly had never shown empathy towards anyone before.

They chatted about this and that and Nell was pleased to observe that Polly was more relaxed than she'd seen her since before Joe was born. Must be the sherry, she thought.

The wireless was on low, and when they turned up the volume for the news they were shocked to hear the terrible announcement that the Japanese had bombed the US Pacific Fleet at their home base at Pearl Harbor in Hawaii.

'Blimey,' gasped Peg. 'That's a shock.'

'What a terrible thing,' added Nell.

'The Americans will come into the war now, I should think,' suggested Peg.

'I don't see that they'll have much choice now that Japan has declared war on them,' agreed Nell.

'We'll have to keep the wireless on in case there's any more news later.' This was Polly.

'It'll be all over the papers tomorrow,' Nell mentioned, 'so we can read about it then.'

'Any more of that sherry going spare, Peg?' asked Polly. She was being more sociable than of late and sounding much more like her old self.

'I think there's enough for us all to have a drop more,' replied Peg, getting up and going over to the sideboard.

Nell was heartened to see her friend on such good form. Her cheeks were flushed and she was smiling. It was probably just a result of the alcohol but it did prove that the old outgoing Polly was still in there somewhere.

'Cheers,' said Nell when Peg had refilled her glass. 'Here's to little Joe's future. May it be a good one.'

'Cheers,' chorused the other two, raising their glasses.

The atmosphere was warm and light-hearted, thought Nell. It was just like old times, before Polly had lost her sense of humour.

When Nell awoke the next morning to hear the baby crying and saw from her alarm clock that it wasn't anywhere near time to get up, she turned on to her side and pulled the covers up over her head to drown out the noise. She'd grown accustomed to these rather too early wake-up calls since Joe had been around. Fortunately, he never cried for long, though, because Polly always attended to him.

Nell dozed off only to be woken again by the sound of Joe screaming. He sounded very distressed, almost as though he was choking. What was the matter with him? she wondered. Polly never left him to cry like this. She did hope that he wasn't sickening for something. Oh for heaven's sake see to him, Polly. I've got to go to work in the morning, she thought irritably as the yelling continued.

It wasn't like Joe to cry for so long. Should she go in to see if there was anything she could do to help? No, she'd better not. Polly might think she was interfering and be offended. At last there was blissful silence. Nell closed her eyes and snuggled down.

But something was going on. She could hear Peg and Tom talking; there were footsteps on the stairs. What was happening out there? They never got up this early. The muffled sound of their voices from downstairs drifted up to her. Perhaps one of them was ill or something.

Worried now, she got out of bed, dragged on her dressing gown and went downstairs, where she found them both in the living room. Peg was sitting in the armchair nursing the baby; Tom was pacing up and down anxiously.

'We tried not to wake you, as you've got to go to work tomorrow,' said Peg thickly, her eyes wet with tears.

'What's happened?' asked Nell nervously.

'Polly's gone,' Peg informed her emotionally. 'That trollop has done a bunk and left her baby. He was crying his little eyes out when I went in there. The poor little soul. It's nothing short of wicked.'

'Are you sure she's actually left?' asked Nell in disbelief. 'Maybe she's just gone out and will be back in a minute.'

'At this time of the morning?' queried Peg. 'Where would she go at this hour?'

'A walk, perhaps,' Nell suggested, desperate to find an explanation.

'Sorry to disappoint you, Nell, but she hasn't just popped out; she's taken all her clothes so she's gone for good,' said Tom gravely. 'She's cleared out. Left without a word of explanation.'

'If I ever see her again, she'll wish she'd never been born, I know that much,' declared Peg, her voice quivering with anger. 'I mean, how could anyone do something like that? How could you walk out on your own child? It's beyond me.'

'I don't know how she could have done it either, Auntie Peg,' said Nell worriedly. 'I really don't. I'm as shocked as you are by the whole thing.'

'It's absolutely shameful,' said Peg, tears falling now.

'There, there, love,' soothed Tom, sitting on the arm of his wife's chair and putting his hand on her shoulder in a supportive gesture. 'I know it's hard, but try not to upset yourself too much. Babies sense these things and we don't want him being in a state as well as the rest of us.'

'No, of course we don't.' She kissed the top of Joe's head, which was covered in fair downy hair. 'This child will want for nothing that it is within our means to give him,' she proclaimed dramatically. 'His mother might not give a tuppenny toss about him, but his grandparents certainly do.'

As Peg's words registered, it all became horribly clear to Nell. Polly's eagerness to have the christening at the earliest opportunity and her request for Nell to be godmother; her more relaxed attitude last night. She'd been happier because she had known she was about to shed her responsibilities. She had planned her departure. She'd gone, easing her conscience with the certain knowledge that her son would be well looked after by his adoring grandparents and with a godmother as back-up support. Nell knew for certain now that Polly had no intention of coming back.

Chapter Nine

Peg was vehement in her condemnation of Polly's departure and refused to even consider the idea that such things didn't always have a rational explanation.

'There's no excuse; no excuse at all,' she held forth emotionally later on over breakfast when Nell tried to suggest that perhaps Polly's judgement had been impaired by some sort of reaction to Joe's birth. 'If a woman is destitute or sick and simply doesn't have the means to look after her child, then maybe I could understand her being forced to abandon it, though I do believe that only death would part me from any child of mine. In Polly's case there is no justification for it at all. She's fit and healthy and has been given a good home here with us. God knows she's had enough support in looking after young Joe. She just doesn't want the bother, the selfish little cow.'

'We don't know what was going on in her mind, though, do we, Auntie?' Nell pointed out, wanting to give her friend the benefit of the doubt. 'You must admit that she hasn't seemed herself lately.'

'There's no point in your defending her, Nell, because my mind is made up. I'm sorry if that seems harsh but I cannot condone her behaviour. I know she's a friend of yours, but what she's done is nothing short of wicked.'

'She could have been confused and not thinking straight,' ventured Nell.

Peg had the warmest of hearts, but her feelings on this issue were entirely governed by the strength of her emotions for her son and grandson.

'Confused, my Aunt Fanny!' she burst out. 'She knew exactly what she was doing. She planned it, she must have done. She even got the christening arranged before she left; no doubt to ease her conscience.'

Nell couldn't argue with that so she stayed silent.

'I knew she wasn't right for my Ed the minute I set eyes on her,' Peg went on, clearly very distressed. 'With her flighty ways and her vulgar turn of phrase. I knew she wasn't our sort from the start, but I made the effort for Ed's sake. She's proved me right, as it happens. And don't think I'm glad about that, because I'm not. I wanted Ed to have a long and happy marriage.'

'Ed!' Nell blurted out, pausing with her porridge spoon in mid-air, her brow creased with worry. 'What is this going to do to him? He absolutely adores her.'

'Yes, he does,' agreed Peg, pale and anxious. 'It's awkward with him being away, isn't it? What are we going to do?'

'Nothing until he comes home on leave,' Tom stated categorically. 'We certainly mustn't write and tell him while he's away at the war and in danger. His spirits need to be kept up, not destroyed so that he gets careless.'

'We can't keep something as important as that from him, though, can we?' said Nell.

'Perhaps Polly will write and tell him herself,' suggested Peg. 'Though I don't suppose she'll have the nerve.'

Nell was certain that Polly wouldn't write and tell him. The way she had calculated her departure indicated that when she had walked out of here this morning, she had intended to cut her ties altogether with this period of her life, with no explanation to anyone. She obviously didn't realise the crippling effect of her actions. If she had, she wouldn't have gone. Surely even Polly couldn't be that cruel.

'But if he doesn't hear from her, he'll wonder why, and worry,' Nell suggested.

'Mm, there is that,' agreed Peg. 'We don't want him worrying. That's the last thing he needs.'

'The mail is very unreliable for the services, so maybe he'll just think that her letters have been held up,' suggested Tom hopefully. 'I really don't believe we should write and tell him, not if it can possibly be avoided.'

Peg nodded in agreement, and Nell knew she must abide by their decision.

'We'll have to tell Polly's parents, though,' Peg mentioned gravely. 'Joe is their grandchild after all, even though they've never shown the slightest bit of interest in him. They need to know what their slut of a daughter has done to him and to my son.'

'Steady on, Peg,' urged Tom. 'There's no need to resort to gutter language.'

It hadn't been suggested by anyone that Polly might have fled to the arms of her parents, Nell observed. They all knew it would be the last place she would go, and that she would have been given short shrift if she had. The Browns had made it clear that they hadn't approved of her pre-marriage pregnancy, and had paid no attention to their grandson whatsoever.

Anyway, as Polly apparently wanted nothing more to do with her son, she wouldn't risk living in the same neighbourhood. God only knew what would become of her, fretted Nell. As far as she knew, she didn't have any friends outside of the area.

Nell didn't want to hurt Peg by mentioning it while the older woman was still so upset, but she was worried about Polly. Her friend was shallow and selfish, it was true, and what she had done was callous in the extreme, but surely there must be a reason for it. Something must have made her want to leave.

Being a mother herself, Peg knew the power of the maternal bond, so would naturally be unable to understand how any woman could abandon her child. Even without such experience Nell found it hard to comprehend. But she was afraid for Polly, rather than angry with her. The grass was always greener for her, almost as though she had a self-destructive streak.

'Gone off and left her baby, you say? Gawd Almighty, what next? First she disgraces us by getting herself pregnant the wrong side of the blanket; now she's buggered off,' said Polly's mother with harsh disapproval. 'She's always been a selfish little madam.'

'She didn't disgrace you by getting pregnant, because Ed married her and no one was any the wiser.'

'Don't make me laugh; they would have guessed she was already expecting, since the wedding was arranged in such a hurry,' claimed Mrs Brown. 'People aren't stupid, you know. They can count and they would certainly have counted the months between the wedding and the birth.'

'It doesn't matter what other people think,' said Peg. 'The important thing is that they were married and respectable long before Joe was born. Thanks to my son.'

'Thanks to your son,' repeated Polly's mother, her voice rising to a shout. 'He was the cause of all the trouble in the first place. Men like him want locking up.'

'It takes two,' Peg came back at her. 'And I'm sure your daughter was a willing party, if not the instigator.'

It was the evening of the same day, and Nell had gone with Peg to see Polly's parents. Tom was looking after the baby at home, and Polly's father wasn't in.

'He should have been more careful and shown some sense of responsibility,' ranted Mrs Brown.

'Responsibility?' blasted Peg. 'You've got the cheek to accuse my son of not being responsible when your daughter has just walked out on her own child? Maybe if you'd taught her to be a dependable human being with some sense of values, she wouldn't have done it and little Joe would still have a mother to love and look after him. It doesn't say much for the way you brought her up, does it?'

'Flamin' cheek,' said the other woman, lunging towards Peg and looking ready to throttle her.

'Calm down, the pair of you!' Nell thrust herself between them. 'This isn't helping at all. You're behaving like a couple of fishwives. Pack it in before it goes too far.'

'Mind your own business!' shouted Mrs Brown, giving Nell a hearty shove to remove her, then grabbing hold of Peg by the upper arms and shaking her hard. 'You evil old cow. It's all your fault. You should have brought your son up decently. You should have taught him some morals.'

To Nell's horror the two older women started wrestling with each other, slapping, punching and pulling one another's hair. Mrs Brown even tried to bite Peg.

'Come on now, Auntie Peg,' said Nell firmly, dragging her friend away forcibly. 'That's quite enough of that.'

'She started it,' claimed Peg, red-faced and dishevelled.

'I know she did, but there's no need to sink to her level,' advised Nell. 'Let's go home. Come on.'

'You're right,' said Peg eventually, allowing Nell to pull her away. Nell could feel her trembling. 'We've done what we came for. We've put the old bag up to date about her daughter. Now let's get out of here before we catch something.'

'Good riddance!' shrieked Mrs Brown.

As a parting shot Peg said, 'It's a good job young Joe has grand-parents who love him on their father's side; there's precious little on his mother's.'

'Get out, the pair of you,' ordered Mrs Brown, pushing them towards the front door and slamming it after them.

'It's no wonder Polly's the way she is,' remarked Peg as she and Nell walked down the street, both feeling a little shaky in the aftermath. 'Imagine having her for a mother.'

'It doesn't bear thinking about,' agreed Nell, feeling a stab of pain as she compared Mrs Brown to her own dear mother.

The peaceful nights continued, and Nell and Peg decided to bring the children home for Christmas. Evacuees had been returning to London in their hordes since the end of the Blitz, and it was generally agreed by the family that there was no point in leaving Lenny and Pansy where they were unless it was strictly necessary. It was arranged that Maud would bring them on the train and stay for the holiday, though the children would remain for as long as the bombs stayed away.

They were given a rapturous welcome from Peg, who was the only one at home during the day. 'It's so lovely to have you home,' she said, hugging them both.

'I shall miss them when I go back,' said Maud, looking sad. 'I've got used to having them around.'

'Stay here with us, then you can see them all the time,' suggested Peg warmly. 'You know you're welcome here on a permanent basis. You don't have to stay in Essex on your own. Unless you're worried about the air raids starting up again.'

'It isn't that,' explained Maud. 'I'm set in my ways at the cottage. I love the village and I value my independence.'

'Yeah, I know you do. Maybe after the war, when accommodation isn't so scarce, you can get a place and be independent here in London, with us close at hand,' Peg told her. 'Tom and I worry about you up there on your own.'

'We'll see.' They both knew she wouldn't leave her cottage in Waterlow until they carried her out.

Peg was in her element with the older children to look after as well as the baby, and the company of her mother-in law, with whom she had always got on very well. So, despite the drama of Polly's disappearance, Ed's continued absence, and the loss of loved ones, this Christmas was a cheery occasion, with paper chains decorating the house and gifts being exchanged, albeit less abundant than in peacetime. They played games, sang songs around the fire and relished the sweets that had been saved up for the big day.

Nell was delighted to have her sister home, and wept for joy when she first saw her. Pansy was still a thin, sensitive girl with a sweet smile and pretty features. But she was growing fast. She was ten now, and Nell was aware that she wouldn't be a child for much longer. She could see the first signs of incipient adolescence already.

Pansy was immediately besotted by the baby, as indeed were the rest of them. Joe never lacked for attention. Even Lenny, who thought babies were soppy, seemed to enjoy having him around, though he would never admit it.

It was surprising how quickly Nell got used to having her sister home, and it soon seemed as though she'd never been away. She seemed to be rather tense, though, and Nell had cause to be reminded of the trauma Pansy had been through, being sent away so soon after losing her parents.

'Are Lenny and I staying here?' Pansy asked her on Christmas night when they were both in bed.

'Unless the bombing starts again,' Nell replied cautiously. 'Why, didn't you like it at Granny Maud's?'

'Yeah, I liked it. It was good. Lenny and me had some great fun,' she said.

'You enjoy being with Lenny, don't you?'

She nodded. 'Oh yeah. Lenny's smashing. I just wondered if we were staying here . . . mostly because of starting back at my old school. It will be like starting a new one again.'

Nell's heart lurched. Had they done the right thing in bringing the children home, she wondered, given the disruption to their education if they had to send them away again? Maybe they should have heeded the government's warning and left them where they were until the war was over.

Then Pansy said, 'I quite liked it at Granny Maud's, but I'm ever so glad to be back. I missed you so much, Nell.'

'And I missed you too, Pansy,' she said with a lump in her throat. 'You can't know how much. I'm so glad you're back.'

'I wish we still had Mum and Dad, don't you?'

'Yes, I do, love. I really do. But we have each other.'

'Thank goodness.'

Whether bringing Pansy home had been the wisest decision remained to be seen, but from a personal and emotional point of view there was no question about it in Nell's mind. They were sisters and needed to be together so soon after losing their parents.

One day in March, a call came through to the news desk of the *Chiswick and Hammersmith Herald,* informing the paper of some sort of disturbance in a butcher's shop in Chiswick High Road. Nell was assigned to the job of covering it.

When she arrived, there was a large crowd outside the shop and a policeman was blowing his whistle like mad for assistance. After asking around among the gathering, Nell discovered that the butcher had a woman customer held hostage in the shop and was threatening her with a meat cleaver.

'She more or less accused him of overcharging her on her mince; suggested he might have tampered with the scales,' she was told by a woman who had apparently been in the shop when the incident had erupted. 'He went absolutely berserk; came out from behind the counter and grabbed hold of her, waving the cleaver and threatening to chop her head off with it. You've never seen a queue disperse so quickly.'

'I'm not surprised,' responded Nell. 'But is he usually a violent man?'

'No, not at all. He's a lovely fella as a rule and never even raises his voice,' the woman informed her. 'A real gent; very well liked and respected round here.'

'It's odd that he should do this now, then, isn't it?' probed Nell. 'She must have really upset him.'

159

'He's recently had news that his only son's been killed in action,' the woman explained grimly. 'It must have gone to his head, the poor devil. He's a widower too. He needs a doctor if you ask me, and something to calm him down.'

Nell made some shorthand notes and manoeuvred her way through the masses to where the policeman was trying to keep the crowd back. She showed him her press card and asked if there was anything she could do to help.

'Perhaps I can talk him round, Officer. Being a woman, it might just do the trick,' she offered. 'I'm quite prepared to go in there and have a try.'

'It's more than my job's worth to let a member of the public go in there,' was his firm response. 'Someone in that state of mind could do anything. I shall go in myself as soon as I get some assistance out here to control the crowd.'

Meanwhile some poor woman gets injured or even killed, thought Nell worriedly.

Gus saw the crowd in the High Road and edged near enough to make out what was going on, just out of curiosity. Then he saw her: Nell, the glorious brunette. She was right up there at the front and perfectly at ease talking to the copper. The way she handled herself, confident and engrossed in the matter in hand, filled him with admiration. She was simply amazing. It would be madness to approach her, and much too risky for himself at a personal level, but he could fight it no longer. Having heard from someone in the crowd what the problem was, he spotted a way to impress her.

'I'll go into the shop, Officer,' he said, having made his way to the front, pretending not to notice Nell.

'No, sir, get back, please.'

'And leave someone to get hurt or killed? Not likely!'

Before the constable could do anything to stop him, he had stepped into the shop. The butcher had the woman on the other side of the counter and was holding her from behind, the meat cleaver in his other hand. A white-haired man in a butcher's apron, who Gus judged to be his assistant, was standing in a doorway behind the counter, looking terrified.

160

Gus could tell at a glance that the butcher had reached breaking point and the customer was scared out of her wits. A small woman with a turban over her curlers, she was wide-eyed and pale with fright.

'Come on now, mate,' said Gus persuasively. 'Let the lady go. You've made your point and she knows that. Let's end this now before someone really does get hurt.'

'I've never cheated anyone out of so much as a farthing,' said the butcher, his voice shaking with emotion. 'I'm a good butcher and an honest businessman of long standing, and she implied that I was holding the scales down when I was weighing up the meat. I wouldn't do that.'

'I'm sure you wouldn't,' Gus tried to placate. 'I expect the lady knows that too.'

'I do know that and I'm sorry,' she blurted out, sobbing with fear. 'People say that some butchers put their thumb on the scales for a second when they put the meat on, and hold it down so it seems to weigh more. I was only mentioning what I'd heard. I wasn't saying that you did it.'

'You suggested it.'

'Sorry I said it. I didn't mean to upset you!' she cried. 'I've been buying my meat from you for years. I wouldn't do that if I didn't trust you, would I?'

'There you are, mate; she's apologised,' said Gus in a tone of quiet persuasion. 'Now why not accept her apology, give me the cleaver and we can all get back to normal?'

The butcher's face crumpled and he started to cry, releasing the woman, who scuttled from the shop.

Gus took the cleaver from the man without opposition. The butcher was sobbing. 'Get back to normal?' he ground out thickly. 'I'll never be able to do that, not now my boy's gone. Twenty-one years old, that's all he was.'

'I'm sorry, mate, I really am.' Leading him outside, Gus said to the policeman, who had now been joined by another constable, 'He needs someone with him.' He looked at the butcher, who was now trying to hide his anguish, because grown men didn't cry in the world he moved in. 'Is there anyone I can contact for you, mate?'

'Can you tell my assistant to keep the shop open, please? People have got to have their meat ration.'

'Course I will.'

'It's all right, sir,' the constable said pointedly to Gus. 'We'll look after him now.'

'He's having a bad time and is in a bit of a sorry state,' mentioned Gus. 'There's no harm done, so go easy on him.'

'Thanks for your help, sir,' said the policeman, politely ignoring Gus' request, and the two officers led the butcher away.

Gus went back into the shop and passed the message on to the butcher's assistant inside, then feigned surprise to see Nell standing outside, the crowd having dispersed and the queue quickly re-forming and snaking out of the shop.

'Well done,' she praised him. 'I thought you were brilliant, the way you handled that.'

'Why thank you, Nell,' he smiled. 'I didn't realise that you were around.'

'I'm always around when there's a story to be had,' she laughed, before adding in a serious tone, 'Mind you, I'd rather this particular story hadn't happened. Isn't it sad about the butcher?'

'Yeah, very.'

'I hope they don't send him to prison or anything,' she went on. 'I know he shouldn't have turned on that woman, but it's only because he was so grief-stricken about losing his son, the poor man. He doesn't have a wife to turn to either, apparently.'

'I should think they'll be lenient with him, but they have to uphold the law,' Gus pointed out. 'You can't have people swinging meat cleavers about with criminal intent, can you?'

She laughed because it sounded comical the way he put it. 'Not really, no.'

'You and I seem to have formed a bit of a habit of running into each other,' he mentioned.

'Mm, we do now you come to mention it,' she said casually. 'Are you not working today? A day off?'

'No such luck. I'm going in to the office now, as it happens. I'm on my way to the station to get the train. I've been out on a job.' He paused before adding, 'I can't say what, of course.'

'Of course not. How mysterious,' she said. 'It all sounds most intriguing. Exciting, really.'

'Not at all,' he told her with a nonchalant air. 'It's just a job. We all have our part to play in defeating the enemy, don't we?'

'Indeed.' She stuffed her pad into her bag. 'Well I must get back to the office and get my report typed up. I can already see the headline: "Brave member of public saves woman in butcher's shop siege".'

'That sounds a bit corny.'

'The subeditor writes the headlines, not me,' she told him. 'And that sort of thing sells papers.' She paused, shaking her head. 'Though these days the problem is finding the paper to print enough copies to sell rather than trying to sell more. We're having to tell our readers to share their copies with friends and neighbours. It's all very worrying. If the paper shortage gets much worse, it could drive us out of business, along with other newspapers.'

'That would be a pity.'

'A calamity, more like,' she said lightly. 'I've found something I love to do and I want to hang on to it for as long as I can.'

'Let's hope it doesn't come to that then.' He paused and looked at her, frowning slightly. 'By the way, I'd appreciate it if you didn't mention my name in the paper,' he said unexpectedly. 'Only in my line of work I'm expected to blend into the background rather than get myself noticed.'

'Oh . . . oh, I see. In that case I'll make sure your name isn't disclosed. I'll just call you someone from the crowd. That'll be sufficient.'

'Thanks.'

'No trouble at all. Anyway, I must go,' she told him. 'See you around, I expect.'

'Er, I was wondering if you might like to go out sometime,' he blurted, much against his better judgement. 'So that we can get to know each other. These accidental meetings must be telling us something.'

'Yes, I'd like that.' Perhaps she could have played a little harder to get, since he'd kept her waiting so long before making a move. But such tactics weren't in her nature.

'That's lovely. When would suit you?'

'Saturday night would be good for me,' she said, without a moment's hesitation.

'Saturday night it is then.' He sounded delighted. 'About seven thirty suit you?'

'That will be fine.'

'I'll come to your place to call for you.'

'I shall look forward to it,' she said with a grin. 'See you on Saturday, then.'

She walked down the road swinging her hips, her dark hair flowing past the collar of her grey coat.

He watched her go, wondering why on earth he was pursuing this course when it was so completely wrong for him, and knowing the answer immediately. She was gorgeous and he was smitten, and to hell with the consequences.

When she was out of sight, he went on his way. But he didn't go anywhere near the station . . .

'He's asked me out at last,' Nell told the family that evening when they were eating.

'You mean that Gus Granger bloke,' surmised Peg.

'That's right.' She looked radiant. 'You remember you all had bets on how long it would be before he asked me to go out with him? Well, he's asked me now, so you were all wrong because it took longer than any of you thought.'

'I still say he's too old for you,' declared Peg. 'You watch your step, love.'

'He's a decent enough bloke,' put in Tom. 'She'll come to no harm with him.'

'He's a man of the world,' Peg opined. 'You can tell that just by looking at him. He's probably known a lot of women.'

'There's nothing wrong with that,' defended Tom. 'I speak as I find and he's always been perfectly pleasant to me.'

'I'm not saying he isn't a thoroughly nice man,' said Peg, ever protective of Nell. 'But I think he'd be better suited to someone older who's been around a bit like he has. Nell is young and fresh; she doesn't have a past as far as men are concerned.'

'Do you mind?' interrupted Nell in a light but definite tone. 'I am here, you know, and I'll form my own opinion. It is just a night out, not a lifetime commitment.'

'We know that, love,' said Peg. 'Sorry to be interfering. It's only because

164

we care about you and know that your mother would want us to look out for you.'

'I know, Auntie, and I appreciate it,' said Nell in an understanding manner. 'But I can look after myself.'

'I'm sure you can. I'll keep my nose out,' said Peg, having no intention of doing any such thing.

'Is this Gus bloke going to be your regular boyfriend then?' enquired Pansy.

'Oh heavens, it's far too early to make predictions like that.' Nell was adamant. 'I'm beginning to wish I hadn't said anything, the way you're all carrying on about it. I am going out with him for one night, so stop making it into more than it actually is.'

Pansy looked worried.

'What's the matter?'

'Nothin',' she said, but there was obviously something troubling her. It was written all over her.

The conversation turned to more serious matters: the fact that coal was going to be rationed.

'We won't feel it so much now with the winter behind us,' said Tom, who had been reading about it in the paper before coming to the table. 'But they reckon there'll be real trouble next winter if they don't resolve the crisis. A shortage of miners is the main problem. They drafted too many of them into the army and war factories. Though there are transport difficulties too, and unrest among the remaining men working down the mines.'

'Oh well. We'd better make sure we've got plenty of hot-water bottles then, hadn't we?' suggested Peg chirpily. 'Though they're not all that easy to get hold of either these days. Oh well, never say die.'

'What's the matter, Pansy?' asked Nell later when she went up to the bedroom to say goodnight to her sister.

'Nothin',' Pansy said again, with a shrug.

'Why are you so worried about my going out with Gus Granger?' Nell wanted to know. 'The others will all be here while I'm out. It isn't as though I'm going to leave you on your own.'

'I know that.'

'Why the long face then?'

Pansy stared at the bedcovers and didn't reply.

'Come on, Pansy, tell me what's the matter. Now that you're back I want you to talk to me about things.'

Pansy looked up, her huge brown eyes like sad pools in her face. 'If you get married you'll go away.'

'Get married!' exclaimed Nell. 'Good grief, I haven't even been out with the man yet, let alone thought in terms of marrying him. That really is taking it too far.'

'You might like him; then you'll think about it.'

'Not for ages. I'm a long way from getting married to anyone, love, I can promise you that,' proclaimed Nell. 'I might not even want to see him again when I've been out with him once.'

'But you'll get married some time, and when you do you'll go and live somewhere else, won't you?' Pansy said anxiously. She paused, staring at her fingernails. 'You'll go away and forget all about me.'

'I will never do that,' Nell assured her emphatically, taking her hand. 'Surely you must know that.'

'I sort of do . . . but you'll live somewhere else, so everything will be different.'

'It depends what the housing situation is at that time,' Nell told her. 'But yes, married people do usually have a home of their own. So I expect I will too, eventually.'

'Will I stay here?'

'No. Wherever I go, I will take you with me while you are still young enough to want to come,' she told her. 'I will never desert you, Pansy. The only reason I sent you to live with Granny Maud was because of the bombs.'

'I know. But people do go away,' said the young girl. 'Mum and Dad did.'

'Well I'm not going to, so you can stop worrying,' Nell told her emphatically.

'Promise?'

'I promise.' She grinned and introduced a lighter note, even though she was worried about her sister's fretting. 'Anyway, you might be grown up before I find someone daft enough to want to marry me. You might even beat me to it and get married before me.'

Pansy smiled. 'Silly,' she said.

'It could happen; you never know.'

'I doubt it.'

'We'll see. Off to sleep now,' she said. 'Nighty night.'

'Night, Nell.'

Tiddles stalked into the room, jumped up on to the bed in a propri-etorial manner and settled down to sleep. Pansy cuddled and stroked him, giving Nell a pleading look because he wasn't really allowed on the beds.

'Don't worry, I won't tell Auntie Peg,' Nell told her. 'I'll put him out when I go to bed.'

'Thanks.'

'It's all right.'

Nell didn't leave the room with an easy mind. Her sister was still acutely vulnerable and Nell wanted desperately to make her life safe and stable. But there was only so much she could do. The powers behind the events that had caused her sister's insecurity in the first place were beyond her control. It was very worrying.

'Well, what do you think?' asked Gus on Saturday night. 'Do you approve?'

'Yes, it's very nice,' Nell replied, glancing around the nightclub he had taken her to in the back streets of the West End. It was dimly lit with a small dance floor and individual tables set around it. Unlike the loud and joyful big band sound, the colourful lights and exuberant gaiety she was used to at the dance halls, here a five-piece band was playing discreetly in the corner. The number was 'The Last Time I Saw Paris' and a few couples were moving slowly round the dance floor, which was hazed with cigarette smoke. Most of the people here were in an older age group to Nell and far more sophisticated. Some of the men were in uniform but quite a few in civvies, which was unusual these days. The civilians were possibly beyond military age; others were in the same sort of reserved occupation as Gus, she assumed. 'I've never been to a place like this before.'

'I didn't think the cinema was a good idea because you can't talk, and I thought it would be nice if we did some of that as we don't really know each other.'

'It was a good choice. I simply adore dancing,' she assured him cheer-fully. 'Though I'm more used to places like the Hammersmith Palais.'

Given her age and class he'd already assumed that, but had deliberately avoided the Palais because it would be packed with servicemen of all nationalities. Not being in uniform himself, he stood out like a sore thumb and was vulnerable to insults. There was also the possibility that Nell might compare him unfavourably with the younger men in uniform. Anywhere too expensive might seem tasteless to a girl with a social conscience like her in these hard times, so he'd chosen somewhere reasonably priced but more intimate than the Palais or the Lyceum. He guessed that anything too ostentatious would be anathema to her.

But he said by way of explanation, 'I didn't suggest that because it's so noisy you can't hear yourself think, let alone talk, and I'd like to get to know you better. Maybe we could go there another time, if you would like to.'

'This is fine really . . . I didn't mean . . .'

'I know you didn't,' he assured her in a gentle tone. 'So relax and I'll order us some drinks.'

As the sizeable gin and orange took effect, Nell began to relax and feel more comfortable.

'You look lovely,' Gus complimented her.

'Thank you.' She was a wearing a white blouse with long sleeves and a boat neck over a royal blue taffeta skirt she'd made out of an old dress. He was looking as traditional as ever in a smart grey suit with a waist-coat and a dark blue tie. 'So do you. But then you're always very smart.'

'A suit and tie is compulsory for the office, so I suppose I'm in the habit.'

Nell was really beginning to sparkle and enjoy herself now. When he asked her to tell him about herself, she didn't hold back about recent tragic events.

'As I said before, I'm very sorry about your parents,' he said sympathetically.

'Yeah, me too. But thank you for you kind thoughts.' She looked at him. 'What about you? Do you live with your parents?'

'Good God, no,' he responded, adding quickly, 'I mean, I left home years ago.'

'Do you see them often?'

'No, not often; they've gone to stay with a relative in Somerset because of the bombing.'

168

'I expect you miss them, don't you?'

A brief hiatus, then, 'Well, yes, of course.'

'Do they normally live near you?'

'In London, but not local to me. Their home is in Plaistow.'

'Is that where you're from originally?'

He nodded.

'East End boy made good, eh?'

'Not really,' he said, studiously modest. 'I've just made the most of opportunities that have come my way.'

'So where do you live now?'

'On the borders of Chiswick and Hammersmith,' he explained. 'I've got a little flat there, it's very central. I'm within walking distance of Shepherd's Bush too, if I want to get the tube there.'

A flat. Blimey! She didn't know any other unmarried person who had their own flat. Everyone in her circle lived at home until they got married, and some stayed there even after that because accommodation was so short. Still, he was older. A man of his age wouldn't still live at home.

'A flat of your own,' she said. 'I am impressed. You're lucky to get that.'

You could get most things if you were willing to pay over the top for them, he thought, but said, 'One of the perks of the job. They have to find us accommodation in London so that we're within easy reach of the office.'

'Of course. I suppose they would do.'

Sensing that he may have made himself seem privileged, which would probably put her back up, given the sort of person she was, he added, 'It's only very small; tiny, in fact. Little more than a rabbit hutch really.'

'Nice, though, to have a place of your own.'

'You won't hear me complaining.'

Anxious to show his sympathetic side, he leaned forward and touched her hand in a comforting gesture. 'I really am sorry about your loss.'

'Thank you.'

'I expect it will get easier with time.'

'So they say . . . but anyway, we mustn't get maudlin on our night out, must we?' She grinned at him saucily. 'Why don't you ask me if I'd like to dance?'

He laughed and she found him devastatingly attractive, his deep velvet

169

brown eyes drawing her to him. 'Why, you forward young hussy,' he teased her.

'Well if I wait for you to ask, I might grow old in the process,' she giggled.

'Come on then,' he said, and the tenderness in his tone warmed and thrilled her.

He led her on to the dance floor where there was a slow waltz in progress. She felt as though she was floating as they moved around the floor.

'I hope they have a jitterbug later on,' she mentioned as they went back to the table.

'I'm a bit out of my depth with that sort of thing, I have to admit,' he told her.

'I haven't had a chance to get to grips with it properly yet either, but I'm dying to learn.'

Her exuberance was captivating and he couldn't wait to have her in his arms again. But if he rushed things too much, she might be frightened off.

'Perhaps we can learn together then,' he suggested.

'Good idea. There are a couple of Americans in here, so we'll watch them,' she suggested.

The last thing he wanted to do was to make a damned fool of himself on the dance floor in front of some of those big-headed Yanks who'd started to invade this country since America had come into the war, showing off their smart uniforms and flashing their money about. But he couldn't tell her that so he said, 'I'm game if you are,' and hoped the situation didn't arise.

They danced the night away, and Nell was so happy she was flying: waltzes, quicksteps, the rumba, a tango, and she even began to master the jitterbug with the help of some American GIs who were only too willing to take centre stage on the floor and demonstrate the dance with their partners. Gus didn't seem very keen at first, but he put a brave face on it and seemed to be enjoying himself when the music came to an end.

'I've had such a lovely time,' Nell enthused when he took her to her front door. He had brought her home in a taxi as they had missed the last train. 'Thank you so much.'

'Thank *you*,' he said. 'I've enjoyed every moment. Can I see you again?'

'Yes please,' she agreed at once.

'I don't think I can wait until next Saturday. How about one evening in the week?' he suggested. 'Are you free on Wednesday?'

'I can be.'

'I'll call for you about seven thirty, then.'

'You'd better make it eight o'clock in case I can't get away from work in time.'

'Sure.'

He kissed her lightly on the cheek, then turned and walked down the street. She stood there glowing by the door before pulling the key through the letter box and letting herself in. What a smashing bloke he was. She was really looking forward to seeing him again.

Chapter Ten

Nell's second outing with Gus was as pleasurable as the first and they began to see each other on a regular basis. They went dancing, to the cinema, had tea at Lyons in the West End and walked in Hyde Park on a Sunday afternoon. It was great fun for Nell, and her feelings for Gus were growing stronger. He became a regular visitor at the Mills home, and seeing Nell so happy, even the circumspect Peg began to warm to the idea.

'It isn't as though the age gap is all that big,' she conceded one morning when the family were together at breakfast. 'There's not twenty-odd years between you or anything. I must say, Nell, the two of you seem so right together it's beginning to look like a match made in heaven.'

'I said from the start he was a decent bloke, didn't I?' Tom reminded her.

'I've never suggested he wasn't, dear,' she pointed out. 'I just wondered at first if he was a bit too worldly for Nell, being quite a bit older and more experienced.'

In all honesty, by the time spring turned to summer, Nell was enjoying herself so much, she didn't care what anyone else thought of Gus. Anyone else, that is, except her little sister, who had taken against him from the start, claiming that he had 'horrid mean eyes'.

'He isn't going to come between you and me, Pansy,' Nell had assured her on several occasions, assuming that this was the reason for the child's dislike. 'I still intend to keep my word. I won't leave you, I promise.'

'I won't come with you if you marry *him*,' Pansy declared hotly. 'I'll stay here with Auntie Peg.'

'Who said anything about my marrying him?'

'You want to, don't you?'

Things hadn't got that far yet, but the idea didn't displease Nell, even though she did sometimes feel as if she didn't really know him. 'He hasn't even asked me, so don't think about it.'

'Anyway, I'm not the only who doesn't like that Gus,' stated Pansy one day when they were all having breakfast. 'Lenny doesn't like him either. Do you, Len?'

'No, I don't,' Lenny confirmed. 'He's a slimy creep.'

'Lenny,' admonished his mother, spooning bread and milk into Joe's mouth as he banged happily with a spoon on the tray of his high chair. 'That isn't nice, especially as Gus is kind enough to give you and Pansy chocolate. It's very generous of him, especially now that sweets and chocolate have gone on to ration.'

'Quite right, Auntie,' supported Nell. 'I shall tell him not to do it any more as they're so horrible about him.'

'Good, that will save us having to make a big thing of saying thank you to him,' Pansy retaliated. 'He only does it to show off anyway, so that you'll like him even more.'

'You don't refuse to take the chocolate, though, do you?' challenged Nell.

'It would be rude to do that, and you'd soon tell us off,' responded Pansy.

'If he's dozy enough to give his sweet ration away, we'd be mad not to take it,' the forthright Lenny pointed out. 'It's funny that he always gives us chocolate, though. Never aniseed balls or acid drops.'

'Why, you selfish young article,' rebuked his mother sternly. 'You should be grateful that he gives you anything at all.'

'I am, Mum, very grateful,' he told her. 'I'm just saying that it's funny that he always gets chocolate.'

'That's probably because he doesn't know anything about kids,' suggested Pansy. 'If he did, he'd know that we like sweets better than chocolate.'

'I'm disgusted with the pair of you,' declared Nell. 'You sound like a couple of spoilt brats, and you don't deserve his kindness.'

The clank of the letter box announcing the arrival of the post ended the discussion.

★ ★ ★

Despite the very best efforts of the forces postal service, the delivery of letters resembled London buses, in that there were none for ages then three or four came at the same time. Which was exactly what had happened to Ed's letters home. There were three addressed to Polly and one to Peg, Tom and Nell jointly, the latter mentioning the fact that Ed hadn't heard from Polly and wanting to know if everything was all right with her and the baby.

'Now what are we going to do?' Peg enquired of Nell, showing the letter to her after she and Tom had both read it. 'We can't just ignore it, can we?'

'I think we should write and tell him the truth without further delay,' said Nell when she'd finished reading it. 'I know you don't agree with me, Uncle Tom, and probably every magazine agony column would advise against giving bad news to someone who's away at the war, but he's obviously out of his mind with worry, and that can't be doing him any good. It's obvious now that Polly isn't going to write to him to explain things.'

Peg nodded. 'Nell's right, Tom,' she said.

'He needs to know what's happening here and that his baby is being well looked after,' Nell went on, her opinion influenced by her friendship with Ed. 'I know we agreed not to tell him, but now that he's been in touch to say that he hasn't heard from Polly and is worried, I think we should. He's got a strong enough character to cope with it. Just think how he's going to feel if we don't tell him and he comes home. He says he's hoping for some leave soon.'

'He can't tell us where he is so we don't know how long it'll be before he gets here,' Peg pointed out. 'Given how long it's taken for these letters to arrive, ours might not reach him in time.'

'At least we'll have tried,' Nell pointed out. 'He'll never forgive us if we keep it from him after knowing that he's concerned about Polly. He'll never forgive me anyway. You're his parents; it's different for you. But I'm his friend, so I see it from a different perspective. I'd certainly want to be told something like that and would expect a friend worthy of the title to tell me. But he's your son so I'll have to leave the final decision to you.'

'We'll talk about it tonight,' said Tom, rising. 'I'll be late for work if I don't get going.'

Nell had it on her mind all day, and when Peg and Tom told her that evening that they had decided to write and tell Ed, she felt even worse, imagining him reading the letter and knowing how hurt and miserable he would be. It was at times like this that she had furious feelings towards Polly. How could she have done this to someone like Ed?

It was Nell's preoccupation with the letter and Ed's problems in general that caused her and Gus to have their first real falling-out that same evening. They were having a drink together in a pub in the back streets near Marble Arch.

'I think you should forget all about Ed Mills' private affairs,' Gus said after he'd coaxed her into telling him what was worrying her. 'It isn't as if you're even related to him.'

'He's a very dear friend, Gus,' she explained. 'I've known him all my life and we're like brother and sister.'

'So you have told me, but strictly speaking, it isn't any of your business; someone else's marriage never is,' he said tartly. 'Your best bet is to steer clear.'

'I have no intention of interfering in his marriage, which appears to be over anyway,' Nell made clear. 'I am simply concerned about his reaction to the news that his wife has walked out on him and their baby. It's a huge thing to have to come to terms with, especially when you're away at the war.'

'You should distance yourself from it altogether,' he advised her in an authoritative manner. 'It's his life, not yours.'

'How can you say that when I've just told you that he's a very close friend of mine?' She was angry and upset now. 'Do you not have a friend you really care about?'

'At this moment all I care about is the fact that you are getting yourself upset over something that is nothing to do with you, and spoiling our evening together.'

'So it's yourself you're concerned about and that's plain selfish,' she snapped.

'All right, so I'm selfish,' he said with a shrug.

'If you're fond of someone you don't just turn away in times of trouble, and I can't turn away from Ed just because it offends you.'

'Are you sure this Ed Mills is just a friend?'

'I certainly am.'

'It doesn't sound like it to me.'

Because her relationship with Ed really was so straightforward, Gus' suggestion stung her and she stared at him furiously. 'How dare you say that there might be anything other than friendship between us? That is horrible.'

'Is it any wonder I'm beginning to have doubts, the way you're carrying on?' he said accusingly. 'You are out with me for the evening and thinking about some other bloke the whole time.'

'I've told you, Ed Mills isn't some other bloke,' she made clear. 'Not in that way.'

'He's a man, isn't he?'

'His gender is irrelevant. He's been a part of my life for as long as I can remember and I hate to think of him being unhappy,' she declared. 'What's the matter with you? Are you made of stone or something?'

'I think you know that I'm not.'

'You're behaving as if you are,' she objected.

He looked at her, his eyes narrowing. 'How would you like it if I was to witter on about some other woman the whole time when I was out with you for the evening?'

'I've told you that Ed isn't another man as such,' she made abundantly clear. 'And I was not wittering on.'

'Yes you were.'

'Well if I'm such boring company, maybe I should I go,' she threatened.

'Don't be so ridiculous.'

'Oh, so I'm ridiculous too, am I?'

'When you carry on like this, yes, you most certainly are,' he informed her brusquely. 'You're behaving like a child; a spoiled one at that.'

'Perhaps you should find someone of your own age then,' was her parting shot before she leapt up and marched across the bar and out on to the street.

Watching her swing across the room, making heads turn, Gus didn't move. He had every intention of going after her but not until she'd had a few minutes to calm down and worry because he hadn't immediately done so. He knew exactly how long it would take her to walk to Marble

Arch station, and he also knew of a short cut so that he wouldn't miss her. He was infatuated with her but not so far gone that he had lost all sense of tactics. He was far too experienced in the ways of women for that.

It was becoming increasingly obvious to him that there was only one way to achieve his aim and get Nell into bed, and that was to make a serious commitment to her. An engagement ring was the very least it would take. On the odd occasion that he'd taken her to his flat, she'd made it clear that anything beyond respectable canoodling was definitely not on her agenda at this stage. Moreover, he'd had to promise not to tell Peg or Tom Mills that she'd even been at the flat with him on her own because they wouldn't approve.

It wasn't that she wasn't passionate and sexy, or that she was prudish. It was simply that she'd had it drummed into her psyche not to succumb to the unmentionable until there was a ring on her finger. The war had created the current climate of live for today and encouraged some girls to be more flexible with their favours, but Nell wasn't one of them, un-fortunately.

Marriage to someone like Nell could be disastrous for a man in Gus' position and he was hoping it wouldn't come to that. Seeing her in the evenings was one thing; living with her quite another, and very damaging to the privacy that was so essential to him. But he'd do it if he had to; though only as a last resort. If he wanted Nell Porter and there was no other way, then that was the price he was going to have to pay. And he did want her; by God he did.

He daren't rush it too much with Tom Mills and his wife hovering in the background like a couple of minders. Falling for someone as good and wholesome as Nell did have its drawbacks, but it added spice too. He wasn't going to wait too long before he moved things to another stage. Patience never had been one of his virtues.

Meanwhile he needed to put things right in the here and now. He finished his drink and left the bar.

Nell's fury drained away as she walked to the station and was replaced by a burning sense of compunction. How could she expect anyone else, espe-cially her boyfriend, to understand the nature of the special friendship she had with Ed? However worried she was about Ed, she shouldn't have let it dominate her evening with Gus. She'd been well out of order and it was no wonder he was angry, especially as she'd said such horrible things. He hadn't come after her, so perhaps she had gone too far and lost him.

The thought frightened her because she didn't want to lose him. Panic rose, and as the station entrance came into view she turned and began to run back to the bar, only to meet him coming towards her.

'I'm so sorry, Gus,' she said, full of contrition. 'I really am. I shouldn't have . . .'

'Wittered on . . .' he suggested, teasing her.

'Yes, all right, if you say so,' she conceded, pleased to smooth things over. 'Will you forgive me?'

'I might consider it,' he told her with a half-smile. 'As long as I don't hear another word about Ed Mills tonight.'

'That's a promise.'

'Let's go back and take up where we left off then, shall we?' he suggested, smiling. She really was the most beautiful girl and he adored her. The fact that she was more of a challenge than he was used to only added to her appeal.

Nell was popular with her work colleagues and they teased her in a friendly way about her romance.

'She's got her head in the clouds, isn't that right, Doreen?' Frank said to Nell's replacement one day when she brought some tea through to the reporters in the main office.

'And why not?' enthused Doreen. 'You're only young once. There's plenty of time to come down to earth later on when the newness has worn off.'

'I admit that I'm smitten with him, but my head isn't so far up in the clouds that I've lost my powers of observation as to what's going on around me,' Nell told them. 'And I noticed that Percy Wood is out of prison now. I saw him strolling along Hammersmith Broadway yesterday.'

'I wonder how long he'll manage to stay out of trouble this time,' said Frank.

'Maybe he'll go straight,' suggested Nell.

'Maybe Hitler will become a monk,' grinned Frank.

'You could be wrong about Percy, you know,' Nell persisted. 'People do change.'

'Not people like Percy,' said Frank with conviction. 'The right side of the law is a foreign country to him. Anyway, he's got someone else pulling his strings.'

'I'd love to find out who it is and get them put away,' stated Nell. 'And that goes for all the big-time black marketeers.'

'You won't get involved in anything like that on my time,' declared Ted, coming out of his office to speak to Doreen and overhearing the conversation. 'You've more than enough to do covering ordinary local events without digging around in the underworld for a story to spice things up. We're a local fireside paper, remember, not the *News of the World*.'

'I wasn't thinking of spicing things up; just getting justice,' Nell told him.

'The same rule applies,' said Ted. 'You could get hurt delving into that sort of thing. There are dangerous men involved in it. You can guarantee that when there's big money being made.'

'Danger doesn't worry me.'

'Well it does worry me and I am your employer, so forget it.' He was adamant.

'It just seems so wrong, that's all,' she went on. 'I mean, we're all only human and most people wouldn't say no to the occasional under-the-counter tin of fruit or extra piece of meat, but dedicated villains making a fortune out of the population's deprivation is wrong.'

'Yes, it is wrong, and there are trained police officers to deal with wrongdoers; not junior reporters on my paper.'

'I should concentrate on your lovely man if I were you,' advised Doreen lightly. 'He sounds a real smasher.'

'He is,' confirmed Nell.

'Oh no! You shouldn't have reminded her of him,' laughed Frank. 'She'll go all starry-eyed again.'

'Starry-eyed or not, I still get the job done, don't I?' she reminded them.

'We can't argue with that,' agreed Frank.

'And when I've had this cup of tea I'm going to have a chat to a war hero back from the front,' she told them. 'I set the interview up the other day.'

'Initiative, that's what I like to hear,' approved Ted, thinking again what a valuable asset to the team she had become.

When Nell got home from work one evening in August, she found Peg looking pale and grave.

'Ed's come home on leave,' she told her.

'Oh, how wonderful.' Nell looked at her, puzzled. 'So why the long face?'

'He didn't get our letter.'

Nell's hand flew to her head. 'Oh no. So he didn't know that Polly had gone?'

'Exactly. We should have taken your advice and written and told him right after it happened, but we left it too late and the letter didn't reach him; it must have got lost.' Her eyes were clouded with worry and sadness. 'Oh Nell, it was heartbreaking; he came in full of beans expecting Polly to be here. Of course, I had to tell him straight away.'

'Where is he now?'

'He's gone out for a walk; he said he needed to clear his head,' Peg told her grimly. 'Oh Nell, I'm so worried about him. The poor boy was devastated.'

'I'll go and see if I can find him,' she offered. 'He's probably gone down to the river.'

'Oh, would you, love,' Peg said gratefully. 'Tom isn't home from work yet and the baby needs seeing to.'

'I'll go right away.'

She found him sitting on a wall in Chiswick Mall in the evening sunshine, staring unseeingly towards Chiswick Eyot, where families of swans were preening with a proprietorial air.

'I thought I'd find you here.' This had been a favourite haunt of theirs as children.

'Some friend you turned out to be,' he said bitterly. 'You could have let me know, Nell.'

She explained why she hadn't, and reminded him that there was a letter in the post to him somewhere.

'Anyway, would it have hurt you any the less for knowing when you

181

were away from home in God only knows what danger?' she asked. 'You couldn't have done anything about it, could you? And it might have upset your concentration and cost you your life, at least that's your dad's theory. I couldn't go against your parents' wishes, Ed. We all only had your interests at heart.'

'I know,' he conceded miserably. 'Sorry, I shouldn't have taken it out on you.'

'That's what friends are for.' She pushed herself up and sat on the wall next to him. 'Though I'm blowed if I know what to say to make you feel any better.'

'Why, Nell?' he asked. 'Why did she go? Was it the usual reason: another bloke?'

'I honestly don't know why she left because she said nothing to me about it at all, but I'm absolutely certain that wasn't the reason,' she told him.

'She always was a terrible flirt,' he reminded her. 'I remember how she was all over me that night at the firm's dance. I'd never met a girl like her before. Talk about forward. It was all her; she took all the initiative. I was like a gormless schoolboy compared to her. She would be the same with someone else.'

Nell shook her head. 'She changed a lot after Joe was born,' she told him sadly. 'So much so you would hardly have known her. She didn't go out anywhere except with the baby to the shops and so on, so she wouldn't have had a chance to meet anyone. She was much quieter than she used to be; almost like a different girl.'

He stared at the river, which was waning with the tide to reveal dark, slimy mud. 'Why would she just go like that?' He put his hands to his head in anguish. 'What sort of a woman would walk away and leave her baby? All right, leave me if she has to, but not a poor defenceless child. That's wicked.'

'As I've just said, Ed, I have no idea why she went. I was as shocked as anyone because she gave me no hint of her intentions.' She paused, mulling things over. 'I've turned it over and over in my mind and I don't believe that her leaving had anything to do with you or Joe, not directly anyway. It was something within her; some troubling influence that made her run away, probably with nowhere to go. She knew her baby would

182

be well looked after, even getting me to be his godmother as back-up support for your parents.'

'And that makes it all right, does it?'

'No, of course it doesn't,' she said sympathetically. 'I'm just pointing out that she didn't leave her baby exposed to danger on a park bench or with strangers.'

'Why are you defending her?'

'I just feel that there must be more to it than there seems,' she tried to explain. 'I suppose I'm just hoping to make sense of it.'

'I wouldn't waste your time,' he advised harshly. 'She's a selfish little bitch who doesn't want the bother of bringing up her son. There's nothing more to it than that.'

Nell shrugged, looking sad. 'You could be right, Ed. I really don't know,' she said. 'Polly was self-centred, I know, but she never struck me as heart-less.'

'She's proved you wrong now, hasn't she?'

'Maybe.'

'I tell you one thing, Nell,' he began, anguish turning to anger, 'if she ever does turn up, she's not going to see Joe. I shall make absolutely sure that Mum and Dad are in no doubt about that.'

'She's still his mother, Ed, whatever she's done. She has a right to see him.'

'When she walked out on him she gave up all rights as far as I'm concerned,' he stated categorically. 'She is not going to pop back into his life just when she feels like it, causing him upset and disruption. She'll never see him again.'

Nell deemed it wise not to comment further on the subject. 'I should concentrate on getting to know your son while you're at home and try to put Polly to the back of your mind if you can, though I know it isn't easy,' she suggested. 'At least when you go back you'll know Joe is in good hands. He's got the whole lot of us doting on him.'

He managed a watery smile. 'He's a fine boy,' he said, swelling with pride. 'I didn't realise he'd be so big. He was crawling about all over the place when I arrived.'

'He'll be a year old in October,' she reminded him. 'He'll be walking soon.'

'I hope he isn't going out to work before I get home again,' he said with a wry grin.

'That's better,' she encouraged. 'You're getting your sense of humour back.'

'I don't know about that. It's just a question of accepting that she's gone and doing my best for Joe, as limited as I am in that while I'm away.'

'That's the spirit.'

'I think we ought to go home now,' he said. 'Mum will be wondering where I am. I shouldn't have taken off like that. It wasn't fair.' He shook his head slowly. 'It was just such a shock I needed to get away and be on my own.'

'If we look sharp, Joe might still be awake.'

'Let's step on it then.'

Together they hurried away from the river and headed towards the town.

It warmed Nell's heart to see Ed taking such an interest in his son over the next few days; getting down on the floor and playing with him and making the little boy chuckle and show off the deep dimples in his cheeks which he had inherited from his father.

On a Sunday morning – if she didn't have to go into work and the weather was fine – it was Nell's habit to take Joe for a walk in his pram to see the ducks on the river. It gave Peg a breather and a chance to get on with preparing the Sunday dinner, and Joe loved it. He would squeal and shout for joy when the ducks came into view and Nell would squeal with him.

'He enjoys this, doesn't he?' observed Ed, who had gone with her this particular Sunday. 'He's a proper little champion. It'll be hard to leave him when I have to go back.'

'Don't even think about it yet,' she advised. 'You've still got a while to go.'

'You're very good with him, Nell.'

'Am I? That's probably because I love him so much.'

'You'll be wanting a baby of your own soon.'

'Eventually I will, yes. I'd love a family of my own,' she said with enthusiasm.

Ed had only met Gus briefly when he'd come to call for Nell the other night, but he hadn't struck him as the family-man type. It was most unfair of Ed because he didn't even know the man, but there was something about him that made him sense that he wasn't right for Nell. Quite what it was, he couldn't be sure. The man didn't dress flashily or behave in an arrogant manner. He was a polite, amiable individual. But somehow his persona didn't ring true. Even his ordinary mode of dress seemed staged somehow. Everybody knew there were spies about, pretending to be ordinary and mingling with the general public. There had been a lot of talk about it since the outbreak of war. Oh really, Ed admonished himself, now he was getting paranoid just because he couldn't take to the man.

Anyway, he had no intention of upsetting Nell with his thoughts, so he just said, 'You'll have to have a word with that boyfriend of yours then.'

'All in good time,' she responded. 'He'd have to make an honest woman of me first.'

'That goes without saying.'

Ed did hope he was wrong about Gus because Nell was obviously mad about him and he didn't want her to get hurt.

Gus was no more impressed with Ed than Ed was with him. In fact he wasn't at all pleased to hear that Nell was seeing a lot of Ed; going for walks along the riverside with his kid and spending time with him at home. The sooner Ed Mills went back to sea, the better.

'It was just a walk by the river with the baby,' Nell said when Gus made his feelings known on the subject rather forcibly that evening on the way to the cinema. 'Surely you can't possibly object to something as innocent as that.'

Oh but he did. Very much! 'Of course I don't object,' he lied. 'I just don't see the necessity for it. If he wants to walk his baby in the pram he should do it on his own.'

'It's me who walks the baby and today Ed came along as he was at home,' she explained. 'That's all there was to it. Anyway, men don't usually walk their babies, do they? It's a woman's thing.'

'Why do you have to walk the baby anyway?' he demanded. 'It isn't as if it's yours.'

'He isn't an it, he's a he,' she admonished. 'And I think you're being really horrible.'

'I was only trying to point out that the child isn't your responsibility,' he told her.

'Not legally he isn't, I'm well aware of that. But from a human point of view he is. Anyway, I'm his godmother. I want to be there for him as much as I can. His mother deserted him, for heaven's sake. It's up to the rest of us to give him plenty of love and attention to try and make up for it. I don't have to take him out, you know,' she informed him. 'I do it because I want to. I love little Joe and enjoy doing things with him.'

'So what else do you and Ed do together?' Gus asked, his jealousy of Ed making him overbearing. 'Living in the same house there must be ample opportunity.'

'If you're suggesting what I think you're suggesting, you're well out of order.' She threw him a furious look. 'How dare you say a thing like that to me?'

Uh-oh, she was on the verge of stomping off again. Prompt action was required. 'I wouldn't dream of suggesting that anything untoward was going on,' he corrected quickly. 'I meant that you must do quite a bit of talking. You obviously know each other very well.'

'Well of course we do plenty of talking,' she told him. 'We eat at the same table; we sit in the same room. But I'm out at work all day and he often goes out for a pint of an evening.'

That was a relief, he thought. 'I didn't mean anything, you know.' He was keen to make amends now. Because he felt seriously threatened by Ed Mills, he'd allowed himself to get careless enough to seem possessive.

'I hope you didn't, Gus, because as I've told you before, Ed is a very dear friend of mine and I don't want that friendship sullied by any sort of insinuation. If going out with you gives you the right to own me, then we'd better finish it now.'

'Don't be silly, Nell, that's the last thing I want.'

'Look . . . I want the two of you to get along because you both mean so much to me, in different ways.' She paused, remembering something. 'In fact, you'll have the chance to get to know each other better on Saturday night, because Peg and Tom are having a bit of a party for Ed at the house and I'd like you to be there.'

Frankly, Gus would sooner chew rusty nails than spend an evening cooped up with the Mills Gestapo, all of them keeping a beady eye on Nell's wellbeing. Ed Mills would be lording it over him too, because he was in uniform and Gus wasn't. Thank God the wretched man was going back to join his ship soon. Being away didn't entirely stop him from being a threat, though, not while there was a postal service in existence. His wife had left him so he was probably looking for someone to replace her, and Nell was the obvious person. Drastic action was needed on Gus' part, and he knew suddenly what he must do to secure Nell's affections.

'I'll look forward to it,' he said smoothly. 'I'd like to get to know Ed and the others better. Sorry I was a bit touchy before.'

'Don't worry about it,' she said, taking his hand in hers. 'I know you didn't really mean it.' She smiled that brilliant smile of hers that made all the effort on his part worthwhile. 'I'm so looking forward to Saturday.'

'Me too,' he said and he meant it now. Suddenly Saturday had taken on a whole new significance.

Most of Ed's pals were away in the services, so the gathering was largely made up of neighbours and friends of the family, though Barney, one of his mates from the factory who the firm had refused to release for military service, was there.

There was a good atmosphere, especially when the booze kicked in. Pansy and Lenny were making themselves useful by taking the sandwiches round and running up and down the stairs to check on Joe, who was, miraculously, sleeping through it. But it was never a quiet house; there were always people coming and going, so he was accustomed to noise.

'So you've seen some of the world then, mate,' Barney said to Ed when some of them were standing around chatting with drinks in their hands. 'It must be a great experience.'

I've experienced plenty of other stuff too, thought Ed. Cold so deep in his bones he could have wept, exhaustion to the point where he could barely keep his eyes open, and fear that paralysed him when the ship was damaged by torpedoes and almost went down. But there was also magnificent comradeship, a new understanding of the elements and the excitement of going ashore in foreign countries.

'Yeah, it is. It's an eye-opener, I can tell you.'

'Is it true what they say about sailors? A different girl in every port and all that?' asked Barney.

It hadn't been for Ed, because he'd thought he was a married man, but the opportunities had been there and lots of the blokes had welcomed them with open arms. Ed had got drunk a few times with the rest of the lads but he'd been faithful to Polly, ironically enough as it turned out, he thought, with a piercing stab of pain.

'Surely you don't expect me to answer a question like that when my parents are within earshot,' he said, laughing it off.

'No, I don't suppose you would,' the other man grinned.

Everyone joined in the laughter. It was a warm late summer evening and the French doors to the small garden were open. Some of the guests were outside, though the lawn now sprouted vegetables instead of grass.

'I think the navy is the service I'd fancy if I was allowed to go in,' said Gus, who was being especially nice to Ed – even though he couldn't stand the sight of him – because he knew it would please Nell.

'I was in a reserved occupation too,' said Ed pointedly. 'But I still went in. I was determined about it. I volunteered, and because the navy needed my skills, the firm didn't have much choice but to let me go.'

'You're lucky, mate,' said Gus. 'My employers just wouldn't release me.'

There were some people, especially the relatives of dead servicemen, who would say that he was the lucky one, thought Ed, but he didn't want to upset Nell so he just shrugged and said, 'Oh well, we all have to do what we're told these days.'

'Let's get this party going,' suggested Tom. 'We need some music to liven things up.'

The man from next door sat down at the piano and everyone started singing, most of it out of tune but with a great deal of heart and unity.

'Are you enjoying yourself?' Nell asked Gus.

'You bet.'

'Thanks for making such an effort with Ed,' she said. 'It means a lot to me.'

'I know it does, which is why I've done it.' He finished his beer. 'Actually, I need to speak to you in private.'

'In the middle of a party, you'll be lucky.'

'It's really important.'

'You don't half choose your moments,' she teased him. 'The house is packed with people. There's not a square foot of privacy to be had anywhere. Even the usable bit of the back garden is full of people, and you want a private word.'

'Where there's a will,' he said, taking her hand and leading her to the front door and out into the tiny garden, closing the door behind them, 'there's a way.'

'What's all this about?' she asked with a half-smile, giving him a curious look.

'I won't keep you in suspense. I'll come straight to the point,' he said in a brisk, efficient tone. 'Will you marry me, Nell?'

She was so shocked she just stared at him. Of course she had hoped for this but she hadn't expected it yet. Nor had she expected a proposal that had been couched in such a way as to suggest that he'd been offering her a job.

'Shall I get down on one knee?'

'No, of course not.'

'What's the matter then?'

'Isn't love usually mentioned in a marriage proposal?' she asked.

'That goes without saying. Of course I love you. I wouldn't have asked you otherwise.' Honestly, why did women always want everything packaged with trimmings? Why couldn't they be content with the bare facts?

Nell let out a nervous giggle because she was feeling so emotional. 'There's no need to sound so aggressive about it.'

'I didn't mean to.' He needed to calm down and turn the romance up or this proposal was going to fail and he was going to look a right idiot. 'I love you, Nell, you must know that,' he said, softening his tone and trying to inject some feeling into it, 'and I want to marry you, more than anything in the world.' He dipped into his pocket and took out a small box. 'I hope you don't think it presumptuous of me to get this, and if you don't like it I can change it.' He opened the box to reveal a ring set with a cluster of diamonds. 'Well, what do you say?'

'Oh Gus, it's beautiful,' she said, warming to the idea now that his attitude had changed.

'Can I put it on the appropriate finger?'

She frowned. 'I would love to marry you, Gus, and I don't want to

189

spoil your big moment,' she told him. 'But I'm afraid my little sister Pansy and I come as a package. I can't marry you unless I can bring her with me after we're married.'

After we're married! Hang on a minute, he almost said aloud. Engagement was one thing; marriage quite another, and he had no plans to venture into that particular minefield unless there was absolutely no alternative.

'Of course you can bring her with you,' he said with feigned sincerity. 'I naturally assumed she would come with you. I'll try to get to know her a bit better before then too.'

'Oh Gus, that is so kind of you,' she praised him. 'Some men wouldn't be prepared to take a child as well.'

'I want whatever makes you happy,' he said.

'In that case, the answer is yes.'

He slipped the ring on her finger and kissed her. 'Shall we go and tell everyone?' he said.

'Let me tell Pansy on her own first,' she requested. 'So that I can explain that I won't be deserting her when we get married. I'll go and do it now, then we'll tell the others.'

He couldn't wait to wipe the smile of Ed Mills' face, and this diamond badge of ownership should do the trick very nicely.

'Whatever you say, sweetheart,' he said with a victorious smile. 'Whatever you say.'

Nell took Pansy up to their bedroom to tell her the news.

'Oh,' said Pansy dully.

'I won't leave you when we get married,' she assured her. 'Gus has said I can bring you with me.'

'Oh,' Pansy repeated in a flat tone.

'I was hoping you'd be pleased for me.'

'I do want you to be happy.' She was sitting on the edge of her bed, picking at her fingernails. 'It's just that everything will change again. I want us both to stay here.'

'We can't stay here for ever.'

'Auntie Peg would probably let us, because Mum was her best friend,' suggested the young girl.

'She probably would, but I love Gus and I want to marry him.'

'Perhaps I could stay here without you.'

'It would spoil it for me if you did,' Nell told her.

'That isn't fair,' objected Pansy. 'Why should I have to live with *him* just because you want to?'

'Why don't you like him?' asked Nell. 'Apart from the fact that you think he's going to take me away from you?'

'It isn't just that.'

'What is it then?'

'I dunno. I suppose it's because he isn't like Uncle Tom or Ed,' she said.

'In what way isn't he like them?' Nell was curious to know.

'He's different. He doesn't make me feel the same as they do,' Pansy tried to explain. 'He makes me feel cold inside.'

'That's only because he doesn't know the family very well yet, and he isn't used to children.'

'He makes me feel the same as Miss Harrison at school does,' Pansy further enlightened her.

This was something of a shock to Nell, because Miss Harrison was the headmistress of the junior school, an authoritarian who terrified the life out of all the pupils.

'Are you saying he frightens you?'

'I'm not sure exactly . . . I don't know what it is. I just don't feel comfortable when he's around. I can't help it, Nell.'

'Look, he's going to try harder to get to know you. Will you give him a chance? It means a lot to me.'

'All right, I'll try.'

'You can be my bridesmaid if we can get the material to have pretty dresses made when the time comes,' Nell told her. 'Would you like that?'

'Yes please.' She was obviously trying her best, but her effort wasn't convincing

But Nell said, 'Good girl. With a little effort on both sides I'm sure you and Gus will soon be the best of friends.'

She wasn't as confident as she sounded, though. Although Peg and Tom welcomed Gus into their home, he wasn't like one of the family and she sensed that he never would be. Pansy was right about him being different; he was an outsider somehow. There was something indefinable about him that set him apart from the people in her world and made her sometimes feel uncomfortable when they were all together.

But she loved him; that was the important thing. So she would go and tell him that they could go ahead and announce their engagement without further delay.

Ed took the opportunity to have a few private words with Gus later on when people were beginning to leave. When Gus went into the kitchen to get a drink, Ed followed him.

'I hope you're planning on treating Nell right,' he said, keeping his voice down so that the others couldn't hear.

'Oh yeah?' said Gus in a questioning manner, meeting Ed's eyes. 'And what exactly do you mean by that?'

'The flash engagement ring might impress her, but it doesn't have the same effect on me.'

'Why would I want to impress you?' Gus asked, with unconcealed victory in his eyes. 'You're nothing to me.'

'Nell's a lovely girl and she's had a hard time, losing her parents and her home. The last thing she needs is someone like you doing the dirty on her.'

'Why would I do that when I'm in love with her?'

'You don't strike me as the type to settle down,' Ed told him. 'You wouldn't be the first man to put an engagement ring on a girl's finger without the slightest intention of following it through to marriage. There are men who think a ring will give them certain privileges, and when it suits them they move on.'

'What do you know about anything? You're not much more than a boy,' said Gus.

'Don't make me laugh,' responded Ed. 'I became a man the day I signed up to go and fight for my country. Seeing action is the fastest way I know of growing up.'

'There's more to manhood than fighting in a war,' claimed Gus. 'And I hope you're not suggesting that I am somehow inferior to you because I am not in the services or that I wangled my way out of it.'

'I'm suggesting nothing as far as that is concerned,' Ed made clear, deeming it wise to keep those particular thoughts to himself. 'But I will say that I hope that the ring you've just given Nell hasn't been used before.'

Gus squared up to him but changed his mind almost immediately, realising that he was in the presence of superior physical strength. Ed Mills was a super-fit sailor and Gus wasn't prepared to risk getting hurt. Not likely! No woman was worth that.

'I don't know what sort of stories you sailors tell each other when you're away at sea, but you're barking up the wrong tree with that one,' he said.

'I hope I am too, for Nell's sake,' Ed told him in an even tone. 'I don't want to receive a letter from her saying she's had her heart broken.'

'It won't be broken by me,' Gus assured him coldly. 'But there wouldn't be a thing you could do about it anyway, would there, since you'll be in the middle of some ocean somewhere, being a man.'

Ed was about to take a swing at him when his father came into the kitchen.

'Oi, oi, that's enough of that,' commanded Tom, standing between the two of them and pushing them apart. 'Whatever the problem is, you're not sorting it in here. We don't have fighting in this house and we don't want the women upset. This is supposed to be a happy occasion and I won't have it ruined.'

'Sorry, Dad,' said Ed and marched from the room.

Watching Ed say goodbye to his son at the end of his leave brought tears to Nell's eyes.

'You be a good boy now for Daddy,' he was saying. 'No running about the streets making mischief.'

They all laughed, because Joe was still only at the crawling stage. He gave his father a beaming smile, revealing some newly acquired teeth, and held his arms out.

'All right. One last cuddle then,' Ed said thickly, taking the child from his grandmother and holding him close. 'Now you be good for your gran and grandad and Nell.'

The little boy squirmed and chuckled, indicating that he wanted some fun. His father lifted him high, then brought him down again with a whoop so that the child was beside himself with delight, cheeks pink, wispy golden hair flying.

'You'd better go, son,' said Peg gravely. 'Time is getting on and you don't want to miss your train.'

Ed nodded, handed the baby back to his grandmother, kissed her, shook his father's hand and gave Nell a peck on the cheek and told her to take care of herself. After he had bent down and ruffled Lenny and Pansy's hair, he was gone, swinging down the street, bell bottoms flapping.

Ed felt most embarrassed as he hurried down the street to the bus stop because tears were running down his cheeks. Never in his life had he felt emotions as strong as he felt for his son. It was everything: love, joy, protectiveness, an aching need to care for him and be with him. He had never felt so vulnerable in his entire life and would give anything to be with Joe to watch him grow up.

How Polly could have left him was completely beyond his understanding. Had she not experienced the same bond he felt with their child? Had she not brimmed over with love for him and experienced ineffable pleasure just at the sight of him and the feel of his smooth baby skin? The mere thought of him being left without his mother made Ed want to cry even more.

The personal sense of pain and rejection he had felt at Polly's departure was as nothing compared to the agony of having to leave his son now. Thank God he had good and caring people to look after Joe. The responsibility of parenthood was immense, but so was the joy.

His reverie was interrupted by two young boys. 'Can we touch your collar for luck, sailor?' asked one of them.

'Course you can,' he said, blowing his nose and composing himself as they jumped up in turn and touched the square white collar on his back.

The mental image of his family standing at the gate would stay in his memory for a long time, he knew that. Mum holding Joe, Dad beside her, Pansy and Lenny with Nell in the middle with her arms around them. He ardently hoped that he was wrong about Gus and that the man treated her right. He really did want her to be happy. Please God, keep them all safe, he entreated silently. Please keep them safe.

Chapter Eleven

One evening in October in a cinema in Kilburn, a slim young usherette was taking the customers' tickets and tearing them in half, then walking neatly down the aisle shining her torch and showing them to their seats. This was the final performance of the night, and when things quietened down the usherettes were allowed to stand at the back and watch the film, or sit down if there were any vacant seats.

When the flood of people became a trickle and eventually petered out altogether once the big picture had started, Polly stood at the back and fixed her eyes on the screen. The main feature this week was a film called *Belle Starr* about the American West's most notorious outlaw. The only good thing about it as far as Polly could see was the fact that it had Dana Andrews in it. He was gorgeous.

She wasn't particularly keen on the film but could enjoy watching anything in the dark and smoky auditorium just to feel people around her. Being here was a whole lot better then moping around on her own in her dingy room in an old house in the back streets of Kilburn with nothing to do but think and feed the gas fire with her hard-earned dosh.

All day she plied her trade as a shorthand typist in the offices of a munitions factory at Harlesden and in the evenings she came to work here. She'd chosen north-west London to flee to because she knew that no one from her old life would ever come here. This region of London had been unknown territory to her until she'd arrived one morning last year looking for a room and a job. The neighbourhood she now lived in had an anonymous feel about it, being made up of large old houses mostly converted into overpriced furnished rooms like hers. This suited her perfectly; now that she was alone, she didn't want to be among families, making her feel even more of an outsider.

Leaving baby Joe was the only thing she could have done under the circumstances, but it hadn't been as easy as she'd previously imagined. She hadn't expected an all-consuming feeling of pain and regret to spoil her freedom. Today had been particularly difficult because it was Joe's first birthday and she'd been thinking about him all day long, wondering if he was happy, what he looked like now, how many teeth did he have, whether he was crawling or walking.

None of that had been part of the plan. As she hadn't bonded with him as a mother should, she'd known she couldn't make a good job of bringing him up, so she'd left, intending to cut all ties with that disastrous part of her life. Physically she had made the break, but she hadn't reckoned on the guilt and anguish of wondering about him and – in a peculiar sort of way – missing him. Still, at least she was free, that was the main thing. The rest could be endured.

It was a question of knowing her limitations, and she'd known without a shadow of a doubt that motherhood was quite beyond her capabilities. So what else could she have done but leave? You couldn't be a good mother if you hated the whole business of being a parent and didn't love your child in that special maternal way that everyone talked about. She'd been stifled and repelled by the whole thing; terrified of the awesome responsibility, the constant attention a baby needed and the fact that she herself no longer mattered as a person because the child always had to come first. She'd resented the loss of her carefree days and the fact that she couldn't even put a bit of make-up on or go to the lavatory without making sure Joe was all right first. The burden of it all had torn her nerves to shreds to the point where she'd actually felt ill. She hadn't wanted to talk; she hadn't been able to eat. All she'd wanted was to escape.

In retrospect she could see that she hadn't given much thought – if any – to Ed because her mind and emotions had been focused entirely on Joe. Ed was all part of the baby package. She couldn't have one without the other. Being brutally honest, she doubted if she had ever really loved Ed. It had been all about lust with him. That was what it was all about with any man, come to that. This so-called 'love' thing people talked about was simply sexual attraction, which she'd had in barrel loads for

196

Ed Mills. And what had he done? He'd ruined her life by getting her pregnant. So much for her dream of a glamorous future now.

In this mood of self-pity, she chose not to remember her part in the affair; how she'd gone all out to get him and used every last vestige of her sexuality to achieve her aim.

Of course, she was well aware that her name would be mud all over Chiswick now for walking out on her child. Well, they could say what they liked about her. She had done the best thing for that baby. And it wasn't as though she hadn't left him in good hands. Peg Mills would make a brilliant job of bringing him up until his dad came home. Polly had even provided a godmother as extra security for him. Between them Peg and Nell would see that he wanted for nothing, and his father would support him financially, so she had nothing to feel ashamed of. And she wasn't going to. Nor was she going to let these sentimental thoughts fester. She'd made her decision and she would stand by it.

Now she came out of her reverie to realise that she'd been so pre-occupied with her thoughts she hadn't noticed that the programme had ended and people were standing for the National Anthem; those who hadn't slipped out just before. When all the punters had gone she went to the staff room to get her coat, said good night to the other usherettes and the projectionist, and left.

The darkness outside was total and she had to wait until her eyes had adjusted to it before she could go on her way, cautiously even then because there were so many hazards in the blacked-out streets. It was so damned annoying to find herself reliving over and over again the moment when she'd left her son. She'd packed her things the night before, then got up before dawn and given him his bottle, changed his nappy, kissed his fore-head and slipped from the house.

And at this moment she was very glad of the blackout because tears were pouring down her cheeks. It was this flamin' birthday thing, she told herself. Once it was over, she would feel better. She'd have to make a determined effort to do so, because she couldn't spend the rest of her life in torment.

Nell was thinking about Polly that same evening and wondering if she had remembered that today was her son's birthday. It seemed so dreadfully sad for her not to be with him today, because he really was the most adorable child; perfect at one year old with a flawless body, cheeky blue eyes and a smile that lit up everything around him. He could now pull himself up and walk tentatively around the furniture, and did so with a large amount of glee. It was a pity his father wasn't able to see him today too. Oh well, it wasn't as though little Joe missed them. He was too young to be aware of such things.

'Well, you've had a smashing day, young man; you've had some lovely presents and blown the candle out on the cake I managed to cobble together without the proper ingredients.' Peg was chatting to Joe, who was in his pyjamas ready for bed and playing happily with some wooden bricks on the floor, assisted by Pansy. Lenny was sitting on the box-end by the fire engrossed in his precious latest issue of the *Dandy* comic, which, because of the paper shortage, had had its weekly publication changed to fortnightly, alternating with the *Beano*. 'But it's time for beddy-byes now, darlin'.'

'Ooh, he's not going to like that one little bit,' observed Tom, who was sitting in the armchair reading the newspaper. 'He hasn't got an ounce of sleep in him.'

'He is tired, though, overtired probably,' remarked Peg. 'He didn't have much of a nap today.'

'I'll take him up if you like, Auntie Peg,' offered Nell, who helped whenever she could and had noticed that the older woman looked weary. 'I'll read him a story from his fairytale book. That usually sends him off to sleep.'

'It might take a while to get him off, love, and you're going out,' said Peg, glancing towards Gus, who had come to call for Nell and was sitting on the sofa waiting for her. 'You don't want to keep your young man waiting.'

Nell looked at Gus. 'Would you mind very much waiting a little bit longer?' she asked, giving him an uncertain smile. 'I'd like to give Auntie Peg a break, and I'll be as quick as I can. We're not doing anything all that special tonight, are we?'

Yes, he did damn well mind. He minded very much indeed. In fact he deeply resented the way Nell fussed over Ed Mills' brat. They were all besotted with the child in this house. It was ridiculous. Joe was only a baby like all

198

the others: noisy, mucky and altogether a flaming nuisance. All this palaver because it was his birthday, and he wasn't even old enough to understand.

Getting engaged to Nell had hardy been worth the trouble and expense. She still wouldn't sleep with him; nor did she treat him as though he was the only person in the world who mattered to her, which he considered his right as her fiancé. She nattered on about her precious job, and the wretched Mills family, and as for this baby; well, anyone would think it was hers the way she carried on. Surely Gus himself was entitled to the whole of her attention. He was the man in her life after all.

'No, of course I don't mind,' he heard himself say now. 'You take as long as you like.'

'Thanks, Gus, you are a sweetheart,' she said, kissing him lightly. 'It's no wonder I fell for you.'

'Anything for you,' he said.

Although he was extremely peeved, she had this way of winning him over, and she had done it again with her sunny smile and expressive brown eyes. This wasn't like him at all. He was usually in control where women were concerned.

Well he wasn't having it! He would have to take a firmer stand with her. He couldn't let a woman rule him like this. The irony of it was, she didn't even know she was doing it. She had no idea of the effect she had on him. It wasn't in her nature to be calculating or bossy or to know-ingly hurt anyone. It was just that she was interested in lots of other things besides him. She loved her job, adored the Mills family and took an interest in current events, the war and practically everything else on the planet. The women he'd been out with prior to her had only been interested in spending his money and having a good time, so he had always had their wholehearted attention.

Oh well, this was the price you had to pay when you fell for a girl as special as Nell.

'I was thinking, Nell,' he began, later that evening when they were sitting in a small pub by the river, 'that perhaps you might like to have your own key to my flat.'

She gave him a puzzled look. 'It's nice of you to offer, but what would be the point of it exactly?' she enquired.

'So that you could call in at any time you like; treat the place as your own,' he explained. 'You are, after all, only lodging with the Millses, aren't you?'

'No. I don't see it that way at all,' she was quick to point out. 'I feel completely at home there.'

'It would be nice to have somewhere to kick your shoes off and feel more relaxed, though, wouldn't it?' he persisted.

'I feel like that at Auntie Peg's,' she made clear. 'As far as I'm concerned, it is my home.'

'Well, yes,' he began, becoming edgy because she hadn't jumped at the chance. 'But I have a flat, and what's mine is yours.'

'Not until after we're married it isn't, Gus,' she said, knowing exactly what he had in mind.

He knew what she meant too, and it was something he intended to work on. He had to take it carefully, though, or risk having the whole Mills clan on his back. 'You'll be quite safe, I promise. Surely you can trust me not to take liberties? It just seems to make sense for us to spend more time there instead of sitting in pubs and picture houses to be together. If you had the key you could come straight from work if you felt like it, even if you got there before me. It would give us longer together. It isn't as though we get any privacy at your place, is it? No chance to be on our own.'

She'd been to his flat only a few times and had felt most uncomfortable there. She was always on her guard, because she knew things would get out of hand if he had his way. Even apart from that, she didn't like the feel of the place. It was clean and well furnished but miserable somehow and impersonal. There was no cosiness; perhaps because he was a bachelor and it lacked a woman's touch. She could see his point about the need for privacy, though. All these outings must cost him a fortune.

'We could go to your place sometimes instead of the pictures, if you like,' she suggested. 'But I don't need the key. I'll come when I know that you'll be at home.'

'I'm offering you a key, Nell, not asking you to move in with me,' he snapped.

'I know and I didn't mean to seem ungrateful,' she said apologetically. 'I was a bit surprised, that's all. I suppose because I've never had a boyfriend with his own place before. It's a whole new world to me.'

'As I have said, it isn't as though you can't trust me, is it?' he persisted. 'I know how strongly you feel about certain things and I respect that.'

Like hell he did. Given half the chance he'd have her in that bedroom saying goodbye to her virginity in a flash. He was a man; and as such he wasn't built for abstinence. It was all very well her wanting to save herself for her wedding night, but what about him?

'Yeah, all right then,' she agreed at last. 'If you'd like me to have a key, go ahead and get one done.'

Don't overdo the enthusiasm, he thought with irony. Honestly, some women would get down on their knees with gratitude to have what he was offering her; he was giving her the run of his home whenever she wanted it. It wasn't something he offered to just anyone. He had to be careful in his line of business. His privacy was paramount, which was why he had taken some necessary precautions before even mentioning the idea to her.

'I'll see to it then.'

'Thank you, Gus.' She didn't expect to be using it much, if at all, but he was keen for her to have it so she'd gone along with the idea to please him. 'It's very kind of you.'

Polly went straight from the factory to her spare-time job one Saturday in November to avoid being alone in her room. It was cold, foggy and dark and she was too early for her shift, so she went into a café near the cinema for a cup of tea to pass the time.

The place was steamy, smelled of stale cooking fat and was none too clean, but at least it was warm. She ordered her tea at the counter and sat at a table by the window with it, wondering how a girl with her good looks and personality could have sunk so low as to be sitting all alone in a greasy café on a Saturday night with only a shift as an usherette to look forward to. The old Polly would have been getting herself dolled up ready to go out at about this time. What had happened to the glamorous life she had yearned for? She was young, free and ready for anything, and there wasn't anything to be had besides boring work and loneliness.

She was definitely meant for better things than this. Elevation from ordinariness was something she had aspired to for as long as she could remember. Nell used to tell her to be content with what she had. Nell . . .

Oh no, she wasn't going to let that train of thought develop, because that would depress her even more. Thinking about Nell led to the Mills family, and that in turn resulted in thoughts of that damned baby, who was nothing to do with her any more. She didn't want to think about him. In fact, she refused to.

'You look as though you've got the worries of the world on your shoulders, and that can't be right. A good-looking girl like you should have the world at her feet.'

She came out of her reverie to see a man who looked to be in his early twenties standing by her table holding a cup of tea and looking at her with unconcealed admiration. This was more like it, she thought; a blatant flirtation. He wasn't bad-looking either; well built, with saucy dark eyes and black hair.

'Perhaps I have,' she said, rolling her eyes at him in her old flirtatious way and feeling all the better for it.

'You wouldn't be in here on your own on a Saturday night if you had,' he said, sitting down at her table.

'I don't remember asking you to join me,' she admonished, though she was very pleased that he had. She was beginning to feel almost normal for the first time since she got pregnant.

'You don't mind, do you?' he asked.

'Would it make any difference if I did?'

'No, not really.'

'You'd better stay where you are then, hadn't you?' she said, immediately at ease with him. 'I have to go soon anyway. I've got to go to work.'

'Are you doing night work in a factory, then?'

'No. Just the evening shift at the cinema. I'm an usherette. By night anyway. I work in an office during the day,'

'Ooh, an office girl, eh?' He seemed impressed. 'I thought so the minute I set eyes on you. That is one classy young lady, I said to myself.'

The boost to her seriously diminished ego was just what she needed. 'I bet you say that to all the girls,' she said

'No. Only you!'

They both laughed, because the remark was so obviously tongue in cheek

'Syd Becks,' he said by way of introduction.

'Polly Mills.' She had kept her married name because of her ration book.

And after that the conversation just flowed. He told her that he was single and had been invalided out of the army because of a chest wound. He worked on light duties as a labourer in a munitions factory, he informed her. Although he had a room in this area, his family lived in Slough.

She told him that she was a single woman whose family had been killed in the Blitz. It was easier than complicating matters with the truth. There was something about him that made her suspect there was more to him than he was admitting to, and he might be some sort of an outcast like herself. It didn't matter to her who he was or where he came from. He fancied her and she reciprocated; that was enough for now.

They were getting along famously when she realised that she had forgotten the time and was in danger of being late for work. 'I'll be in dead trouble,' she told him.

'That's my fault. Sorry,' he said.

'You're not to blame. I've enjoyed your company.' She had been so glad to have someone to talk to and to feel all her old impulses flowing again, she had lost track of time. But she wasn't going to tell him that. 'But I'd better look sharp now or they'll give me the sack.'

'Can I see you again?'

It was music to her ears. 'Yeah, if you like,' she said with feigned casualness. 'I'm not working tomorrow.'

'Neither am I, as it happens. So perhaps we could meet here in the afternoon,' he suggested. 'It'll probably be closed as it's a Sunday. But if we meet outside we can soon find something to do. We can go to the West End if you like for a wander around. It's only a short bus ride from here.'

'Yeah, that would be nice. See you tomorrow then,' she said, and left the café and hurried up the street to the cinema in the swirling fog, her mood much improved. In fact she felt better than she had in ages. Almost like her old self. Thank God she was free to enjoy life again!

They went to the cinema in Leicester Square and queued for ages to see *The Road to Morocco* with Bob Hope, Bing Crosby and Dorothy Lamour.

Afterwards they had tea in Lyons, chatting companionably.

On the bus on the way home in the evening she said, 'I've had such a nice time, Syd.' Because he was so easy to get on with and obviously keen on her, she saw no reason to hold back. 'Thank you.'

'Thanks for coming,' he said, squeezing her hand. 'I've enjoyed myself too.'

He insisted on seeing her safely to the door of the rooming house.

'Would you like to come in?' The fog of yesterday had cleared and it was a crisp moonlit night, so she could see his handsome profile, albeit dimly. 'I've got a bottle of Camp coffee and some milk and sugar. My room is very basic . . . well, a bit scruffy to be honest. But I've got a gas fire we can put on to make it cosier.'

He looked hesitant.

'There are no rules about visitors,' she assured him. 'The landlord doesn't live here and he couldn't care less what his tenants get up to as long as they pay the rent.'

When he still didn't respond, she felt as though she'd been too pushy and said in a prickly manner, 'Please yourself. I was only being friendly.'

'It isn't that, Polly,' he said, lowering his voice almost to a whisper. 'I haven't been honest with you.'

'Oh yeah. You're married, I suppose.'

'No, nothing like that.' He leaned towards her and put his mouth close to her ear. 'I wasn't really invalided out of the army. I came home on leave and never went back.'

'You mean you're a deserter . . .'

'Shush, not so loud,' he urged her in whispered tones. 'But yeah, that's it in a nutshell. And if I come in to your place I'll be putting you at risk because it's illegal to harbour deserters.'

'I suppose it would be,' she said, sounding unconcerned. 'But who would know about it?'

'They could catch up with me at any time,' he said furtively. 'They have ways of finding people like me. I spend my whole life looking over my shoulder'.

She took her key out of her handbag.

'Come on in, for goodness' sake, man, and forget about people being after you,' she said in a firm tone.

'You're taking a chance.'

'I'll risk it,' she said breezily, opening the door and ushering him inside.

After they'd made love, Polly and Syd sat in bed, smoking, drinking watery Camp coffee and talking, the gas fire making the room warm and cosy.

'I just couldn't face going back off leave that last time,' he confided. 'I suppose people would say that I lost my bottle and just brand me as a rotten coward.'

'Yeah. I reckon they would,' agreed Polly, who had never been known for her tact. 'But you can't help the way you are, can you? None of us can.'

'I just couldn't stand seeing any more killing; the blood, the stench of rotting human flesh, seeing mates die. Life means nothing out there, Polly. Death loses its meaning too because there is so much of it.' He paused, staring into space as though reliving the scenes. 'The fear was terrible. I was in absolute terror from morning to night. I just couldn't help it.'

'It must have been awful for you,' she sympathised. 'I'm glad I'm not a man. I'd probably do the same thing as you if I was and they sent me away to fight.'

'In the end I knew I couldn't do it any more,' he went on, seeming to need to talk about it. 'So I said goodbye to my folks in Slough as though I was going back off leave in the normal way, got the train into London and stayed here instead of getting the connection to join my unit. It's easier to melt into the background here with so many people passing through. There are ways of earning a living without papers, and no questions asked, too.'

'You poor thing.' She could feel him trembling against her. 'Shush,' she said, feeling sorry for him, which was unusual for her as empathy normally escaped her. 'Try and put it out of your mind. You mustn't let it haunt you or you'll drive yourself mad. What's done is done, so put it behind you.'

'You'd be better off not getting mixed up with someone like me,' he advised her. 'I'm just a rotten deserter.'

'We're two of a kind in a way, Syd. I haven't been honest with you either,' she explained, and went on to tell him the truth about herself and her circumstances.

'I just couldn't love that baby as a mother should, no matter how hard

I tried,' she confessed. 'I hated being a mother, absolutely loathed the whole thing. So I ran away, which makes me just as much of a coward as you are.'

'You're not the only woman to do that,' he said, in an effort to console her. 'You hear about that sort of thing.'

'It's usually when the mother is destitute, though,' she pointed out. 'I was far from that. I had a husband and a home and support from my in-laws. But I couldn't stay.'

'Far be it from me to blame you,' he told her. 'I'm in no position to judge anyone. And as we're being honest with each other, I might as well tell you that I don't really work in a war factory either. I can't get a job through the usual channels because I can't show them my papers, so I earn a living doing odd jobs at places where they don't ask questions. Cash on the nail and no paperwork involved. I do the cleaning in pubs and clubs, sometimes a spot of maintenance if there's anything that needs doing.' He inhaled deeply on his cigarette. 'My name isn't really Syd Becks either.'

'You're Syd Becks to me and I don't want to know any more than that,' she said. 'It'll be simpler that way.'

'You're right. The less you know, the better,' he agreed. 'You don't want to get involved in my mess.'

'You sound as though you regret what you did.'

'I'll say I do,' he admitted without hesitation. 'I hate living my life on the run; always watching my back; afraid of getting caught. Not being able to have a proper job. Most of all I hate the way I feel about myself and what I did.'

'Ashamed?'

'Not half!'

'You'll just have to tell yourself that soldiering wasn't right for you,' she suggested. 'The same as mothering wasn't right for me. It's just the way we are. Some people have all the right boxes ticked in their make-up. Others don't. You can't help the way you are; none of us can.'

'Being a mother is a hell of a lot different to being a soldier, though,' he pointed out. 'I mean, nobody wants to fight in a war, except a regular soldier perhaps. None of my mates wanted to be there and they were probably as scared as I was, but they stuck it out for the sake of their

206

country because they knew it was their duty. I didn't, so I've lost all my pride and self-respect.'

'If you feel as bad as that about it, you could always turn yourself in,' she suggested.

'I could do, but there's one thing stopping me from doing that,' he said.

'What's that?'

'I'm too much of a coward.'

Polly burst out laughing suddenly. 'What a pair we are,' she said. 'A right couple of drop-outs.'

Her laughter infected him and they both giggled until they were shedding tears.

'Oh Polly, you're a tonic,' he told her. 'You really are. You've cheered me up no end.'

'I feel a lot better since meeting you too,' she said with sincerity. 'I think we're good for each other.'

'I think so too.'

Because there hadn't been an air raid for such a long time, Nell was startled to hear the siren. She was on her way back to the office after covering a church bazaar to raise money for war orphans in Hammersmith. When the heavens opened with a sleety rain and the heel came off her shoe simultaneously, she found herself rummaging in her bag for the key to Gus' flat, which was just round the corner from where she happened to be.

What a blessing that she'd finally agreed to take the key. Somewhere out of the wet to have a short break was just what she needed. She could shelter from the rain, wait for the air raid to end and try to fix her shoe before she continued on her way.

His flat was over a greengrocer's shop in a small parade. It had its own private entrance. She didn't bother to knock because it was still only late afternoon and she knew he would be out at work; she just let herself straight in and went up the stairs.

It felt rather strange being in someone else's home when they weren't there; she felt intrusive even though he had invited her to come at any time. It was very still inside and smelled a bit musty, the air tinged with stale cigarette smoke and another familiar scent which she couldn't quite identify.

She had only ever been here before briefly; never long enough to use the facilities. Vaguely recalling having seen the bathroom once when the door was open, she went in there to find a towel to get the worst of the wet off her dripping hair. She gave it a good rub, shook her sodden raincoat over the bath, hung it on the hook on the back of the door and went in search of the kitchen to find something with which to mend her shoe.

It was an old building with high ceilings, sash windows and heavy interior doors, all of which were closed. She turned the handle of what she thought was the kitchen door and pushed. It didn't move. At first she thought it was stuck, but after turning the handle and giving the door several hefty shoves with her shoulder, she realised that it must be locked. How odd! She could understand him closing all his doors before he went out; it was supposed to be safer in case of fire. But to lock them seemed a bit extreme.

However, when she tried the door next to it, it swung open easily on to a bedroom, as did the door to the living room and finally the kitchen. It was just that one door that was locked. Oh well, Gus must have his reasons. She found a wooden spoon in one of the kitchen drawers and managed to do a temporary repair on her shoe by banging the heel back on to the tacks it had worked loose from. She'd have to take it to the shoe mender tomorrow to get it done properly. But this would do for now.

She could hear distant explosions outside so the raid was obviously in full swing. Going over to the window, she looked down into the street to see that it was still raining heavily. She could see drops running down the glass, and people in the street in the gathering dusk had their umbrellas up. Damp and shivering, she toyed with the idea of making a cup of tea to warm her up while she waited for the rain to ease off and the all-clear to go. But it wouldn't be right to use Gus' precious tea ration, even though she knew she would be welcome to it. He was very generous like that. The rationing never seemed to bother him.

The rain was beating on the windows as she wandered into his living room, cheerless and sombre with dark brown furniture and heavy flecked wallpaper in an assortment of dull colours. The gloomy atmosphere here was depressing and she couldn't wait to leave. Despite the driving rain and the continuing air raid, she fetched her raincoat from the bathroom and hurried down the stairs and out into the street, glad to be away from the place and vowing not to call in there again when Gus wasn't at home.

Naturally she didn't hurt Gus' feelings by telling him that his flat gave her the creeps, but she did mention to him that she'd been there, when he walked her home from the pictures that night. He seemed absolutely delighted that she'd taken him up on his offer.

'I told you that key would come in useful, didn't I?' he beamed. 'You should have made yourself some tea and put your feet up for a while. There were biscuits in the cupboard too.'

'I didn't want to use your rations,' she explained. 'Anyway, I had to get back to the office.'

'Oh well, another time,' he said casually. 'And never worry about using my rations. As I said the other day, what's mine is yours, as far as I'm concerned.'

'Thanks, Gus. It's kind of you, especially as we haven't even set a date yet.'

'You found everything you needed to dry yourself off?' he said in an enquiring manner.

'Yeah, luckily. I was soaked, so I was very glad of your bathroom towel.' She paused, remembering something. 'I tried one of the doors thinking it was the kitchen and it was locked. I wrestled with it for ages before I realised. Why on earth would you keep one of the doors locked inside your own flat?'

'Locked?' He gave her a dark look. 'Of course it wasn't locked. Why would I lock one of my inside doors?'

'Exactly.'

'It must have been stuck.'

'I don't think so, Gus. It felt locked to me,' she claimed. 'I struggled with it for ages and had to give up in the end. It didn't matter, though, because I found the kitchen elsewhere. I wasn't sure which room was which initially.'

'The door was not locked,' he denied again, his voice rising with anger.

'All right; keep your hair on,' she retorted. 'It makes no odds to me either way.'

'I'll have the key back,' he said, surprising her. 'I'm not having you poking around and accusing me of locking doors.'

'I wasn't poking around, and there's no need to get so upset, Gus,' she said in a tone of mild admonition. 'What you do in your own home is none of my business. It couldn't matter less to me if you keep every door in the place locked. I wish I hadn't mentioned it now. It was only a casual comment.'

'I need the key to leave with a neighbour in case of an emergency, and it's almost impossible to get one cut these days,' he explained, cursing the carnal desire that had led him to give her unlimited access to the flat. 'I wasn't able to get another spare one done as I'd intended, so I was going to ask for it back anyway.'

She took the key out of her bag and handed it to him, glad to be rid of it and keen to defuse the tension.

'Good, now that that's out of the way can we please drop the subject and talk about something more interesting?' she said. 'Like Christmas arrangements.'

'Yes, all right. What do you have in mind?'

'Auntie Peg told me to ask you if you'd like to join us for Christmas Day.'

'Oh, that's really nice of her,' he responded, but he sounded doubtful.

'You don't sound too keen.'

'Of course I'm keen,' he said sharply. 'You know that I always want to be with you. But . . . er, I won't be able to make it, I'm afraid. I'm ever so sorry.'

'Oh, that's a shame.' She couldn't hide her disappointment that he was planning to spend Christmas without her. 'I didn't realise you had already made other plans.'

'Duty calls, I'm afraid.' His mood was still somewhat aggressive. 'There's something I feel obligated to do.'

'Really?'

'I have to go down to Somerset to see my folks,' he explained. 'I'm taking a few days off work so that I can travel before the holiday when the trains are running or I won't be able to get there.'

'Oh well, it can't be helped, but I must admit that I was looking forward to our first Christmas together.'

Together! That was a joke. He wouldn't get near her with the Mills police around. 'Sorry, sweetheart, but I'd feel really guilty if I didn't go,' he apologised. 'It wouldn't be right of me not to make the effort at Christmas time.'

'Of course you must go,' she said approvingly. 'You only have one mum and dad. I'd make sure I spent Christmas with mine if they were still around.'

'I'm glad you understand,' he said, putting his arm around her and giving her an affectionate squeeze. 'I'll make it up to you when I get back. I promise.'

'Don't you worry about me,' she assured him. 'I'll be fine with Auntie Peg and Uncle Tom and the others. You make sure you enjoy yourself with your parents.'

His parents! He hadn't seen them for years and had no plans to do so. They were no more in Somerset than he was. He didn't even know if they had survived the Blitz. The East End had been heavily bombed so they might not have. It didn't matter to him one way or the other. Plaistow was merely the place he had originated from; it meant nothing to him, and nor did the people in it. He'd moved on from there a long time ago. His parents were just a memory; a memory that didn't come into his mind very often.

The thought of playing happy families on Christmas Day with Tom Mills and his family was too awful to contemplate – even if it did mean being with Nell – so he'd had to come up with a convincing excuse pronto.

Games with those ghastly children on Christmas afternoon and sitting round with the family in the evening listening to the wireless and strug-gling to make conversation, with a glass of brown ale and a wartime sausage roll, wasn't his style at all, especially as a good-night kiss and cuddle at the front door was all he would get from Nell with her minders around. No woman was worth putting himself through that. Not even Nell.

Now he said, 'We'll go out somewhere nice when I get back to London.'

'When will that be?'

'The day after Boxing Day,' he said, thinking fast to make sure his story was convincing. 'By then, with a bit of luck, the trains will be running normally again after the holiday; normal for wartime anyway, which isn't saying much.'

'You don't have to do anything special to make it up to me, Gus,' she told him. 'I really mean that. You're doing the right thing and I'm proud of you.'

She really was the sweetest and – fortunately for him – the most gullible of women, he thought. 'Thanks for being so understanding,' he said.

Chapter Twelve

'You decided not to send it after all then,' observed Syd when he arrived at Polly's place for Christmas dinner and noticed that the clockwork toy car she had bought as a present for her son was still on the shabby sideboard, one of the few pieces of furniture in the room. Besides this there was a bed and a wardrobe, two well-worn armchairs and a dining table and chairs. Polly had managed to get hold of a second-hand wireless set, which was on top of the sideboard. In the corner there was a partitioned-off area containing a small cooker and a sink.

'That's right,' she replied. 'There's no point in unsettling him, is there? It'll be better for him if I don't make contact.'

'He isn't old enough to understand, though, is he?' Syd pointed out, taking off his coat and hanging it on a peg on the door before sitting down in an armchair and putting the shopping bag he was carrying on the floor.

'Not now he isn't,' she agreed. 'But it'll be best for him if I don't set a precedent for later on, when he does know what's what.'

'Kids think their presents come from Santa Claus until they get quite big, though, don't they?' he pointed out, knowing how much she had wanted to send the present to Joe.

'There is that, I suppose,' she said, unable to hide a hint of wistfulness. 'But it's too late now, and I think I did the right thing in not sending it.'

'You must trust your own judgement,' he said tactfully. 'I wouldn't dream of interfering.'

He knew that she had been agonising over this for days. She pretended to be as hard as nails – and she was in some ways; by her own admission she was very self-seeking – but she was vulnerable as far as her little boy was concerned, though he doubted if she would ever admit it.

Syd had grown fond of Polly. She accepted him for what he was and he did likewise. They were both fully aware of the fact that they were flawed human beings; neither of them had anyone else, so they were glad of each other's company. Although they were lovers, they were pals too, and this was the first time he'd ever experienced such a thing with a woman.

Past relationships had tended to be fraught with tension and jealousy but this was a very easy-going one. He came and went as he pleased, sometimes staying overnight, other times not. Occasionally they went to the pub or the pictures; on Sundays they would take the bus to Hampstead Heath for a walk or go to the West End; other times they stayed in her room and listened to the wireless. If she wanted to be on her own she wasn't afraid to tell him so and there was no offence taken. Similarly if he didn't see her for a few days she didn't go on at him about it. Doing two jobs took it out of her and she was quite often exhausted. He understood that she needed to sleep and made himself scarce. It worked very well between them.

Now she was saying, 'Anyway, they probably wouldn't have given it to him if I had sent it; they hate me that much.'

'You don't know that, Polly.'

'It's obvious. I'd hate me too if I was in their position,' she said.

'They won't be any too happy with you for leaving Joe, that's for sure, but that doesn't mean they hate you,' Syd pointed out. 'I'm sure your friend Nell wouldn't have turned against you altogether.' Polly had confided in him fully about her past life. She'd seemed to need to talk about it and he was a good listener. 'She sounds nice from what you've told me about her.'

'She is nice, *very* nice; that's why she would hate me,' Polly tried to explain.

'Genuinely nice people don't hold grudges against their friends,' he said. 'They try to understand them; try to find it in their hearts to forgive.'

'Nell is a good person; really good, I mean. Not one of these self-righteous do-gooders. She seems to get everything right somehow; feels all the right things at the right time. So she wouldn't be able to understand why I left Joe because it's something she would never do herself.'

'You can't be absolutely certain that she wouldn't understand,' he suggested. 'She sounds the type who would have a damned good try anyway.'

'I'm not saying that she wouldn't try. I know she would do her damnedest but she wouldn't be able to understand,' Polly told him. 'Loving a baby would come naturally to her because she genuinely cares about other people. That's one thing I've never been able to quite get the hang of.'

'Oh Polly, you don't half put yourself down.'

'I'm only saying it like it is, Syd. I've had plenty of time to think since I left. I always knew I was different from Nell but couldn't work out why. I wanted to be like her because she is so popular, and the reason people like her is because she cares about them, or most of them anyway. I don't do that. I'm only really interested in myself.'

'You've taken an interest in me.'

'Mm, that's true. I must be going soft in my old age,' she said, laughing it off. 'Anyway, don't let's spoil Christmas Day by picking at old wounds. Let's have our dinner and get drunk.' She grinned. 'Though being that I'm not much of a cook and all I have had to manage with is a gas ring and an oven barely big enough to hold a chipolata sausage, maybe we should do that in reverse order.'

'Whichever way round we do it will be all right with me,' he assured her, taking a couple of bottles of spirits from his bag. 'I managed to get the ingredients to help us forget our troubles; that's one of the few perks of working at licensed premises.'

'You didn't nick it, did you, Syd?'

'No. Course I didn't,' he assured her. 'They gave it to me as a Christmas box.'

'Well done,' she praised. 'Sorry I haven't got any decorations to cheer the place up. There were none to be had in the shops. I looked every-where.' She paused with a sad look in her eyes. 'Of course, Christmas cards are a thing of the past for me.'

'Me too, but I've got one for you, and a present,' he said, producing an envelope and a package wrapped in newspaper. 'I couldn't get any wrapping paper, but happy Christmas anyway.'

'Thank you, and a happy Christmas to you. I've got a present for you too, but let's open them when we sit down for dinner, shall we?' she suggested.

'Suits me.'

Polly couldn't help comparing this Christmas Day favourably with the abysmal one she'd had last year a few weeks after she had walked out on Joe. She hadn't spoken to a soul all over the holiday and had been glad to get to the cinema on Boxing Day evening to do her shift so that she was among people.

She felt so relaxed with Syd. He was a bit rough and ready but he was quite nice-looking, and he was kind-hearted and good company. At least he'd taken the edge off the grinding loneliness with which this room – and indeed her life – was synonymous.

'Why don't you pour us both a large drink, while I put the vegetables on?' she suggested.

'Certainly,' he said, going over to the sideboard where the glasses were laid out ready. 'Christmas Day is no time to stay sober for people like us.'

'You never said a truer word, Syd Becks,' Polly agreed. 'The sooner we get blotto, the better.'

On Boxing Day, Nell, Peg and the older children came out of the Chiswick Empire and jostled through the crowds to the bus stop, having decided to take the bus rather than walk all the way home because it was so bitterly cold. They were all still smiling with thoughts of the pantomime.

'It was a good show,' said Nell.

'Not half,' agreed Peg.

'My favourite was the fairy godmother,' said Pansy, 'and I loved the dancing girls.'

'Buttons was the best of the lot for me; at least he made us laugh,' put in Lenny. 'There was too much singing and dancing the rest of the time. Every five minutes they were bursting into song. I thought, "Oh no. Not again."'

'Maybe you're getting too old for the pantomime,' his mother suggested.

'Don't say that, Auntie Peg,' put in Nell. 'When these two outgrow the panto, we won't have an excuse to go.'

'By the time they have properly outgrown it, Joe will be old enough to go, so we'll be all right for a good few more years,' grinned Peg.

'I wonder how Uncle Tom is getting on at home looking after him,' remarked Nell.

'He'll be in his element, I expect,' said Peg. 'Knowing how he loves that boy.'

'Joe will be keeping him on the go, that's for sure.'

They stood in the bus queue, hugging themselves against the cold. Dusk was just beginning to fall and the temperature was dropping, but the air was clear and still. Nell was feeling better than she had all over Christmas. Christmas Day itself had been almost unbearable, but Boxing Day brought a sense of relief because the whole thing was nearly over. Maybe one day she would be able to enjoy Christmas again, but memories of her parents were still too raw.

Thinking along these lines, she could see that it was probably just as well that Gus had gone away. She had been on the verge of tears all day yesterday, so wouldn't have been much company for him. She'd kept her mind occupied by playing with Joe, and Gus would have been bored stiff, bless him.

The bus came and everyone piled on, chattering and laughing; mostly they were the pantomime crowd discussing the show. Nell and the others managed to get a seat downstairs and Nell found herself by the window next to Peg; the children were sitting in front of them.

A sudden shriek from Pansy resounded throughout the bus. Then she and Lenny started poking and pushing each other and were jointly reprimanded by Peg.

'He started it,' claimed Pansy, turning around looking indignant. 'He was pulling my plaits really hard.'

'Pack it in. Lenny,' admonished Peg.

'I only gave them a little tweak because she prodded me first.'

'No I did not, and it wasn't just a little tweak. You nearly pulled them off my head,' she cried hotly.

'Didn't.'

'Yes you did.' She craned her neck to look at her sister. 'Tell him, Nell. Tell him to stop pulling my plaits and telling lies about me. Nell . . . are you listening to me?'

Silence. Nell was glued to the window, her eyes wide with disbelief.

'Nell . . . I'm talking to you.'

'What was that?' Nell responded at last, turning away from the window.

'It's just these two squabbling again. Take no notice of them,' explained

217

Peg. 'They're never happier than when they're quarreling, and if we inter-vene they start defending each other.' Peg turned her head towards Nell and gave her a considering look. 'Nell, whatever is the matter, dear? You look as though you've seen a ghost.'

She hadn't seen a ghost. But she had seen Gus walking along the street; just ambling along, as though he had all the time in the world. The simplest explanation was that he'd come back sooner than he'd planned from Somerset. Perhaps he'd caught an early train this morning. But that wasn't very likely. Even if the trains were running, the service would be restricted because of the holiday; he'd said that himself. The more plausible reason for him being in London today was that he hadn't been away at all and had lied to her all along.

'I'm all right,' she said now, struggling to gather her wits and pay atten-tion to what was going on here. 'Will you two kids stop playing up, please? You've had a lovely afternoon out. Don't spoil it.'

They made the usual protests, but Nell wasn't listening. Her mind was full of burning questions. If Gus had come back early, why hadn't he been round to let her know? And if he hadn't been away at all, why had he lied to her about it?

'Me in Chiswick High Road on Boxing Day?' said Gus, sounding outraged at the suggestion. It was a few days later, and they were walking down the street on their way to the pictures. 'Not me, sweetheart. I was miles away in Somerset on Boxing Day.'

'But I saw you, Gus.'

'You couldn't have done.'

'I did.'

'It must have been someone who looks like me,' he insisted. 'It defin-itely wasn't me. I might have a few tricks up my sleeve but I can't be in two places at once.'

'You must have a double, then.'

'Perhaps it was getting dark,' he suggested.

'It was beginning to, as it happens,' she admitted.

'There you are then,' he said quickly, and she detected a definite note of relief in his voice. 'It's hard to see anything at all in the damned blackout.'

'It wasn't dark,' she made clear. 'It was early dusk.'

218

'I don't care if it was broad daylight with the sun beaming down.' His voice shook with fury. 'It was *not* me you saw. I was *not* in London at all over the holiday. How many more times must I tell you?'

'Why are you getting so cross?'

'Because you are accusing me of being somewhere I wasn't,' he replied furiously.

'I'm not accusing you of anything,' she denied. 'I am merely mentioning that I saw someone I thought was you. And I was surprised because you told me you were going away and not coming back until the day after Boxing Day.'

'Which is what I did,' he said. 'Are you calling me a liar?'

'No . . .'

'Yes you are,' he cut in sharply. 'You are suggesting that I lied to you about going to Somerset.'

'No. Not necessarily,' she said. 'You could have come back early or something.'

'But I didn't.' He was beside himself with rage.

'For goodness' sake, Gus. There's no need to get into such a temper about it. I was obviously mistaken. I'm sorry.'

'I should damned well think so too,' he said with emphasis. 'Honestly, you don't half get some funny ideas.'

'All right, don't go on about it.'

'Well, no man wants to think that his intended doesn't trust him,' he said, sounding peeved.

'Let's forget all about it and enjoy the rest of the evening, shall we?' she suggested, just to keep the peace, but she was seriously beginning to wonder if she could trust him. He was far too anxious in his denial to convince her that he was telling the truth.

'Yeah, let's do that.'

'Thank goodness for that.'

'I'm sorry I was a bit sharp just now,' he said, sounding contrite and slipping his arm around her.

'Don't worry about it,' she said lightly.

'That's my girl.'

She was extremely uneasy, though. It had definitely been him she had seen on Boxing Day. She was as certain of that as she was about the door in his flat being locked when he'd insisted that it wasn't. The two incidents in themselves weren't important. The fact that he'd lied to her so vehemently about them was. Why would he do that? Suddenly she felt as if she didn't know him at all.

Then he said, 'I'm such an old misery-guts. I don't deserve a beautiful girl like you,' and she melted.

The best thing she could do was to put the two insignificant happenings out of her mind. She was engaged to him, and if she wanted to stay that way she would have to give him the benefit of the doubt and have faith in him or there would be no point in continuing. Without trust, how could any relationship survive?

It was evening and the engine room mess was thick with cigarette smoke, some of which was being exhaled by Ed. He was on his break, and as always when his mind wasn't focused on the job, his thoughts turned to home. He had a mental image of Joe and smiled to himself, his heart full of joy. He simply must survive this war and get back to him; he had to do it! There had been times lately, though, when he'd seriously doubted if he would make it, because HMS *Benwall* had taken a real battering.

Here we go again, he thought, as the alarm bell sounded throughout the ship and the call came for action stations. The men in the mess dispersed immediately and Ed went back to the engine room. There was a series of terrific explosions, every sound down here magnified by the water. Suddenly Ed was knocked off his feet as the ship rolled and juddered after a crash, and the sudden increase in temperature told him that there was a fire down here somewhere. He guessed that the ship had been hit by a torpedo. Before he had a chance to locate the fire, however, another blast knocked him out completely.

When Ed came round, the room was full of smoke and he was coughing, his throat feeling raw. Hearing the call through the loudspeaker, 'Anyone below?' he responded with a cry, but it was too weak to be heard. Sweating and choking, he dragged himself on all fours through the smoke to the ladder and started to climb, his chest rasping and his breathing restricted to the point where he could only gasp. Somehow he managed to reach the lower deck and pulled himself up on to the floor.

The order to abandon ship reached his dulled senses but he didn't have the strength to reach the next ladder to the upper deck. There was no one else around, but he could hear the sounds of chaos above: running footsteps and men shouting; alarm bells ringing.

With a supreme effort born of terror, he finally managed to crawl to the ladder and started to climb. Every iota of energy was expended as he took it one rung at a time, and finally opened the hatch to the upper deck.

'Blimey, mate. You're cutting it a bit fine, aren't you?' exclaimed one of the deck hands, helping him speedily to his feet. 'She's going down fast.'

Ed stumbled over to where the men were being lowered overboard into lifeboats while bullets rained down from enemy aircraft above. There was a sudden piercing pain in his leg and he was lifted into the air.

The next thing he knew he was in the water, the breath sucked out of him by the bitter cold. He couldn't see anything in the pitch dark. Unable to swim because his limbs were paralysed by the shock, he sank down into the bottomless ocean.

'Personally, I think you should get any idea of turning yourself in right out of your head this minute,' Polly advised Syd one evening in March. 'God only knows what they would do to you if you were to do a damned silly thing like that.'

'You've changed your tune,' he commented. 'I remember you once telling me that giving myself up was worth considering as I feel so bad about deserting.'

'Yeah, maybe I did, but I've got to know you better since then and I care about what happens to you,' she explained.

'I sometimes think it will be worth the punishment just to stop feeling so ashamed.'

'That's just plain stupid.' She was adamant. 'All you have to do is stick it out until the end of the war. You'll be all right then.'

'I won't be safe even then. They'll still be after me,' he told her. 'Desertion is a crime and the slate isn't going to be wiped clean just because the war is over.'

'It'll be easier, though, surely, to get back into normal society when peace comes,' she suggested. 'People will be looking forward, not back. Who is going to worry about a soldier who did his bit but wasn't able to stay the course?'

'A lot of people, I should think, especially those whose sons and husbands were killed in action,' he opined. 'Anyway, I don't think I'll ever have any peace of mind until I've owned up to what I've done.'

'Of course you will.' She was emphatic about it. 'You're a young man with your life ahead of you. You mustn't let the past spoil your future once the war is over.'

'I'll always be a deserter, but if I give myself up, at least I can take the punishment, whatever it is,' he suggested. 'That might take some of the shame away.'

'Don't even think of doing something so stupid.' Polly's concern was almost entirely for herself. She was terrified of losing him. He was all she had now and she didn't want to be alone again. She couldn't bear the thought of going back to how it had been before Syd had come into her life.

'I don't suppose I will when it comes down to it,' he said dismally. 'Once a coward, always a coward.'

'You'll really upset me if you carry on talking like that,' Polly rebuked. 'You're always telling me not to do myself down, and you're doing the same thing to yourself.'

'I'm only saying what's true.'

'*You are not a coward*. How many more times must I tell you?' she tried to convince him. 'You stuck it out for as long as you could. You went to war; you saw your share of action. Some men never see any if they work in the cookhouse in a home barracks somewhere. Anyway, some people have more stamina than others for that sort of thing. You can't help it if you're not one of them.'

'That's one way of looking at it, I suppose.'

'I know I'm a selfish cow but I don't want to lose you, Syd,' she admitted soulfully. 'You've been a rock to me these past few months and I don't know what I'd do without you.'

'You'd be all right,' he assured her. 'You're tougher than you think. You've got good looks on your side as well. You'd soon find someone else.'

'Not someone who understands me like you do,' she pointed out. 'We're two of a kind, you and me.'

'I know we are. But you can stop worrying,' he said, 'because I'm not going anywhere. Talk is easy. Doing anything about it is something else altogether.'

'Thank God for that.'

He paused, frowning. 'Not unless they come for me, of course, then I won't have a choice.'

'Stop scaring me.'

'That's the last thing I want to do, but it's a possibility we must both keep in mind,' he said gravely. 'So don't rely on me too much.'

'Oh Syd, you're really getting morbid now. Pack it in, for goodness' sake.'

'I'm just being realistic, Polly. It could happen and you must accept that,' he told her. 'I can offer you love and loyalty in bucketloads. But I can't offer you security.'

'Who can, in wartime? None of us know if we'll still be here tomorrow, do we?'

'That's true, but I have the added complication of possible capture,' he reminded her.

'If that happens, it happens. But there's no need to ask for trouble, so promise me that you'll forget about this crazy idea of giving yourself up.' She was desperately in need of reassurance.

'All right, I'll try to put it out of my mind,' he sighed. 'I'd probably never have the nerve anyway.'

'You'd have the nerve for anything if you had to, Syd Becks,' she told him in a firm tone to buck him up. 'But you don't have to do something daft like that. So come and give me a cuddle and forget all about it.'

'How can I resist?' he said.

'Don't even try.'

'As if I would.'

'That's better.'

'This is a lovely cup of coffee, Gus,' approved Nell. 'It's such a treat to be able to have sugar, and biscuits with it too. Delicious!'

'I'm glad you like it.'

'I hope this isn't putting too much of a strain on your rations,' she said.

'I've told you before not to worry about that.'

'I hope you haven't been paying the earth on the black market for sugar and biscuits for my supper,' she said.

'Of course I haven't,' he was quick to deny. 'You know I don't approve

223

of that sort of thing. As I've told you before, Nell, I don't have a sweet tooth, never have had, so I can let other people have my share of sweet things.'

'Which is lucky for us, especially Pansy and Lenny, who get a regular supply of chocolate.'

'Exactly.'

They were ensconced on the sofa in his flat in front of the gas fire, playing records on his gramophone. Although Nell wasn't keen on spending time here, she couldn't avoid it altogether, especially as he always paid when they went out. He was an extremely generous man and a real gentleman when it came to picking up the bill; he wouldn't allow her to go anywhere near her purse when she was with him. As it happened, that was just as well, because by the time she had paid Peg for hers and Pansy's keep and taken care of clothes and pocket money for her little sister, there was precious little over for anything else.

She was very lucky to have him, she appreciated that, which was why she tried to put the occasions when she'd doubted his integrity out of her mind. After all, the door she had thought was locked had been wide open when she'd been here since, and when she'd thought she'd seen him from the bus window it *had* been dusk, and it had only been a fleeting glimpse. It must have been someone who happened to resemble him.

'Would you like another cup of coffee?' he offered as she drained her cup and put it on the small table beside her.

'Not for me, thanks,' she said.

'Sure?'

'Positive. I really enjoyed that one, though. A lovely treat! You spoil me.'

'You're worth it,' he said, putting his cup down and slipping his arm around her.

The scratching sound of the record reaching its end interrupted the emotion of the moment, and he got up to change it.

'I might as well go and wash the coffee cups while you do that,' she said, getting up and collecting the crockery on to a tray. 'Won't be a minute.'

In the kitchen, she put the cups on the wooden draining board, but instead of getting on with the job of washing them, she found herself wandering out into the small hall and standing outside the room which she'd thought had been locked. Once again the door was wide open, almost as though Gus was making a statement, proving that he had nothing to hide.

Try as she might, she just could not erase the memory of struggling to open it and knowing that it was locked. How could she have imagined something like that? Unlike most interior doors, which were not fitted with a locking device, apart from bathrooms, this one was, she observed. That was odd in itself.

Intrigued, she poked her head inside, not daring to put the light on because it seemed too intrusive. In the glow from the hall she could see the usual contents of a spare room: a couple of suitcases, an old chest of drawers, a folding ladder and other oddments of furniture, all of which couldn't be more commonplace. But she knew suddenly and with absolute certainty that the door *had* been locked when she'd been here before. Which meant that – no matter how much she wanted to deny it – Gus had lied to her.

The knowledge puzzled her because it was such an odd thing to lie about. Unless he had had something in there he didn't want anyone to see.

'What are you doing out there, Nell?' he called to her from the living room. 'Are you cleaning the cupboards out or something? You've been gone ages and I'm missing you.'

'Just coming,' she responded, slipping back speedily into the kitchen. She rinsed the cups and saucers under the tap, dried them and went back to the living room, where he was waiting for her with open arms.

'At last,' he said. 'What kept you?'

She knew there was no point in asking him why he had lied to her, because he would only deny it and lose his temper again. 'I was just clearing up and putting everything away,' she said, feeling ill at ease and sensing that it wouldn't be a good idea to show it. This was no way to behave towards the man she loved and was engaged to marry, suspecting him of being dishonest and snooping around in his spare room.

But there was something not quite right here and she was going to keep a shrewd eye open to see if she could find out what it was. The reason for his deceit was probably quite innocent, but she needed to know.

★   ★   ★

It was coming up to Lenny's thirteenth birthday and he was hoping for a new bike.

'Can I have a proper grown-up one, please,' he requested hopefully one evening a week or so later. They were all sitting around in the living room. Nell and Peg were knitting, Tom was reading the newspaper, and Lenny and Pansy were having bread and cheese and cocoa for their supper.

'We'll do our very best, son, but we can't promise anything for definite because everything is so hard to get hold of at the moment,' his mother told him.

'We might be able to find a second-hand one,' suggested Tom.

'That's a possibility,' Peg agreed.

'The one I've got now is miles too small for me and I feel a right idiot on it,' said Lenny. 'I need a proper grown-up bike with a crossbar.'

'You know we won't let you down if it can possibly be avoided,' said Peg. 'We never have done so far.'

'I know, Mum,' he said.

'Are you going to have a few friends in for a birthday tea?' she enquired.

'Give over,' he snorted disdainfully. 'I'm far too old for that sort of thing.'

'Oh really?' said Peg with a twinkle in her eye. 'I thought you were going to be thirteen, not thirty.'

'I'm not a kid, you know.' Lenny was fed up. His voice kept going funny, and other embarrassing things had happened to him lately. He would die of embarrassment if his mother ever got to find out about them. She'd come into his bedroom the other day when he was getting undressed and he hadn't known where to put himself. It was all right for his mates to know, because the same things were happening to them and they had a good laugh about it. But your mum? Not likely! Anyway, all of these changes proved that he wasn't a kid any more. 'I'm beyond children's tea parties. I'd rather be out with my mates.'

'You could have your mates here for tea,' suggested Pansy. 'It would be a bit of fun.'

If looks could kill, she would have withered and died. 'They wouldn't be seen dead at a tea party,' he informed her. 'They'd think I was a right sissy if I asked them to come to tea.'

'I don't see why. Parties are fun. I like them anyway,' said Pansy.

'That's because you're a girl,' he stated categorically. 'Anyway, you're still a kid, so you would do.'

'I'm not,' she protested hotly.

'No offence, Pansy, but you are.'

Huh, that was what *he* thought! He wouldn't say that if he knew what had happened to her a few weeks ago. But she couldn't tell a boy that she had started her periods, which – in her opinion – meant that her childhood was over. That was how it had felt when it had happened anyway. She'd felt quite poorly with tummy ache and was apparently going to have this happen to her every month. Nell had been very kind; had said it was natural, nothing to worry about, and she wouldn't feel bad every time.

But everything was changing. Lenny was always going off with his mates from the boys' school and she missed him terribly. Her body was altering its shape too. Nell had said something about her having a brassiere soon. Oh, the humiliation of it all. 'I'm turned twelve and you've no right to say that I'm still a kid.'

'All right, big girl,' he teased her, chuckling. 'Don't get your knickers in a twist.'

'That's enough, Lenny,' rebuked his mother, seeing Pansy turn scarlet. 'We don't want that sort of talk in this house, thanks very much.'

'He's only pulling your leg, Pansy,' said Nell. Her sister was at such a sensitive age, especially where Lenny was concerned. Ostensibly she could hold her own with him, but he did have the power to hurt her. 'Take no notice of him.'

'I don't care what he says,' declared Pansy, but Nell knew that she did care very much indeed.

Taking in the scene, Tom was also very much aware of changes afoot, and his heart ached for Pansy. Lenny was spreading his wings and didn't have so much time for her these days. She obviously still adored him and was finding it painful.

They were both growing up. Lenny was all arms and legs, turned crimson with embarrassment at the slightest remark about his appearance, and his voice was beginning to break. It was time Tom had a chat with him about the facts of life, which he probably thought he knew, having heard an exaggerated version from the boys at school. Doubtless he would be far too embarrassed to listen to his father.

There had always been a special place in Tom's heart for Pansy, and it pained him to see her hurt. But with the onset of adolescence and then adulthood it was inevitable that she and Lenny would drift apart. Their closeness had both pleased him and caused him concern over the years. Now, she might be showing the beginning of womanhood, but she still had that lovely shy smile, the same as her mother.

One thing was certain: the fat really would be in the fire if the childhood friendship between Pansy and Lenny ever developed into anything more. God only knew what would happen if the truth ever came out.

A knock at the front door interrupted his reverie.

'Will that be Gus for you, Nell?' asked Peg.

'No, I'm not seeing him tonight,' she replied.

'I'd better go and find out who it is then, hadn't I?' suggested Tom. 'Seeing as no one else seems willing to move.'

'If you wouldn't mind, love,' said Peg. 'I'm right in the middle of a row and I don't want to drop a stitch. Nell's busy knitting too.'

'Consider it done,' he said, getting up and leaving the room.

'You don't see Gus every night, do you, Nell?' commented Peg in a companionable manner.

'No. We have a few nights off during the week.'

'A good idea. It keeps things fresh, doesn't it?'

'You need some time to yourself no matter how much you love someone.'

'You'll get precious little of it when you're married.'

'Exactly,' said Nell.

At that moment Tom came back into the room whey-faced and trembling.

'What is it, Uncle Tom?' asked Nell, frowning.

'Tom . . .' began Peg. 'Whatever is the matter? Who was it at the door?'

'It was George from next door,' he told her shakily.

'And . . . ?'

'It's Ed's ship. George heard it on the news on the wireless,' he said. 'Ed's ship has gone down.'

Chapter Thirteen

Whatever their private thoughts on the matter, no one in the Mills household ever so much at hinted at the possibility that Ed might never come back. Even after they had had official notification that he was lost at sea, presumed dead, there was a collective refusal to give up hope.

'Just because he's missing doesn't mean that he definitely drowned,' Peg was often heard to utter in the weeks following the news. 'It's probably complete chaos when a ship goes down and no one knows where anyone is.'

'He could have been picked up by another ship and hasn't been able to let anyone know,' suggested Tom supportively, reminding Nell of the couple's utter devotion and the strength of their marriage. It was almost as though they were one person.

'Course he could,' Peg agreed. 'I reckon he'll just come walking in that door one day. I'm his mother and I would know if he hadn't made it, believe me.'

Nell admired their faith but was fearful for them. She didn't know if Peg really did believe that Ed was still alive or was afraid to face up to the alternative. Either way she went along with them. Until they heard for certain to the contrary, hope was still possible. She herself prayed on a regular basis for his return. For her personally, life without Ed Mills in it was unimaginable.

Meanwhile, spring came and Lenny had his much-longed-for bike with a crossbar, albeit second-hand, while Pansy's embarrassment was complete when she was bought her first bra. The house resounded with little Joe's noisy exuberance and he was a constant source of joy and entertainment to them all.

229

Still as keen as ever on her job, Nell was always on the lookout for material with which to inform and entertain their readers, and kept her ears and eyes open to that end. One day in June she found herself with an unexpected lead when she overheard some women on a bus discussing a local hero, a publican of advanced years in Hammersmith, who had risked his life by jumping off the bridge into the Thames to save a drowning child.

Interest immediately aroused, she wasted no time in obtaining the necessary details from the gossipers and, back at the office, got on the telephone to arrange an interview. The heroic publican said he would see her the next day in the saloon bar when the pub closed after the lunchtime session. With the customers gone, he could give her his full attention.

Eager as ever, she arrived a little early for the interview. The pub was still open. It was one of the larger of Hammersmith's public houses, and the main entrance opened into a reception area with bars leading off. She was about to go into the saloon bar when she saw something through the partly open door to the public bar that turned her blood cold and stopped her in her tracks.

Gus was sitting at a table in the corner, smoking, drinking and talking with three other men, one of whom was Percy Wood. *Percy Wood?* How come Gus was on friendly terms with him? They were all too deeply immersed in their conversation to notice Nell staring at them through the doorway. Gus in a local pub during a working day instead of in an office somewhere in central London, and with a known criminal? What was it all about?

Shaken and uncertain what to do, she sensed that it wouldn't be wise to confront Gus or even let him know that she had seen him. She darted outside and went across the road, where she hid behind an ancient horse chestnut tree. Because the pub would be closing soon, she knew that it wouldn't be too long before the men emerged.

With her heart thumping chaotically, she tried to make herself invisible as the foursome came out of the pub and stood outside talking; luckily for Nell seeming oblivious to anything going on around them. There seemed to be some sort of an argument in progress between Gus and the two strangers. Percy just stood aside and watched. The row became heated; voices rose – though not so much that Nell could hear what was being said – and one of the men pushed Gus, while the other shook his fist close to his face as though warning him.

Eventually the gathering dispersed. Gus and Percy went one way and the two strangers went the other. Keeping her distance, Nell followed the former, feeling compelled to do so in order to shed some light on this startling development. They turned the corner and got into a saloon car that was parked in the road. With Gus in the driving seat, the car moved away.

A car? Gus had a *car*! He'd kept that well hidden. He was obviously using it illegally, because only those people whose occupations meant that they must be instantly mobile – such as doctors and others of that ilk – were eligible to keep a private vehicle on the road in wartime. If his mysterious job put him in that category, he wouldn't have been able to resist showing it off.

It was beginning to look very suspicious indeed. If Gus was involved with Percy, he was probably dabbling in the black market. If he had an important job, why wasn't he at work in the middle of the day? Maybe he was doing more than just dabbling. Maybe the job he was supposed to have didn't exist and his means of earning a living was illegal.

It was all becoming horribly clear. The locked door in his flat and his fierce denial of it, followed by his sudden request for the key to be returned immediately after Nell had mentioned it. Maybe he'd had unlawful goods stored in there and didn't want to risk having her nosing around another time when he might have cause to lock the door again.

What was she to do? She couldn't talk to anyone about it without incriminating Gus, and she might have got it all wrong. There could be a perfectly innocent explanation for his association with a known criminal and for secretly running a car, though she couldn't imagine what it might be. She needed time to think. But for the moment she reminded herself that she had a job to do, and hurried back towards the pub.

'You seem a bit quiet tonight, sweetheart. What's up?' asked Gus one evening a couple of days later, the first time she'd seen him since the incident at the pub. They were at his place.

'Nothing.' She struggled to sound normal.

231

'It isn't like you to be so subdued,' he persisted. 'You're usually such a bright spark.'

'I'm not being quiet intentionally.'

'Are you sure there's nothing the matter?'

Something was very much the matter, but she couldn't tell him that because she had no proof. Since seeing him so unexpectedly with his dubious friends, she had thought of nothing else. The whole thing was eating away at her; the lies he had told her that had rocked her faith in him and which she'd tried so hard to ignore until now. What was a relationship without trust? Even if she did find out for certain that he was involved in criminal activities, how could she report her own fiancé to the police?

'Quite sure. I'm absolutely fine,' she said now.

'Why are you sitting over there, then?' he wanted to know. She was seated somewhat stiffly in the armchair while he was on the sofa. 'We usually snuggle up together over here.'

Dutifully she went over to him and sat down by his side, but when he put his arm around her and drew her close, she instinctively pulled away. The distrust she now had for him was taking its toll on her and she didn't want him to touch her.

'What's the matter?'

'Nothing.'

'Why are you being so cold towards me, then?'

'I'm not.'

'You are. You can't bear me to touch you.'

'Perhaps I'm tired or something.'

'Have you gone off me?'

'Don't be silly.' The turmoil she was in was making her irritable. It wasn't in her nature to be deceitful, but in this case she had to make an exception, for the moment anyway. 'I suppose I just don't feel like being mauled.'

'Mauled! Is that the way you think of it when I touch you?'

'No, no, of course not,' she corrected quickly, angry with herself for allowing her feelings to influence her words. 'It must just have been a slip of the tongue.'

'I should damn well hope so, too.' He was enraged. 'That isn't the sort of thing you should be feeling about someone you're engaged to.'

'Look, Gus. Let's just put this down to the fact that I'm not very good company tonight, shall we?' she suggested. 'It's no reflection on you. I'm in a funny mood for some reason. But I think I would like to go home now.'

'Go home.' He was appalled. 'It isn't even nine o'clock yet.'

'All the better. Perhaps an early night will do me good, and I'll be more like my normal self when I see you next.'

'Oh well, I'm not happy about it but if it's what you want, we'll go,' he grumbled.

'There's no need for you to see me home.'

'Of course there is,' he disagreed. 'I wouldn't dream of letting you go alone.'

'I want to be on my own, Gus,' she insisted, almost shouting. 'So please just leave me be.'

'Oh . . . oh well, if that's the way you feel, you can suit yourself,' he retorted, his expression a mixture of bewilderment and anger.

'I'm sorry.' She touched his arm. 'I'm not fit company for anyone tonight. I'll see you tomorrow.'

'I'm busy tomorrow night,' he said in a truculent manner. 'It'll have to be the night after.'

'Whenever suits you.'

She hurried from the flat, relieved to get away. As she made her way home through the dark streets, she knew she couldn't continue in a relationship with a man who deceived her on a regular basis. But she had to know one way or another if he actually was up to no good or if there was some perfectly innocent explanation for the deceit. By the time she got home she knew exactly what she was going to do to find out.

The next morning she was in position early to make absolutely sure she didn't miss him. She was in a back street off the parade of shops where his flat was situated, just out of sight around a corner. Her common sense told her she was going to have a long wait, because if her suspicions were correct and he didn't have a proper job in an office in central London, he probably wouldn't leave home early, if at all. By the very nature of their business, gangsters wouldn't work regular hours.

Fortunately it was a fine summer's morning, so at least she didn't have inclement weather to contend with; just her nagging conscience. She felt mean and underhand at what she'd been driven to do. But she needed to know, and how else could she find out? He would admit to nothing; that much she was sure of. Nine o'clock passed; ten o'clock and eleven. Passers-by glanced curiously at the young woman in a cotton frock and sandals hanging around in the street with no apparent purpose. Housewives went by with their empty shopping bags and came back with them brimming over, and still she was there. She alternated between sitting on a low wall and standing about, shifting from one foot to the other.

They would be none too pleased with her at the office for not turning up for work this morning, but this was something she'd felt bound to do, and she would wait here all day if necessary. As it happened, it wasn't, because in the early afternoon Gus emerged from his front door and headed along the main road in her direction. With nerves tingling, she dived into an alleyway and waited for him to pass, then – keeping at a safe distance – she followed him.

Coincidentally, Nell wasn't the only one engaged in surveillance that day. Polly was at it too.

She was at the end of the street where the Millses lived, hoping for a glimpse of her son. Having some leave from the office due to her, she had decided to come to Chiswick to do some observation. She had guessed that Peg would take the baby out for a walk in the afternoon, as was customary, and had got here in plenty of time.

The return to her home ground had been awful; she'd felt as though she had 'Child Deserter' printed all over her in large letters. She had dreaded being seen by someone who knew her – especially anyone who was acquainted with her parents – but the need to see her child had been so strong as to be undeniable. It must just be curiosity. It couldn't be anything else, as she didn't have any maternal feelings, which was why she was skulking about in the street like a potential burglar instead of looking after her baby inside the house.

The sun felt warm on her arms, but her legs were aching from standing up, so she sat on a garden wall, unable to enjoy the sunshine because of the butterflies in her stomach. Oh come on, Peg Mills, you silly old bag, she said to herself, impatient already. Take that child for his afternoon outing.

Her breath caught in her throat when the front door opened and Peg emerged. Polly could only see the top of her because of the privet hedge. Standing well back out of sight, she waited for her to emerge into the street with the pram. Instead she saw her come out of the gateway holding the hand of a small boy and dragging a pushchair with the other. Shock waves went through Polly. She'd known that Joe wouldn't still be a baby, of course, but she realised now that she hadn't fully envisaged him as the little person he was. That tiny baby she had left who did nothing but feed, scream and fill his nappy was now walking on his own two legs and looking like a real boy. He even had trousers and shoes on. It was incredible!

Joe ran off, and Polly could hear the high-pitched tinkle of his laughter from here. Peg tore after him, picked him up and put him in the pushchair, then they walked up the street in the opposite direction to Polly.

She knew she should leave it at that. She had achieved her aim and seen him. Now she must go home. But she was in thrall to her emotions and unable to walk away, so she found herself following them, guessing that they were heading for the park.

Nell was careful not to get too close to Gus as he turned off the main road and led her through the back streets, travelling quite a distance from his flat, then turning in to an alleyway between some houses. The alley was secluded, with high back-garden walls, and overgrown with bushes at the sides. For a moment she lost sight of him. Gingerly she edged into the lane and saw him by some lock-up garages.

So this was where his illegal store was kept, she thought miserably, desperately wanting to be wrong about him but finding it increasingly impossible. He must have had an overflow when he'd stored stuff in the locked room at the flat. He looked furtively around and she dodged behind a bush.

He disappeared inside the garage and closed the doors. She toyed with the idea of confronting him there and then, but forced herself to hold back because she needed to think about her next move properly. The whole thing was so dreadfully upsetting, her mind was in turmoil.

Moving cautiously back to the end of the alley, she hid behind a bush and waited. Quite a time elapsed before he emerged and opened the garage doors, going straight back inside and backing the car out. She guessed the vehicle was loaded with his ill-gotten gains. He was probably going to make some deliveries to contacts who would buy and sell on at high prices. Also small-time crooks like Percy Wood, who would shift the stuff on the streets.

The garage doors were closed and carefully padlocked, then Gus got into the car. As the vehicle rolled slowly past Nell's hiding place and moved on to the road and out of sight, she wanted to break down and sob her heart out. The man she had fallen in love with was a fake. She didn't need to break into his garage to prove to herself what was in there. Whatever it was, it wouldn't be legal. She knew Ted Bigley would kill to get his hands on a story like this. Ironically, she'd stumbled on the scoop of a lifetime, but she knew she wasn't going to use it. Choking back her tears, she composed herself and headed for the office.

The items from the playground in the park – the swings and slide and so on – had been destroyed in the Blitz and wouldn't be replaced until after the war, so Peg was playing with Joe on the grass with a small ball. She rolled it to him and he scooped it up and immediately dropped it, which made him squeal with delight.

'Butterfingers,' she said playfully. 'Come on then, let's have another go.'

The process was repeated again and again, and each time Joe dropped the ball, Peg said, 'Whoops,' which amused him greatly and he tried to copy her. Then he ran across the grass and fell over, whereupon he let out a scream loud enough to wake the dead. Peg rushed over and assessed the damage. 'Aah, is it your knee, darlin'? Let Gran kiss it better for you.'

As Peg cuddled and fussed him, Polly observed the whole thing from the other side of the water fountain, just near enough to hear some of what was being said. She was sitting on a bench ostensibly reading a newspaper, which she had picked up from the news-stand on the way here. Every time Peg looked in her direction, she concealed herself speedily behind it.

When Peg finally put Joe – still wanting to play – in the pushchair and headed off towards the park gates, Polly didn't go after them. She stayed where she was until she managed to stop crying, then headed for the station.

⋆　⋆　⋆

'Why don't you get the boy back if you feel that strongly for him?' suggested Syd that evening after she'd told him about the emotional events of the day. 'You are still his mother, so they can't stop you from claiming him.'

'No, I wouldn't do that,' she told him.

'Why not?'

'I'm not a maternal woman.'

'If you don't feel a mother's love for him, why have you been in tears most of the time since I've been here?' He was perched on the arm of her chair companionably.

'Don't ask me. I haven't got a flamin' clue what makes me tick. Maybe it's because he looked so lovely and cute.' She gazed into space wistfully. 'He's such a fine healthy boy, Syd. You should see him. He runs about and everything.'

'Kiddies do tend to do that sort of thing when they get a bit bigger,' he said, teasing her. 'It's funny, that.'

She gave him a playful slap. 'I know that, you fool. It gave me such an odd feeling seeing him running about. I know it sounds silly, but I hadn't imagined him as an actual little person, having remembered him only as a baby.'

'I suppose it's only natural to remember him as he was when you last saw him.'

'His grandmother is very kind to him,' she went on, looking into space. 'She obviously thinks the world of him.'

'So do you, from what I can make out.'

'I was just pleased to see him thriving. It gave me a nice feeling, you know.'

'Supposing you'd seen your mother-in-law being unkind to him. What would you have done then?'

'I don't know.'

'I do. You'd have been over there sorting her out and taking your boy away from her.'

Polly's eyes filled with tears again. 'It's all hypothetical anyway,' she sighed. 'He's obviously being very well looked after, as I knew he would be when I left.'

'Go and get him, girl,' Syd advised her in a strong tone. 'Don't leave it too late. Don't miss out on all of his childhood.'

237

'Oh yeah, and what have I got to offer him? Tell me that,' she asked, casting a disapproving eye around. 'One dingy little room; no garden, and I'm out at work all day.'

'Mm, there is that.' He pondered for a moment. 'Couldn't you try to get back with his father for the sake of the boy?'

'Are you trying to get rid of me, Syd Becks?' she asked jokingly, trying to lighten the atmosphere and lift her spirits.

'You know me better than that. I just want things to be good for you,' he explained. 'As much as I would like to, and believe me I would very much, as a deserter on the run I'm not in a position to offer you anything of material value. I can't take you and your child on and make a decent home for you both. I just live from day to day hoping that I don't get caught.'

'I know that, Syd.'

'But that little boy is your flesh and blood, and a child needs its mother.'

'Don't say that, please,' she urged him, clasping her hands to her head in despair. 'I feel bad enough already. Don't make me feel even worse.'

'It isn't too late to put things right,' he suggested kindly. 'You could write to your husband and tell him that you're sorry for what you've done and say you want to make a go of things. If you can get that sorted, you can move back in with your in-laws.'

'You don't understand. Even if he would have me back, which I doubt, I couldn't go back because I can't do mothering,' she said, starting to cry again. 'I don't want to; it just isn't in me. I'd only let Joe down again.'

'He's your child, Polly. He must come first. What you want personally doesn't really come into it,' he dared to suggest. 'At least, that's what I've always believed.'

'Which is why I left,' she wept. 'I've told you, Syd, I still put myself first and I always will. I can't help it, don't you see?'

'I'm trying to, Polly, I really am,' he said, 'but what about your boy in all this?'

'He'll be all right. He's with good people. I made sure of that.'

'Okay, so you always put yourself first and you reckon you can't change. So let's look at the problem from a selfish point of view,' he suggested.

'For your own personal comfort, wouldn't you rather be in a decent house with a garden and a good family than living from hand to mouth in this grotty little room in a house with shared lavatories?'

'Of course I would, the same as anyone else, but I can't go back. I can't live that sort of life. It just isn't in me to be a mother, and if I moved back in I would have to step back into that role with all its responsibility.'

'Did you love the boy's father?'

'Probably not. I fancied him rotten, though. Which is why I ended up in trouble.' She paused, mulling the situation over seriously. 'He wouldn't have me back. Not in a million years.'

'How do you know?'

'He's very family-orientated,' she explained. 'He would think that abandoning a child is the worst sin in the book.'

'A lot of people would agree.'

'You as well?'

'Generally speaking, yes,' he admitted. 'But I can see that it isn't a straightforward matter in your case. Anyway, I'm in no position to judge you and I wouldn't dream of doing so.'

'You can't help but disapprove, though, can you?' she challenged. 'It's only natural.'

'I suppose there is something in what you say, but it isn't so much disapproval as lack of understanding,' he told her. 'To me a child is such a precious gift I can't fathom how anyone wouldn't want to be with him. You've explained how you feel and I accept that, but it's hard to actually comprehend, because I can't get inside your head. You're a very complicated girl, Polly.'

'I don't want any of that other life, especially motherhood.' Fresh tears began to flow. 'I don't know why I'm the way I am. It's something I can't do anything about. For now I just want to be with you, Syd. I can't take all that other stuff on board.'

'You'd better not go there again, spying on him, if it's going to upset you so much.'

'Perhaps not.'

'Make that definitely not, I would say,' he said, looking at her tear-stained face, her red swollen eyes. 'Just look at the state you're in.'

'Thanks for being so good to me, Syd,' she wept. 'I don't know why you put up with me.'

'Oh, come here, you daft thing,' he said, putting a comforting arm around her and holding her close. He was worried, though. She was so acutely vulnerable at the moment and he couldn't promise to always be around for her.

Nell was in a state of turmoil that night too. She really didn't know what to do about Gus. Having had her faith in him shattered so completely by his lies and deceit, she felt as though she didn't want to see him ever again. But hiding away from him wasn't the answer. She had to bring it to a proper conclusion. She could write and tell him it was over between them, but that was the coward's way out.

There was only one decent way to deal with it. She would tell him to his face when she saw him tomorrow night. For all that she had loved him enough to wear his ring, she couldn't be with a proven liar and criminal.

It was Saturday the next day, and when Gus came to call for her he asked her if she would like to go out dancing. A crowded dance hall was the last place she wanted to end her engagement, so she suggested that they go to his place since they couldn't talk at hers.

'I hope you're in a better mood than last time we were together,' he remarked as he let them into the flat. 'I never did know what I'd done to upset you.'

She didn't reply. As she walked past the spare room on her way to the living room, a smell wafted out to her; the smell she had noticed the day when she'd been here alone. Now she realised it was the smell of new tobacco, which was familiar to her because she had sometimes been to the tobacconist for Ted when he'd wanted cigarettes. Gus had obviously had a stash of cigarettes stored in there.

'If you don't mind, I'll get straight to the point, Gus,' she said in a brisk manner, though she was very nervous. 'I have something important to say to you.'

He looked at her. 'Oh?' he said. 'You'd better get on and say it then, hadn't you?'

She twisted her ring off her finger, trembling slightly, and put it down on the table. 'I'm very sorry to do this, but I have to tell you that it's over between us.'

He looked absolutely astonished. 'What on earth are you talking about?'

'Don't make me say it again,' she said. 'It was hard enough the first time.'

'But you can't just end it like that.'

'I have to, I'm afraid.'

'Why . . . Did you fall out of love with me all of a sudden?' he demanded, angry rather than hurt.

'It isn't as simple as that.'

'Why then?'

'Because I found out you've been lying to me,' she explained, meeting his angry glare without wavering. 'I don't want to be with someone who isn't straight with me.'

His eyes narrowed on her. 'In what instances have I lied to you?' he wanted to know.

'On several occasions, but I suppose the biggest deceit was telling me you had some hush-hush government job, which I suppose accounts for most of the other lies.'

'Oh yeah, and what brings you to this conclusion?'

She had no option but to tell him. She'd decided beforehand to be honest.

'So you've been spying on me?' he said incredulously when she'd finished.

'Once the seed of doubt was sown, I had to. I didn't want to judge you unless I knew for sure,' she told him through parched lips. 'But you've no need to worry. Your secret is quite safe with me. I have no plans to shop you to the police. I wouldn't do that to someone I once loved. But I can't be a part of your life any more knowing how you earn your living; knowing that while other men of your age are away fighting for their country you are having an easy life, lining your pockets as a small-time crook. Not even doing a proper day's work. God only knows how you managed to get out of conscription.' She paused, remembering something Frank had once told her on the subject. 'Though perhaps I do have a fair idea, on thinking about it.'

He didn't try to deny it or make excuses. Now that the truth was out his mood was one of arrogance. 'It wasn't too difficult for a man like me,' he explained boastfully. 'My contacts are so comprehensive there is nothing I need that I can't get.'

'I'm not impressed.'

'Small-time crook?' he said in a mocking tone. 'Is that what you think I am?'

'Of course. Who else would spend their days meeting known black marketeers in pubs, keep a car hidden and store bulk cigarettes behind a locked door in their flat.'

Vanity prevailed. 'You're wrong,' he said, and for a moment hope rose in her heart that there might be a legitimate explanation for all of this. 'A crook I am. But I am not small-time. I am very much big-time. I control a lot of people this side of the river.' He displayed his conceit with pride. 'I can lay my hands on anything from forged papers to hooky fags and chocolate.'

'Small-time, big-time, it's all the same to me,' she informed him. 'It's illegal so I don't want it in my life – not even second-hand. It makes me shudder to think that every time you bought me a drink or a cinema ticket you paid for it with dirty money.'

'I knew it was a mistake falling for Miss Respectability of nineteen forty-three,' he said viciously. 'You were always too much of a prude for me. Not my type at all.'

'Why did you pursue me, then?'

He looked at her with lazy contemplation. 'Because you're gorgeous . . . and you were a challenge,' he explained. 'Now you are a threat, and that's a pity because I really am fond of you.'

'How am I a threat?' she asked, feeling uneasy. 'I've told you I won't go to the police.'

'Unfortunately your word isn't enough for me. I'm not going to risk having my way of life wrecked by some prissy bit of a girl who fancies herself as a pillar of the community.' He looked at her in a superior manner. 'I don't think you realise what a powerful man I am. I can get anything done. *Anything at all.*'

'Meaning?'

'I can make people disappear.'

A bolt of fear shot through Nell and she realised what a fool she'd been in wanting to be straight with him. 'Are you threatening to have me killed?' she asked, her mouth so dry with nerves she could hardly speak.

'Oh no, not *you*,' he told her. 'I don't want *you* dead. I haven't finished with you yet, not by a long chalk. I never walk away from a challenge.'

His last comments barely registered against the gravity of the first. She was even more frightened now. 'Who do you mean then?' she asked fearfully.

'Nobody, if you keep your mouth shut,' he replied. 'But if you go anywhere near the police, you won't see your little sister again, except to identify her body.'

'Oh no, not Pansy,' gasped Nell, her brow beaded with cold sweat. 'Don't you dare touch her. Do what you must to me, but leave her out of it.'

'If I end up behind bars, your sister will go to meet her maker. And don't think you can get me put away to stop me carrying out my threat, because I shall arrange everything beforehand so she will only be safe if I stay a free man.'

Nell was almost too frightened to speak or move. How could she have been so stupid as to put her sister's life at risk? How could she have fallen for such a man, who was now repulsive to her? How gullible she'd been to be taken in by his good looks and charm. When she'd found out that his work was unlawful, she hadn't realised that he was dangerous too.

She threw herself at him, punching his chest.

'Don't you dare harm so much as a hair on my sister's head,' she screamed at him, beside herself with fear and anger. 'Kill me if you must, but leave her alone! I haven't told anyone what you're up to. If I'm out of the way your freedom is assured. No one else need be involved.'

'I'll be the judge of that,' he responded. 'Meanwhile I shall feel safe in the knowledge that you're living in fear for your sister.'

'Don't you even speak her name.' She was still pounding his chest with her fists. 'You're not fit to live among decent people and breathe the same air.'

At first he took the blows as though mildly irritated, but suddenly his mood changed and he grabbed her arms in an iron grip, his mouth close to hers so that she could smell alcohol and nicotine on his breath. 'Ooh, nice. I like a woman with a bit of spirit. I'm glad to know that little Miss Prim and Proper can be as common as the rest of us when she wants to be.'

'I gave you my word that I wouldn't go to the police,' she said. 'I won't say a thing to anyone. Just promise me that you won't touch Pansy.'

'I'm promising nothing,' he made clear. 'You know what you have to do to ensure her safety.'

'If anything happens to my sister, I'll make sure you hang,' she threatened.

'You'll get nowhere against me and my contacts in the underworld. The only way you can keep your sister alive is to keep your mouth shut. I'm sorry it's ended like this, because as I've said, I really am fond of you.' Without warning, he threw her against the wall and slapped her so hard around the head her ears rang and she saw stars. Then he hit her again and again, even harder. 'Now get out of here quick, before I really lose my temper.'

Nell didn't need to be told twice and left without another word.

Outside she was sick in the gutter. There was blood in her mouth from the cut on her lip his blows had inflicted. Being afraid for your own life was one thing. Being in fear for someone you loved was much worse. She was absolutely terrified for Pansy and at her wits' end to know how to deal with it. Gus couldn't be trusted to keep his word and could have Pansy killed anyway as a way of frightening Nell to ensure her silence. Who knew who else he might harm to protect himself?

She knew she was in deep trouble and that this situation was far too dangerous for her to deal with on her own. She had to protect her loved ones even if it meant revealing the truth to them. Trembling and nauseous, she made her way home.

'I'll kill him,' was Tom's initial reaction when a bruised and bleeding Nell told Tom and Peg what had happened. Fortunately, Pansy and Lenny were already in bed. 'I'm going round there right now to wring his flamin' neck.'

'You'll do no such thing,' ordered Peg, gently bathing Nell's sore face. 'He isn't worth hanging for. Calm down and we'll work out what to do between us.'

'I'm sorry to dump this worry on to you both,' Nell apologised. 'I wanted to spare you, but now it's turned really nasty I thought you needed to know, for your own safety. Who knows what he might do to save his own skin?'

'You did the right thing,' Peg assured her.

'It's my fault for falling for him,' said Nell. 'If I hadn't we wouldn't be in this mess. Now I'm in fear for my sister's life, and all because I was taken in by him. How could I have been so stupid? I feel terrible. My sister is in danger because of me.'

'If anyone is to blame it's me, for introducing him to you,' Tom pointed out.

'Don't try and make it easy for me, Uncle Tom,' Nell told him. 'The whole thing is my fault and I'll never forgive myself if anything happens to Pansy.'

'That sort of talk will get us nowhere,' Peg pointed out. 'We have to decide what to do.'

'We'll have to go to the police,' decided Tom. 'We can't deal with this on our own. As you say, we can't take his word for it that he won't harm her, even if you do keep to your side of the bargain.'

'We can't go to the police,' Nell reminded him, wringing her hands. 'He'll have Pansy killed if we do that. That is why I don't know which way to turn.'

'We'll have to ask for police protection for her,' Tom suggested. 'Explain to them that we won't tell them what we know about the black-marketeering unless they promise to do that.'

'Even if they do agree, they can't be with Pansy all the time. And it won't be good for her to know that she's in danger. It would make her a nervous wreck.'

'There is that,' he nodded.

'The way I feel at the moment, I don't want to let her out of my sight ever again,' Nell confessed. 'But she can't live her life with someone guarding her the whole time.'

'No, she can't.' Tom scratched his head. 'But perhaps between us and the police we might be able to manage it without her realising until the danger is over.'

'It won't be over,' she told him. 'It'll be a life sentence for her. If he can pull strings from behind bars, he will never let up. Even if they were to hang him, he'd probably leave instructions with his minions.'

'I'll kill him,' said Tom again, pacing the floor and puffing on a cigarette. 'That will solve the problem once and for all.'

'It would solve nothing,' Peg disagreed. 'Stop talking so daft. You don't have it in you to kill a fly, let alone a man.'

'There just doesn't seem to be a solution,' said Nell despairingly. 'He's got us by the throat whichever way we look at it. If only Ed was here. He'd sort it out.'

'Yeah,' said Peg, her eyes filling with tears at the mention of her missing son.

'Pansy is safe for the moment,' said Tom. 'We can sleep on it and discuss it again in the morning.'

'Sleep,' said Nell. 'I don't think I'll ever sleep again.'

'Me neither.' This was Peg.

'I feel the same, but I suppose we need to rest our bodies even if we don't go to sleep.'

Neither Peg nor Nell could possibly know how deeply affected Tom was by all this. He would do anything to protect Pansy; anything at all, because she meant the world to him. He'd give his life for her if necessary. But he couldn't see how that or anything else would help with a man like Gus Granger calling the shots.

Tom was also finding it hard to come to terms with the truth about Gus. He had always seemed such an ordinary sort of a bloke down at the ARP; well liked by all the chaps too. Who would have thought he would turn out to be a hardened criminal?

In a back-street pub in Paddington, a group of four men sat around a table deep in conversation but keeping their voices low.

'He's getting far too greedy and above himself for my liking,' said one of them.

'And mine,' said another.

'He's been warned to stay on his own turf on more than one occasion,' said one of the others. 'But does he take any notice? No, he still pushes his luck.'

'It's greed, pure and simple,' said a man who was smoking a cigar. 'He must think we're a right lot of mugs.'

'He's trodden on my toes once too often now,' declared the first man.

'I mean, I don't object to anyone making a good living. We're all in the same business, after all, but there is a certain code of conduct and he's overstepped the mark again.'

'You don't take the bread out of another man's mouth,' said one of them.

'Course you don't,' said another. 'You can con the punters as much as you like, but you've got to be straight with your own.'

'Has he never heard about honour among thieves?'

'If he has, he's chosen to ignore it.'

'He'll have to be dealt with,' said the first man. 'Are we all agreed on that?'

'No question about it.'

'The sooner the better; like right away. He can't be allowed to get away with it any longer.'

Agreement among the group was unanimous. They carried on talking until a suitable plan was hatched, then they left the pub, got into a car and drove away along the dark London street.

Chapter Fourteen

Syd didn't have a wireless set so kept up to date with the news by means of the daily paper, both morning and evening. He often took the latter to Polly's with him if he hadn't finished reading it. She never so much as glanced at it herself but didn't mind him doing so when they were together as long it didn't distract his attention from her for too long.

'Well stone me,' he muttered to himself the following evening when something in the paper caught his attention. 'You wouldn't believe such a thing could happen outside of the films, would yer? Dear oh dear, as if there aren't enough people copping it because of the war; we don't need murders happening outside of it.'

'What are you on about?' Polly asked.

'Some bloke was shot dead in a crowded pub last night while people were enjoying themselves,' he informed her. 'They were having a singsong.'

'Why didn't somebody stop it happening if there were so many people around?' Polly asked.

'Nobody knew about it,' he explained, his eyes glued to the page. 'There was a silencer on the gun and the first anyone knew about it was when the man had slumped to the floor and someone nearly tripped over him.'

'What about the people he was with? Surely they must have seen something.'

'He was in there on his own, according to this. Having a drink at the bar.'

'Blimey. That's shocking. Have they caught the killer?'

'No, not yet. The police think it was an underworld killing, which to my mind means they probably never will find out who did it. Those sort of people live in a closed world, and use professional killers to do their dirty work,' he said, reading on. 'The victim was a gangster. He'd been living in various places under different names for years; a right villain by the sound of it.'

'Was it in the East End?'

Searching the article for more details, Syd said, 'No . . . west London. Hammersmith, as it happens. Over near your neck of the woods somewhere.'

'Give it here; let's have a look.'

'Don't screw it up and lose my place,' he said, handing her the paper.

'Good God,' gasped Polly when she found herself staring at a photograph of a man she recognised. Someone she'd met first in a pub; a pal of Tom Mills from the ARP. It was obviously an old photograph, because he looked younger, but it was definitely Gus Granger; she remembered him particularly because he'd had his eye on Nell. 'Phew, that's a turn-up for the books.' She put her hand to her brow. 'Ooh, that's made me come over all queer.'

'It is a bit gruesome, I know.'

'No, it isn't just that, Syd. I knew him,' she spluttered. 'The murdered man.'

He looked shocked. 'How did you get mixed up with someone like that?'

'I didn't get mixed up with him,' she explained. 'I met him a couple of times, that's all. He was a friend of Ed's dad.'

'I hope it was only a couple of times,' he said. 'It wouldn't do to get on friendly terms with anyone from that sort of world. He was a bad 'un by the sound of it.'

'He seemed very interested in Nell but nothing ever came of it, not while I was there anyway; just as well, as it turned out. He looked like such an ordinary bloke, too. He wasn't flash as you imagine a gangster to be.'

'He wouldn't dare to look the part in wartime,' suggested Syd. 'In case he got noticed and sent into the army. He'd try to melt into the background by looking like a regular sort of a chap, especially as he was known to the police all over the place.'

'I suppose so.'

She handed the paper back and Syd immersed himself in it, commenting on various items of general interest: war news from abroad, new and stricter fire-watching rules that had been issued by the government.

She made all the appropriate noises in reply but she was miles away; in Chiswick to be exact. The item in the paper had reminded her of them all: of Nell, the Mills family, and of course little Joe. She felt so dreadfully sad suddenly.

'Shall we go out tonight, Syd?' she suggested. 'I fancy losing myself in a good film.'

'Whatever you like, sweetheart,' he said in his usual amicable way. 'I don't mind what we do as long as it makes you happy.'

Syd was such a lovely fella, she thought, and so good to her. She really didn't know what she would do without him.

The first Nell knew about Gus' death was when word of the shooting came in to the news desk. The office was buzzing with it, being a local story. She didn't realise it was Gus until the subeditor assigned Frank to the job of covering it and he came back with all the details, including the victim's name and address. Gus Granger was just one of his many false names, Frank managed to find out from a contact in the police.

Although she was horribly shaken, Nell managed to gather her wits sufficiently to do the right thing. She went straight to the editor and told him that the murdered man was the fiancé she'd talked so much about, then she went to the police.

She told them everything: about her relationship with Gus, and his terrible threat when she'd confronted him with what she'd found out. She wasn't charged for withholding information, as she explained that she'd known nothing of his criminal activities up until that point. She also told them about his secret lock-up garage and the car.

'It's a terrible business, but at least young Pansy is safe now,' said Tom later when they were talking about it after the youngsters were in bed.

'The sort of man he turned out to be, he won't be missed,' added Peg impulsively. 'To think that we welcomed him into this house and tried to make him feel like one of the family. Ugh, it makes me feel sick to think about it. Good riddance to bad rubbish, that's what I say. Isn't that right, Nell?'

It wasn't quite as simple as that for Nell, because she had been in love

251

with him. Up until just a few days ago she had worn his ring with pride and expected to share her future with him. The dream had been shattered the minute she had realised that he wasn't what he seemed, but still his death was a shock and a cause for sorrow. Naturally it left a void. The man had been a part of her life. Now she was alone again without that someone special. It was very hard to take.

'That's a bit harsh, Auntie,' she pointed out. 'He was a human being, when all is said and done.'

'Only just, by the sound of it,' Tom put in.

'You'll soon find someone else, a pretty girl like you,' encouraged Peg, realising that she could have been a bit more sensitive just now. 'That probably doesn't help much at the moment, because I know you thought the world of him, but just concentrate on the fact that Pansy is safe.'

Nell had to admit that it was an immense relief. It wasn't in her nature to wish anyone dead, but as Gus' death meant that Pansy would be safe, how could she grieve too deeply for him?

'I don't particularly want to meet anyone else at the moment. I think I'll steer clear of men for a while, Auntie Peg,' she said. 'But yes, it is a huge relief about Pansy.'

'Funny that Pansy never took to him, despite all the chocolate he gave her and Lenny,' mentioned Tom.

'Lenny didn't like him either,' said Peg.

'Gus must have laid it on a bit too thick with them to win their favour and they saw through it. Kids can be surprisingly perceptive,' said Tom. 'The rest of us were taken in by him. He even won you over eventually, didn't he, Peg?'

'Eventually,' she admitted. 'I was wary at first but only because of his age. I never dreamt he would turn out to be a flamin' crook of the worst kind.'

'Anyway, it's over now,' said Nell, needing to put an end to the subject because every word cut deep into her wound. 'I have to get on with my life and put it behind me.'

'That's the spirit, dear,' said Peg.

'Hear, hear,' added Tom.

★ ★ ★

As the summer days began to have that damp, slightly earthy feel of early autumn about them and the fourth anniversary of the outbreak of war coincided with the Allied landing in Italy, Nell strove to put the whole Gus episode out of her mind and get on with things as best she could, even though she still felt hurt, humiliated and empty. She threw herself even more avidly into her work, took on more knitting for the navy, gave Peg extra help with Joe, spent time with her sister, and found a new hobby . . .

Her love affair with words, which had begun when she joined the paper, was her salvation now as she struggled to heal her broken heart. In spare moments she practised making words slot together in an interesting way by writing about her thoughts on various subjects, endeavouring to make the pieces entertaining. The process was engrossing and calming and she tried to improve her technique and expand her vocabulary. Finding the best way to express a feeling or event was enthralling.

Along with her interest in writing, she also became an avid reader and regularly had books on loan from the library. It was a whole new world for Nell, though getting hold of paper to write on wasn't easy as the shortage continued.

Because of the Porter sister's circumstances – losing their parents at such a young age and then being parted by evacuation – there was a closer bond between them than perhaps there might have been had their parents lived.

Having spent so much of her spare time with Gus while the love affair lasted, Nell now wondered if her attention to Pansy might have been allowed to slip. With this in mind, she decided to make up for any possible deficit, and started off by taking her sister to Oxford Street to get her a new winter coat. They went on a Saturday morning when Nell had been given the day off in lieu of some Sundays worked.

Having purchased a cherry-red coat for Pansy, they went to Lyons for a cup of tea and a bun.

'I'll be glad when you stop growing, young lady,' said Nell jokingly. 'It's an expensive business, keeping you clothed.'

'I'll be going out to work soon myself so I can pay for my own things,' Pansy pointed out.

Nell didn't brush her comment aside as though it wasn't valid, because that was how the system worked for girls like them. With the receipt of your first pay packet you were totally responsible for yourself financially and expected to pay your way at home as well. She remembered her own early days as an office junior, longing for clothes she couldn't have because no matter what other expenses she had, she had to put her money towards the household budget on the table every Friday night. It wasn't that her mother was hard; it was just the way things were done in working-class circles.

'Yeah, that's true.'

'It must be a bit of a nuisance for you, having to support me as well as yourself,' Pansy remarked, old enough now to be aware of such things.

'Not at all,' Nell assured her. 'I'm your sister, so it's no more than my duty.'

'If Mum and Dad were still alive, you wouldn't have got lumbered,' said Pansy.

'I don't consider myself to be lumbered,' Nell informed her emphatically. 'I'm happy to do it for you until you're old enough to do it yourself.'

Pansy sipped her tea then emitted a sigh. 'I wish I could be like you,' she said.

'Who says you're not?'

'I don't even look like you,' she said. 'I don't have that lovely dark hair. I'm stuck with mousy brown.'

'It isn't mousy brown. It's a lovely light brown colour like Mum's was,' said Nell. 'You're going to be a really good-looking girl when you've finished growing up.'

'Huh, that's a good one,' snorted Pansy. 'I'm just a skinny, mousy-haired nobody.'

Nell reached across the table and rested her hand on her sister's. 'Don't put yourself down like that. It upsets me to hear it.'

'I'm only saying what's true,' she said. 'All the girls in my class are prettier than I am.'

'Rubbish,' disagreed Nell, regarding her sister's smooth-skinned young face with its small features and huge brown eyes. She was at the transitional stage so not at her best, but Nell could see a beautiful woman eventually emerging from the metamorphosis. 'They all probably think you are better-looking than them.'

'No they don't. They know they're gorgeous and they're always showing off about it.'

'Your time will come,' said Nell.

'The reason Lenny keeps going off without me is probably because I'm not pretty enough,' she said.

'Lenny is going off without you because he's growing up,' explained Nell, remembering the agonising uncertainties of her own adolescence and how vital appearance was at that age. 'You'll be doing the same thing yourself before very long. You'll have the boys queuing up to ask you out, believe me. Give it a year or two and you'll wonder what you ever saw in Lenny Mills.'

'I'll never think that,' she said.

'In that certain way, I mean,' Nell explained. 'You'll probably always be friends because you've grown up together.'

'We haven't stopped being friends,' Pansy made clear. 'It's just that he doesn't want to be with me much now. He thinks I'm boring, I expect.'

'Give him time and a bit of space, love,' Nell advised. 'You're both going through a lot of changes.'

Pansy made a face. 'You're telling me.'

'It's all very natural,' Nell said kindly.

'I want to be like you,' said Pansy again. 'You always know what to do.'

'That's only because I'm older than you,' Nell pointed out. 'Anyway, you showed better judgement than I did over Gus. You knew there was something not quite right about him from the start.'

'He was creepy,' said Pansy, frowning as she remembered. 'I knew he was only being nice to me to impress you. I would have hated it if you'd married him and made me go to live with you.'

'Well it didn't happen, so I think it's probably best forgotten,' suggested Nell.

'Yeah. Sure.' The exuberance of youth finally prevailed over Pansy's wistful mood as she moved on swiftly. 'I can't wait to wear my new coat.'

'Let's go to the pictures tonight,' suggested Nell spontaneously. 'You can wear it then.'

Pansy's face lit with pleasure. 'Oh could we, Nell? I would love that,' she enthused.

'We'll do it then,' said Nell. 'And I'll do your hair a bit special for you too if you like. Let's take it out of the plaits for a change and you can wear it loose.'

'Yes please,' Pansy said excitedly.

Seeing her pleasure and realising how much power she herself had to colour her sister's life just by giving her some of her time, Nell said, 'It'll be just you and me, kid. Not Lenny or Auntie Peg. We'll tell them that we're having a sisters' Saturday night out.'

'Smashing,' Pansy said happily.

At that moment Nell understood just how easy it was to get sidetracked into neglecting someone else's feelings when you were a little too wrapped up in your own.

They saw a film called *The Gentle Sex* about seven girls from different backgrounds who were conscripted into the ATS. It was a pleasant, interesting and easy-to-watch film, though quite thought-provoking in parts.

'Did you enjoy it?' asked Nell as they made their way slowly out of the cinema with the crowds.

'Yeah, I loved it,' said Pansy, linking her arm through her sister's as their eyes adjusted to the dark. 'I want to join the ATS when I'm old enough.'

Which was exactly the reaction the film-makers hoped for; the idea was obviously to tempt young women into joining up, thought Nell, but she said, 'The war will be over and done with long before then.'

'If it isn't, I will definitely join,' Pansy said lightly. 'I loved the bit where all the ATS girls were walking down that long road singing.'

'I enjoyed that bit too,' Nell smiled. 'They were a smashing crowd of girls.'

'I'm glad you haven't gone away in the forces,' Pansy said. 'I would hate that.'

For the second time that day Nell was reminded of how important she was to Pansy. Soon Pansy would broaden her horizons and be more independent, but for now her big sister was vital to her. Nell hoped she lived up to the responsibility she had inherited from their mother. Arm in arm, the two girls headed homewards, chattering about the film and happy to be together, although Nell couldn't help worried thoughts of Ed entering her mind.

★ ★ ★

256

'You've been out spying on that boy of yours again, haven't you?' guessed Syd one wet Sunday evening in October when he arrived at Polly's to see that her eyes were red and swollen.

She nodded.

'I told you not to do it again if it upsets you so much.'

'I know you did, but it was his birthday; his second.'

'All the more reason to stay away,' he said. 'It's bound to upset you.'

She gave a hopeless shrug. 'I didn't see him anyway. I suppose they stayed in as it was so wet.'

Syd rolled his eyes disapprovingly. 'Don't tell me you stayed there after it came on to rain,' he said.

'I just kept hoping they might come out, so I waited a bit longer then a bit longer still,' she explained. 'Anyway, a drop of rain never hurt anyone.'

'You can't go on like this, Pol,' he warned with genuine concern for her. 'You'll make yourself ill, or get arrested for loitering or invasion of privacy or something.'

'I'm not doing any harm,' she pointed out. 'He doesn't even know I'm there.'

'You're doing harm to yourself, not the boy,' he told her. 'Look at the state you've got yourself in.'

'I'll be all right. I'm as tough as old boots.'

'In some ways maybe,' he agreed. 'But not when it comes to that boy of yours. Honestly, Pol, you'll have to get a grip of yourself. Either get back into his life or let him go.'

'I've told you it isn't that simple.'

'I know it isn't, and I sympathise with you, I really do. But you can't spend the rest of your life hanging around the streets trying to catch a glimpse of him.'

'I know, and I will try and keep away.' She paused, composing herself and affecting a change of mood. 'I don't feel like staying in tonight. What do you fancy? The pub or the pictures?'

'Let's toss for it.' He produced a penny from his pocket. 'Heads or tails?'

It was Monday afternoon and every inch of Peg's washing line was in use, running the length of the back garden. You didn't get many bright and breezy days like this in October, so she was delighted not to have wet

257

washing all over the house, on clothes horses and lines strung across the bathroom and the kitchen, creating steam everywhere. It was a real treat, especially after the rain yesterday.

'Some of this is dry enough for ironing,' she muttered to little Joe, who followed her everywhere.

'Dry,' he repeated.

'Yes, that's right, darlin',' she said, feeling and unpegging some items and putting them in a basket, then raising the line with the clothes prop so that the rest would catch the wind, the sheets billowing in the breeze. 'Your talking is coming on lovely. You're a clever little boy and I'm proud of you.'

'Pussy,' he said, spotting Tiddles on top of the coal shed and running over, whereupon the cat shot to the end of the narrow garden out of reach. The two-year-old's tendency to demonstrate his loving nature was a bit too much for the tabby cat. 'Oh, he's gone. Why's he gone?'

'That's what cats do, darlin'; they're free spirits,' Peg said, but Joe was already running down the path after Tiddles.

Peg called him back. 'Come on now, love,' she said. 'You can see the pussy later. We're going indoors now. It's chilly out here and you'll catch cold if we stay out any longer.' She shivered, the basket she was holding resting on her hip. 'Some of the washing needs to stay out here for a bit more of a blow . . . Joe, are you coming or am I going to have to come after you?'

Full of devilment, the little boy ran away; he loved being chased. Peg put the washing basket down and caught him by the cabbage patch, sweeping him up in her arms, whereupon he struggled to get down to do the whole thing again. 'No. No more,' she said firmly. 'We're going inside.'

She picked up the basket, took his chubby little hand with her free one and turned towards the house.

'Oh my Lord,' she said suddenly, dropping the basket and clutching her chest as she looked towards the back door. 'Oh my good Gawd. You nearly gave me a heart attack.' And with that she burst into tears.

'Is that any way for a mother to greet her son?' grinned Ed.

Peg flung her arms around him. 'Oh, Ed, where've you been? And what are you doing creeping up on us like that?'

'I didn't creep up on you. I got the key through the letter box and called into the house half a dozen times. Then I realised you were out here.' He grinned at her. 'Where else would you be on a dry Monday afternoon but seeing to your washing?'

'Where else indeed!'

'I enjoyed watching the two of you together,' he said. 'I hardly recognised him, he's grown so much.'

Peg pulled away from her son and paid attention to Joe. 'Here's your daddy, darlin',' she said thickly. 'Daddy's home.'

The little boy was wary and clung to his grandmother's leg.

'Hello, little 'un,' said Ed, holding out his arms. 'Come and see your dad.'

Joe wanted to stay with Peg.

'You're not shy, young man, so don't kid us that you are,' said Peg affectionately. 'Come and say hello to Daddy.'

'You don't remember me, son, but we used to have good fun together,' added Ed persuasively.

'Give him time,' Peg advised. 'He's a bit overwhelmed, I think. He isn't normally a shy child.'

Father and son stared at each other long and hard, then Joe took one cautious step, then another until Ed could reach him. His father lifted him up and held him close. 'Oh, it's so good to see you, son. So very good.'

Peg turned away because she didn't want to embarrass her son, who had tears running down his cheeks.

Peg made some tea and they sat in the living room chatting and exchanging news while Joe played with his toys on the floor. When it was time for his nap, Peg took him upstairs to his cot.

'So what happened after the ship went down, son?' she enquired.

'I was in the water for what seemed like for ever, clinging to a bit of wreckage. Then I got picked up by a merchant ship and taken to Cape Town because that was their next port of call,' he explained. 'I had a bit of time there to recover, then I joined another Royal Navy ship and got back here when they did. I thought the navy would let you know that I was safe.'

'No, we haven't heard a word except to say that you were missing,' she told him.

'No wonder you nearly passed out when you saw me.'

'I was shocked because you appeared so suddenly; not because I really thought you were dead,' she explained. 'I'm too stubborn to believe that. I knew somehow that you'd be back. Call it mother's intuition if you like.'

'For a while back there I thought I really was a gonner. I went under just after the ship went down.' He shuddered at the memory. 'It was the most awful feeling when I couldn't get to the surface. I was struggling and choking down there, expecting to see my life flash before my eyes. But eventually somehow I got my head above water. It took them ages to thaw me out when I was finally picked up.' Noticing that his mother looked worried he said, 'But I'm fine now. I'm one of the lucky ones.'

'Yeah, yeah, I know that, son.'

'No word from Polly, I suppose,' he speculated.

She shook her head. 'Sorry, Ed. I wish I could tell you different,' she said.

He shrugged but she could see the hurt in his eyes. He asked what else had been happening. She brought him up to date, then told him about the drama with Gus.

'What a shocker,' he said. 'How is Nell?'

'She's being Nell and getting on with things. You know what she's like. She's got plenty of guts and is always on the go. She works far more hours than she needs to. It's her way of getting through it, I suppose.'

'She must have been shattered, though.'

'Not half. She was very frightened too, when she thought Pansy was in danger. We all were; then to find out that Gus was dead, murdered just like that.' She puffed out her lips. 'It must have been one hell of a trauma for her. I mean, she was engaged to him, and very smitten at one time.'

'She certainly was. I didn't take to him at all, though,' admitted Ed. 'He seemed a bit of a fake to me the minute I clapped eyes on him. I didn't say anything to Nell because I hoped I was wrong. I thought it might just me being biased. She was so happy with him I didn't want to spoil it for her. I wish I had, as things have turned out.'

'She wouldn't have listened to a word against him anyway,' said Peg. 'You don't when you're keen on someone. He really was a nasty piece of work, though.'

'I'll have to try and cheer her up while I'm home.'

'How long is your leave?'

'Ten days. I shall probably sleep for the first two of them,' he said. 'And I'd like to go to Essex for a couple of days to see Gran before I go back.'

'That's thoughtful of you.' Peg gave a wry grin. 'We'd better let her know you're coming or you really might give her a turn, a woman of her age.'

'Perhaps I'll take Joe with me,' he mentioned thoughtfully.

'That's a very good idea,' she approved. 'I'm sure Maud would love to see him.'

He stretched lazily. 'Oh, I can't tell you how good it is to be home, Mum,' he said.

'I *can* tell you how good it is to have you here,' she responded, wiping a tear from her eye. 'There's no feeling on earth to beat it, son, and that's a fact.'

Nell had just got home from work and was hanging her coat up on the hall stand when someone grabbed her from behind and put their hands over her eyes. She let out a shriek.

'Guess who?' said her assailant.

'Ed!' she squealed, swinging round to face him. 'I'd know that voice anywhere.' She drew back and looked at him, then threw her arms around him and hugged him, tears streaming from her eyes. 'Oh Ed, it's so good to see you safe and well. Oh, it's the best news we could ever have.'

She drew back and they looked at each other, both beaming though Nell was crying.

'Oh not you as well. Why does everyone take one look at me and burst into tears?' Ed asked in a jovial manner, though his voice was ragged with emotion.

'Because we're so pleased to see you,' she told him, dabbing at her eyes with a hanky.

And then they were all around him, vying for his attention: Lenny, Pansy, Peg and Tom; everyone so excited and joyful to have him home. It was as though a warm celebratory breeze was blowing through the house.

'Mum told me about Gus,' said Ed later that same night when the others were in bed. He and Nell had stayed in the living room chatting. 'What a thing to happen, eh? It must have been dreadful for you.'

'Yeah, it was,' she told him gravely. 'I would have given a lot to have had you here. I remember thinking that at the time.'

'I wish I had been, too,' he told her. 'I hate to think of you going through that on your own.'

'I wasn't on my own, not really. I had to tell your mum and dad in the end when Pansy's life was threatened. I tried to keep it from them, but when it got so dangerous I didn't have a choice.'

'You told them, but you had to go through the emotional side of it on your own,' he pointed out. 'The pain of the end of a relationship; then his death.'

'I'm still a bit raw now, to tell you the truth,' she confessed. 'I keep myself busy and that helps, but there's only so much you can blot out that way. I was such a fool to fall for him. I keep asking myself why I didn't suspect before that he wasn't what he seemed.'

'Why should you? He behaved like any normal bloke when he was with you.'

'Looking back on it, there were signs. I mean, all this business about having a secret job in the civil service was a bit far-fetched when you think about it.'

'Not really. I'm sure there *are* people employed in mysterious work for the government. Dad was fooled by it anyway,' he reminded her. 'It was him who told us about it in the first place. It was bound to seem plausible, with him and the rest of them at the depot accepting his occupation as a fact. Anyway, there's a lot of secrecy about these days because of the war, and people are doing all sorts of unusual jobs you wouldn't hear of in peacetime.'

'There were plenty of warning signals that I chose to ignore,' Nell admitted ruefully. 'I noticed things he said that didn't quite add up, but I was in love with him, and you know how that blinds you to the truth.'

'Don't I just,' he said with emphasis. 'Though in my case, I knew that Polly was no angel from the start. I was fully aware of the fact that she was flighty, shallow and selfish. I just didn't realise that she was cruel too.'

'I often wonder about her. What she's doing; how she's getting on. Do you?'

'Not if I can possibly avoid it,' he declared harshly.

'You don't mean that.'

'I do. I don't want her in my thoughts, but she creeps in sometimes, of course,' he admitted. 'How can it be otherwise when you've been in love with someone?

'It can't, and don't I know it.'

'But that is a matter of the heart. As far as my intellect is concerned, Polly has ceased to exist. Anyone who can desert a child is more than just selfish; they're downright wicked.'

'I think that's going a bit far, Ed,' Nell admonished. 'We don't know why she left.'

'Yes we do. She left because she was too selfish and unfeeling to face up to her responsibilities.'

'There could be more to it . . .'

'There's no point in your making excuses for her, Nell,' he cut in, his voice rising. 'I don't want to hear them.'

'All right. Keep your wig on. I was only saying . . .'

'Let's change the subject, shall we? Just the thought of that woman gets me riled, and I don't want to take it out on you.'

'All right, enough said.' Nell yawned and stretched. 'We should go to bed. It's late and I have to get up early in the morning.' She grinned. 'Of course I realise that you'll probably spend the best part of tomorrow in bed, won't you?'

'Quite a large slice of it, I hope,' he grinned. 'When I've caught up on some sleep I can enjoy my leave properly.'

'Is it tiring, being at sea?'

'Exhausting. Still, I'm not complaining. At least I've got to see something of the world.'

'And got quite a ducking in the process.'

'I'm here to tell the tale, that's the important thing. You can't expect to come out of a war unscathed, especially when you think of what some of our boys have suffered.'

She nodded in agreement. 'You got a good suntan out of it anyway,' she said lightly. 'It suits you.'

'Glad you approve.'

'Apart from sleeping, do you have any other plans for your leave?' she enquired chattily.

'Yeah, I'd like to go to Essex to see Gran at the weekend. I'll take Joe with me.'

'Lucky you,' she responded impulsively. 'I love it there.'

'Why not come with me then?' he suggested on the spur of the moment.

'Don't be daft. I didn't say that so that you'd invite me,' she blurted out, embarrassed. 'It was just a casual comment.'

'I know it was, but it would be a good idea.'

'No, honestly, Ed. It's very kind of you to offer, though.'

'Kind doesn't come into it,' he said. 'I have an ulterior motive.'

'Really?'

He nodded. 'I might need some help with Joe, and I know that you're something of an expert in that department.' He knew he would never persuade her unless she thought she could be of practical help; she was the sort who wouldn't want to impose. In fact he was asking her because he thought a break would do her good. 'Mum tells me he's a bit of a handful at times.'

'Aren't they all at that age.' She was only too happy to help, but wasn't sure if she would be in a position to. 'I work Saturdays, though,' she told him.

'From what I've heard, you've worked enough seven-day weeks to entitle you to a weekend off.'

'I'll have a word with the editor tomorrow,' she said. 'But I can't promise anything.'

'Remind him of all the hours you've put in; that might do the trick,' Ed suggested. 'After what you've been through, you need a break, and a bit of fresh air will do you good.'

'It will be fresh, too, at this time of the year,' she said with a wry grin. 'Fresh bordering on freezing, I should think!'

Chapter Fifteen

Waterlow was beautifully bleak when the three of them arrived that Friday afternoon in November. The sky was iron grey, the rolling white clouds tinged with ominous black patches and fringed here and there with rays of light. A cold wind blew through the village, whipping the surface of the water into frenzied little waves and filling the air with the earthy smell of the countryside, the tangy scent of pitch and paint from the boatyard also pleasantly detectable. To say that the weather was bracing was an understatement.

But Maud's welcome was such that they soon forgot the temperature outside. Bonhomie exuded from her every pore. Peg had left a telephone message for her at the village shop, so Maud was well prepared for the visitors, with beds made up, cakes baked and a roaring fire in the front parlour.

'Ooh, how lovely it is to see you all,' she trilled after hugging them each in turn. 'How you've grown, Joe, and look at you in uniform, Ed; so smart and handsome. All the nice girls like a sailor, so they say, and I bet they all like you. Ooh yeah, not half! What a relief they got you out of the sea in time.' She turned to Nell. 'And as for you, young lady, you're still as pretty as a picture and I'm so glad you came.'

If ever a journey had felt worthwhile it was this one, thought Nell. 'I'm here as a sort of nanny to his lordship for the weekend,' she explained lightly.

'Why you're here don't matter,' beamed Maud, the lines in her face deepening with the broadness of her smile. 'You are here, that's what counts.'

Naturally they had come armed with their ration books, and after greetings had been exchanged and tea and seed cake consumed, Nell went to the shop to buy food so that Maud wouldn't be left short by their visit. She also thought it appropriate to slip away briefly so that Maud could have some time alone with Ed and Joe.

'How come you were able to travel down this afternoon and get here before dark?' Maud enquired later that evening over a delicious supper of shepherd's pie with gravy and carrots.

'My boss was in a good mood,' explained Nell. 'He gave me an extra day off so that we could make a long weekend of it.'

'It was the very least he could do, Gran, seeing that she works every hour there is normally.'

'Don't make it sound like a hardship, because that's the last thing it is,' Nell admonished mildly. 'I work hard because I enjoy the job so much.'

'You're the sort to put your back into your work whatever it is,' opined Maud.

'If someone is paying you, it's the least you can do; that's the way I look at it,' said Nell, helping Joe with his food. 'In your mouth, darlin', not all over yourself, the table and the floor.' She looked at Ed and Maud. 'He's ever so tired. I think we ought to put him to bed as soon as he's finished.'

A furrow appeared in Ed's brow.

'Don't panic,' she told him lightly. 'I'll get him ready for bed. You can put him down.'

'Why don't the two of you do it together while I get on and do the dishes?' Maud suggested.

'I'm not leaving you to do the washing-up on your own. It wouldn't be fair,' protested Nell.

'Nonsense. It won't take more than a few minutes and I think you'll be much more useful on Joe's bedtime duty,' smiled Maud. 'Ed isn't used to it.'

'Honestly, anyone would think I was a complete idiot,' he objected good-humouredly. 'I mean, how hard can putting a two-year-old child to bed be?'

Some time later, after lots of warm milk, the entire contents of his fairytale book read alternately by Ed and Nell, the tiredness detected at suppertime now having disappeared completely, Ed had his question answered.

'He seemed so tired before,' he said.

'He still is,' Nell observed. 'He's gone a bit past it, that's all.'

'I'll be asleep before him at this rate,' said Ed, who was sharing the bedroom in the eaves with his son. 'If he doesn't soon go off, it'll be time for me to get in beside him.'

'He's almost there,' said Nell in a hushed tone, stroking the child's forehead with infinite gentleness.

'It's a good job you did come to Essex with me,' Ed whispered to her. 'I wouldn't have had a clue how to get him to sleep. I take back what I said earlier.'

'Your gran would have helped; in fact she'd probably have taken over altogether,' suggested Nell.

'That was what I didn't want,' he confided. 'She's getting on a bit for that sort of caper.'

'I doubt if she would agree with you about that.'

'Maybe not. But she isn't so used to him as you are,' he said. 'You're brilliant with him.'

'I've been involved with him since the day he was born, so he knows me really well.' She looked at Joe, carefully removed her hand and kissed him lightly on the forehead. 'I think we can go downstairs now, Ed.'

He followed her out of the room, leaving the door ajar so that the light from the stairs would comfort Joe if he happened to wake up in the night.

'Thanks, Nell,' he said, outside the bedroom.

'A pleasure,' she said, and meant it. For the first time since Gus' death she felt almost like her old self.

The next day, Ed took the opportunity to do some odd jobs for his grandmother. Using the toolbox that had belonged to his late grandfather, he mended the lock on her bathroom door, fixed her back gate, which had been pulled off its hinges recently by the wind, mended a fence, got plenty of coal in from the coal shed to last her a while and drew water from the well.

While he was busy, Maud and Nell took Joe to see some of Maud's friends in the village so that she could show him off. Then they met Ed at the pub, where the landlord turned a blind eye to Joe as there weren't many people in and they were only staying for one drink.

In the afternoon a watery sun slipped from behind a cloud, bathing the village in a pale light that streamed in through the cottage windows. Nell and Ed wrapped up well and set off for a walk with Joe while Maud took a nap. They walked down the hill past rows of cottages, some with seafaring artefacts in their gardens: a small boat, some ropes, a sail. At the quays they showed the little boy the fishing smacks and barges and watched the fishermen tending to their nets; the yachts in the boatyard were laid up for winter. Then they went to a quieter part of the river and let him linger awhile watching the ducks before leaving the waterside and continuing on across the heath. Here the trees were still tinged with some coppery colours, a carpet of fallen leaves rustling underfoot as they played chase and hide-and-seek with Joe, who squealed with delight and roared with laughter.

It was great fun but exhausting, and that night after Joe was in bed Nell and Ed collapsed into chairs by the fire, pleasantly tired, their cheeks glowing from the fresh air. Maud made them all some cocoa but said she was going to take hers upstairs to drink in bed.

'It's a bit early for bed, isn't it, Gran?' remarked Ed.

'Not for an old gel like me it isn't. Anyway, I like to read in bed. I got a couple of good books this time from the library lady who comes round the village on her bike,' she explained, standing by the door to the stairs which led straight out from the parlour. 'See you both in the morning.'

'Sleep well,' said Nell.

'From me too,' added Ed.

'Oh, I've had such a smashing day, Ed,' said Nell effusively after Maud had gone. 'All that lovely fresh air has made me feel as though I've had all the London smoke and grime blown out of me.'

'I enjoyed it too.'

'We had some fun, didn't we?'

He nodded. 'That's something you and I have always done a lot of.' He paused thoughtfully. 'I never had fun with Polly, now I come to think about it.'

'Oh.' Nell looked surprised. 'I thought your relationship was based on fun.'

'If you mean sex, yeah, there was plenty of that,' he admitted, unabashed. 'But we never had a good laugh together like you and I did today.'

'Strange,' she remarked.

'It might have been because it was all over too quickly for us to get around to being friends,' he said. 'We were too besotted with each other in the beginning; then she got pregnant and she was none too happy about that, so it was all deadly serious. Then I went away to sea and she did a bunk while I was gone. Not exactly the most enduring of relationships, was it?'

'Not really, no.'

'It was good while it lasted, though, especially at the beginning,' he said reflectively. 'I was young and inexperienced and living from day to day with no thoughts of the future. Being with Polly was the most exciting thing that had ever happened to me at that time.'

Nell nodded.

'She was my first serious girlfriend and for a while I was infatuated with her. You grow out of these juvenile things, especially when you're away at the war.'

'Maybe if she'd stayed you would have made a go of things,' she suggested.

'Who knows what would have happened?' he responded. 'I would have done my best to be a good husband even though I hadn't planned to get married that young.' He paused and gave her a half-smile. 'Still, whatever her faults, Polly gave me the greatest gift of all. I just couldn't imagine life without Joe now. Because I feel so strongly for him, it hurts me to think of her deserting him.' He raised his eyes. 'Being a parent doesn't half sharpen up your protective instincts.'

'I'm sure it must do.'

'Anyway, that's enough about me,' he decided, looking at her. 'I don't know why it is, but I always seem to end up pouring my heart out to you.'

'I'm a good listener.'

'You certainly are. But what about you? You've been through the mill recently. Would it help to talk about it?'

'Thanks, but no,' she said without hesitation. 'I want to put the whole Gus episode down to experience and try to forget about it.'

'Very wise.' He gave a slow smile. 'I don't know, Nell. You and I are a right couple of disasters, aren't we? Neither of us showed good judgement with the opposite sex.'

269

'As it happened, no we didn't,' she agreed.

There was an odd, uncomfortable silence; something that Nell had never experienced in Ed's company before. Puzzled by it, she stared into the fire, watching the flames flicker and glow. He did the same, and she wondered if he felt awkward too. They were both lost for words suddenly. There had never been such a thing between them before. It was strange.

Upstairs Maud was in bed but she wasn't reading. Contrary to what she'd said to Ed and Nell, she'd finished her book the other night and had nothing she hadn't read before. Still, that didn't matter as long as her absence downstairs helped to get things moving for Ed and Nell, something that needed to happen and was as plain as day to her but they seemed unaware of.

Just good friends, my eye! That might have been true once, but there was more to it now. She'd never seen a couple more right for each other than those two, and they seemed oblivious to it. If ever two people needed each other, it was them. They had both been hurt and badly let down. Now that was behind them, a future together was there waiting for them. Life was too short to dally about something as important as that, especially in these dangerous times.

The reality was that they had to find their way for themselves. It was all very well for Maud to see it, but she couldn't show it to them. About the only thing she could do was to make sure they had a little time on their own together tonight and tomorrow before they went back to London.

'What is the matter with you tonight, Syd?' asked Polly, observing him across the pub table. 'You've had a face like a broom handle all evening.'

'Have I?'

'You know damn well you have. It isn't like you to be such a misery-guts.'

'Sorry.'

'Don't be sorry. Just cheer up, for goodness' sake, man,' she urged him. 'It's Saturday night and we're supposed to be out having some fun together.'

'Would it help at all if I were to get you another drink?' he offered.

'Yeah, that might go some way towards it,' she replied. 'A gin and orange if you can get it; if not, anything with a bit of a kick in it, and let's see a smile on your chops, please.'

He took her empty glass and went up to the bar. They were in her local, which was packed to the doors, and he had to fight his way to the counter. Someone was playing the piano but it could barely be heard above the raucous roar of talk and laughter.

'A gin and orange for her ladyship,' he said on his return, putting her refilled glass on the table.

'You managed to get it. Well done! Thanks, Syd. You're a real sweetheart.'

'A pleasure.'

'So now perhaps you can crack your face and smile.'

'I'll give it a try,' he said.

'You'll have to be a lot more convincing than that,' she told him when his attempts to brighten up failed completely. 'That wouldn't fool anyone. What is it? What's up?'

'Nothing.'

'Don't lie to me, Syd,' she urged him. 'I know there's something. Come on, out with it. You might as well, because I shall keep on at you until you do.'

'All right, you asked for it.' He cleared his throat nervously. 'The thing is, Polly,' he began, taking large swallows of Dutch courage, 'I've got something to tell you; something that you're not going to like one little bit.'

She threw him a shrewd look. 'Oh yeah, well if I'm not gonna like it, don't tell me. I think I'd rather not know.'

'I have to tell you.'

She frowned. 'Have you got another woman?' she asked. 'Is that what you're trying to tell me?'

'No, nothing like that.'

'That's a relief,' she said. 'As long as it isn't that, I can cope with it, whatever it is.'

Anything except this, he thought, but she had to be told, so he braced himself and said, 'I'm going to give myself up.'

The colour drained from her face. 'Oh no, Syd. Not that old nuisance again.'

'Yeah, that again.'

'What's put that stupid idea back into your head?' she asked through dry lips. 'You promised me you'd forget all about it.'

'I tried, but it just wouldn't work.'

'You'll have to try harder then, won't you?' she said in a brittle tone.

'It won't make any difference. Giving myself up is something I know I must do, Polly,' he said, his tone deadly serious. 'I'm sorry to go against your wishes, but I can't live with myself any longer this way. It's not negotiable, I'm afraid.'

'And never mind how I feel about it,' she snapped.

'It isn't like that.'

'What is it like then?' she demanded, on the verge of angry tears because her life was about to be disrupted and there was nothing she could do about it. She could tell by his determined attitude that he wouldn't change his mind. 'You go off to ease your conscience and I'm left with no one.'

Syd knew Polly was flawed, but her unveiled selfishness over this serious issue surprised even him. 'I feel bad about leaving you, but . . .' he began.

'But you're going to do it anyway,' she cut in heatedly.

He nodded. 'Yeah, that's right. Surely you must be able to understand why I have to do it.'

'No, I don't. Not at all. In fact I think the whole thing is absolutely ridiculous,' she ranted. 'Everyone knows the war is almost over. If you give it a bit longer, all the boys will be back home and you won't feel so threatened.'

'I'll always feel threatened while I'm on the run, and I'll always be on the run because I've done wrong.'

'Rubbish, I've told you before . . .'

'I feel like an outsider, and I hate that because I used to have a lot of good mates,' he cut in emotionally. 'It isn't only about feeling threatened; it's about feeling guilty too.'

'Misplaced in my opinion.'

'That's up to you. I can't change the way you see it. It's something within me and I have to do what I know is right,' he said with an edge to his voice. 'Anyway, the war isn't over yet, not by a long chalk, and if you bothered to read the paper to keep up to date with what's happening, you would know that.'

She flinched because it was so unlike him to be tough with her. He was usually so kind, and let her have everything her own way. 'We haven't had an air raid in ages and everyone is talking about what's going to happen after the war,' she burst out, recovering but very angry with him. 'They've even appointed a Minister of Reconstruction. Whatsisname . . . that Minister of Food bloke Lord Woolton got the job, so they must be expecting an end to it at some point in the not so distant future. See, I do know what's going on. You're not the only one around here who can read a news-paper, you know.'

'In that case you will know that there are still men dying on battle-fields abroad,' he came back at her gravely. 'How do you think that makes me feel; the poor devils losing their lives while I'm having it easy here?'

'You shouldn't have deserted in the first place if you feel so strongly about it,' she said harshly.

'Do you think I don't know that? I've told you why I didn't go back off leave,' he reminded her. 'It was a big mistake and now I want to put it right.'

'You're just being selfish.'

'*I'm* being selfish? Hark who's talking,' he burst out, his eyes hot with rage. 'You don't give a toss about what's going to happen to me. All you can think about is yourself, and how this will affect you.'

'Of course I care what's going to happen to you,' she objected. 'I'm not that much of a hard-nosed bitch.'

'You've got a funny way of showing that you care.'

'You know I'm not the sloppy, sentimental type.'

'You don't want me to do it because you don't want to lose your boyfriend, someone who is useful to you,' he went on, brushing her comment aside. 'Never mind that the rest of the women in the country have to manage while their men are away doing their bit.'

'I've never pretended to be a nice person. I am the first to admit my faults. You know that very well,' she reminded him. 'And yes, you're right: I don't want you to go because it will leave me on my own and I shall miss you something awful. But you're completely wrong when you say I don't care about what happens to you, because I do – in my own way.'

He shrugged.

'We're good together. Why spoil it?' She looked at him soulfully. 'Please don't do it, Syd.'

'I have to, Polly. I'm sorry.'

Polly's misery at the thought of being all alone again manifested itself in anger so strong it was as much as she could do not to throw her drink in his face. But gin wasn't easy to come by these days, and she wasn't going to do anything so foolhardy as to waste it. 'Oh well, if you must you must, I suppose,' she said miserably.

'I'm not going on a picnic, you know,' he pointed out. 'It won't exactly be a barrel-load of laughs.'

'Which is why it's so flamin' stupid for you to do it at all when you stand every chance of getting away with it if you could just wait a bit longer.'

'How many more times must I tell you that I can't do that? I wish I could but I can't.' He sipped his beer slowly, looking at her with a grim expression. 'I don't know what will happen to me, so don't feel that you have to be faithful to me,' he told her solemnly. 'If you meet someone else, you go ahead and make a life for yourself. I'd sooner that than have the worry of your being all alone. I know that you're not good at being on your own.'

'Are you . . . are you saying it's over between us?'

'No. I'm saying that it can be if you want it to,' he explained. 'I don't know what the future holds for me, so I can't ask you to wait. I don't want you to be lonely on my account. I don't want that on my conscience as well.'

'Oh Syd,' she said in a softer, more affectionate tone, taking his hand and looking into his eyes. 'Why do you have to be so damned decent?'

'If I was decent I wouldn't have deserted in the first place, would I?' he pointed out.

'Being decent has nothing to do with it. You'd done your bit and you'd had enough. Basically you're a good man. I just wish you weren't, then you would stay here with me.'

'I wish I could too,' he told her ardently. 'And I mean that from the bottom of my heart. But it just isn't possible; not any more. I have to take whatever punishment is dished out to me. I have to find some sort of peace within myself.'

'That's the last thing you'll find once you're branded a deserter,' she said, tactless as ever. 'A living hell is more like it.'

'You don't understand.'

'No, I don't suppose I do,' she sighed, tears rushing into her eyes. 'But I do know that I'll miss you, Syd Becks. Very much indeed!'

'I know,' he said gently. 'I know.'

'I suppose your gran wants Joe to herself for a little while,' suggested Nell the next morning. She and Ed were out for a brisk walk along by the waterfront. 'That must be why she suggested that we go out for a walk on our own.'

'It's only natural; she doesn't get to see him all that often,' responded Ed.

'Of course it is, and I must say it's rather nice for us to be able to stride out like this for once without being restricted by Joe,' she remarked. 'I feel as though I must breathe in as much country air as I can before we go back to London. Sort of store some up to last me.'

He laughed. 'I don't think it works that way,' he said.

She gave him a playful slap, chuckling. 'Of course it doesn't, you twerp,' she grinned.

'I don't need to store up any fresh air,' he told her. 'You get a lot more than you need at sea. This is just a half a nostril compared to that.'

'Don't mention the dreaded S word,' she said. 'It reminds me that you'll be going back soon.'

'Do I take it that you'll miss me then?'

'You know I will,' she replied, feeling the need to add quickly, 'We all will, especially your mum.'

They fell silent, walking on by the river, its waters dark and muddy under the heavy skies. The tide was out and the river bed was layered with smooth mudbanks upon which small boats were grounded. Fishermen stood around in groups talking and smoking, apparently unaffected by the cold weather. Heading on to the heath, the wind gathered strength, whistling through the trees and sending the leaves flying.

'I'm glad you and Pansy are living at our place,' Ed said out of the blue. 'I like to think of you all together while I'm away.'

'I shall have to try and find us a place of our own as soon as the housing shortage eases up,' she remarked. 'I can't expect to stay there indefinitely.'

'Why not?'

'It wouldn't be fair to your mum and dad. They don't want lodgers cluttering up the place for ever.'

'You're not lodgers, you're friends, and they love having you,' he assured her. 'And I'm not just saying that to ease your mind. Mum has told me that she was dreading the idea of your moving out to marry Gus.'

'Really?'

'Oh yeah.'

'Someone was pleased about the outcome, then.'

'Of course not,' he was quick to correct. 'You know Mum better than that. The last thing she would want is for you to be unhappy, no matter how much she enjoys having you.'

'I know.' Nell paused, remembering. 'I have a feeling she didn't think that Gus was right for me from the start, even though he did work his charm on her eventually.'

'I didn't either.'

'Oh?' She halted in her step and looked at him. 'You didn't say anything when you were home on leave.'

'You were so happy and excited,' he explained, meeting her eyes. 'I couldn't bring myself to spoil it for you. Anyway, I only had a gut instinct to go on. It proved to be right as it turned out, but I thought it was just me being biased. I suppose what it comes down to is that no one is good enough for you in my opinion.'

'It's nice of you to look out for me,' she said. 'But I'll be twenty-one next year.'

'Old enough to make your own decisions, eh?'

'And my own mistakes,' she added. 'Though hopefully I'll get it right at some point.'

A peculiar silence ensued. An elderly man walked his dog nearby but Nell and Ed were almost oblivious. This was a pivotal moment and they were isolated within it. Nothing else existed; not the weather or the scenery or the dog barking nearby. The feeling of intimacy was almost unbearable, the atmosphere fraught with emotion.

'Come on, give us a hug for friendship's sake,' Ed said at last, putting his arms around her. He had obviously found it necessary to clarify the nature of their relationship.

'I wish you didn't have to go back, Ed,' Nell blurted out, her voice quivering.

'Me too.' He forced a laugh and eased the tension by saying in a jokey manner, 'Now don't you get yourself mixed up with any more gangsters while I'm away this time. I don't want to come home to find you've got married to some con man with Al Capone tendencies.'

'All right, you. Don't rub it in,' she admonished in a light-hearted manner.

'Just teasing.'

They drew away from each other and walked on, neither saying anything. Nell was trying to come to terms with the change in her feelings towards him. She felt as though she was falling in love with him. How could that be so when they had been friends all their lives? It was crazy!

Ed was having similar thought about his own feelings. It was like fancying your sister, an incestuous thing. He loved Nell; he always had. But not in that way, for goodness' sake. He enjoyed being with her, liked to talk to her and look out for her. Now he found himself wanting more. Pull yourself together, mate, he admonished himself. She's had enough trouble with her love life recently; don't inflict more on her just because of some biological malfunction. She needs friendship, not complications.

Slipping his arm through hers in a matey sort of a way, he said, 'Come on, slowcoach, let's get a move on; all this hanging about is freezing me through to the bone.'

'Flipping cheek,' she objected in their old chummy way, quickening her pace. 'If anyone is slow around here it's you. Being at sea must be taking its toll and slowing you down on dry land.'

'Saucy bitch,' he retorted.

They hurried onwards arm in arm, chatting and laughing; back to normal. Though it wasn't quite the same as before. It never could be again.

Peg and Tom gave Nell a gold watch for her twenty-first birthday in May of the following year. She was thrilled to bits because she'd never had a watch before.

'You'll sprain your wrist if you don't stop turning it up to look at the time,' Peg joshed. 'I bet you've been doing that all day at work.'

'I have.'

'It's got a good fastener, love,' she added. 'It isn't going to fall off and get lost, so you don't need to keep checking.'

'I know that, but I just love looking at it,' Nell explained excitedly. 'It's so kind of you to give it to me. I don't know how you managed to get hold of it with everything being in such short supply. It must have cost a fortune.'

'It's worth every penny,' said Peg.

'Hear, hear,' added Tom.

'We wanted you to have something really special for your twenty-first,' Peg told her. 'It's the most important birthday of them all. The day you officially come of age.'

Nell had come of age the day her parents had died. She'd had to grow up fast then. But she didn't spoil the moment for them by mentioning it.

'Do you like the brooch, Nell?' asked Pansy, who had saved up her pocket money and bought Nell a gilt leaf with shiny stones.

'I love it,' Nell assured her, guessing that Peg had had a hand in it. 'You're such a sweetheart to get it for me.' She looked at Lenny, who had used his sweet coupons on a box of chocolates for her. 'I love the chocolates too. We'll share them later on.'

'Good,' said Lenny, who was now a tall adolescent who would be leaving school at the end of term.

'You bought them for Nell, not so you could get your paws on them,' admonished his mother.

'Greedy pig,' added Pansy.

'Don't be so mean to him,' Nell said. 'It was kind of him to get them and I wouldn't dream of eating them all myself.'

It was the evening of her birthday and she'd just got home from work. Her colleagues in the office had put together and given her a necklace. She'd adhered to office tradition and bought everyone on the team cakes at teatime, though the fanciest things she could find were some rather stale and tasteless buns. Ted and the others had taken her to the pub round the corner at lunchtime for a drink to mark the occasion. Everyone had been so warm and friendly. She'd been very touched.

One of the best treats of all was the card she'd had from Ed, which had arrived a week ago. At one time it would have pleased her; now it positively thrilled her. It was all totally pointless since to him she was just a friend, but he was more than that to her and there was nothing she could do about it. He hadn't been home again since that last leave, but she knew for certain that she wouldn't feel any different when she saw him again.

'Will somebody lay the table, please,' requested Peg. 'It isn't much in the way of birthday fare, Nell, just bangers and mash. But I've got a tin of peaches and have made you a cake, albeit a wartime one, and Tom and I will take you down the pub later to buy you a birthday drink. Lenny and Pansy will baby-sit Joe, won't you, kids?'

'Course we will,' said Pansy.

'I don't suppose we've got a choice, have we?' said Lenny, who was at an age to find home and everything in it immensely boring.

'No, you haven't,' confirmed his mother.

Nell was pierced by a sudden memory of her eighteenth birthday when they'd all gone to the pub and she'd met Gus for the first time. The intensity of the memory shocked her as she recalled the initial impression he had made on her. She really had been quite bowled over by him. How odd that seemed now when she couldn't imagine what she had seen in him.

Thoughts of that night reminded her of Polly too; she'd been full of herself and loud with complaint about the discomfort of pregnancy. What had happened to her? Nell wondered, feeling a stab of sorrow. Polly would have had her own twenty-first birthday recently, as there was only a matter of weeks between them in age. How could someone disappear as completely as she had? Nell wouldn't have thought it possible before Polly had gone.

Oh well, Gus was dead and Polly had vanished from all of their lives with not so much as a note, so there was no point in dwelling on any of it. But for all that she disapproved of what Polly had done, Nell did hope she was all right.

Polly was standing amid a bank of young people lining the dance floor at the Lyceum. The lights were low, the crowd dense and the air was a fog of cigarette smoke. Polly was hoping someone would ask her to dance soon. She didn't want to stand here like a lemon for much longer. It was too humiliating.

One good thing about the war was that it had produced a tasty assortment of men, servicemen of many different nationalities: Canadians, Polish, Norwegian to mention just a few. Polly's favourites were the Americans. She liked their looks, their uniforms, their fat wallets and – most of all – their generosity with the contents. They were friendly and good fun. People said they were oversexed and overpaid, which suited her down to the ground. She certainly wouldn't say no if she had the chance to nab one.

Twenty-one years old and she was still out on the prowl, trying to find a decent boyfriend because she didn't want to be alone. What a sad state of affairs that was. There had been no one since Syd, and life was bleaker than she could have imagined without him. She hadn't heard from him and didn't expect to at any time in the future. That was the arrangement they'd had when they'd parted. He'd understood that she had to look after her own interests and find someone else to be with. No luck so far, though. The few dates she'd been on hadn't come to anything.

At the moment she was surrounded by girls in groups – many of whom appeared to be younger than she was and, although she hated to admit it, as good if not better looking giggling and speculating about their chances here tonight. Polly had none of that sort of camaraderie; she was here alone.

She hadn't had a female friend since Nell. Women didn't seem to take to her. They never had. Probably saw her as a threat, she thought conceitedly, because she was prettier and sexier than they were. There was also the fact that a lot of the girls of her age in the office were married or engaged, so they didn't need to come out to find someone to get fixed up with.

Of course, she herself was married in the legal sense. She was Mrs Mills on her ration book but she hadn't worn her wedding ring since the day she left or behaved in any way like a married woman. She'd put all of that behind her.

Suddenly she wanted it back with a passion. She didn't want to be standing in the ranks hoping to be chosen for a dance, and something more too with a bit of luck. She wanted to be in the little house in Chiswick with her boy asleep upstairs. The spying in the hope of catching a glimpse of Joe had ceased when Syd had left. It was just too painful to cope with on her own. 'You've made your bed and now you must lie on it,' her mother would say if she was here, and that was what Polly was doing.

What of Nell? she wondered. She was probably married and settled down by now. Could even have a kiddie of her own. Nell had been such a good pal. She was the only female friend Polly had ever had who hadn't got tired of her and abandoned her. Yet the two of them had been so completely different. Nell had been such a caring person, irritatingly so at times, always worrying about people Polly couldn't have cared less about.

It had always been a mystery to Polly how anyone could be genuinely concerned for some stranger who looked ill or distressed at a bus stop, or someone taken poorly on the tube. But she couldn't count the times she'd been held up on her way somewhere with Nell because her friend had felt compelled to be a Good Samaritan while Polly would have preferred to turn a blind eye and go on her way. It had been infuriating and she used to tell Nell so. Oh yes, they'd had their differences, and plenty of them.

But now Polly's thoughts of Nell were all of a kindly nature. Friends like her didn't come along very often, and Polly had turned her back on her as well as on little Joe. No! She wouldn't allow herself to go down that road, stirring up her conscience and getting all upset. She had done the right thing, the only thing she could have done under the circumstances. The situation was irreversible, so best forgotten.

So here she was alone at a dance hall hoping to pick someone up for romance and company. That showed stamina if nothing else, she thought, especially as she didn't feel all that well. She'd been feeling a bit run-down and peaky for a while as it happened; tired and off colour, and she had a persistent cough she couldn't shake off. It was probably the result of a lack of proper nourishment because of food rationing. Most of the population needed a tonic.

Ooh, things were looking up. There was a tall American heading her way with that look in his eye. Thank God for that. He was exactly what she needed to perk her up.

'Would you like to dance, honey?' he asked politely.

Not half, she thought, but she said in a girlish manner, 'Yeah, all right then. If you like.'

This is more like it, she thought as he led her on to the floor, which was heaving with couples, some of them jitterbugging. She was young, free and single and had a red-blooded GI after her. Just what the doctor ordered!

Chapter Sixteen

As Nell stood, still and tense, in Chiswick High Road with her face turned towards the cloudless sky, watching the robot aircraft scuttle over the rooftops with flame spurting from its tail, she was already transferring the sight into words, something that had become almost second nature to her now.

When the killing machine was almost overhead and people darted into doorways or crouched behind walls, some preferring to lie face down on the ground, Nell stayed where she was, her strong sense of journalism prevailing over concern for her own safety and making her reckless.

'Take cover quick, love,' warned a woman who had just ducked into a doorway. 'The flamin' things are lethal.'

The flying bomb fell to earth after a heart-stopping moment of silence that sent even the indomitable Nell diving to the ground. Scrambling to her feet when the danger was over, she dusted herself down and hurried off in the direction of the crash. In her report for the paper she would omit the actual location, as was customary in wartime.

It was late June 1944, and after nearly three relatively quiet years Londoners had found themselves under fire again this past couple of weeks; this time from enemy rockets with harsh sounding engines that sped across the Channel heading for London. After the high hopes of victory generated by the Allied landings in France, this unexpected carnage was a bitter disappointment to everybody, especially the people living in London and south-east England. The damage these monsters caused to property was immense and the human casualty rate extremely high, because they came down at all hours of the night, and daytime too, when people were out and about.

Now Nell enquired of someone in the street and was told the exact locality of the explosion. It was further away than she'd expected, and she had a long walk through the back streets to get to it. By the time she got there, the emergency services were already making headway. Her heart lurched when she turned a corner into the bombed street. Ahead of her, what had once been a terraced row of houses similar to the one she had lived in was now a smoking ruin.

A group of women in aprons and turbans stood across the street, looking sad and bewildered.

'Terrible, isn't it?' Nell said to them.

'Shocking,' responded one of them.

'Many casualties?' Nell enquired tentatively.

One of the women nodded. 'Too many. Some of 'em fatal an' all,' she said tearfully.

'What a way to lose your neighbours,' said another woman, puffing anxiously on a cigarette.

'We're a close-knit community around here,' added a third. 'Everybody is missed.'

'Oh please God, no,' an onlooker gasped as the rescue men carried out a stretcher with a blanket covering a shape so small it could only be that of a child. 'It's one of the kids. Oh Jesus wept . . . I can't bear it; it's wicked.'

'Come on, Elsie,' urged one of her friends, putting an arm around her. 'Come over to my place for a cuppa to steady your nerves. There's nothing useful we can do here. We're just upsetting ourselves even more by staying.'

As she led her neighbour away, someone explained to Nell that the woman was especially distraught because relatives of hers had lived in one of the bombed houses.

Almost in tears herself, Nell turned and walked away with leaden steps, heading back to the office. She didn't need names and personal details. She'd seen enough. To stay longer could verge on voyeurism.

By the time she reached the High Road, the all-clear had sounded and people were going about their business as though nothing untoward had happened. There was a feeling of determination among the population generally to defy Hitler by not allowing the flying bombs to ruin their lives; similar to the spirit so prevalent during the Blitz. What else could anyone do but carry on despite their grief? There simply wasn't an alternative.

'I saw at least ten Doodlebugs go over on my way home from work,' boasted Lenny at the meal table one evening. He was now fourteen and fancied himself as a bit of a lad. Gainfully employed as an errand boy in a munitions factory, he was planning to join the navy as soon as he was of an age to do so. 'It could have been more than ten. I lost count there were so many. One of them exploded very near to me an' all. In fact, you're lucky to have me at all here, I can tell you. I nearly had my lot and that's the God's honest truth.' He held up his finger and thumb about half an inch apart and there was real drama in his tone. 'I was that close.'

'How is it you always see so many of the flippin' things?' asked Pansy with an air of disbelief. 'I don't come across as many as that on my way home from school.'

'Probably because there aren't so many of them about at a time when children come out of school,' he suggested, having absolutely no idea but keen to sound knowledgeable. 'It's the workers the Germans are after. That's the difference between us now, you see, Pans. You're still a kid, whereas I'm a working man.'

Nell nearly choked on her food at that one, observing his adolescent body: endless limbs, pimples on his chin and a fine dusting of fluff above his boyish upper lip.

'A man, my eye,' expressed his mother.

'I go out to work and pay for my keep,' he said in a challenging manner.

'I know you do, son but you've a bit more growing up to do before you can call yourself a man,' she told him.

'You haven't even had your first proper shave yet,' his father chipped in lightly.

'Honestly, Tom,' admonished Peg. 'Do you have to be so personal, embarrassing him like that in front of everybody?'

'Huh. It'll take more'n that to embarrass me,' declared Lenny, his cheeks turning such a bright shade of crimson Nell could almost feel the heat from across the table.

'Of course it will. It isn't as though I said anything to show him up in front of strangers, is it?' Tom defended himself. 'It's only between us, and we're all family.'

It wasn't strictly true, of course, but Nell was warmed by the natural way Tom had included Pansy and herself.

'Anyway, you can stop telling your mother all these porky-pies about the Doodlebugs,' his father went on. 'You know how much she worries about us all.'

'They are *not* porkies,' the boy denied hotly.

'Exaggerations, then,' clarified his father,

Nell thought that was probably closer to the truth. Everybody, it seemed, had a Doodlebug story, and youngsters like Lenny tended to embroider them hugely to make them more exciting in the telling. 'Horrific' was more the sort of adjective Nell would use to describe these eerie pilot-less aircraft that were doing their best to destroy London. But Lenny was an exuberant young boy, and as such saw the whole thing as an adventure.

'Nobody believes a thing I say in this house,' he complained. 'All you ever do is take the mick.'

'That's what families do to each other, son,' said his father. 'It's all in fun and will stand you in good stead for the future, because you'll be able to take a joke.'

'You don't have a choice if you live in this house,' Lenny grumbled. 'But one of these days you'll take me seriously. Just you wait and see.'

As it happened, they did have cause to take him very seriously indeed in September when a bomb landed in Chiswick one evening with an explosion that reverberated all over London. Lenny, who just happened to be in that particular street at the time, was caught in the blast and thrown high in the air, sustaining a broken leg and a substantial number of cuts and bruises.

As well as sick leave from work and special attention at home, the incident gave him a great deal of credibility with his pals, and he gloried in it. But he persisted in claiming that it hadn't been a Doodlebug that had caused the explosion; he insisted that it was something altogether more sinister and dangerous.

'There was no warning; just a bright flash in the sky, a loud bang and then an explosion. I ought to know, I was there. It was different to a Doodlebug, I swear.'

Indeed, over the next few weeks the rest of the populace heard extra-loud bangs that shook London so violently it didn't seem possible that any of it could remain standing. The blasts were rumoured to be caused by exploding gas mains, since there had been no official explanation for them. It wasn't until November that the Prime Minister finally admitted that the enemy had been using a long-range rocket called the V-2 for some weeks.

'See? I told you, didn't I?' said Lenny triumphantly to all those who had doubted him.

'You did too, son,' agreed his mother.

'We all thought you were a hero anyway,' said Pansy, her eyes full of admiration.

Nell felt an ache inside. Her sister's adoration of Lenny showed no sign of abating.

As well as being cold and uncomfortable, fire-watching was also extremely boring. But it was a public duty and Nell took her turn on the roof of the office building where she worked one night in December, partnered by her colleague Frank.

Dressed for the weather, the two of them were swathed in thick coats, scarves and gloves, each wearing a tin hat. The night was cold and clear, the navy-blue sky woven with searchlights. The siren had sounded some time ago. As fire-watchers, their job was to spot and put out any fires they could manage in the immediate vicinity. They would be on duty until dawn, then home to try to grab some sleep before going into the office as usual.

'Nothing much doing on our patch tonight so far,' remarked Frank as they sat huddled on the roof.

'Plenty a bit further away, though,' said Nell. They could see right over Chiswick from their rooftop position, and there were explosions all around.

'Mm.'

'It must be a bit of a worry for you, having to leave your wife at home on her own while you're out doing this,' mentioned Nell to make conversation.

'Yes, it is rather,' Frank confirmed. 'Fortunately her mother lives just across the road, so they keep each other company. And it isn't as if we have to do this every night.'

'No. Thank goodness,' Nell said. 'Spending every night up here would drive us up the wall.'

'We haven't heard anything in the office about your love life lately,' Frank said chattily.

'I don't have one, that's why.'

'Once bitten, twice shy, eh?' he speculated. 'After that awful business with the gangster.'

'It left its mark, of course,' Nell admitted. 'But it's more that I just haven't met anyone else I want to go out with.'

'You will,' he said.

Since that weekend in Waterlow a year ago, there had been only one man she wanted to be with, and he looked upon her merely as a friend. But she said, 'I expect you're right. These things take time and I don't want to rush into anything.'

'I don't blame you.'

Their conversation was interrupted by the drone of an enemy plane growing louder. Before they had time to gather their wits, there was a flash followed by a thunderous explosion nearby that rocked the building so violently, tiles came off the roof and crashed to the ground, almost taking the two fire-watchers with them.

'Are you all right?' asked Frank in the hush of the aftermath.

'I'm still here, anyway.'

'Blimey, I thought we'd had it that time.'

So had Nell, which reminded her yet again that life really was too short to waste in dwelling on negative thoughts of the past. Near misses like the one they had just had were a part of everyday life at the present time, but each one really brought home to her the transience of life and the privilege of survival.

Since she'd been on her own, Polly didn't make a fuss when she wasn't feeling well, as there wasn't much point with no one around to sympathise; she just carried on regardless as a rule. But she'd felt poorly for months and it was really cramping her style now. She'd lost her chance with that lovely GI because of it when she hadn't felt well enough to keep a date. She hadn't been able to let him know, so had had no alternative but to stand him up. Not that it had mattered, because she'd felt too rotten to care.

This morning she felt unable to get up and go to work. She'd been coughing and sweating all night and now felt weak to the point of light-headedness. This wasn't the first time she'd taken time off lately either. There had been too many other days when she'd been too ill to make it into the office. To make matters worse, she hadn't been able to validate her absence with a doctor's certificate, so the supervisor had been none too pleased.

Polly couldn't be bothered with all that doctor malarkey. Paying money to be told what she knew already was a waste of time. There was also the thought that while she kept away from the medical profession, she could tell herself that there was nothing wrong with her apart from being a bit run-down. Once she sought professional advice, all pretence would be lost. She didn't need a doctor to tell her what was wrong with her.

What was she to do? she asked herself, lying in bed between sheets that were odorous from her sweat because she hadn't been in a fit state to take them downstairs to the communal sink to wash them, and her spares were in an even worse state. She was alone with no one to turn to for help. She'd turned her back on everyone who would have been there for her now, and she was growing weaker by the day. Assistance was now urgently required and she didn't know where to go to get it.

A persistent banging on her door forced her to drag herself out of bed to see who it was.

'You wanna get that cough seen to sharpish,' shouted the woman from the next room furiously when Polly opened the door. 'You've had me awake half the night and it's been going on for weeks and weeks. As if it ain't bad enough with ruddy explosions stopping us from getting our rest, I have to put up with you hacking your guts up all night and every night.'

'Sorry,' said Polly, with uncharacteristic meekness.

'Oh.' Polly's submissiveness seemed to surprise the woman, and she bit her lip, looking a little sheepish. 'Look, love, I don't want to seem harsh, but I have a hard day's work in a factory ahead of me and I need my rest of a night.'

'Yeah. Of course you do. I quite understand,' responded Polly.

'Do something about it then,' advised the neighbour, obviously at the end of her tether.

'I just can't seem to shake it off,' Polly explained. 'I've tried all sorts of cough mixture from the chemist but nothing seems to shift it. It's really getting me down, to tell you the truth.'

'I should go down the doctor then,' suggested the woman, who looked pale with exhaustion. 'I know you'll have to dip into your purse, but at least he'll give you some proper medicine to clear it up. I know I must seem hard, but I've got to get some sleep in between the ruddy Doodlebugs. I'm going to work now and I feel half dead. I shall fall asleep at my machine at this rate.'

'I'll get it seen to, I promise,' said Polly, wanting the woman to go because she was feeling faint. 'Sorry to have bothered you.'

'And I'm sorry to have to come knocking on your door like this when you're not well,' said the woman, looking guilty. 'We're all sick and tired of this rotten war, and someone coughing all night is just about the last straw.'

Polly nodded feebly.

'You look as though you need a doctor anyway, for your own sake,' observed the woman, looking at Polly more closely. 'It would be in your interests as well as mine to get that cough sorted. There are times when the chemist just isn't enough.'

'You're right. I'll go down the doctor's later on.'

'I'd appreciate that. Must go. Ta-ta.'

'Ta-ta.'

Closing the door, Polly struggled back to the bed and lay down, her skin suffused with sweat. When the feeling of dizziness had subsided, she sat up and coughed into her stained rag handkerchief, the fresh emission of blood forcing her into a decision. There was only one option open to her, and that was what she must do, no matter how difficult it was going to be.

'Surely this will be the last wartime Christmas,' Peg said to Nell when they were together in the kitchen washing the dishes after Sunday dinner a week or so before Christmas. 'I know we say that every year, but the war can't drag on for another whole year, can it?'

'No, of course it can't,' said Nell with her usual optimism as she dried a plate with a tea towel. 'All the signs of victory are there. Even the blackout restrictions have been relaxed into half-lighting. There's no way the government would allow something like that unless they thought the end was near.'

'Yeah, I suppose you're right,' agreed Peg, sprinkling some more soda crystals into the washing-up water. 'But people are worn out and run down. Everybody you meet seems to have a cough and cold or sore throat.'

'At least we've managed to get a few things for young Joe for Christmas morning.'

At that moment the little boy – now three years old and full of life – burst into the kitchen,

'How many more days now till Father Christmas comes?' he asked.

'The same as when you asked me ten minutes ago,' Peg replied with a wry grin. 'Eight days.'

'Ooh, it's taking ages,' he said longingly. 'I can't wait for him to come.'

'You'll have to be patient for a little while longer, darlin',' Peg told him, putting a dish for drying on the wooden draining board. 'He likes boys and girls to wait nicely. He doesn't like them to drive their gran mad by asking every five minutes how much longer.'

'Does he know?'

'Course he does; he knows everything.'

The boy's eyes widened with awe.

'I'll take you over the park when I've finished this if you like,' suggested Nell. 'It might help to use up some of that excess energy of yours.'

'Yippee.'

'Can you do me a favour, Joe? Go in the other room and ask Pansy to come out here and help with the wiping up to speed things along,' Nell asked him. 'Tell her she isn't going to wriggle out of it again.'

He trotted off just as there was a knock at the front door. Nell went to answer it.

'Mrs Brown,' she said in surprise, recognising Polly's mother and sensing trouble, because she never came to call.

'Can I come in, please?' the woman requested. 'I wouldn't have come if it wasn't important.'

With a terrible sense of foreboding, Nell stood aside and ushered her inside.

★   ★   ★

291

'What are *you* doing here?' demanded Peg when Nell took the unexpected visitor straight into the kitchen. 'Don't tell me your conscience is troubling you for ignoring the existence of your grandson for all this time.'

'No, nothing like that.'

'Why have you come then?' asked Peg, drying her hands on the tea towel. 'You must know you're not welcome here.'

The woman was whey-faced and nervous. 'Yeah, I'm very well aware of that. It's Polly . . .' she began.

'I don't want to hear her name mentioned in this house after what she did,' Peg cut in.

'She's . . .'

'I don't want to hear it. Get out; go on, clear off, you old bag,' bellowed Peg. 'I don't know how you've got the bare-faced cheek to turn up here.'

'But . . .'

'Your daughter abandons her child and you never once lift a finger to see if he's all right.' Peg was beside herself. 'You ought to be hiding your head in shame, not disturbing decent people on a Sunday afternoon.'

'I've come to . . .'

'I don't care what you've come for; you're not staying,' interrupted Peg heatedly. 'I want you out of this house this minute.' She pointed to the door. 'Go, before I really lose my temper.'

At that moment Pansy appeared as requested, and was delighted to be sent straight back into the other room by her sister, who was far more concerned about the current drama than Pansy wriggling out of her share of the chores.

'Let her say her piece, Peg,' urged Nell, putting her hand on Peg's arm in a gentle gesture of restraint. 'It's obviously important or she wouldn't have come.'

Peg stood erect with her arms folded, glaring at the other woman. 'Go on then, spit it out, and then go and don't come back . . . not ever,' she ordered.

'It's Polly,' explained Mrs Brown, and Nell noticed how tired she looked. 'She's dying . . . of TB.'

There was a stunned silence.

'Oh,' gasped Peg at last, clearly shaken. 'I'm very sorry to hear that. That's awful.'

'The thing is,' began Mrs Brown wearily, 'she wants to see her little boy one more time before . . . before the end. She isn't well enough to come here, so she's hoping that you'll let me take him to our place.'

Silence throbbed through the room. Nell's breath was short and her legs felt weak; this was her friend, a young woman in the prime of life. For a moment she thought she was going to pass out, but she managed to stay upright and take hold of Peg as she leaned against the sink to steady herself.

'That's terrible,' said Nell at last, tears rushing into her eyes. 'Really awful. I'm so sorry, Mrs Brown.'

'That goes for me too,' added Peg.

Polly's mother gave a helpless shrug. 'It was a God-awful shock to us, I can tell you. We hadn't heard from her since she left the area. Not a word in all that time, so we had no idea where she was. Then she turned up on the doorstep out of the blue, in a bad way. She came to us because she didn't have anywhere else to go.' She shrugged again. 'You can't turn your own away at a time like this, can you? No matter what differences you've had in the past.'

'That's very true,' said Peg gravely.

'Is there nothing they can do to save her?' asked Nell.

'Nothing at all. Consumption shows no mercy,' Mrs Brown replied sadly. 'About all my husband and me can do is to make her comfortable in her last days. We'll have her at home with us until the end.'

'It's a pity you weren't more supportive to her earlier on,' Peg burst out emotionally. 'She might not have felt the need to vanish into thin air if you had.'

'That's none of your business,' Mrs Brown came back at Peg, though there wasn't a lot of fight in her.

'She deserts my grandson and it's none of my business?' said Peg. 'I think it is.'

'Look, I came to tell you that my daughter is dying,' reminded Mrs Brown, looking worried and worn out. 'I thought you might show a little compassion.'

'Yeah, well I'm very sorry, of course,' mumbled Peg, who was feeling totally devastated, for all her front. 'I don't like to think of anyone dying before their time. It must be awful for her, and for you and your husband.'

'There are no words to describe how we feel,' confirmed Mrs Brown. 'But about her seeing her son one more time . . .'

'I'm very sorry, but I can't allow you to take young Joe out of this house.'

'Polly is still his mother,' Mrs Brown pointed out.

'She didn't think of that when she left him, did she?' Peg reminded her. 'She lost the right to call herself his mother the day she walked out on him. Never once bothering to find out how he was.'

'That doesn't alter that fact that she is his mother,' the other woman persisted. 'Do you have a heart of stone? Would you not grant a sick woman her last wish?'

'I'm very sorry for Polly, of course, but I'm the one who looks after Joe and I won't have him upset,' Peg explained. 'I'm responsible for him and I don't think the deathbed of a mother he doesn't even know is a suitable place for a three-year-old to be.'

Nell took Peg's arm gently. She could see how upset Peg was by the shocking news. Her voice was hoarse and her neck suffused with red blotches. 'Couldn't you consider granting Polly's dying wish, Auntie Peg? It can't do any harm.'

'Of course it can. Subjecting him to the misery of a sickroom and having to see someone in distress wouldn't be good for him, not to mention the germs he might pick up. I know death has become commonplace because of the war, but it's our duty to protect the little ones from it as much as we possibly can. A deathbed reconciliation could traumatise the child for the rest of his life.'

'Polly only wants to see him,' explained Mrs Brown. 'She doesn't intend to cuddle him or have him know she's his mother, not now with her being so poorly. He's too young and she's too sick for anything of that nature. She knows it could have a bad effect on him, and that's the last thing she wants. He'll have to be told the truth later on, of course, but for now all she wants is to see him one last time. It would mean so much. I know my daughter has done wrong, but she is still a human being.'

'I'm not refusing out of spite,' explained Peg, almost beside herself with conflict. 'I am doing it to protect Joe. I take my responsibility towards him very seriously in his father's absence. Surely you can see my point?'

'Perhaps Polly could see Joe outside your house through the window,' suggested Nell, looking at Mrs Brown. 'Is she strong enough to go to the window?'

'Only just, but I expect she could manage it if she had to.'

'I'll take him round there, Auntie Peg, if you'd rather not,' offered Nell. 'She could wave to him from the window and he'll just think she's a stranger being friendly.'

Peg thought about this. She wasn't a hard-hearted woman and she was deeply moved by Polly's fate. But she was fiercely protective of her own and thought the world of her grandson. Maybe her concern for him had caused her to be overly protective to the point of cruelty to Polly, and she didn't want that.

'Well I suppose that would be all right,' she agreed finally. 'But I'll come with you, Nell. We'll take him together then let him have a bit of a runaround in the park while we're out.' She looked at Mrs Brown. 'We'll be round in about half an hour. Does that suit you?'

'Yeah, that will be fine,' said Mrs Brown. 'Thanks ever so much.'

Peg nodded.

'I'll see you out,' said Nell politely, and led Mrs Brown to the front door.

'I'll tell you when they arrive,' said Polly's mother. 'You go back to bed and save your energy until they get here.'

Polly tore her eyes away from the street and struggled from the window back to the bed, where she lay down, panting from the exertion and with an effort pulling the eiderdown over her. This was where she spent her days now. Her parents had been very good to her since she arrived home and treated her better than she deserved, looking after her and doing everything they could to make her comfortable. They had even brought her bed downstairs so that she didn't feel isolated all day upstairs in the bedroom.

She hadn't realised that her mum and dad had had it in them to be so kind, and having had plenty of time lately to reflect, she wondered if maybe she hadn't always been the easiest daughter to bring up, never doing as she was told and always getting into trouble at school. She couldn't count the times her mother had been sent for by the headmistress because she'd been involved in some dire prank or other.

As she'd got older she'd been even more of a headache to them; often coming home late at night, never telling them where she was going and usually out chasing boys, then finally committing the ultimate disgrace by getting herself pregnant. It was no wonder they hadn't always been warm towards her, especially as she'd been so rude to them the whole time. They must have been at their wits' end on occasions.

'They're here,' said her mother now, helping her across the room to the window. 'There's your boy, and a fine lad he is too.'

Polly pulled back the net curtain. Oh my God, Nell was there too, and Peg, and between the two of them was a small boy with shiny red cheeks and a smile beaming from under his blue bobble hat that matched his muffler. He was the absolute image of his father.

Polly smiled and waved, and Joe did the same. The feelings that swept over her were ineffable and never before experienced. She hadn't been an emotional person until she'd had Joe; she had always been able to float over such complexities, and still could as far as most things were concerned. But not when it came to the small person out there in the street. This little miracle was her creation, and he didn't even know who she was. She wanted to go out there and wrap her arms around him and tell him she loved him more than anything else in the world and that she regretted leaving him.

But for once in her life she was going to do what was best for someone else instead of herself; her child was her priority now. He was happy and settled. Let him stay that way. Let him enjoy his Christmas. She waved again and smiled, then let the curtain fall back into place and staggered back to the bed, burying her face in the pillow while she sobbed. Her mother slipped quietly from the room, knowing that that was what her daughter would want. Polly's father was having a Sunday afternoon nap, and knew nothing about it.

At the park, Nell and Peg played hide-and-seek and chase with Joe. Having never known such things as swings and a slide that used to be here, he didn't miss them and had a whale of a time running Nell and Peg off their feet.

When it was time to go, he said, 'Will the lady be at the window on the way back to wave at us?'

'We're not going back that way,' said Peg quickly.

'Why?' He was at the 'why' stage.

'Because it isn't on our way home.'

'I want to wave to her again,' he said. 'She looked nice.'

'She won't be there,' said Nell, hoping to satisfy him.

'Why?'

'I don't know. I just know she won't be, so trust me on this one and stop all this "why" business,' requested Nell.

'Why?'

'Will you crown him or shall I, Auntie Peg?' said Nell, making a joke of it.

In fact she had been profoundly moved to see Polly at the window, a hollow-eyed shadow of her former self, smiling and waving at her beautiful, healthy son. It had been one of the saddest things Nell had ever witnessed.

'Forget all about the lady at the window,' said Peg. 'And if you ask me why, I'll explode.'

'Actually, Auntie Peg,' began Nell, 'will you and Joe go on home without me? There's something I'd like to do.'

'All right, love, we'll see you later,' said Peg knowingly.

'You've got a visitor, Polly,' said Mrs Brown.

'Nell,' croaked Polly, lying back against the pillows, her eyes red and swollen from crying and looking sunken in her skeletal face. She looked apprehensive.

Nell went over to the bed and sat down on a chair beside it, trying not to show how shocked she was at her friend's altered appearance: the emaciation and terrible pallor, the frailty of someone so young. 'Hello, kid,' she said. 'It's been a long time.'

'Am I in for a rollicking?' asked Polly.

'No. I'll spare you that.'

'You must hate me for what I did, though,' suggested Polly.

'I was angry with you for causing us all such worry, but I didn't hate you. Never that.' She took her friend's bony hand in hers. 'You could have let me know that you were all right even if you didn't tell me where you were. We were mates, remember.'

'Yeah, I know. I got it all wrong as usual,' Polly said

'Why did you leave, Polly?'

She didn't answer for a while; just lay back staring at the ceiling as though trying to gather her strength. 'I couldn't cope with being a mum; just hated the whole thing,' she explained eventually. 'Being responsible for a baby frightened the life out of me. That's the only way I can describe it.'

'You would probably have got used to it as he got bigger,' suggested Nell.

'Who knows? It was the wrong time for me then. I wanted to be free. And yeah, I know it was selfish, but that's the way I am and I can't change anything. What was done was done. There was no going back, even though I wanted to after a while. I knew I wouldn't have been any good to him. By the look of him Peg's done a brilliant job, helped no doubt by you.'

'He's just a part of the family; everybody gives a hand, though he isn't a baby any more so he just mixes in with the rest of us. We all love him to bits, but Peg is the one who is actually bringing him up.'

'I knew he would be well looked after.'

'Would you have gone if you hadn't been sure of that?'

'I'd like to think I wouldn't, but that's something I can never be really certain of. I mean, how can anyone know something like that for sure?' She stared ahead of her. 'Anyway, it doesn't matter any more because I'm getting my punishment.'

'Is that how you see your illness?'

'Of course. Don't you?'

'No. You don't have to have done something bad to get TB,' Nell reminded her. 'It's a very common illness. I just feel so desperately sad that this has happened to you.'

'Don't worry about me,' Polly said with a hint of her old spirit, though her eyes were brimming with tears and Nell could see through the act to terrible weakness and fear. 'I shall fight on until the end, moaning about my lot until my last breath. You know me, I like to get my own way, and this time I can't.'

'Oh Polly . . .' Nell was distraught.

'Don't. You'll start me off again, and I've only just finished one session.'

'Is there anything I can do?' asked Nell, gulping hard to curb the tears. 'Anything at all.'

298

'Yeah, there is as it happens,' Polly replied, composing herself. 'Tell my boy, when he's old enough to understand these things, that I did love him even though I had a bloomin' funny way of showing it. Not a day went by when I didn't think of him and wish I hadn't left.' She gave Nell a bleak smile, remembering. 'You can tell him that I used to hide outside his grandmother's house just to get a glimpse of him. And seeing him today has made me so happy; sad, but very happy too.'

'Why didn't you come back if you felt as strongly as that about him?' asked Nell.

'I'm not sure. I was ashamed, I suppose; didn't have the courage to face up to it,' she said. 'But I didn't think I would be right for him either. I'm not a natural mother; too selfish, you see. I expect I was thinking of myself as usual.'

'Oh Polly.'

'Thank Peg for me,' she went on. 'Tell her that she's doing a great job.'

'Will do.'

There was a pause as both women became engrossed in their own thoughts.

'Is Ed still away at sea?' asked Polly.

Nell nodded.

'What message can I give you for him?' Polly said, looking helpless. 'I know he will never be able to forgive me for going off and leaving Joe. What man could?'

Nell maintained a diplomatic silence.

'Just tell him I'm sorry I went off, for what it's worth,' she said. 'Ed and I never had a marriage based on love. It was always just lust. He deserved better. Tell him that.'

'I will.'

'Thanks for coming to see me, Nell,' said Polly, her voice losing strength. 'I'm so glad I've seen you again. I missed you something awful. You're the only real friend I ever had.'

'I missed you too.'

'I was a selfish cow.'

'I can't disagree with you about that, but it didn't stop me liking you,' Nell told her. 'We had a lot of fun together. Do you remember Miss Crow?'

'How could I ever forget?'

Nell recalled all the happy times and the laughs they'd had. The past was all Polly had now, and Nell wanted her to remember the nice things. She stayed for quite a while, reminiscing and bringing Polly up to date with her own news. But when her friend seemed to tire and then erupted into a violent coughing fit, Nell left with a heavy heart.

Christmas was overshadowed for Nell by Polly's awful fate but she entered into the spirit for the sake of the others, Joe in particular. Now of an age to understand the festive season, he careered about the house excitedly with the toys they had managed to get for him, including a wooden pull-along horse, a home-made teddy bear, and his favourite of all: a scooter that Nell had got hold of second-hand. Once he had the hang of how to do it, he was up and down the street on it, taking the odd tumble now and then.

On Boxing Day the whole family apart from Lenny ('A pantomime at my age – I'd be a laughing stock among my mates') went to see *Aladdin*. Joe didn't really understand what it was all about, but joined in, shouting and squealing along with everyone else at the colourful entertainment on the stage.

Unaware that just a few miles away his mother was taking her last breath, he had a wonderful time.

Polly's funeral was a week or so after Christmas. There weren't many mourners at the graveside; just her parents and a few relatives. Nell was there, though, paying her last respects. It seemed ironic somehow that Polly had died so tragically young, because she'd always wanted to be different. She had always yearned for stardom and longed for more than it was possible to have; all those dreams of being somebody special: an actress, a singer, anything that would make her stand out from the crowd. Ordinariness had never been enough for Polly, but in the end she would have been grateful just to stay alive.

Apart from her parents, few people would be saddened by her death. Nell was no stranger to grief, but hot tears meandered down her cheeks as they lowered the coffin into the ground on this bitterly cold winter's day.

Chapter Seventeen

Along with the rest of the population, Nell had wanted peace to come with a passion. For nearly six years she had yearned and prayed for it with aching fervour. But now that it was here and the euphoria had passed, along with the celebrations, there was an aspect of the war that she missed very much indeed: her job in the newspaper office. She'd known from the start it wasn't permanent, of course, but that did little to fill the gap now that it was a reality.

The editor had been most flattering to her; he'd told her that he was sorry to lose her because she'd shown real flair as a reporter and had made an important contribution to the paper. As much as he would like to keep her on, her predecessor had returned from the war and needed his job back.

Nell was sympathetic to all of that, and wouldn't dream of depriving any returning soldier of employment. It was just that her new position in the stenographers' pool at a canned food factory seemed somewhat tedious in comparison. However, she did find a spare-time outlet for her creativity.

She picked up a second-hand typwriter for sale very cheap. It was old and battered; the M key didn't work at all, and several others took some persuading. But at least it enabled her to produce well-presented articles she could submit to newspapers and magazines for publication. She'd written in her spare time ever since she discovered she had a talent for it, but had never sent any work out; mostly because she lacked the confidence, the fact that it was handwritten adding to this.

Peg let her use a corner of the kitchen table to work on when everything was cleared away of an evening, and she tapped away whenever she had an idea. Although they tried to be supportive of her, her eagerness to spend time on this activity was a bit beyond the understanding of the Mills family.

'Haven't you had enough of a typewriter after sitting at one all day?' asked Peg one evening when Nell heaved the machine up on to the table.

'I would if I was typing someone else's words, but these are mine and it's a different thing altogether. I just love doing it, Auntie.'

'So . . . will this stuff you're typing be in the papers and magazines?' asked Peg naïvely.

'That's the aim.'

'Will you be famous?'

'Hey, steady on. I don't even know if I'll manage to get anything accepted,' Nell replied. 'I think it's very hard to break in.'

It was indeed; everything came back in the stamped addressed envelopes she supplied, along with a rejection slip. Although this knocked her back, she was too deeply attached to the creative process to stop writing. Each new piece generated a fresh supply of energy and optimism, and she continued to send them off with renewed hope in her heart. They were mostly light-hearted observations of everyday life in these austere times with everything in shorter supply than during the war.

Nineteen forty-five was a year of change in the Mills household. Not only did Nell have a different job, but Pansy left school, going to work as a junior clerk in an office and – with reluctance and much persuasion from Nell – signing on at evening classes for shorthand and typing.

'It'll stand you in good stead for the future,' approved Nell. 'Shorthand typists are always in demand.'

'I'd rather work in a dress shop,' Pansy complained. 'At least you get to talk to people. Office work is boring.'

'Give it a chance, love,' urged Nell. 'If you really don't like it later on, then try something else. But you'll get better pay than in a shop in the long term.'

Because the repatriation of all the troops was such a massive task for the government to organise, Ed's much-awaited homecoming didn't happen until early in the New Year of 1946. Peg had been saving up and storing tinned goods for ages for the party. It was a real humdinger, with tinned salmon sandwiches, sausage rolls, cheese straws, a barrel of beer, an assortment of spirits and the man next door playing the piano. There was singing, dancing and hilarious games of sardines and murder. At some point in the small hours there was a long line of revellers doing the conga up and down the street.

'It's a good job your mum invited the neighbours, isn't it?' Nell remarked to Ed when the guests had all gone home and the rest of the family were in bed. She and Ed had flopped into armchairs in the living room enjoying a quiet few minutes before turning in. 'We must have been making one heck of a racket.'

'She plays safe by inviting them but I doubt if they would have complained even if she hadn't,' he said. 'I don't think anyone minds a bit of noisy merrymaking with so many welcome-home parties going on. It beats being kept awake by bombs.'

'I'll say.'

They lapsed into an easy silence; both nicely relaxed having had a few drinks.

'I've been thinking about Polly all evening,' Ed mentioned unexpectedly. 'She would have had a whale of a time tonight. She loved a good party, didn't she?'

'She certainly did.' Nell had volunteered to be the one to write to Ed with news of Polly's death at the time. She'd given him chapter and verse on her last sad meeting with her friend, passing on Polly's message to him. They had talked more about it since he'd been back too. 'I'm glad you can think of her in kindly terms now.'

'There's no point in harbouring a grudge against someone who's died, no matter what they've done,' he said. 'I still can't believe she's gone. She was always so full of life.' He shook his head. 'Much too young to die.'

'Because I saw her when she was so terribly ill, it has probably made it easier for me to accept,' Nell told him. 'It broke my heart to see her like that, though.'

'The poor girl,' he sighed, shaking his head slowly. 'From what you've said, she died full of regret, too.'

'Yes, she did.'

'Shame.' He sighed. 'Still, there's no point in dwelling on it and upsetting ourselves even more. Let's talk about something else,' he said in a rapid tone, and she could hear the sorrow in his voice, despite his efforts to conceal it. 'You, for instance. You've changed your job and found yourself a hobby.'

'That's right. It doesn't seem as though I'll ever get anything published, but it keeps me occupied of an evening,' she said lightly. 'As long as I've got something to say, I'll carry on saying it even if no one ever gets to read any of it. I don't understand why I want to do it so much. I suppose it must be some need in me to communicate.' She paused thoughtfully. 'Every time I post a new piece off, I feel as excited as I did about the first one; as though this is the one that will do it for me.'

'One day it will.'

'Well, it doesn't do any harm to have a dream, does it?'

'Are these pieces you write about real life?'

'That's right,' she confirmed. 'Just everyday life from the point of view of an ordinary working girl. I hope they are written in such a way as to be entertaining. But I'm up against experienced journalists. I was just a junior reporter on a local rag.'

'Perhaps you'd have more luck with stories; you know, the stuff you make up?' he suggested.

'Fiction is a different thing altogether. I think you have to have a special kind of imagination to do that,' she told him, thinking it over. 'I doubt if I could write about something that hasn't really happened to me. Total invention is beyond my meagre capabilities.'

'Have you tried?'

'Well, no. I've never even given it a thought.'

'Perhaps you could look into it at some point.' He shrugged. 'But who am I to advise you when I know nothing about such things? It's another world to me.'

'Maybe it's not such a bad idea,' she said meditatively. 'I'll give it some thought anyway.'

'Regardless of what happens about publication, it's nice to have something special that you can take an interest in,' he said. 'That's your thing; something not everyone can do.'

'I'm glad I found it, and I wouldn't want to be without it. I'd probably have been quite content with secretarial work had I not got the job at the paper,' she told him. 'That's where I found I could do things with words, where I got the writing bug, and once bitten there's no shaking it off. Writing and wanting to get published go together for me, though I think there are people who do it just for the love of it because it's a very nice thing to do.'

'You keep writing and sending stuff out,' he advised. 'One of these days we'll see your work in print.'

'It would be such a thrill.' Her eyes became glazed for a moment as she savoured the idea, then she changed the subject. 'But what about the future for you, Ed? I suppose you'll go back to Barker's after you get demobbed, won't you?'

'I shall go back initially but I don't fancy staying there indefinitely,' he surprised her by saying.

'Really? I thought you were set to stay there for life.'

'I was at one time, but not now,' he said. 'I'd like to do something different.'

'Are you thinking of going in the navy as a regular, then?' she asked, trying not to look depressed at the thought of it.

'No, that isn't an option for me because of Joe. I wouldn't mind for myself, because I enjoy life at sea, but I'm not going to leave him. I want to see him grow up and be an everyday part of his life; not just someone who comes back from foreign parts every now and then. He doesn't have a mother. I don't want him to grow up with only a part-time dad.'

'I think that's very wise. You'd both miss out on so much if you were away.'

'You learnt something new when you went to work at the paper and it's given you an ambition,' he went on. 'I suppose that's what's happened to me too. I've been away, experienced other things, had my horizons broadened. The war is over and we're at the beginning of a new era. I feel it's the time for a new start; a fresh challenge. I want to make something of myself, and I'll never do that working in an engineering factory.'

'You want to be one of the bosses? Is that what you mean?' she enquired.

'Not necessarily,' he replied. 'It's more that I want to give Joe the best life I possibly can. I want him to have more than a job on the shop floor at Barker's will allow.'

'What about promotion?'

'There is the possibility of that later on, but it's very slow and you don't earn that much more money unless you get on to the management, and that isn't likely to happen. If it did, it would take years. I'm not sure that I'm prepared to wait that long.'

'I see.'

'The problem is, Nell, I don't have any real capital,' he continued, absorbed in his ideas. 'I've got a bit to come in back pay, from when they couldn't get our wages to us, but not enough to do anything major with. I shall keep my eyes open for any interesting opportunities, though. Something that wouldn't take too much to start up.'

'It seems that the war has turned us into a couple of dreamers,' she remarked.

'It does seem to have,' he agreed. 'Still, what would life be without dreams, eh? You keep trying with that writing of yours. I've got every faith in you.'

'Thanks, Ed.' She paused. 'Mine isn't a life-changing ambition like yours. Getting a small piece accepted for publication wouldn't mean that I could give up my proper job. It would take more than a few hundred words in print to do that.'

'You'll have to get more than that in print then, won't you?' he suggested.

'There would probably be no stopping me if I got something accepted, once I'd come down off the ceiling,' she laughed. 'I'd be so excited they'd hear me squealing in Scotland.'

He smiled. 'I'd be that proud of you, they'd probably hear me too,' he added.

'That's nice.' Looking at him, she noticed how sun-tanned and lean he was; thinner than he used to be, but it suited him because he was so trim. 'It's really good to have you home, Ed,' she said with feeling. 'The waiting seemed never-ending.'

'You're telling me.' He looked at her. 'Why don't you and I have a night out together on our own next Saturday to celebrate my being back?' he blurted out impulsively. 'We could go dancing if you fancy it. Let our hair down and have some fun. If I can drag you away from your literary works, that is.'

'It's hardly that.'

'Well, anyway, what do you think?'

'I think it would be smashing.'

'Right. We're on,' he confirmed. 'Meanwhile I think we should get some shuteye.'

'Yeah, I agree,' she said, yawning and rising. 'G'night, Ed. See you in the morning.'

'It'll probably be dinnertime before I get up.'

'Preferential treatment for you at the moment,' she told him. 'Your mum's so pleased to see you, I think she'd let you lie in till teatime if that was what you wanted.'

'It won't last long, so I might as well make the most of it.'

She smiled. 'Night, then.'

'Night.'

What in God's name are you playing at, man? Ed asked himself when Nell had left the room. The woman is like a sister to you; what are you doing suggesting a date with her? It's almost indecent. But it wasn't really a date as such, was it? he reasoned. Just a night out together for two close friends.

Nell was so very special to him; so lovely inside and out, with her dark eyes and pretty face, her caring personality and interest in the world around her. Most women of her age had one thing on their mind: finding a suitable husband. There was nothing wrong with that. It was how society worked. It was built around marriage and men wanted it too, but not, in his experience, with the same eagerness as women, who were burdened with the label 'spinster' if they were still unmarried at about thirty.

But there was more than that to Nell. She was different from any young woman he'd ever known, and there had been a few in various ports around the world. He remembered with pleasure his visit to the beautiful city of Rio. What a welcome the girls had given the sailors when they'd docked in the harbour . . .

Things had been sweet and simple between him and Nell before he had complicated matters by allowing his feelings for her to become more than entirely platonic. Now he'd let his heart rule his head and invited her out. Still, she wouldn't look on it as a date as such, would she? They knew each other too well. They were a part of the same family, for heaven's sake; even lived in the same house.

As long as he kept things friendly, didn't overstep the mark and made sure that Nell was left in no doubt that he didn't have designs on her, all would be well. Why shouldn't they go out and have fun together when they enjoyed each other's company?

What about her? How did she feel about him? he found himself wondering. There had been moments when he'd felt it flow both ways. But he wasn't going to pursue that side of it, because what they had as friends was too special to risk.

Upstairs in bed, Nell was mulling over Ed's invitation. Although she was thrilled, she knew it wasn't a date as such. She and Ed didn't do dating. He'd made it clear when they were in Waterlow that he wanted them to be just friends. But a night out dancing would be fun. As long as she didn't allow herself to read more into it than there actually was, things would be fine. She was really looking forward to it. In fact she couldn't wait for Saturday to come. But meanwhile there was something else on her mind that she wanted to look into; something that would keep her busy until then . . .

'Peaceful, isn't it, Tom, with just the two of us,' remarked Peg on Saturday night. They were both relaxing in their armchairs with the wireless on at low volume. 'Young Joe asleep in bed and the others out enjoying themselves.'

'Where is it they've all gone?' enquired Tom, who had been preoccupied with the newspaper when the youngsters had been clattering around, bickering over their turn in the bathroom, then giving themselves a final once-over in the mirror over the fireplace before the house was suddenly quiet.

'Nell and Ed have gone dancing, Lenny's gone out with his mates to the firm's social club and Pansy has gone round to her friend's house; to giggle and gossip as young girls do, no doubt. So it's just you and me: a proper old Darby and Joan.'

'We could do with a night out ourselves sometime, just the two of us,' he suggested. 'Now that Ed's home he can stay in and do the baby-sitting for his son.'

'He did ask me if we minded, and it isn't as if he's out every night of the week,' Peg said, defensive of her beloved elder son. 'He doesn't just take it for granted that we'll look after Joe.'

'I know that, and I should hope not either,' said Tom. 'You do more than enough for all of them. You're always running about after one or the other.'

'They're family,' she reminded him. 'They're my life . . . after you, of course.'

'You don't need to point that out to me,' he told her. 'No man could have a more devoted wife.'

'We're a good team, you and me.'

He nodded, looking at her with affection. The tar-black hair she'd had as a girl was now almost white, she was plumper than she'd been on their wedding day and her face was a mass of laughter lines. But she was still a handsome woman, with her bright darting eyes and olive skin.

Peg was what he would call a truly good person, and he loved and admired her for her energy and endless capacity for help and understanding. She was a far better human being than he would ever be, and she meant everything to him. There was nothing she wouldn't do for her family.

'Unusual for Nell and Ed to go out dancing together, isn't it?' he said casually.

'Yeah, I suppose it is really, now you come to mention it,' she agreed. 'Perhaps they were both at a loose end so decided to team up for the evening. There's nothing more than that to it, I don't think. They're just friends.'

'It wouldn't matter if there was more to it,' he remarked. 'There's no blood tie between them.'

'That's true. There's nothing I'd like more than for them to get together as a couple, but I think they've known each other too long for anything like that,' she said. 'They're more like brother and sister.' She paused in her knitting, resting it on her lap and looking into space thoughtfully. 'Now with the other two, Lenny and Pansy, there's definitely a spark there; on her side anyway. She had a right face on her when he went out all spruced up tonight.'

'She's just a kid; she'll grow out of it.'

'I expect she will, and I hope so for her sake, because Lenny is spreading his wings and taking an interest in other girls.'

'It's only natural.'

'Exactly. But it's hurting her.'

'She'll find someone else soon enough, I expect,' Tom suggested. 'You know what young girls are like.'

'I certainly do; she's becoming a very attractive young woman too. So she won't have any trouble finding someone, as long as she gets over this crush she's got on Lenny.' She picked up her knitting again and clacked away. 'You never know, Lenny might begin to see her in a different light at some point in the future. It wouldn't matter, because as you say, the girls aren't related to our boys.'

That was just the trouble, thought Tom worriedly.

The Palais was buzzing on Saturday night, the dance floor a moving mass of couples, jiving, jitterbugging and quickstepping to 'You're Nobody Till Somebody Loves You'. It was smoky, brightly lit and crowded, the colourful decor and curtains capturing the mood of wholesome fun and gaiety. The air was pungent with cigarette smoke, cheap perfume and perspiration.

Near the band there was an area where people could jive and jitterbug while the rest tripped lightly round the floor to the more traditional quick-step. Although many of the American troops had gone home at the end of the war, there were still some at various bases around the country, and they were well represented here tonight, as were men of the British forces. There were the handsome, the less so and those who were definitely out of the question, as well as a large number of gorgeous girls. But Nell and Ed were too engrossed in each other to take much notice.

'It's just as well I'm in good shape,' said Ed, leading Nell off the dance floor near the band, where they had been jiving to everything with a beat all evening. He mopped his brow with a white handkerchief. 'Or I'd have strained all my muscles trying to keep up with you.'

'You're loving it,' she said.

'I am,' he admitted. 'It's wonderful.'

The lights were dimmed and the band struck up with the last waltz, 'Who's Taking You Home Tonight?'

'There you are, a nice slow one,' she told him. 'That will give you a chance to recover before we start to walk home.'

'May I have this dance, please?' he asked, laughing as he pretended to be formal.

'I might have to think about that,' she replied, slapping him playfully on the chest. 'Why are you bothering to ask all of a sudden?'

'Just thought I'd do things properly, as it's the end.'

'Yes, I'd love to dance with you,' she said, entering into the spirit.

When they went on to the floor and moved slowly under the coloured revolving mirror ball in the ceiling, with Nell's head resting on Ed's shoulder, neither of them came up with any wisecracks. In fact they didn't say a word. Nell was lost in the moment, wishing it could go on for ever. The feeling was there between them again, so strong.

But when the music ended and they got caught up in the crowds heading to the cloakroom to get their coats, it was as though nothing had happened. Ed was back to his old matey self. Maybe what had happened was just her imagination, she thought. After all, it wasn't something that could be seen or even described. It was a feeling of warmth and sweetness; of wanting to be with him.

In her heart she knew she hadn't imagined it. She was falling in love with him, and she sensed he felt something too. But her intuition told her most strongly that any initiative to change the nature of their relationship had to come from him or the whole thing could fall apart and she would lose a friend. So for the time being anyway, she had to play a waiting game.

Nell wrote her own name and address on a large envelope and stuck some stamps on it. Then she folded it and slipped it inside another large envelope addressed to a well-known women's magazine. The envelope also contained her first finished attempt at fiction, and she was thrilled to have found that she could do it. It was neatly typed and double-spaced, and contained a brief covering letter addressed to the fiction editor.

Having taken Ed's remarks to heart, she had purchased several women's magazines and studied the stories within them to get the general idea of the sort of thing that was needed. Some were romantic; others not. All were light and entertaining. Immediately inspired, she had tried to come up with some ideas and found she had a very fertile imagination now that she had switched to this genre.

Whether her story was worthy of publication remained to be seen, but she had found an outlet for her creative leanings; that was the important thing. Sticking the flap down securely, she went to get her coat and walked down the street to the postbox. She paused for a moment before slipping the envelope through the opening, wishing it luck silently, then dropping it in with a sense of excitement and achievement. She didn't know how long it would be before she heard back, but she would certainly be taking a special interest in the arrival of the postman after some time had passed.

Oh, wouldn't it be the most wonderful thing, to have it accepted for publication? If they paid her for it, she would be a professional, technically speaking anyway. Even if it was only sixpence she would be more thrilled than anyone could imagine. Keep your fingers and toes crossed, girl, she thought as she walked back to the house in the cold winter's night.

When she got in, there was a heated discussion in progress in the living room, mostly between Ed and his father, though the others – excluding Joe, who was in bed – were there too. Nell slipped in and sat down on a chair beside her sister, who was reading one of the magazines Nell had bought to study for her project.

'You're a skilled worker the same as I am. We're both damned good tradesmen,' Tom was saying in an angry tone. 'You should be proud of it, not hankering after something else that pays more money.'

'There's nothing wrong with trying to better myself, Dad,' claimed Ed.

'Oh, so the shop floor isn't good enough for you now?' snapped Tom. 'I'll have you know that it's a very honourable trade.'

'I fully accept that, but I've got a child to support and I want him to have the best in life that I can give him.'

'Oh, so I didn't give you a decent life on my earnings, then, is that what you're saying?'

'No, of course it isn't. You're deliberately misunderstanding me. I had a wonderful upbringing and I thank you for it,' Ed declared. 'Times were hard for you and Mum during the depression, I know, but I was always well looked after and had a happy childhood. But we're living in different times now and I don't want to feel as though I have to stick with the same job for the rest of my life.'

'It's always been good enough for me,' stated Tom.

'I know, Dad, and I admire what you do. But that doesn't mean it is necessarily the best thing for me, not in the long term anyway,' Ed pointed out reasonably. 'We're all made different.'

'After all that training, you'd throw it away for a few quid extra?' said Tom accusingly.

'There's nothing wrong with him wanting to better himself, Tom,' Peg intervened defensively. 'I like to see initiative myself. You should be encouraging him, not having a go at him.'

'But he's just after more money.'

'What's wrong with that?' she wanted to know. 'As long as it's earned honestly.'

'There's more to life than money,' insisted Tom. 'There's pride in your work, and job satisfaction.'

'Look, I haven't said I'm definitely going to come out of my trade,' Ed pointed out. 'I was only saying that if a good opportunity came up in another field, I might be interested.'

'As long as it paid well.'

'Of course; that's the whole idea.' He was becoming angry now at his father's refusal to even consider his point of view. 'I'm not fool enough to make a move if it wasn't well worth my while. I've got a child to support. I've got responsibilities. It's my duty to get the best I can for him.'

Nell could see that they were both het up and overreacting to each other's every word.

'It's the flaming war,' declared Tom, his temper rising. 'It's made people greedy.'

'Ooh, fat chance of that,' put in Peg with a wry grin. 'There's nothing to be greedy with. Everything is scarcer than it was when the war was on. It's nothing short of disgraceful the way we are forced to live.'

'I mean that people have tasted other things and now they're not content with their lot.'

'The government are promising us a better world, and people want to have some of it,' she said. 'And why not, I say. It's been hard what with the depression and then the war. Why shouldn't people have higher expectations?'

'If I were you, Ed, I'd go back in the navy,' Lenny piped up. 'That's the life. Out there seeing the world.'

'Who asked your opinion?' This was Ed.

'No one.'

'Well keep your nose out of it then.' Ed was uncharacteristically irritable because he and his father seemed to be worlds apart suddenly, and he wasn't used to that; they'd always got on well. 'This is a conversation for grown-ups.'

'Which I am.'

'Show it then by keeping quiet.'

'Oh, I'm getting out of here,' Lenny reacted huffily. 'I'm going round my mate's house to be with people who value my company.'

'Don't be late,' warned his mother.

Lenny gave an eloquent sigh. 'I am sixteen, Mum,' he reminded her pityingly.

'I don't care if you're sixty-four,' said his mother. 'Don't be late coming home to this house.'

Sighing and shrugging, Lenny left the room mumbling about the unfairness of it all.

'Would anyone like a cup of tea?' asked Nell in a bid to lower the temperature.

'What a good idea,' approved Peg, exchanging a look with her. 'We'll all have one. It might calm you two men down.'

When Nell left the room, the debate was still in full swing and the temperature rising. One thing she did know for certain was that Ed would want to discuss this with her later on when the others had gone to bed. He might be reluctant to move things to another stage between them at a personal level, but he valued her opinion and respected her views even though he didn't always agree with them.

As she filled the kettle and put it on the gas stove to boil, her thoughts returned to the envelope she had just slipped into the postbox, and excitement rose up inside her.

'Dad's far too set in his ways,' Ed complained to Nell later on when the others had gone to bed. He'd sought her view of the matter as she'd guessed he would. 'He simply refuses to open his mind to anyone else's ideas.'

'He's entitled to his opinion, Ed.'

'And I'm entitled to mine,' he stated heatedly. 'But oh no, there was nothing like that. I was just told I was greedy and that was that. He didn't even try to understand my point of view.'

'You were both far too agitated to be reasonable.'

'You're ambitious,' he remarked, looking at her thoughtfully. 'And no one could ever accuse you of being greedy.'

'That's a different thing altogether,' she told him. 'I just happened to discover that I could do something and I'd like to succeed at it. It has nothing to do with money; it's more about personal achievement.'

'Are you saying that if someone wanted to pay you for your writing, you wouldn't grab it with both hands?'

'No, I'm not saying that at all,' she made clear. 'I'd be thrilled, of course. A few coppers earned from my writing would mean more to me than someone giving me a hundred pounds. It would mean that someone thinks my work is good enough to be published. By the sound of it, you just want to get rich in whatever way you can.'

'All right, so I want to do well for myself. I haven't worked out a way to do it yet, but it all comes down to the same thing in the end,' he said. 'We both want to improve our situation.'

'No. I just want to get my work published,' she told him. 'I don't want to improve my life in any other way.'

'Okay, so I'm the greedy one,' he said, his voice rising. 'What is so terrible about wanting more money?'

'Nothing, so long as the need for it doesn't take over your life,' she replied.

'I need to have a serious attitude towards it or I'll still be at Barker's in twenty or thirty years' time,' he pointed out. 'I don't want to look back when I'm old at what might have been if only I'd had the guts to give it a try.'

'As long as you stay true to your principles — and I know you always would — I think you'd better start looking for a way to get rich, because you won't rest until you've given it a go. Win or lose, you need to try, and good luck to you.'

He laughed. 'Trust you to hit the nail on the head,' he said. 'I need to put my thinking cap on. There will be plenty of opportunities around once things in the country generally begin to improve, so I'll keep my ear to the ground.'

She hadn't told anyone that she had posted her first story tonight just in case she was disappointed. She didn't want to tempt fate. But she was so excited about it, she couldn't resist telling Ed.

'Well done,' was his genuine response. 'I said you should give stories a try.'

'Thanks to you, I did, and I've got a real feel for it, Ed,' she said.

'In that case, I'm sure you'll get good news soon.'

'I do hope so.'

'Will you stop going on about it,' urged Peg, in bed beside Tom. 'So the boy has got ambition. Don't try and make him feel bad about it. Why not be proud of him. I know I am.'

'I'm proud of him the way he is now,' he told her. 'He's done his bit in the war, he's got a steady job at Barker's to go back to, and he's being a good father to young Joe. I won't be so proud if he throws his training away and gets some flash job as a salesman or something because he thinks he can get rich.'

'Salesmen have been known to do well,' she pointed out, 'if they work hard. Nothing comes from nothing, as you very well know. Whatever he finally decides to do, he'll have to put his back into it. Anyway, there's nothing wrong with going into sales.'

'There is when you've been given the training that Ed has, and have the special skills.'

'I shall slap you in a minute, Tom Mills,' she warned. 'You can't live Ed's life for him. You have to let him do what he wants, and make his own mistakes.'

'It's just that . . .'

'It's just that you think your son has to have the same views as you about everything,' she cut in. 'It doesn't work like that. Times are changing, Tom, and we have to adapt to them. Ed is your son, yes. But he's also his own man.'

'Yeah, I suppose so.'

'Now can we go to sleep, please?'

At that moment there was a knock on the bedroom door.

'Come in,' said Peg.

Ed put his head round the door. 'I heard you talking so knew you weren't asleep. I just wanted to say sorry, Dad, for getting a bit stroppy downstairs earlier.'

'That's all right, son.'

'Night, then.'

'Night,' they chorused.

'There you are,' said Peg when Ed had shut the bedroom door behind him. 'That's the sort of man your son is. One who takes the trouble to come and apologise before we all go to sleep.'

'He didn't say he'd changed his mind, though, did he?'

'No, he didn't, and that's because he's got a mind of his own, and I personally admire him for that. He came to say sorry, and that's enough. You can't have everything.'

'No, of course you can't,' Tom said, sounding pleased despite himself. 'He's a good lad at heart. Both our boys are.'

'Shame we didn't have any daughters of our own,' Peg mentioned. 'But we've got the next best thing in Nell and Pansy.'

'Mm,' muttered Tom, very glad that the light was out so she couldn't see the look in his eyes.

Nell's disappointment when her story was returned to her with a rejection slip was out of all proportion to the actual event, she admitted to herself. It was as though all the hope had been punched out of her. She hadn't realised until she opened her self-addressed envelope just how high her hopes had been. The pages that had been alive with the voice of her imagination were now just dull pieces of paper with failure emanating from them.

She stared at the brief letter from the fiction department, searching it for any clues as to why they hadn't wanted to use her work. But it was just a polite note thanking her for submitting her material and saying that unfortunately it wasn't suitable for publication in their magazine. No explanation as to *why* it wasn't suitable.

To her shame, she felt close to tears. This was ridiculous. People had far worse to deal with; indeed, she herself had had her share of trauma. But somehow none of this helped. It was a different sort of pain, but it did hurt. It was the end of a dream.

When she told Ed, though, after the others had gone to bed, he didn't seem to see it that way. 'Oh, I'm ever so sorry, kid; better luck next time.'

'Next time? There won't be a next time,' she declared haughtily. 'I'm obviously no good at it or they would have wanted to use it. I would have thought that was obvious.'

'Wouldn't you get better the more you do of it? That's how it is with everything else.'

'It's different with writing. You either have the talent or you haven't,' she said tartly. 'And I obviously haven't or the story wouldn't have come back.'

'All right. Don't snap my head off. There's no need to take it out on me.'

'Sorry.'

'Look, Nell, I'm not going to pretend to know anything about the world you are trying to break into, but even I have heard of rejection slips,' he told her.

'Of course you have. I've just told you that I've had one,' she reminded him.

'No. I mean other people get them in sackloads. Aspiring writers receive them all the time when they're starting off. I heard something about it on the wireless once.'

'If you think I'm going to waste my time again just to be humiliated, then you can think again.'

'It isn't like you to give up so easily,' he persisted.

'You know nothing about it,' she said huffily, her disappointment still raw. 'Nothing at all.'

'I've already admitted that,' he said. 'But I do know you, and I know that you're not a quitter.'

'I am as far as this is concerned,' she said. 'In fact I feel like chucking the typewriter in the river.'

'If you keep trying, you might eventually be able to afford to get one with an M key that works.'

She smiled despite herself. 'It isn't funny.'

'No, but your attitude towards it is,' he grinned. 'It isn't often you get narked, but this has done it good and proper. I've never seen you so ratty. It's a wonder your hair isn't standing on end.'

'I'm going to bed,' she said. 'Good night.'

'Nighty-night.'

By the time Nell went to sleep, she had the germ of an idea for another story swimming around in her head. Excited and inspired, she got out of bed quietly so as not to wake Pansy, took a pencil and piece

318

of scrap paper from her drawer and crept down the stairs to make a few notes.

Good old Ed, he did talk sense when he wasn't going on about making money.

Chapter Eighteen

'Just look at those two enjoying themselves out there,' observed Peg, looking out of the kitchen window into the back garden while she washed the dishes at the sink. 'It's a treat to see them, even though I'll have the devil's own job to get the grass stains off their clothes.'

'Sometimes they are more like a couple of old pals than father and son,' Nell responded, smiling at the sight of Ed and Joe play-wrestling on the lawn in the spring sunshine one glorious Saturday afternoon in early May.

'Mm, they are at times,' agreed Peg. 'Though Ed is firm when he needs to be, and he does quite often need to be now that Joe is growing up and getting cheeky.'

'I can hardly believe that he'll be five in the autumn,' mentioned Nell, drying a plate and putting it away in the cupboard. 'It hardly seems any time since he was a baby.'

'He'll be off to school in September,' sighed Peg wistfully. 'I shall miss him something awful during the day; I love having him around.'

'I'm sure you will.'

'He's ready for school now, though. He needs more than I can give him at home.'

Pansy appeared in the doorway. Now going on sixteen, she looked smart and pretty in a white blouse and plain black skirt worn with perilously high heels, her face made up and her brown hair luxuriant and loose. 'I'm going to Hammersmith to have a look round the shops,' she announced.

'Don't forget that it's your turn to clean the bedroom,' Nell reminded her.

'I'll do it tomorrow morning.'

'You will too, I shall make sure of it,' warned Nell. 'You've got to do your share around here.'

'I'll do it, I promise, so give over nagging, will you, sis,' she said with a careless giggle. 'Anyway, I've got to go. I'm meeting the girls. See you later.' And she was off out of the front door, her heels clattering down the path.

'She's full of life these days,' said Nell. 'Always wanting to be out with her friends. She's really come out of her shell lately, and I couldn't be more pleased.'

'She's at the age to want to be out,' said Peg. 'Lenny's the same. He never seems to be at home. Let them enjoy the fact that they're young and it's peacetime, I say.' She stopped suddenly, looking out of the window. 'Look at the daft pair now.'

Following Peg's glance, Nell saw Ed with Joe on his back galloping around the garden, with Joe shouting, 'Giddy-up!'

'Sweet,' observed Nell. It delighted her to see the way Ed was with his son, somehow managing to have fun like a five-year-old whilst retaining his authority. Joe pushed his luck sometimes when he got overly exuberant, but even then he knew his dad was the boss. Ed devoted his time to Joe at weekends, playing with him, reading to him, taking him out. It couldn't have been easy at first, having been away so long and having to build a relationship with Joe more or less from scratch, but he had proved to be an excellent father.

Ostensibly, things hadn't changed between Nell and Ed since the night of the dance when she'd realised she was in love with him. He was still affectionate, but in a friendly, brotherly way which she knew in her heart was forced. She could wait. He'd come round to the idea of their being together eventually, when he accepted the change in their feelings for each other; she was sure of it.

When Ed had left Barker's to go into the navy, Marian Barker, the daughter of the factory owner, had been an insignificant schoolgirl who was occasionally seen around the factory and didn't warrant a second glance. Now she was a gorgeous, long-legged redhead with suggestive green eyes and a figure that almost brought the shop floor to a stand-still when she walked by.

Ed was still biding his time at Barker's while keeping an eye open for an opportunity to change direction and he didn't recognise her when she walked through the factory en route to her father's office one day the following week. He was aware that there must be something different about this particular female, though, because the appearance of a woman with her looks on the factory floor would normally produce a chorus of wolf whistles and other vulgar appreciation. But as the boss's daughter, she was treated to a respectful silence, the men ostensibly busy with their work and only daring to look at her from the back after she had passed by.

Much to Ed's amazement and the amusement of his workmates, Marian took a fancy to him; she would stop by his workbench and flirt with him outrageously. Ed treated it as a joke and played along with her, but being only human, he was flattered to be singled out for so much attention by a girl who could have anyone.

'Are you working in your dad's office or just visiting?' he asked one day when he met her in the corridor. 'You seem to be spending a lot of time here lately.'

'Just helping out to keep Dad happy; well, I'm supposed to be helping out, but I do as little as I possibly can,' she explained with a wicked gleam in her eye.

'Doesn't that put more of a load on to the others?'

'No, not really. There isn't much for me to do. Dad invented a job for me just so that he can keep an eye on me here at the factory. I'm not really needed. He thinks that being here under his beady eye will keep me out of trouble.' She laughed and rolled her eyes at Ed. 'Which just goes to show how little he knows about me.'

'I bet you give him a few headaches.'

'I do my best.' She looked at him under her lashes. 'Are you going to ask me to go out with you on Saturday night?'

'No.'

'Why not?'

'I hadn't thought about it.'

'Think about it now, then,' she urged him saucily.

'I doubt if your father would approve of your going out with a member of his workforce.'

'It has nothing to do with him. I don't have to have his approval about anything any more.' In her attitude, Ed could see a classier version of Polly and was immediately on his guard. 'I'm a grown woman and I go out with whoever I please. Anyway, he likes tradesmen. He was one himself back in the Stone Age.'

'Surely you wouldn't want to embarrass him, though,' suggested Ed. 'He is your father, after all.'

'My dad doesn't get embarrassed.'

That's just as well with a daughter like you, thought Ed, but he said, 'I find that hard to believe. Everyone gets embarrassed at times.'

Marian shrugged. 'What does it matter anyway?' she said carelessly.

'A lot, from where I'm standing.'

'You won't get into trouble over it, if that's what's worrying you,' she assured him. 'That would upset me, and Daddy wouldn't want to do anything to annoy his darling daughter.'

'The poor bloke,' Ed said lightly. 'I bet he doesn't know if he's coming or going with you as a daughter.'

'Look . . . let's stop mucking about. You're the best-looking bloke this side of the river, and I'm the prettiest girl,' she stated categorically. 'So let's get together and have some fun. You know you want to.'

'Fancy yourself, don't you?'

'Not half as much as I fancy you.'

Definitely another Polly; trouble with a capital T, he thought. 'I'm flattered, but I'm not free to go out with you. I have a young son . . .'

'But no wife to hold you back,' she cut in, grinning. 'You see, I've done my homework.'

'Then you'll realise that I can't go out just when I feel like it,' he said.

'That's easily solved; get a baby-sitter,' she suggested airily. 'I'm sure your mother will be more than happy to oblige. I know she's nice and handy.'

'You really have been nosing around, haven't you?'

'It isn't difficult to get information in a firm like this. Not when you're the boss's daughter, anyway.'

'Why should I take advantage of my mother's good nature by asking her to baby-sit for me, when she looks after my boy all day while I'm at work?'

'Because you're a young, virile man and you've had an offer you can't refuse.'

'Saucy cow.'

'I like it, I like it!' she cried, her eyes bright with enthusiasm. 'A man who speaks his mind. Oh yes!'

'What makes you so sure that I want to go out with you anyway?' he challenged.

'Every man on the workforce would jump at the chance, and you're no different.'

'You've got some front; I'll say that much for you.'

'I'm no shrinking violet, it's true,' she admitted. 'That sort of attitude gets you nowhere.'

'What exactly do you have in mind for this proposed outing?' he enquired. 'Only I can't afford to take you to the sort of places you're used to.'

'The pictures, for a drink; anything will do as long as we are together,' she told him. 'I've got plenty of money to spend, but I suspect that you're the sort of man who would take a dim view of the woman paying.'

'I certainly would.'

'You can pay then. It doesn't worry me one way or the other. We can just go for a walk if you like,' she said with a casual air. 'I don't care what we do so long as I can get to know you better.'

'You don't exactly play hard to get, do you?'

'What a waste of time that is,' she replied. 'If I want something I go all out to get it.' She rolled her eyes at him. 'I've never been known to fail.'

'I'll let you know when I've investigated the baby-sitting situation,' he told her.

'Okay,' she agreed. 'I'll be waiting. I shall seek you out tomorrow and I'll expect an answer.'

She turned and walked away, swinging her hips in an exaggerated manner.

Ed was under no illusions. Marian was a girl who was used to getting her own way about everything. She was rich, spoilt and ruthless; not his type at all. But on the other hand, a one-off night out with her might be fun.

Rejection had become a way of life for Nell. She received one several times a week in a fat self-addressed envelope; sometimes two at a time,

325

because she sent her stories to a number of magazines before finally giving up and stashing them away in a drawer. It still hurt, but somehow the ideas kept coming, so she kept on writing and submitting and putting herself through the misery of rejection time after time. It was almost like a compulsion with her.

But when Ed came in late one night when she was just about to pack the typewriter away and told her that he was dating Marian Barker, her writing dream was pushed to the back of her mind so effectively it didn't seem to matter one iota. She couldn't have been more hurt and shocked if a rock the size of a football had been thrown at her head.

Of course, she had noticed that he'd been out more than usual of an evening lately. But he'd answered the family's casual enquiries by saying that he was meeting some mates for a pint.

'I wanted you to know before I tell the others,' he said, feeling compelled to give her an explanation even though there was no reason why he should.

'Why is that?' she asked stiffly.

'Because you're my closest friend.'

'So close you found it necessary to lie about your new relationship; to pretend you were going out with your mates.'

He looked sheepish. 'Yeah, that was wrong of me,' he admitted. 'But I knew Dad wouldn't approve and I didn't want to get into a row about it, so it was easier to tell a fib. It was just a bit of fun anyway at first. Not worth mentioning.' He sighed. 'There's no privacy in this house, so the odd white lie is almost inevitable.'

'Why are you making it public now?'

'Because things have moved on and it's become more than just a bit of fun,' he explained. 'She's invited me home for tea on Sunday to meet her folks.'

'In other words, it's serious.'

'She wants it to be an accepted fact that we're a couple. Put it that way.'

'And you?'

He shrugged.

'Do you love her?'

'No,' he said without hesitation.

'So why are you leading her on?' Nell wanted to know.

Ed looked at her shiftily.

'Oh, I get it. It's the money, isn't it? If you were to marry into the Barker family you'd be set up for life,' she said accusingly. 'You'd get taken into the firm on a high salary and given all the status and lifestyle you've been thinking about so much lately.'

'Steady on, Nell,' he urged her. 'Marriage hasn't been mentioned yet.'

'That's the intention, though, isn't it?' she surmised. 'And you daren't bring it up yet in case her father guesses what you're up to. She must have blokes after her all the time for her money.'

'She came after me, not the other way around, as it happens,' he made clear. 'She asked me to go out with her. She was all over me, in fact. You can ask any of the blokes at work if you don't believe me,' he invited. 'They pulled my leg something rotten about it.'

'You weren't slow in snapping up the offer, though, were you?' she said.

'She was so pushy I thought it would be a laugh; I thought it would just be a one-off,' he explained. 'But she was dead keen from the word go, and before I knew what was happening I was seeing her on a regular basis'.

'And then the material gain dawned on you?'

He lowered his eyes.

'Oh Ed. Are you that greedy for money you'd stoop to such a level?' she asked, bitterly disappointed in him.

'It isn't a question of greed. It's a matter of making the most of your opportunities.'

'Now you're just making excuses for yourself.'

'I'm just being practical.'

'And what about Joe in all this?'

'It's him I'm doing it for,' he pointed out. 'I'd be better able to provide a decent life for him.'

'Oh, please . . . don't use an innocent child as an excuse.' She looked at him in a questioning manner. 'Anyway, how does the lovely Marian feel about your having a child?'

'It's still very early days, but she seems quite happy about it. She knows that he is my priority. I made that clear from the start,' he told her. 'There is no way I would take it any further if she wasn't willing to accept that.'

'I believe you about that, at least.'

'Actually, Marian suggested that I take him with me on Sunday, but he's going to a birthday party and I don't want him to have to miss that. They'll meet him another time.'

'So you're going to Sunday tea to meet the family and they'll take you to their hearts because everyone does,' she speculated. 'But will you really be able to live with yourself knowing that it isn't a social occasion but a glorified job interview?'

'Now you're being ridiculous and making me out to be really unfeeling,' he objected.

'That's what you'll be if you go ahead with this.'

'Look . . . if things were to work out between Marian and me, it would just be a leg up,' he tried to explain. 'What I make of it would be entirely up to me. I have no intention of sitting back and waiting for it all just to drop into my lap. I'd work my arse off for the firm, but at least I'd have a chance of progression, an opportunity to show what I can do. People like us have to seize our opportunities when we can, because we don't have many of them.'

'We don't have as many chances as the better-off, I admit, but they do exist. You make your own luck in life, and if you've any sense of decency, you don't use other people's feelings to do it.'

'Marian started it, and she's leading the way now, so she's hardly the victim; she would never be that anyway, because she only ever does what suits her,' he pointed out sharply. 'Make your own luck, you say; that's exactly what I'd be doing, because I would work hard. A chance has come my way; what I make of it is up to me.'

'If you say it often enough you might even begin to believe it,' Nell said sadly. 'What's wrong with an honest day's work for a decent wage?'

'Ooh, you're a fine one to talk,' he came back at her, rattled by her attitude. 'Who is it who spends all her spare time trying to better herself?'

'I am *not* doing it for that reason and you know it,' she reacted angrily. 'I do it because it's something I enjoy, and if I can get paid for it so much the better. But it would be the fulfilment of a dream, not the satisfaction of greed.'

'Neither will it be that for me.'

'If I ever do achieve success it certainly won't be because I've had a leg up, as you call it.'

'I take it I don't have your blessing, then?'

'If you love Marian or think you might learn to in the future, then I wish you the very best of luck,' she told him. 'If not, I think you're letting yourself down, and I'm disappointed in you. But what you do has nothing to do with me.'

'At least that's one thing we agree about,' he said grimly, and left the room without saying good night.

Over the years they had known each other, naturally they had had disagreements. But never as serious as this, thought Nell, her eyes swimming with tears as she packed up her papers and put the typewriter out of the way in the cupboard under the stairs so that the kitchen table was clear for domestic use the next day.

There was nothing wrong with what he was doing, Ed told himself as he got undressed for bed, in the dark because Lenny and Joe were asleep. Nell had no right to make him feel guilty about it. Anyway, he had a long way to go before there was any possibility of marrying Marian. The meeting with her family was only the first step. It was a giant leap forward, though, he was forced to admit. If all went well on Sunday, he would be on his way to becoming one of the Barker clan.

No, it was *not* wrong, he reminded himself over and over again. Nell's words refused to stop eating away at his conscience, but over this issue he wasn't going to let her opinion influence him. This might be the only chance he ever got to improve things for himself and Joe, and it wasn't as if he expected anything for nothing. He was planning to give his all to the job at Barker's if he was given more responsibility. That was all he wanted: the chance to prove that he was capable of more than what he was doing at the moment.

He refused to be put off by the fact that he wasn't actually in love with Marian or ever likely to be. She was mad about him and he found her entertaining; surely the rest would come. Once committed to her, he would never let her down.

So yes, what he was planning on doing was perfectly decent and acceptable, and he refused to think otherwise just because Nell disapproved.

★   ★   ★

329

The sight of a bulky self-addressed envelope in the post the next morning was just another nail in the coffin of Nell's dreams after a sleepless night trying to come to terms with the removal of all her hopes of being with Ed as a couple. What was the rejection of a short story compared to the loss of the man you loved? Absolutely nothing, she told herself. Taking the envelope upstairs unopened, she stuffed it in the drawer with all the other failures, and got ready for work wondering how she was going to be able to bear living in the same house as Ed now that he was courting Marian Barker.

Pansy had a boyfriend to Sunday tea that same week. His name was Brian.

'Would you like another slice of seed cake, Brian?' invited Peg, wanting to make him feel welcome. She encouraged the youngsters to bring their friends home as often as they wanted, firstly because she enjoyed having them and also so that she could make sure that they weren't getting into bad company. 'Or perhaps you'd like some more bread and butter. I can easily cut more, and there's jam.'

'I'd love another slice of cake, please, Mrs Mills,' said Brian politely. 'It's lovely.'

'Thank you, son,' she said, delighted with the praise. 'I'm told I do a very good seed cake.'

'My mum isn't very good at cake-making,' he confessed. 'My dad says her sponge cakes would make good stepping stones.' He blushed and added quickly, 'She makes other things all right, though; dinners and that.'

Peg thought he was a smashing boy; so polite and easy to get on with. He had light brown floppy hair and shandy-coloured eyes which were mostly focused on Pansy with adoration. Pansy seemed keen on him too. Peg was pleased to see her looking so happy and was relieved that she seemed to be over her crush on Lenny, who – she suspected – was also finding his way with the opposite sex, though he hadn't yet brought a girl home. Knowing Lenny as he was at this age, he probably suspected that such a thing would meet with the disapproval of his 'hard man' mates.

'I'm sure she does, love,' responded Peg now, cutting a slice of cake and sliding it on to Brian's plate.

'I'm going to tea at his house soon, aren't I, Bri?' announced Pansy, sounding delighted at the idea.

'Yeah.' He looked at her and they both turned pink. 'Next Sunday probably.'

Peg thought it was sweet. It was all very juvenile, of course, and probably wouldn't last long, but in bringing Brian home to Sunday tea, Pansy was making a statement saying that he was her chosen one, for the moment anyway.

She wondered if perhaps next Sunday they would be entertaining Ed's new girlfriend. As he had gone to her home today they might be asked to return the compliment. That had been a turn-up for the books, him getting in with the boss's daughter. Tom was none too happy about it, and suspected that Ed was doing it for all the wrong reasons. But Peg didn't agree. Ed wouldn't do a thing like that. He'd been brought up right and was a man of principle.

'You'd better avoid the cake when you go there, if you value your health,' chortled Lenny with a wicked grin. 'Especially your teeth.'

'Oh you,' admonished Pansy, glaring at him before smiling at Brian. 'Take no notice of him, Brian. He's just showing off. He doesn't know how to use the manners his mother taught him.'

'Flippin' heck, it was Brian who mentioned his mother's cakes in the first place,' Lenny reminded her indignantly. 'It was him who said they weren't up to much.'

'It's all right, Lenny; no offence taken,' assured Brian, blushing again.

The poor boy, thought Peg, his face was on fire every few minutes. 'Just get on with your tea and stop being so cheeky,' she ordered her son, knowing what a little devil Lenny could be when he was in the mood.

'I was only joking,' he said, looking aggrieved. 'Honestly, I can't even have a bit of fun in this house. If someone else makes a joke everyone laughs. If I do I get told not to be cheeky.'

'Oh, you poor hard-done-by little thing,' teased his mother. 'Get the violins out, someone.'

Everyone laughed, except Lenny.

Pansy was glad that their numbers were depleted this Sunday teatime because it could be very daunting for a visitor with them all talking and joking and the stranger not knowing where to put himself. They weren't exactly a quiet family.

But luckily Ed had gone to tea at his girlfriend's house, Joe was at a birthday party and Nell had gone to stay with Granny Maud in Essex for a few days. Pansy didn't know what had happened to her sister to send her away in such a hurry. It was all very sudden. After having a face like a poker for a couple of days, she'd packed a bag and gone to Waterlow.

Of course, there was still the biggest mickey-taker of them all to contend with. But Pansy had warned Brian about Lenny, and Brian wasn't the type to take offence, fortunately. He was actually more confident than he seemed, even though he could blush for England. Usually she would be put off by that because it might make him seem a bit drippy, but he was so gorgeous in every other way, it would take more than a red face to make her change her mind about him.

What she'd ever seen in Lenny, she couldn't imagine. She still valued him as a friend, but as for anything else, no thanks, not when there were boys like Brian about. Her passion for Lenny had been a thing of child-hood, she could see that. Now that she was an adult and had opened her mind to a world outside of the Millses' front gate, she saw things in a different light and she liked what she saw.

No one could be more pleased that Pansy's crush on Lenny had finally run its course than Tom. In fact he was thoroughly relieved. If those two had had romantic inclinations towards each other as adults he would have been forced to break his promise to Pansy's mother Alice and tell them that they were, in fact, brother and sister.

If this came out, it would break Peg's heart, tear his family apart and damage Alice Porter's reputation in the eyes of her daughters. And for what? A single event which both parties regretted and never repeated.

Neither he nor Alice had been promiscuous. This one infidelity had been the only time either of them had been unfaithful to their respective spouses. It had come about because Alice's husband had been a cold fish and the poor woman was never shown much warmth. Tom had felt a bit too sorry for her one night and things had got out of hand between them when he'd comforted her. Just the once was enough to get her pregnant, but she had been insistent that Pansy be brought up as her husband's child.

For all his faults Alice had loved Ernie, and Tom's devotion to Peg was the most important thing in his life. So he and Alice had vowed that no

332

one else would ever know about their indiscretion, and they would put the truth behind them.

There had been many times over the years when Tom had wanted to acknowledge Pansy as his daughter, especially immediately after Alice had died. He loved Pansy with all his heart. But the price of the truth for all of them was too high and must not come out unless that was made impossible by a liaison between Pansy and Lenny, which now seemed unlikely given the appearance of Brian at their tea table.

He was recalled to the present by his wife asking if he wanted more tea.

'Yes please, love,' he said, reminded of how very much she meant to him. He knew she would try to understand and come to terms with it if he was to tell her the truth, and one day he would – when Lenny and Pansy were old enough to accept it.

Much to Ed's surprise, things were going very well for him at the Barkers' smart detached residence in Turnham Green, where tea with dainty little sandwiches and cakes was being served on fine china crockery at a table dressed with pure white embossed linen. He was being gently quizzed by Mrs Barker, which was to be expected as Marian was their only child. Ed was determined not to feel intimidated by it. After all, it wasn't as if he was after Marian's money, as such.

'So who is looking after your little boy at the moment?' enquired Marian's mother.

At least Ed was spared the irritation of posh accents, which were noticeably absent in this well-to-do family, probably because George Barker was a self-made man and he and his wife had both come from fairly ordinary backgrounds. Ed found that rather difficult to imagine, given their present comfortable circumstances. 'He's at a birthday party,' he replied.

'Oh, how lovely,' she said. 'I suppose you'll have to get back to collect him later?'

'It's only two doors down from us,' he explained. 'So Mum will get him if I'm not there.'

'Does your mother look after him a lot?'

'Yes, she does actually,' he said, meeting her eyes as though daring her to criticise. 'She brought him up completely while I was away in the navy.'

'We all had to do what we could to help out during the dark days of the war,' Mrs Barker said, her tone implying to him that things were different now.

'I think that still applies,' he said in an even tone, 'among families anyway. Mum's role as grandmother means a lot to her and she enjoys looking after Joe whenever I'm not around.' He paused for a moment. 'And when I am around as well, come to that. We all pull together in our house.'

'Does she have him all day when you're at work?'

'That's right.'

'It must be very tiring for her,' she remarked. 'You don't have the same energy when you get that bit older, you know.'

'Ooh, you'd better not let her hear you say that,' he said, making a joke of it but seriously defending his position. 'Getting older is something she refuses to recognise. She's full of life, my mum.'

'Good for her,' chipped in Mr Barker.

His wife wasn't about to be diverted from her course. 'You're a widower, I understand, Ed.'

'Give over with the questions, for goodness' sake, Mum,' interrupted Marian with an edge to her voice. 'Anyone would think he's in court, the way you're carrying on.'

'I'm only taking an interest, dear.' She was very much on the defensive.

'No you're not,' disagreed Marian rudely. 'You're being downright nosy.'

'It's quite all right, Mrs Barker,' Ed said, grimly polite. 'It's only natural you would want to know something about the man your daughter is going out with.'

'Which football team do you support?' asked George Barker in a timely diversion.

'Fulham,' replied Ed.

'Good boy,' said George with a wry grin. 'Any other answer and I might have had to throw you out.'

'I like to support a local side,' Ed told him.

'You could have said Brentford.'

'A lot of people do around our way, but I followed my dad as a boy and have stayed with them. Dad's always been a Fulham supporter, win or lose.'

334

'Here's hoping next season will be a good one for them.'

'I'll second that.'

Ed sipped his tea, looking towards the other man and meeting his steely gaze. George Barker was smiling with his mouth but not his eyes. The expression in them was clear: he was warning Ed not to play around with Marian's feelings. Ed stared back unwaveringly, because despite his motives, he intended to do right by Marian. He had no reason to be intimidated by her father.

That same Sunday afternoon, Nell and Maud were sitting on wooden kitchen chairs in the sunlit back garden of Maud's cottage, eating doorsteps of homemade bread and jam and drinking tea from large mugs. The small garden was a riot of colour. Maud was a keen gardener but not a conventional one, which meant that everything was pleasantly haywire. Hollyhocks bloomed in abundance among marigolds, lupins, antirrhinums and pansies, while climbing roses ran riot on trellises and walls. Occasionally vegetables could be found growing among the flowers.

However, the main vegetable patch was at the bottom of the garden, and from here Maud produced a tasty assortment for the table. Among other things Nell had been treated to while she'd been staying had been the tenderest of beetroots, the sweetest lettuce, and mouth-watering new potatoes and carrots.

Maud was the only person Nell had confided in about Ed. No one at home had any idea. They never thought of her and Ed in any terms other than friends. But Maud had guessed that something had happened to send Nell here so unexpectedly. She had told her she was surprised that the two of them hadn't got together yet, since they were clearly made for each other. That was when Nell had broken down and told her the whole story.

'He wants his brains testing,' had been Maud's response. 'I shall tell him so an' all when I see him.'

'He's free to do as he likes,' Nell had reminded her. 'It's nothing to do with me.'

'Does he know how you feel?'

'I've never actually told him in so many words, but he must have seen it in my eyes,' she told her.

'Maybe you should have spelled it out for him a bit plainer, then,' suggested the old woman.

'What good would it have done? He's set on getting in with this girl because of who her father is. I don't want him to be with me unless he really wants to be. He's so determined to make something more of himself, I can't compete with that. Anyway, I wouldn't want to be with someone who could do something as callous as that.'

'It'll all end in disaster,' Maud predicted. 'Serve him damn well right too.'

'He has to find out for himself, and by the time he does it will probably be too late,' Nell had said. 'If I were to put up a fight for him and try to stop him from doing what I consider to be the wrong thing, he'd always blame me for holding him back and cheating him of having this "other life" he wants so badly.'

After all the outpourings and discussions, somehow the days had passed in this idyllic village in the company of this lovely lady. Nell had gardened with her, walked by the river, and together they had gone to the little pub on the waterfront and sat in the garden outside with a drink, watching the boats come in and out, the seagulls soaring and swooping, the waters coming and going with the tide.

Now Nell said, 'I'm so grateful to you for letting me stay. It's been so soothing and has helped a lot. I needed to get away so badly.'

'I've enjoyed your company,' Maud assured her. 'I'll miss you tomorrow when you go.'

'I don't want to go back, back to hearing him talk about her; to smelling her perfume on him when he comes in and seeing traces of her lipstick on his collar.' She looked at her watch. 'He'll be at the Barkers' place at this very moment as it happens, worming his way in with them.' She shook her head sadly. 'Oh Gran. I never thought he could do such a thing.'

'Neither did I, love, neither did I,' Maud said sadly. 'It isn't how he's been brought up to behave. But don't spoil your tea by thinking about him.'

'It's time Pansy and I moved out of that house anyway,' Nell went on, thinking aloud. 'It was never meant to be permanent. I shall move heaven and earth to find us a place now.'

'Don't do anything rash.'

'Given the housing shortage, I won't be able to,' she said with a wry grin. 'But I'll make a massive effort now. Living in the same house as him will be just too painful.'

Maud was at a loss to know what to say to Nell to comfort her, because nothing really could at this stage. She would have plenty to say to that scallywag of a grandson of hers, though. What was he thinking of?

The atmosphere at the Barkers' house was pleasantly sociable now that the ice had been broken and Marian's mother had stopped giving Ed a genteel version of the third degree. George Barker and his wife were actually very nice people, Ed decided. But Marian was the boss in that household, no doubt about it. He was shocked by how rude she was to her parents. His own mother would give him a clip round the ear – even now – if he spoke to them like that: 'Oh don't be so stupid, Daddy,' and 'Mummy, will you please stop going on and on. You're like a cracked record and you're getting on everybody's nerves.'

Whatever Marian wanted, Marian got; that seemed to be the rule in this family. Clothes, outings, limitless spending money were all hers for the asking. Her father was even talking about buying her a car later on when they were more readily available. It wouldn't end there, either. Ed guessed that whichever man she chose to settle down with they would accept whether he was an opportunist or not. Her mother might ask a few questions and her father might dish out the odd warning look, but when it came down to it they didn't stand a chance against their daughter. They had obviously spoiled her from the day she was born and this was the result.

Now they were all in the elegant sitting room with its polished wood furniture and smart soft furnishings. George was telling Ed about how he had started the firm when there was a sudden interruption.

'Daddy, stop being so boring,' ordered Marian. 'Ed doesn't want to hear about your silly past.'

'I do, as it happens, Marian,' corrected Ed. 'In fact I find it very interesting, and not at all silly.'

'You don't have to say that just to be polite,' she said, glaring at her father. 'No one could possibly be interested in what the old duffer has to say. Stupid recollections of dim and distant bygone days. Who wants to know about that?'

This was too much for Ed. 'Don't be so rude to you parents, Marian,' he rebuked, looking at her coldly.

'What!' Her eyes were wide with shock that someone should dare to stand up to her.

'You heard,' he said angrily. 'Your parents are good people and you owe them everything. The least you can do is show them a little respect, for goodness' sake.'

The silence was painful in its intensity until a shocked Marian said, 'Don't you dare tell me what to do. You're in my house, so mind your own business.'

'I'm in your parents' house, actually.'

'Same thing.'

'No it isn't. Not at all.'

'Now, now, you two,' ventured her mother 'We don't want any arguments to spoil the afternoon.'

Ed was quiet and thoughtful for a while, then he stood up in a purposeful manner and addressed his comments directly to Marian's parents.

'I'm very sorry but I'm afraid I am going to have to ruin the afternoon completely,' he began, glancing from one to the other while Marian sat in the chair throwing him a look of pure fury. 'The sad fact is, I am here on false pretences.'

'Really?' said Mrs Barker. 'What do you mean by that?'

'I am not in love with your daughter,' he stated boldly, 'and have been going out with her only in the hope of getting promotion at the factory.'

'Why, you . . .' began Marian.

'I'm sorry,' he said, meeting her furious stare. 'But you made it all too easy for me. You made all the running. I would never have been tempted by such a thing if you hadn't pursued me so relentlessly. Everywhere I went, you were there. It was you who asked me out, not the other way around, and I suppose I was rather flattered and just got carried along with the whole thing. You are, after all, a very beautiful girl.'

'Get out,' she ordered, flushed with temper. 'Go on. Get out of this house immediately.'

'Not until I've finished what I have to say.' He turned to George Barker. 'I really am very sorry about this, mate. I'm ashamed of myself for letting things go this far. It was always against my better judgement and I'm very glad I've come to my senses before any real damage has been done.'

'What about me?' shouted Marian. 'What about the damage to my feelings?'

'You'll live,' Ed told her. 'It was all just a game to you anyway. You'll have no trouble finding someone else. You need to change your ways before you settle down with anyone, though. Or I pity the poor bloke, whoever he turns out to be.'

'Of all the cheek . . .'

'Just being honest.' Ed turned to her mother, who was sitting dumbfounded next to her husband. 'Thank you for a lovely tea, Mrs Barker,' he said. 'It was very nice to meet you.'

'I enjoyed meeting you too,' she responded impulsively.

'Why are you being nice to him after what he's done to me, you stupid woman?' ranted Marian, glaring at her mother.

'That's enough, Marian. I won't have you speaking to your mother like that,' rebuked George Barker sternly.

Marian's eyes bulged. She couldn't remember the last time her father had raised his voice to her, and it stunned her into silence.

'Well, I'll be off now,' Ed told them. 'Thank you again for the hospitality. It really was a lovely tea.' He looked at George. 'I'll call in at the factory for my cards whenever it's convenient. I presume you'll want me to finish.'

'You've a week's notice to serve,' George reminded him.

'I didn't think you'd want . . .'

'Well you're wrong, because I do.'

'Okay, I'll do that then.'

As he walked out of the house and headed for the bus stop, Ed felt normal again for the first time since before the sham of a relationship with Marian had begun. How could he have been such a fool as to get involved? Greed plain and simple was the answer to that.

He'd wanted the easy way to a better life. Not that being with Marian could ever be described as easy; she was utterly self-centred, and he hadn't wanted to be with her anyway. She would be a nice girl if she wasn't so spoilt, but she wasn't right for him in any way whatsoever. Thank God he was out of it. He was out of a job too, he reminded himself gloomily.

Oh well, better that than being with a woman he didn't love for the rest of his life.

Nell was just getting into bed when her door creaked opened and Maud appeared.

'There's someone downstairs, Nell.' She paused, listening. 'Hear it? Hear that noise? We've got burglars.'

'I can't hear anything.'

'Listen.'

Concentrating hard, Nell could hear someone moving about. 'You're right,' she said in a whisper. 'There is someone down there.'

'I'm going down,' Maud declared, picking up a china ornament from the dressing table and brandishing it. 'I'll soon sort them out.'

'I'll go,' said Nell firmly. 'You stay here.'

'Not likely.'

'We'll both go then, but I'll go first,' said Nell in a whisper. 'Youth before beauty, as they say.'

'You cheeky madam.'

'Don't turn the light on or we'll frighten him away,' suggested Nell. 'We need to catch him and get him locked up.'

Cautiously they made their way down the creaky stairs in the dark and through the wooden door into the living room, which was flooded with light.

Before Nell could stop her, Maud pushed past her and hurtled towards the armchair, where the back of a man's head was visible.

'Gotcha, you bugger,' she uttered, sitting down heavily on the intruder.

'Blimey, Gran. Steady on,' said Ed. 'You could crush me to death coming down heavy like that.'

'Oh, it's you,' said Maud, rising and putting the ornament down on the sideboard. 'What the hell do you think you are doing, boy, creeping around and frightening decent people half to death? You could have given me a heart attack. You're bloomin' lucky you didn't get clubbed.'

'Sorry. I was trying not to wake you,' he explained. 'I let myself in with the key that we keep at home. The lights were off and it was quiet, so I thought you were asleep. I missed the train to link up with the ferry so had to walk from Colchester, which is why I'm so late.'

'We would have been asleep if you hadn't frightened the wits out of the pair of us.'

'I tried not to make a noise while I made myself some cocoa,' he explained.

'Oh well, no harm down, and it's nice to see you whenever you arrive.' She followed his eyes as he looked at Nell, who was standing nearby in a pair of red and white striped pyjamas. 'Well you obviously haven't come at this hour just to see me,' said Maud. 'I'll go back to bed and leave you to it. Don't stay up all night or you'll be tired tomorrow.'

'Well . . . what happened at the tea party?' asked Nell when Maud had gone.

'I lost my job,' he told her.

'Don't tell me you didn't manage to impress Mr and Mrs Barker,' she said.

'I think I can safely say that I'm not their favourite person,' he replied.

'You must be losing your touch,' she said. 'Most people succumb to your charm.'

'So did they until I told all three of them what I was up to and that I couldn't carry on with it.'

She gave him a half-smile. 'At last,' she approved. 'That's more like the Ed I know.'

'I'd sooner be out of a job than with the wrong woman for the wrong reasons.'

'Thank goodness for that,' she burst out. 'Welcome back to the world where you belong.'

'I am feeling better, I must admit,' he told her, looking pleased. 'I seemed to have lost my way for a while.'

'You certainly did. But it must have been a shock for them, your coming out with it like that,' she remarked. 'I don't suppose Marian was any too pleased.'

'I'll say she wasn't. She isn't used to not getting her own way.' He paused thoughtfully. 'The Barkers are nice people, though. I was sorry to spoil the afternoon for them.' He spread his hands. 'But some things just have to be done.'

She nodded. 'So you'll be looking for a new job, then?'

'That's right.' He looked at her, and everything she felt for him she saw reflected in his eyes. 'But there is something far more important than that,' he began uncertainly. 'Nell, I know we've always been best pals, but it's been more than that for me for some time now.' He cleared his throat nervously. 'I didn't want to acknowledge it because I was afraid it might spoil what we had – that special friendship we both value so much – so I tried to ignore it and got involved with Marian.' He paused, looking at her. 'The fact is, I've fallen in love with you, Nell, and I can't pretend to be just your friend any longer. You're the woman I love and want to spend the rest of my life with – if you'll have me.'

She didn't say anything; just went into his arms.

About time too, thought Maud, who had her ear pressed to the other side of the door to the stairs. She went up to bed with a smile on her face.

'Well, is it in there, Nell?' asked Peg excitedly one morning in early December. Nell had made a pre-breakfast dash to the newsagent's and come back clutching several copies of a well-known women's magazine.

'Yeah,' beamed Nell, opening the magazine and spreading it out on the kitchen table. 'It's in here.'

'"Something Special" by Nell Porter,' Peg read aloud from the page, then hugged Nell tearfully. 'Oh Nell, I'm so proud of you. Well done, love!'

'Thanks, Auntie Peg.'

The envelope containing the story had lain unopened in Nell's drawer, where she'd stuffed it, thinking it was a rejection, before she rushed off to Essex full of heartache over Ed and Marian. She hadn't got around to opening it for a couple of weeks in all the excitement of her engagement to Ed. When she did, she found a letter from the fiction editor saying that if she would like to work on the story further with his suggestions in mind, he would be interested in buying it. She'd done as he'd asked with pleasure, and here it was: her very first short story in print. It was such a thrill!

The other members of the family began to appear in the kitchen for breakfast.

'Cor, that's smashing. Congratulations, sis,' said Pansy, looking at the

342

magazine. 'Can I take a copy to work to show the girls? Oh, and I can't wait to show Brian's mum. I'll take a copy over to his place tonight.'

Tom appeared and picked up on the excitement, offering Nell his heartfelt congratulations. Even Lenny was impressed. 'Cor, fancy living in the same house as someone famous,' he said.

'Hardly that,' said Nell modestly.

'I don't know anyone else who knows someone with their name in print.'

'I told you you'd do it if you kept trying, didn't I?' said Ed, appearing ready for work in a suit and tie.

George Barker had been so impressed with Ed's honesty and his ambition to get on, he'd asked him to stay on at the factory with a view to promotion to management as soon as a vacancy became available. He'd thought that Ed's enthusiasm, as well as his engineering skills, made him an ideal candidate to help take the firm successfully into the new era. Ed had been offered the position of workshop manager shortly afterwards.

'Yes, you did,' she confirmed, putting her arms around him. 'You always had faith in me.'

She had faith in him too. Integrity had finally won out, and she knew he would do well with the opportunity that had come his way in such a roundabout manner. Meanwhile they had their spring wedding to look forward to. Hopefully, too, there would be more stories . . . and more exciting moments like this.

Joe came bounding into the room and ran into Nell's arms. She was so looking forward to being Ed's wife and Joe's mum. She couldn't love the boy any more if he was her own flesh and blood. And perhaps one day he'd have a little brother or sister to play with.

Into this happiest of moments came a sudden piercing memory of her own mother. But on this occasion it didn't make her feel sad; it made her smile, because it was almost as though Alice was here, sharing in her daughter's joy.